# AWAKEN

A FAMILY DESTROYED. A POWER AWAKENED.

PART OF THE ABERRATION SERIES

RICHARD M. LALCHAN

RENEW
YOURMIND
PUBLISHING
RENEWYOURMIND.NET

Cover Artwork by Marcus Silversides

Paperback – ISBN- 978-1-7385316-0-8
Ebook – ISBN-978-1-7385316-1-5

Fiction / Science Fiction
Printed in the UK by Book Vault

www.RichardMLalchan.com

*To my dad, who never got to see the final product.*

*"Science is a great tool, and so is a hammer, but not everything is a nail." Aaron Paul*

PART ONE

# CHAPTER 1

## BAD NEWS

Family was extremely important to Ben Harman until his was destroyed.

The colours on the living room walls screamed neutrality, interspersed with elegantly framed photos of cheerful people. And that of his one-year-old daughter Alice, whose faint cries could be heard through the baby monitor positioned on his lap; and his beautiful wife Lydia, whom he adored and always thought he was punching above his weight in marrying her. His friends mostly agreed. The beautiful photo of their wedding as the best man and ushers held her up.

And there was that one he adored. It was one of those natural, organic photos. Very simple. Lydia was standing by a solid oak tree on the grounds of the stately home they'd hired from a friend for their wedding. Wearing a soft white dress with meticulously embroidered white roses, she looked absolutely radiant. Ben in his dark blue three-piece wedding suit, gazing at his beautiful bride. The photo was tightly cropped at their faces, and the look, especially from Lydia, was that of pure, unbridled love. Everyone commented on that photo, like it was something to aspire to. Ben loved gazing at it. He sometimes drifted off from his writing and stared at that photo—he always kept a small copy to hand in his wallet—bringing back such happy memories.

He pinched himself often. 'How blessed am I to have this wonderful family?' It was his greatest desire and joy to love, protect, care for them…and to grow. They were planning on a large family, both excitedly looking forward to training up their children God's way; to know the truth; to embrace the real world and to counteract the bed of lies they felt often promulgated by society at large.

However, today, two Section One officers sat opposite him in their smart and tightly fitted uniforms. One was tall and lanky, the other vertically challenged and stout. It was almost as if they were chosen to play "good cop, bad cop."

But none of that mattered today. The message they had to deliver, Ben, in his heart of hearts, already knew.

A single tear began its journey down his weary face, even before they gave him the news that three hours ago Lydia Harman, his wife of two years, had been found dead in her lab. Investigations were ongoing, but the conclusion thus far was that she'd died of asphyxiation from inhaling a poisonous gas in a tragic accident.

The walls seemed to close in on Ben as he cradled the baby monitor, staring at the crystal clear image of his daughter, now in a peaceful slumber. 'She'll never get to see her grow up, to see her turn into a beautiful woman,' he thought. A few other tears appeared, motivated to find Ben's chin before falling into his lap. One splashed on the monitor. He didn't even have the energy to wipe it off.

"Will you be OK, Mr Harman? Is there anyone that can be with you?"

It was the short, stout officer who uttered these words in a well-trained manner. His face was a picture of compassion, though tinged with a trace of formality. Not his first time delivering such news. Ben continued staring at his child's face, not having heard the officer.

"Mr Harman? Can we call someone for you?" The officer repeated.

Ben's mind went back to his small family...and now his sense of failure. Recalling his late father's words, and still reeling from the fact he also died too early, not even a full year ago at the age of 51, Jacob Harman gave this advice, as he drifted toward death:

"It's your God-given responsibility to lead and protect your family. There can be no bigger responsibility than this."

Those words had always weighed heavily on him.

Ben, being an only child, was often lacking in confidence. While his parents' love for him was undeniable, the absence of siblings left him with a perpetual need to excel in everything he did, leaving little room for error or experimentation. Jacob and Esther would always say the right things to their son, always encouraging and attempting to build him up, but their actions or subtle expressions didn't always match up.

One time, just past his tenth birthday, Ben was with a few other learning groups at Sab City Library. He loved these sessions as he got to meet many interesting people. Once a year, the session would culminate in an awards ceremony that they all looked forward to. Each student would receive a reward for their behaviour, knowledge, and application.

Ben, as a dedicated learner, loved researching and satiating his curiosity. His reward was often being voted top student. However, on this occasion, he finished in third place overall. He could already sense his parents' displeasure, even before arriving home.

"That's OK honey. You can't win all the time," his mum had said, trying to hide her expression of sadness as she gave him a hug. She didn't succeed. Ben noticed. There it was. Just as he expected. Though he didn't know that for them, the disappointment was most certainly not in their precious son whom they loved deeply, but in the fact they were medically unable to have more children. They would admit this heaped more pressure on Ben, and they weren't always successful at controlling their feelings as much as they tried.

Some sixteen years later, that pressure weighed heavier than ever, as Ben may just have to accept failure in heeding his father's parting advice.

Tall, lanky officer stood up and moved toward Ben, putting a hand on his shoulder, repeating his question.

"Mr Harman? Are you OK? Is there someone who can be with you right now?"

"Er...sorry..." Ben snivelled, slightly startled that he'd not even noticed the officer get up. He sniffed as he pulled out a tissue. "No. Thank you. My neighbours will be back soon."

"How long will that be?" the officer asked.

"About nine o'clock," replied Ben.

"Well, that's only a few minutes," the officer said, checking his wrist, the body suit displaying the time amongst a plethora of other data. "We'll wait with you until then," he said as he sat back down next to his colleague.

"You don't have to, but thank you."

Struggling to contain his emotions, he realised he couldn't recall much of what the officers had shared about how his wife had died. He wasn't sure he wanted to hear, but knowing it was important, and Fabio & Olivia, his dear friends, and neighbours would most certainly ask him, he ventured,

"Can you tell me again what you know? I just can't remember much at the moment."

"Of course, Mr. Harman," replied short, stout officer as he looked at his colleague then started from the beginning.

## CHAPTER 2

## EXCEPTIONAL SCIENTIST

Four hours earlier

At this unearthly hour, Sendo eXperiences' labs were completely deserted, eerily like a ghost town. Two security personnel stood between reception and the main entrance, while no 'normal' lab staff would be working at five in the morning.

Lydia Harman was not normal. In fact, despite only working at Sendo a little over two years, they still echoed a prior testimonial which described her as such:

'Lydia is a rare breed. Someone who has exceptional talent and has the pure dedication and self-discipline to achieve whatever she sets her mind to.'

Glowing praise indeed, and at just twenty-two years young, her ability to grasp complex information was way beyond her years.

She dragged her chair across the floor, her long dark hair

swishing as she moved, setting her eyes on the results of her latest experiment.

"Come on. This must work now. 53rd time lucky." she muttered to herself as she looked down at the display.

Disappointment.

Again.

She let her head fall toward the desk. Her fists clenched, a scowl appearing, drawing her cheekbones higher.

"God, please let the next one work," she pleaded. Then, as if a switch flipped, she lifted up her head as a smile washed over her face.

"As a wise person once said, it's not the events in life that shape us, but our reaction to them. OK. 54th time's a charm." Never one to dwell on the past, she quickly went in to preparation mode to being the 54th test.

Around her, the lab was typical, in that everything was white and clinical. The desk where Lydia sat was one of those vast 270° desks with display screens curved around to give the sense of being enclosed by all the data. She had custom designed it to help her focus. And working on the kind of experiments she did—that of helping solve Sendo's terraforming challenge—she needed to focus. One mistake could set them back months, if not years. But Lydia was the perfect fit for this job. With her personality and temperament, she not only coped but excelled under pressure.

Beyond her impressive desk were large windows looking into the neighbouring labs. And below one of those windows in a corner was a large electron microscope, and next to that were white metallic cupboards with a multiplicity of drawers and storage compartments. The whole lab had a slight smell of pine, often the case first thing after the cleaners had done their stuff.

A small video monitor displayed a cot with a slowly moving child. Lydia always kept a live feed of her daughter Alice, running anytime Ben was asleep or in another room. Some thought she was paranoid. She probably was. But if she was questionable on the scale of normality, what she'd observed of Alice put her daughter right off the scale.

Out of the corner of her eye, Lydia noticed the low hanging mobile in Alice's cot. Not an unusual site. But as she stared, bringing her full attention to it, she noticed that the mobile and all its constituent parts were being drawn down towards the child. However, Alice was not touching it.

"What the heck?" she exclaimed, with no small amount of confusion. Lydia did a double take to make sure she wasn't going mad. Many would have the excuse of not being fully awake at this hour. Not Lydia. She had all of her faculties on high alert. Just as normal.

"I need to record this," she said as she tapped a button, instigating a red glow around the video feed.

Alice pulled the mobile closer and closer towards her, without using her tiny hands–as the mobile was originally set too high for her to touch. It drew nearer as her left hand reached out and pulled at a little sheep hanging next to a black and white cow.

With a big smile and wide eyes, she stuffed the sheep in her mouth, causing the rest of the mobile to strain as it was pulled. Then she let go.

'Thwack!'

Along with the cow and several other animals, the mobile went flying back up and flipped over the bar it was connected too. There was no way she could reach that by stretching out her hand now. But she didn't need to.

Again, as Lydia watched, the mobile untangled and hung down. The cord the animals were attached to was being stretched as the collection of mammals made their way back down toward the smiling child's face. A faint gurgling noise could be heard through the speakers. As soon as Alice touched the cow, Lydia stopped recording and played it back.

"This is...impossible. How is this possible?" she mulled. Switching from loving parent to scientist, she called up a CT scan of her daughter's brain comparing the three-month charts to the live one that was currently running—as most homes and offices had this technology and an assortment of other healthcare monitoring facilities built right into them.

Although not an expert in neuroscience, Lydia had more than enough knowledge to spot anomalies and regularly charted the growth of her daughter with the wonderful array of tools she had at her disposal.

A program was running, contrasting the past three months with the current scans and projecting trends into the near future. The green bar reached completion, then the results were displayed on another screen. Lydia could see the projected development of Alice's brain over the next three years.

'If what I'm thinking is true, this is unprecedented,' she thought. And as she focused her gaze on the results, her mouth dropped open. She clenched her shoulders, attempting to massage her neck, as she gradually understood what she was looking at.

The image of Alice's brain showed that a specific area of her parietal lobe would expand at an unprecedented rate. It already had in the past three months.

Leaning back into her ergonomic chair, her left arm balanced on the armrest; she moved the other absentmindedly to scratch her head.

"If I'm reading this right, this means her sensory perception will increase in a way that...wow...that not only increases her visual acuity...ALL her senses will increase. And if she can physically move a small mobile when she's just one, following these projections through, hmmm...let me see...this indicates external projection of her senses. I mean...imagine what she could manipulate when she is five, ten, or twenty!" she said to herself.

Lydia hastily rose, inhaling deeply to replenish her lungs. So many mixed emotions swirling around her already busy mind. She paced around the lab, her beige court shoe pumps making a rhythmic clunk, clunk on the marble floor.

'I'm not sure if this is good or bad,' she thought. 'If others know about this, they will definitely want to test her like crazy—and to be honest, as a scientist, I couldn't blame them.'

She stopped pacing as a scowl invaded her face.

"But no child of mine is gonna end up being a lab rat," she declared as she looked back at the screen, showing the projections. 'What will Ben think?' She had to tell him, not wanting to have secrets. She loved him too much for that, but she also didn't want to worry him—he was certainly the more worrisome of their family—but these were projections that weren't confirmed yet.

'But,' she thought to herself, swinging back and forth like an angel and demon were sitting on her shoulders, 'I have a recording of our daughter manipulating reality...right now! No future projection. Seen it with my own eyes!'

As she was wondering what to do next, her thoughts were quickly interrupted by a stark buzzing sound coming from the control panel on her desk. Walking back round inside the curved unit, she noticed a red light flashing perfectly in sync with the noisy buzz. She furrowed her brow, confused as to what was happening.

"Not seen that one before. What's that about?" she quizzed. Her eyes glanced at the windows beyond her desk, but knowing that at this time early in the morning, she would be on her own in the lab.

Another light flicked on.

"That's a gas leak warning! What the heck!" she shouted as quickly the air became thick with an invisible assailant to her respiratory system. Lydia struggled to breathe. She knew this was bad as she bent over, holding herself up by the back of her chair. If the gas leak warning light flashed four more times, it would initiate a lock down. Local first, then the whole base. She knows, she knows this, but she stumbles, missing the chair armrest and falling to the ground, unable to hit the panic button under her desk to alert security.

A strange smell enters her nostrils that she can't place. Her mind is now in full on panic mode as she drifts in and out of consciousness. With the alarm blaring across the laboratory, the warning light flashed for the fifth time. Sturdy metal shutters drop from the ceiling, going from left to right across the lab, making a deafening crunch as they locked into place. Lydia barely notices.

Lying prostrate, her mind drifts to her daughter. Clenching her fists and attempting to push up from the floor, she tried to get one last look at Alice, the monitor still displaying the feed from her cot.

'Ha...rumph!' she mutters, struggling with all her might and sounding as though she had a mouth full of marshmallows. Her last adrenaline rush was not enough to push her to the correct angle to view the monitor. She strained as she used all of her cognitive powers to remember the last look on her daughter's face...and Ben.

'I'm sorry Ben! I should have told you more how much I love you and was so blessed to have you in my life,' she thought, tears running down the side of her face, pooling on the floor, as more and more of the toxic chemicals entered her lungs.

"God, if there's still time to get me out of this...Otherwise, please protect Ben and Alice. Comfort them. I trust You," she offered as her last prayer as the alarms continued their announcement, providing Lydia with a pulsing sensation in her brain. Then everything seemed to go quiet. The exceptional scientist lay motionless on the floor of her lab. Her breathing slowing.

If she could have looked up to the screen, she would have seen Alice lying in her cot, staring straight back at her mother, holding out her hand, as though beckoning her to grab it. Her baby face was static, holding a nondescript expression; neither smiling nor frowning.

With the lab in lockdown, there was only one security window not covered by the solid grey industrial steel shutters. The window, about the size of one of the lab's display screens, looked on into the adjoining lab. Within the next hour, Lydia's colleagues would start showing up for work. But for now there was one solitary figure standing stoically, looking right into Lydia's lab. He was a short man with dark olive-coloured skin and patterned markings on his face, which could have been tattoos. His green eyes were wide and full of curiosity. He may well have been standing there the whole time Lydia was breathing in the toxic gas.

But even now, instead of rushing to override the security locks and attempting to save the life of the brave scientist, MendipT muttered something unintelligible to himself. Then he turned around and walked away as if nothing exceptional had just happened.

# CHAPTER 3
## BEDTIME STORIES

They looked so real, swimming steadily around the room. It didn't make sense—fish floating in the air—but as holographic lamps go, it was very impressive. Waving his hand, making the fish swim faster, Ben Harman looked on lovingly toward Alice as she climbed into her bed. The nightly ritual of listening to his daughter read was made even more precious since the death of his wife five years ago.

The warm red glow from the bedside lamp caressed the top of the cabinet, flowing over a full glass of water, lapping at the translucent Reeder waiting to be called into use. Ben watched Alice get settled in, resting her back against the headboard, the noise of the sheets making those comforting bedtime sounds. He stretched over her, pulling the sheets to cover her legs. Stifling a yawn, Ben asked Alice,

"So what'll it be tonight, monkey?"

As a writer, Ben was delighted that Alice was a passionate reader. Frankly, she couldn't get enough of it. He noticed she would often choose stories that were way over her reading age. Staring at the words for ages. Her five-year-old mind trying desperately to comprehend the message the book was communicating to her. Or so Ben thought.

Alice had always been a special child. Not just special in the way that all children are special to their parents. Of course, that was the case. Ben doted on Alice. But Alice was different. Apart from possessing a higher mental age than any of the children from their Learning Group, Ben noticed that at certain times, when she was concentrating hard, a strange thing happened. Objects in close proximity to her became very warm. He'd tested this in various situations to make sure he wasn't going mad. He wasn't.

At one point, they were in the garden together, making a play-tent. He put the pipes together and threw over the canvas. When he crawled inside, Alice was there already preparing tea with her brand new birthday party tea set. She'd taken it out of its box, which was sitting in the shade. It should have been cold. But on touching it, Ben could feel its temperature had noticeably risen. Far higher than the effect of warm human hands coming into contact with it.

He'd brought some more toys into the tent. One by one, he handed them to Alice. As she took each one—seemingly unaware of his ongoing experiment—he took them back and made a note of the distinct change in temperature. It was definitely warmer. It made no sense. He intended to have her evaluated discreetly to avoid exposing her as some kind of freak.

He'd often humorously wondered if there really was a 'School for Gifted Youngsters' and whether he should prepare her for it. Instead, he pictured his beautiful daughter like the sun. She raised the temperature of everything around her, making them radiant too.

Ben smiled as he thought about that analogy—then pictured someone getting too close to the sun. He quickly wiped the image from his mind. At least her 'sun effects' did not burn things, just made them warmer, and it was good that—so far at least—it didn't seem to affect any of the other children she played with, or their parents.

"I want to read about Ruth," replied Alice.

"Again?"

"Yes, I like Ruth," she said as she leant across and picked up the Reeder, its display kicking into life as it touched her skin.

"You read about her last night," said Ben.

"No, I didn't, silly. It was Naomi."

"But that's in the same book, honey–and don't call me silly. Naomi is Ruth's mother," corrected Ben.

"I know that. Sorry, Daddy. But it's Ruth I want to read about," she replied apologetically.

Holding the Reeder—which weighed next to nothing—in her left hand, the device tracked Alice's eyes. The pages turned whenever she reached the bottom right. They flicked through to the page she wanted.

"Ready?" Ben asked.

"Yes," she replied contentedly.

"OK. Go for it."

Ben settled himself next to Alice after kicking off his shoes. Leaning back into the headboard, putting his arm around her, drawing her close, he closed his eyes as she began to read.

Ben wasn't sure who fell asleep first, but the whack as the Reeder slipped off the bed and hit the floor woke him up.

Getting up and walking around the bed, he picked up the Reeder, turned it off, and placed it back on the bedside table. He tucked in the still sleeping Alice, giving her a kiss on the forehead, then headed for his office, his impending deadline at the forefront of his mind.

Ben needed to keep awake to finish writing the content for a website that had to be with the client the next morning. The clock showed 7.30 p.m. Sitting down at his desk across the hall from Alice's bedroom, he grabbed a can of Astir containing just the right chemicals to keep him awake and alert for up to two hours. That should be all I'll need, he thought as he scrolled through the content on his display, editing as he went. It wasn't an extensive project, and he was almost done, but as it was for one of his most demanding clients, he liked to go over things again and again to make sure it was the best he could produce.

The time was now 10 p.m. Ben waved open his Basecamp and typed the brief message to his client. Adding the attachment to his hard work, he tapped send. Waving the console into sleep mode, he dozily wandered across to Alice's room before intending to head to bed himself.

As he got to her room, the door slightly ajar as normal, the light he expected to see emanating from the lamp Alice always kept on for comfort was not there. All he saw was a dark room with a very slight glow from the streetlights outside.

Why are the lights off? He thought to himself. She never likes the dark. Alice loved to watch the holographic vignettes of fish swim around her room if she couldn't sleep. It had a very calming effect on her, making her feel like her entire room was underwater.

Opening the door, Ben walked slowly across the room to the side of the bed. He could see her shape under the covers. He reached the lamp, tapped it and the light came back on, throwing a yellow glow across the room and providing an aquatic sensation. Looking at the bed, he pulled back the covers, and to his shock, Alice was no longer there.

"Alice?" Ben called out, not quite shouting, but enough to get her attention if she was still in the room. Stooping, Ben looked under the bed. Nothing.

He called out again.

"Alice, monkey, where are you?" No response. He called out and quickly opened the far wardrobe before rushing to the bathroom. "Monkey, this isn't funny anymore. Where are you?"

Still no response. The bathroom was equally empty of Alice. He pulled the door to his bedroom, looking under the bed, in the wardrobe and the en-suite, all to no avail. Panic kicked in. 'Lord, I really could do with some help right now,' he prayed quietly. There was no hint of her wanting to get away, and they'd had such a lovely time as usual reading together before bed.

Ben continued looking around the house, now in a more frenzied state. He looked round all the doors and windows. He refused to consider the possibility of her being kidnapped, yet no signs of forced entry were found. All the windows and doors were closed or locked, as was normal. How is it possible that my little monkey isn't here? It makes little sense.

He suddenly remembered his heat sensor, with which he could quickly scan to see if she really was in the house. He ran back upstairs to his bedroom and grabbed the HeatFind from his drawer. It glowed to indicate it recognised his fingerprint and Ben selected 'heat map.'

Holding the oblong object horizontally in his hand, he pointed the lens around the room as he moved it slowly. The screen would light up red to display any heat signatures. Currently, it displayed a very dark version of the room with the occasional lighter pixels.

Ben inched out of his room and directed the inbuilt camera around the house. Still nothing. He moved downstairs, holding the device in front of him as he walked, wanting, hoping for a flicker of red to light up the display. Nothing.

He went outside. Still holding the HeatFind in front of him, directing it around his house, then at the neighbour's. The screen flickered red as expected bodies were being picked up. He counted them. Nothing untoward there, but still he would knock and see if anyone knew anything.

Walking up the path of Fabio and Olivia's home, Ben knocked lightly on the door. After a short while, a tall man in light coloured chinos and a check shirt opened the door.

"Hey Ben. You OK man?" Fabio said in his strong Italian accent.

It was obvious there was panic all over Ben's face.

"It's Alice......she's gone..." he cried.

"Gone where, Ben?" queried Fabio.

"That's just it. I don't know." Ben's eyes were struggling to hold back the tears.

"What's going on, Fab?" a female voice broke through the stifled conversation.

"It's Ben. He says Alice is missing?" Fabio relayed.

"Where could she be?" asked Fabio, directing his focus back to Ben. "I'm sure she can't have gotten far. Let's go look."

"Oli. I'm gonna go with Ben and have a look," he directed up the stairs to where his wife was.

"OK. Just a minute. Let me come too." Ben heard a shuffling and moments later, Olivia appeared wearing a thin stripy jumper and jeans. As soon as she saw Ben, she wrapped him in a warm embrace.

"We'll find her Ben. She can't have gone far. Tell us what happened." Ben led them out but responded to Olivia over his shoulder.

"Thanks, but you don't understand. She's gone. There's no way she could have gotten out of the house on her own. I locked the front door. None of the windows or doors were open. When I say she's gone, I mean she's...like...vanished."

Olivia looked at Fabio. Fabio looked back at Olivia, exchanging quizzical looks between themselves.

"She can't have vanished. That's impossible," Fab said as they approached the door to Ben's house. He led them in.

"I know," said Ben, almost under his breath.

All three of them entered the house as Ben led them straight to the kitchen.

"I checked the heat signals of the entire house. Nothing," he said in resignation, setting his eyes on Fabio.

"Would you look upstairs, Fab? Check the windows for yourself. Olivia, want to look downstairs with me? You check the lounge, and I'll do out back...and check the windows too."

"Of course," they both said as they headed off in different directions.

Fabio headed up the stairs. 'I sincerely hope she's OK,' he thought to himself. 'It makes little sense Alice disappearing like that.' Looking around, he could see nothing seemed to be damaged or broken into. There's something going on here. There's something we're not seeing.

He reached Alice's bedroom. Opening the door, he surveyed the scene. Everything is normal. Looks like a typical five-year-olds' room—albeit a tidy one. Walking past the bed, he traced his hand over the covers, then pulled them back. Nothing untoward here. He replaced the covers and walked past the bed to the windows. Seems to work just fine.

He opened first the small window, then the larger one to the right. His hand traced along the edge of the window to spot any signs of a break-in. Absolutely perfect. There's nothing wrong here. They, whoever "they" are, didn't get in through the windows.

# CHAPTER 4

## SEARCHING

Fabio Brown did everything meticulously. Maybe it was his army upbringing that had instilled in him a strong sense of discipline and the desire to do things right and see them through to the end. This led him on to his current job managing Sab City Library.

Although a book-lover, it was management that was his passion. He saw it as an opportunity to have an influence over every area of a business. To look at and analyse what was working and what wasn't and to make tiny changes and watch the progress. To think, implement, test, analyse then repeat.

Fabio didn't like to be defeated by a problem. He looked at every angle until it was resolved. Some problems however, just couldn't be solved.

"This is weird," said Fabio to himself. "There must be a completely normal explanation. I wonder if Ben got confused and left her at a friends, though he doesn't leave her with anyone these days after Lydia...and I don't blame him. I just don't know what's going on."

He walked into Ben's room, scanning it with his eyes. Just as in Alice's room, there was nothing to suggest foul play. No paper was out of place. It was just as he would expect it to be.

After checking everything obvious, he left the room closing the door and headed for the bathroom. He followed the same process checking the windows and trying to see if there was anywhere to hide. Nothing. Nada!

"Ben there's nothing. no one's tried to break in here!" he shouted down as he began to descend the stairs. "Ben?"

"Out here in the garden, honey!" It was his wife's voice which he followed leading him through the kitchen to the garden. Olivia was sitting down on a chair with a worried expression trying to comfort the tearful Ben.

"There's nothing," repeated Fabio as he reached his wife.

"We know," replied Olivia. "There's no sign of anything downstairs either. To be honest it's most peculiar," she said.

"I don't mean to sound funny, Ben, but you haven't dropped her off somewhere and just forgot to pick her up? Like I don't think you ever would do that...what since Lydia and all, but I have to ask," queried Fabio.

Ben understood. Perfectly. He had no desire to get mad at his friend and neighbour for suggesting he could forget about his only daughter. It was a perfectly sensible question, especially coming from someone like Fab who left no stone unturned.

"No," said Ben. "She's been with me all day. We were out together at a show...then we came straight back...we had dinner, watched one of her programs...I put her to bed. We read...she read, as she normally does, and I only left her when she fell asleep."

"Where did you go?" asked Olivia.

"I just went to my room. I had to finish off the Tranget job. Next time I went back in her room to check on her...maybe a couple hours later, she was gone." Ben's voice was just audible over his tears which were flowing freely now.

"I never heard anything so strange. I don't understand how she could just disappear. You've seen the place. There's no sign of break in," Olivia puzzled.

"I admit. It does seem weird," offered Fabio. "Something doesn't add up. Have you called Section One?"

"Yes. I messaged them. They should be here soon," Ben replied as he rested his head on his knees, whilst Olivia placed her arm on his shoulder.

"We'll find her," she said. "She can't have gone far. I'm sure when Section One get here they'll give a logical explanation. You'll see."

Ben didn't respond. Just held his head tighter slightly rocking back and forth, trying to get any crumb of comfort from his body.

"What if I never see her again?" he muttered through his tears. "I've lost Lydia and now Alice."

"I'm sure that's not gonna be the case, Ben. Like Oli said, I'm sure there's a logical explanation. Let's wait and see what Section One have to say. At the end of the day, God's got it all under His control." Fabio offered.

They all waited, almost frozen in time for the next couple minutes before a knock on the door startled them.

"Fab, d'you wanna get that?" Olivia asked, before watching her husband head towards the front door.

Section One was set up after a significant governmental restructuring of the late 21st century. November 5th, 2086 will forever be remembered as "Guy Fawkes 2" or "GF2.0," a monumental day that brought together years of activism, protests, and civil unrest that hadn't been witnessed in centuries.

Grievances centred around concerns that successive governments had been using academia and the media to exert increasing control over citizens through nudging and other behavioural science techniques.

Large-scale coordinated cyber and physical attacks were carried out against major media headquarters and top universities, resulting in their decimation.

While reports suggested potential indirect involvement of opposing government and media elements, concrete evidence was lacking. The attacks, largely tech orchestrated, resulted in remarkably minimal loss of life.

The government, in response to public demands for change, went through a complete overhaul, significantly diminishing its role and completely changing how it interacts with citizens.

Power was decentralised to local communities, placing greater responsibility on people to govern their own lives within their locales.

The police, military, and the judicial system were integrated into a single organisation called Section One. They worked much closer together, and over the next few decades this became the primary function of government, releasing much of the rest of managing society to the people themselves.

The next day Ben was still out of his mind with worry. He'd hardly slept. Section One came and went. They'd tried to help as much as they could, but there was no evidence of anyone tampering with the locks or windows in Ben's home.

In fact one of the only theories left to them was that Ben had taken her himself and left her somewhere. But there was simply not enough evidence to suggest that, and with all the positive character references Ben had, it just didn't fit, not aside from the fact he had no motive—that they were aware of at least.

There wasn't much more he expected Section One to be able to do. Alice wasn't the only child to go missing. There were several unsolved cases on Section Ones' books. It wasn't quite enough to be an epidemic, so they hadn't gone the route of setting up a separate task force, but it was becoming a bit more frequent than the odd missing person.

Each time the situations were different. Alice's case didn't match any of the others, so after going through the usual routine of taking down the particulars and questioning all concerned, there wasn't much more they could do.

Ben needed to get out. He left the house and went for a wander down into the park to clear his head. He was in autopilot mode as he walked through the gates and headed for the woods as he'd done hundreds of times before.

He thought of all the stories he had read of missing children and some of the nasty things that had happened to them. He knew he shouldn't let his mind wonder, but he couldn't help it. He suddenly felt warm.

It was a grey day, not cold but certainly not hot. The warmth Ben felt seemed unnatural, like walking into a heated shop on a cold day. It was as he walked past a particular tree he noticed it.

Walking backwards and forwards to check he wasn't going mad, Ben worked out which tree it was. As he stepped closer he thought of Alice and how her touch had made objects unnaturally warmer.

"I wonder if this is the same thing?" Ben pondered to himself. He walked to within touching distance of the tree and then around it. What he saw took his breath away.

Looking down he saw his beloved daughter Alice sitting quietly hugging her knees whilst staring at her toes, still wearing her night dress she had on when he'd left her last night.

"Monkey!" Ben exclaimed. "What are you doing here?"

There was no immediate response. Alice was slowly rocking backwards and forwards, seemingly in a daze. Then suddenly she tilted her head up towards him.

"Daddy!" She cried out, immediately jumping up and hugging her father. Ben picked her up, wrapping his arms tightly around her.

"How did you get here? I've been worried sick? Are you all right?" He asked, tears streaming from his eyes.

"Daddy? You brought me here, silly," she replied matter-of-factly.

"When? When did I bring you here?" he enquired ignoring the fact she'd called him silly.

"Yesterday. We went for walk. Can we go home now?" Alice asked, confused.

"Of course, Monkey. Have you eaten? Are you OK? Are you hungry? Let's go home and eat."

"Daddy. You're asking lots of questions!" She asked, drawing her brows together.

"I know, Monkey. I'm just so pleased to see you again. I didn't know what happened to you. Let's go home and we'll get something to eat. Then we can talk about what happened," Ben said.

"OK, Daddy" Alice replied calmly.

# CHAPTER 5

## DISCOVERY

Ben and Alice arrived back at the house just as Olivia was peering out the window. Spying them, she shouted down, "Ben! What's going on?"

"Look who I found!" Ben shouted back with a sense of relief, yet still having so many questions going round in his head that he'd deal with later.

"I'm coming down!" shouted Olivia as she hurriedly slammed the window and ran out to meet Ben and Alice.

"So where have you been?" she asked excitedly, throwing her arms around Alice and giving her the biggest bear hug.

"I've been in the park," said Alice, unaware of the worry and commotion her vanishing had caused.

Before Olivia could ask anymore questions, Ben thought he should end it whilst he could. He wanted to find out what happened himself first. "Yes, we're going to find out all the details...aren't we, Monkey? But after we've had something to eat."

"Yes, Daddy, but we only went to the park," she replied with the same beaming smile as when Ben found her.

"I'll catch up with you later, Oli. Thanks so much for your help...really appreciate it. We'll find out...I'll let you know what this is all about once I know myself," he declared, as he opened the front door and started walking in.

"Don't forget to let Section One know..." Oli said over her shoulder having started to head back to her own front door. Ben turned to listen as she continued. "...I forgot to say, they sent someone round this morning looking for you. Just a routine follow-up, but they'll need to know," she said before stopping, turning fully and beaming, "So glad she's back!"

"Thanks, Oli. Yeah, me too," Ben smiled, as he followed Alice back into the house.

"Let's get you changed, Monkey," he said straining to hold off the interrogation for now.

"Can I wear my red dress? Please, Daddy!" Alice pleaded.

The red dress in question was one that her grandmother had given her on the occasion of Alice's fifth birthday just a few months ago. She loved it more than any of the others and would wear it to bed if her dad would let her.

"Of course, Monkey," said Ben, just happy for her to get out of the nightie that she'd obviously been out in all night.

As Alice was changing, Ben's mind wandered.

'What was she thinking? Why did she say I brought her to the park?' Racking his brain, he tried to remember anything out of the ordinary from the night before. Nothing was forthcoming. How was it possible for him to take Alice away then to come back with no recollection of what happened? He needed answers, and he wanted to get them before Section One came back.

Alice finished changing, then grabbed her toy rabbit—affectionately named Boris after an imaginary goldfish she had—as they headed downstairs toward the kitchen. Ben prepared some food, which was hastily scoffed down.

Still sitting at the table, Alice was playing with Boris whilst Ben cleared away the plates.

"Monkey...now you've eaten, Daddy just wants to find out what happened last night. OK?"

"Sure, Daddy. We went to the park." She'd said this a few times. He tried not to get annoyed. It wasn't her fault after all.

'Why can't I remember?' thought Ben. Stopping his washing up, and drying his hands, he turned Alice's chair to face him as he stooped down. Looking up into her dark brown eyes, sunk deep into her olive brown skin, he enquired, "Do you remember me reading to you?"

"Yes. We read about Ruth," she replied.

"Yes, that's right. What happened after that?"

"You woke me up and then we went for a walk in the park," Alice said.

That was the worrying bit. Ben could only remember going to his office after reading with Alice, finishing the Tranget job and heading back to check on her—only to realise she wasn't there.

Alice could read the concern on her dad's face.

"You OK, Daddy?" she asked.

"Yes, Monkey. I just don't remember going for a walk with you...I remember having a can of AsTir to keep me awake," he carried on—more to himself than to Alice—"so I could get my work done. I must admit, I can't actually remember doing the work itself, only sending an email...The email!" he exclaimed. "I wonder what I actually sent to the client? Hopefully, I didn't botch this up."

Ben stood up quickly. A bit too quickly as he stood still for a few moments to settle the inevitable head-rush.

"Follow me, Monkey. I just need to check something. Let's go to my office," he said as they walked out.

"Sit here for a moment," he said, seating Alice down in his large office chair, not wanting to let her out of his sight.

"Yes, Daddy," said Alice, happy enough holding her toy rabbit in her lap, occasionally lifting it up to her mouth to whisper something in its ear. It was warm.

Ben waved his hand in front of the sleek black console, forcing the display to come to life. His Basecamp software still open, he moved his hand towards the Tranget deck, tapped the virtual folder and did the same on the "Email the Client," option.

His last sent email was at the top of the list. He tapped it and read out loud:

"'I enclose the final draft of the copy for the Tranget sub site, as discussed. All the changes have been implemented. I hope they are to your satisfaction. Any further questions let me know. Ben.'"

"Phew! I can't quite remember writing it...but at least it's OK. Not even a spelling error...that's always embarrassing when that happens."

Alice was paying no attention. Too consumed by Boris.

"Right," said Ben out loud, but to himself. "At some point between writing that email and heading to your room, something must have happened. No. No. that can't be right. It was 10 p.m. when I found you," he said, turning toward Alice but continuing to think aloud "...and it was 7.30 p.m. when I woke up after falling asleep in your room then headed to my office. I remember checking the time. So some time between 7.30 p.m. and 10 p.m....I can only assume I took you out to the park. I'm sure someone must have noticed? It must be caught on camera somewhere. I'll have to message Section One."

Ben stooped in front of Alice. Looking lovingly at her sitting obediently in the chair, he asked, "Can you tell me exactly what happened, Monkey...after I came into your room and woke you up...then what?"

"You said we were going to the park," she replied, twisting her hair round her fingers and swinging her legs.

Ben chewed the inside of his mouth "Did I say why?" he asked.

Alice was visibly tired now. He wouldn't keep her for much longer, but the grilling she'd get from Section One would be much tougher.

"You said I had to meet them by the tree..." Alice responded.

"Them?" he queried worryingly. "Did I say who they were and why you had to meet them?" A hint of panic understandably rising in his voice.

"No," Alice replied.

"Did you see them?"

"No. I sat down by the tree. I was tired. I went to sleep," she responded wearily.

"What happened then?" Ben questioned.

"I don't know, Daddy. I was asleep!" said Alice, baffled by her dad's question. "When I woke up, I saw you and was happy," she smiled.

"Was that this morning, Monkey?"

"Yes, Daddy."

Alice, though tired, answered much of Ben's questions matter-of-fact, like it was the most normal thing in the world to go to the park in the evening still in her nightie and meet some strangers.

Ben knew his daughter doted on him. She completely trusted him, so if he asked her to come to the park to meet someone, she would do it unquestioningly. It reminded him of Abraham and Isaac, recorded in the Old Testament. He believed she would follow him even unto death. Whilst this was a positive indication of the very close bond they held, he couldn't help but feel concerned, that with what happened last night, what if there were more occasions where he simply wasn't aware what he might ask her to do?

Ben tried to summarise what had happened:

"So I took you to the park, said you had to meet them, whoever they are. You then fell asleep and when you woke up, I was looking at you?" he said.

"Yes, that's it, Daddy."

"You didn't wake up in the night? no one else saw or took you anywhere?"

"No, Daddy." Alice yawned

"OK, Monkey. I'm just trying to find out what went on," he tried to say without showing his frustration. "You can go to bed now."

Ben, still none the wiser, followed Alice up the stairs as she headed towards her room. This time as she climbed into bed, still in her red dress, he sat on the chair watching her fall asleep, not daring to take his eyes off her. Though Ben knew he couldn't do this forever.

He accessed his ComTel and messaged Section One to let them know Alice had been found. An almost instantaneous response was sent back thanking him for letting them know and that they would send someone round within twenty-four hours to assess the situation.

Wanting to check his console to find out if anyone else had had similar experiences, but not wanting to leave Alice, Ben switched on the monitor in her room. Lydia had used the same one the very last time she saw her daughter. It was old now, but he couldn't bear to change it. It still worked.

Disappearing into his office now in the comfort that he could still keep his eyes on his daughter via the screen, he waved his hand in front of the Console, bringing it back to life.

Pulling up a browser, he typed in the phrase missing time experiences. He knew it was roughly between 7.30 p.m. and 10 p.m. that aside from emailing, he couldn't recall his actions. He was slowly coming round to the idea that he must have taken Alice to the park. There was currently no other explanation.

He waded through the search results, some recounting tales of people missing whole days, to some, just like him, a few hours.

It suddenly occurred to him he hadn't actually checked the attachment he sent to his client. The email was OK, but what had he actually written for the project?

Swiping his browser out of the way, he called up his Basecamp and tapped open the email. He saw two attachments. The first was as expected. He quickly scanned through it to make sure it was all his content. It was.

Selecting the second attachment, he attempted to open it, but a password requestor popped up. That's strange, he said and instead opened up the meta-data as he was so used to doing to avoid scam emails. He noticed it signed COB. 'What's COB?' he wondered.

Looking at the data, he noticed the location given—where he assumed the attachment originated. It was the Complex—an out-of-world colony, part of five regional communities over 700 light years from Earth. It made no sense to him, so he selected the attachment again and almost absentmindedly typed in the password "Alice51,"—the year of her birth.

The attachment opened full screen. Ben's eyes nearly bulged out of their sockets as he took in the images and text assaulting his senses via his screen. He panicked. Standing up quickly, nearly knocking over the chair, he rushed into Alice's room, lifted her left arm and under her armpit saw a tiny red mole... exactly as he'd seen on the attachment.

In frustration, he buried his head into his daughter's side, wrapping his arms around her. She didn't stir. Feelings of anger growing within him, the only saving grace being now he knew exactly what happened between 7.30 p.m. and 10 p.m. yesterday evening.

# CHAPTER 6

## THE SHUMEN

2114 - 49 YEARS BEFORE PRESENT DAY

Looking at him, you'd be forgiven for thinking he was older than he was. Tall with long spindly legs covered by a tight fitting pant-suit, his dark olive brown skin, not completely smooth, definitely showing signs of wear and tear, but that could also have been the markings he had over the left side of his face. It looked like a series of tattoos. Across his chest was displayed a sharp gold criss-cross pattern beautifully embroidered into a dark blue gown, very reminiscent of archaic religious garb.

The man was fervently pacing back and forth within the confines of a relatively small room in the bunker. This was MendipT, and his irritability was getting annoying.

"Will you just stop!" shouted SentiN, sitting on a burgundy antique-looking sofa, opposite his friend and colleague. "You're triggering my sinuses!"

SentiN was dressed similarly. In fact, it was the Shumen's uniform. Being a community-oriented people, they embraced uniformity in both looks and indeed thoughts as a way of belonging.

This was one of the many reasons they were chosen by Sendo eXperience to be the first inhabitants of the forth-coming Complex–an out-of-world colony to be built as part of five regional communities over 700 light years away from Earth. Chosen, being the operative word.

Sendo had actually run a two year long competition where hundreds of people groups had applied to become the new tenants. The criteria were:

- No involvement in wars, either civil or international, within the prior 100 years
- Less than 100,000 population in total in one location
- Less than 20% gene mix with other people groups
- Completely self-governed
- Carrying no debt
- Financially self-sustaining
- Above average levels of productivity
- One dominant worldview

Many people groups matched several of the criteria and had put themselves forwards. But the area where the majority fell was that of self-governance and gene mix. Some were subject to larger nations' laws, even if indirectly through supra-national groups. Others had full-on mixed with other local— or not so local—people groups diluting their indigenous gene pool.

Only three groups matched all the criteria. Each was invited to 'battle it out'—as the promotional material had put it— through a series of long-term tasks, testing their ability to deal with the kinds of challenges that would be thrown at them living in a brand new colony hundreds of light years from Earth.

The bunker MendipT was pacing in was a replica of the forthcoming Complex, of which construction was due to start in six years' time. It was now 2114. The replica, having recently been completed, would be home to the rest of the Shumenic people, due to move in any day now. But MendipT was having second thoughts. Though, to be honest, this was not uncommon for him.

"We're going to lose control!" he snorted contemptuously. "We are a proud people, and we are signing our lives away to be controlled by a jumped up corporation who shares no values with us."

He stopped pacing and leant against the wall, almost to steady his mind as well as his body. He looked exasperated, though tried not to show it.

SentiN was perhaps, right at this moment, even more exasperated with his friend. With frustration building, he muttered through clenched teeth,

"Why are you saying this now? We've had two years to learn everything there is to know. Our people are literally about to move in here," he swept his hand out for emphasis, "and you come to me with this!"

He clasped his fists and leant forward in the chair. SentiN was the closest the Shumen had to a leader. Their rivalry meant that MendipT always felt his friend, who he'd grown up with, so often had the upper hand. He knew he was the more hot-headed one, whereas SentiN was cool, and calm—which frustrated him even more.

MendipT was always trying to fight him, or someone. He was the kind of person who could argue with a wall if he wanted. 'Definitely an outlier,' SentiN surmised, and a thought occurred to him he must have been holding himself back during the two-year competition, as there's no way the Shumen would have been chosen with such a rebellious individual as MendipT. Perhaps that's why it was all coming out now. He had held back, and SentiN was now reaping the *rewards* for that.

SentiN took a deep breath. MendipT just stared into space.

"Look. Sit." He motioned to the seat next to him. MendipT sat, though kept his eyes looking straight ahead. SentiN continued. "We are going to be the first people group of such a great size to live on a completely constructed colony. We will run the place. Our more in-depth training is still on the horizon. You have already gone through the initial sessions, so you are aware of our dependence on each other, not on Sendo."

Leaning back in the chair, he pulled up his foot to rest on his knee. It looked painful with his long legs, but he was so used to it, it felt comfortable for him.

MendipT's expression hadn't changed. SentiN tried a different approach.

"The people look up to you. They need to see a confident MendipT. One eager at the prospect of our people's future. Remember," he went on, "hundreds of other groups applied, but only we, the Shumen, won. Now the Complex will be ours to run as we see fit. What's not to like?"

For now, MendipT calmed down. "I know, Brother." They weren't blood brothers, but their relationship down the years —even if they were drifting apart latterly—suggested otherwise. "We just need to be careful. We've drifted into this. I'm not saying I didn't like it at the beginning. I'm not even saying I don't like it now, but we need to keep our eyes open, brother. That's all I'm saying," he concluded, much more controlled as he wiped a piece of dust from his chest.

"Noted, Brother. Noted," SentiN replied, knowing it was not even worth arguing and pleased that his friend seemed less agitated.

"It's time, gentlemen," came a smooth female voice from a panel on the wall.

SentiN and MendipT had been waiting for a Sendo representative to outline the next steps for their people to enter the replica Complex. Both men stood up together and headed towards a door from where the voice appeared to emanate.

What they knew so far was that every procedure that would happen when they finally moved into the real Complex in several years' time, would be replicated. Sendo wanted it as realistic as possible. This included air pressurisation—all mimicked at least—and, originally, it included cryogenic preservation for whilst the people were travelling to the Complex.

However, recent advances in Faster Than Light transportation, known as FTL, rendered that unnecessary. This was a relief to SentiN, who hadn't relished the idea of being frozen, not knowing what his resurrection would be like, and that's assuming it happened without a hitch. Regardless, they were about to find out the exact itinerary so they could relay it to their people.

It was a momentous occasion and despite MendipT's reservations, a big part of him was excited by the prospect. Though another part of him had already been making preparations in case things didn't work out the way he wanted. His back-up plan, which–if it worked–and it was a big 'if', would place him in control of not only his people, but with a little luck, potentially Sendo as well.

## CHAPTER 7

## MUSEUM TRIP

2163 - Present day

"It's freezing!" said Sabine rather dramatically, taking her jacket out of her bag and wrapping it around her shoulders. It was chilly in Sab City Museum but certainly not freezing. Seven years after her overnight disappearance, Alice, now twelve, didn't feel the cold as much as her friends. She was happily wearing a t-shirt and jeans and thought nothing of it.

The museum, having been recently refurbished, stood as an imposing presence to the east of Sab City. Designed and run by Sendo eXperience, whose head office was just the other side of the library, it was certainly a striking structure.

The main brick building was surrounded by hundreds of perspex slats, which, when viewed at certain angles and in just the right light, made the building appear to disappear. Naturally, a building that vanished every now and again could lead to many a nasty accident. So Sendo wisely thought of that and painted a red luminescent line around each outside edge, giving it a quite bizarre and childish cartoonistic feel. Despite many wondering who'd signed off on that design decision, most people, rather surprisingly, viewed it favourably.

Inside, Sab City Museum was just as innovative. Many sections were designed to be changed at the push of a button or two. Partitioned walls could change in height, width and even location; pathways guiding visitors through the exhibitions could be reset at a touch; lighting could completely transform a bleak grey exhibition area into a warm, bright and sunny space.

From the control rooms on the ground floor, the museum curator and designers, as well as the on duty manager, really had complete control over each and every aspect of the museum. This was a raison d'être for Sendo. In every experience they created, they wanted their client to have maximum impact and total control.

Alice smiled at Sabine as on they walked, away from the rest of their Learning Group to a replica of the European Union original treaty underneath a large map of Europe in 2017.

"So, all of these countries used to be joined together?" Sabine asked Ben, one of the responsible adults accompanying them on their Learning Groups' history trip. Before Ben had a chance to respond, Alice chimed in.

"Sort of. They were still separate countries, though some shared the same currency—you know, money system, but there was a group that was effectively a government for all of them."

"But why would they do that? What did the government do?" Sabine quizzed. Again, before Ben had a chance...

"It was all about being big back then. They didn't really see the power of individual nations—let alone individual people to be able to determine their own direction in life. They thought that people couldn't be trusted to make decisions for themselves, so they put in lots of rules and regulations that the people had to follow. Isn't that right, Dad?"

Ben was constantly amazed at the intelligence of his twelve-year-old daughter. She could easily be at least triple her age from some of the things she came out with. 'She must have got that from her mother,' he thought, smiling to himself.

"Yes, that's sort of right, monkey. There were different groups that effectively managed Europe and worked out trade deals with other parts of the world, amongst other things. It was started with good intentions, though; to maintain peace after two particularly destructive world wars. But like many things that grow big over time, the original vision got swallowed up in bureaucracy..."

"Buroc..what?" asked Sabine screwing her face up.

"You know, er, administration, making stuff happen," he replied.

"Oh Right!" Sabine acknowledged as Ben continued.

"...and all the admin, has a natural tendency to create a greater distance between the law-makers and the people they make laws for. Like I say, it's not all done out of bad intentions. Some people really wanted to see positive change happening. But regardless, all that started to change in 2019 when we, as part of the United Kingdom at the time, took ourselves out from being managed by the European Union."

"United Kingdom?" quizzed Alice. "What's that?"

Ben responded to a rare bit of information that must have passed her by.

"You know, England, Scotland, Wales, and Northern Ireland?" He replied.

"Yes, of course," Alice said, thinking she vaguely recalled hearing something about it.

"They all used to be effectively one country..." Ben continued.

"...called the United Kingdom!" finished Sabine as if to show she knew something Alice didn't. Though in reality she hadn't heard of the UK before either.

"So we did the same thing as Europe?" Alice asked.

"Yes, honey. It's like you said, there were different views on things back then. If a country focused on making sure its own people were looked after first, and perhaps didn't want to join other global organisations, this was seen as selfish. They called it isolationism. They just didn't see that the ability to self-govern could give more opportunity to embrace other people and countries different from themselves instead of trying to get everyone to conform to being the same."

Ben was in full flow now, not even noticing Sabine as she was making funny faces, whilst moving from one leg to the other like a penguin.

"There were some people who predicted it would actually lead to more peace, stability, and co-operation, but only a few and they weren't generally the ones listened to. It definitely proved many people wrong—not that they ever admitted it." He continued, well in his element.

"I want to look at the GF2.0 exhibition," said Sabine, now being more obvious with her state of boredom. "...not seen that before, and..." she twirled around to face Alice, perking up slightly, but with hesitancy she asked, "Wasn't your granny involved with that?"

Alice glanced at her dad as if to say, 'you respond...that's above my pay grade.' Ben looked back at her in perfect understanding. "There's been lots of rumours, Bine. She was a remarkable lady."

Then he sighed, changing the subject and looking around the room. "Where are the others?"

"They're still with Olivia at the Mars exhibit," Alice replied.

"OK. We'd better wait for them and all go together. I know the others wanted to see GF2.0 too." But Alice and Sabine were getting stir crazy, waiting for the others.

"Dad. We're going to the bathroom," moaned Alice, as Sabine and her were already speeding away.

"OK, Monkey. Don't be long," he warned as he shifted his eyes toward the girls. "I'll be right here," he said, unaware it would be the last time he would see his daughter in a long time.

⏃

The Learning Group that Alice and Sabine belonged to comprised several other families, a few of whom were blood related. Ben often saw it as one big family with a few stragglers. He was one of the stragglers. They mostly lived near each other and had grown up together. The children, of which by now there were quite a few, all played together—and fought together, as children do—as well as learned together.

It wasn't like that in all the Learning Groups, however. There were some parents who, despite nearly eighty years passing since GF2.0, always harkened back to the 'good ol' days' they'd heard about from their parents and grandparents. "They had it easy," they'd say, as they could drop their kids off at schools in the morning and not have to think about them for several hours until they had to pick them up later, and if there were after-school clubs, well...that was even better.

In Ben's Learning Group, they'd shared good times—and bad. Had a few fallings out, but their shared Christian faith held them together throughout life's little...and big, ups and downs. The love and support that Ben had felt from his extended family, especially since losing his wife Lydia, had kept him sane. It meant so much, keeping him from more regularly visiting those dark places in his mind.

With his command of the English language through his job and passion, Ben adored regularly taking Alice, Sabine and several of the other children for English lessons. His equal love of history lead him to where they were today in Sab City Museum.

# CHAPTER 8

## THE BOY

A BANK OF DISPLAY SCREENS CONTINUOUSLY flashed, showing images of various locations around the museum. One showed a group sitting in the theatre area, then flashed to the west stairwell. Another showing the main reception area before flicking to the AutoJet park and back again.

Robert Tomulski, a middle-aged man of Polish descent, stared at them, his head moving from one screen to the next as if captivated by what he was looking at, but really trying to spot anything that looked out of the ordinary.

His rugged figure gave away a previous life spent throwing an oval-shaped ball across green grass. He'd had to give it up several years ago due to a recurring cruciate ligament injury. But even though he could still keep himself fit, he was no match for Frank.

"Do we have confirmation?" enquired Robert, turning around to face his colleague.

"The boy is a go. He said it's as good a way as any," Frank responded.

Turning back around and touching the side of his head, Robert issued the following order.

"The boy is in play. Stand by and wait for my command."

Frank Marcos had worked for Sendo eXperience for many years in various positions. Now, as Head of Security in one of their most recent *experiences*, it was his job to protect the investments and assets of the company. He carried out his job with pride and, as typical for security personnel at his level, an army background was a given.

His body looked like it had been designed specifically to withstand most kinds of physical assault. He'd taken many punches, not to mention been directly shot at, at least fifteen times—and lived to tell the tale. He could not have been better suited to the role had it been designed for him.

Robert felt his jacket pocket vibrate. Pulling out his ComTel, he answered with a slight sense of frustration.

"I'm kinda in the middle of something right now. Everything OK?" Ignoring his emotive response, the woman on the end of the line said rather directly,

"Hi Honey, you were gonna let me know what time you're back tonight as we have Brian and Donna coming round for about 8 p.m. remember?" There was a little frustration in her voice, too.

"Eight o'clock sounds fine. I should be home by seven, and I'll pick up some wine on the way back."

"Could you also grab some dessert, honey...?" she asked.

"You want honey for dessert?" Robert smirked, then quickly his expression changed.

"Don't be smart. It doesn't suit you. I won't have time to prepare dinner and dessert tonight."

"OK. Sure, I'll see you at seven."

With that, she hung up.

All the while, Robert was on the phone, he hadn't taken his eyes off the screens. Now his full concentration returned, he was focused on one screen only. That one contained a medium close-up of Alice Harman.

Alice stood leaning against the wall, waiting for Sabine to emerge from the bathroom. She had always wondered why her older female friends in particular, and it seems Sabine, took so long in bathrooms whenever they went out together. She never did. Went in, did what she needed to, got out. Simple.

She busied herself looking around at the different people milling about in the museum. It wasn't super busy, but there were enough characters for Alice to gaze at using her wonderfully vivid, imagination.

She could stand for hours taking in each person and crafting intricate stories about their life. Right now, a couple was sitting on a bench across the hall. She, was tall with dark curly hair. He was slightly shorter, with a bushy beard and light, slightly greying hair. "Recently married. Must be," Alice surmised out loud. They weren't especially into *culture*, but it was something to do together on a Saturday afternoon. Hand in hand, they ate a sandwich in silence, but with a knowing, comfortable smile.

A family—Alice presumed it was a family—was staring at a holographic map. The woman looked like she was of Asian descent, whilst the man had a bit of Eastern Europe about him. They had three children, the little girl who was pulling at her mother's dress to get her moving. Alice imagined they were a very studious family, who took in every detail of each exhibit they looked at. The little girl reminded her of Sabine; always wanting to move on to the next thing. Never sitting still.

Then there was a little boy sitting on his own, looking quite disconsolate. She wondered why he would be alone and expected at any moment for his parents to wander into view.

She looked, but no one came. She thought he couldn't be much older than six. Getting a little concerned, she decided she would go over to him, but just then Sabine sauntered out of the bathroom.

"Hey," Alice said, moving towards Sabine, shoving her bag at her. "Hold this a minute, Bine. Be back in a sec."

"Er...OK," muttered Sabine quizzically as she gripped the bag, eyes fixed on Alice as she wandered across the hall.

Alice headed toward the boy, who was still sitting quietly and staring at his feet. He was looking quite smart in a shirt and trousers and carrying a small reversible rucksack.

"Hey little man. You OK?"

He looked up without responding while seemingly taking in every detail of Alice's face.

"I...I've lost my group. I think they went that way." He motioned round the corner.

"Was it your mum and dad?" Alice asked.

"My mum. Dad had to go to work."

"That's OK. Let's look for her together," she smiled at him as she put her hand on the boy's shoulder as they walked off round the corner, then along a corridor and about to turn right when...

"That's it!" exclaimed the boy. "That's where they went!"

The black door was solid, what seemed like wood, and had no signage on it whatsoever. There was a small glass window towards the top, but this was blacked out, defeating the object of a window, Alice pondered. The door was indicative of a control room door rather than entry to a specific public exhibition.

"Are you sure?" she asked.

"They said they were going to be in the room round the corner as I was putting my shoe back on. They were sad I was taking too long," the boy explained, a clear sadness in his tone.

"OK. Well, no bother. Let's go in and see," Alice replied, still guiding him towards the door.

"OK," he acknowledged.

Alice opened the door and walked in, observing banks of display screens and flashing lights against the back wall. Sitting down on two high-back chairs in front of a large control panel were two men. They were staring intently right at them.

"Hello," said Alice softly, as though she were in a library. "This kid says his mum and group were..." Her voice trailed off as she motioned round to the boy who was nowhere to be seen.

Frank, the man closest to her, turned round, stood up, towering over her. Taking two steps towards her, he said calmly,

"Alice, isn't it?"

"Er... yes. Who are you?" she replied.

A pause bordering on uncomfortable ensued as Frank weighed up what he was going to say next.

"We've been waiting seven years for you," were his carefully selected words.

"You what?" Questioned Alice, naturally confused.

"I'm going to be blunt. We need you to come with us. We need your help with something that is going to be life-changing. You will have the opportunity to change things in this world for the better. Like I say, we've been waiting a long time for this moment," Frank explained.

Alice's skin started to tingle, a sign that she was heating up from within. She didn't hear everything he said. She heard 'life-changing,' and 'better world,' but the rest was clouded by a sense of wanting to get out of the room.

In a panic, she spun and grabbed for the door handle, only to realise...there wasn't one. She pushed the door, then when nothing happened, she barged it with her shoulder, then tried to get her fingers down the side to pull at it. Neither Frank nor Robert moved.

Robert had turned around to face Frank, giving him a questioning look, then he turned back to observe Alice in her predicament. Frank tried to calm her down.

"That door is solid wood with a metal inner core and, as you can see, there's no handle. It's a security door and won't open unless we tell it to. Look, we won't hurt you. That's not why you're here. We just need you to do some things for us," he said.

Alice, slumped against the door, partly resigned that she wasn't getting out unless they wanted her to, but she was also looking for a window of opportunity.

"You know…" she started, pointing at the cameras "…that my dad and friends are out there and will be looking for me?" She quickly thought, hoping this would be to some advantage. It wasn't.

"Yes, of course. We thought of that, and right now," Frank motioned to the monitor pointing at her dad and Sabine, "right now, they are being told that you have been taken ill and rushed to a Health Improvement Centre."

Alice watched the screen, observing an older woman in a smart suit begin talking with her dad. Shortly after that, her eyes welled up as she recognised a look of panic on his face. As she continued watching, he rushed away, out of sight of the camera. Just as that happened, the screens went blank.

"Why are you doing this?" Alice shouted. "Why me?" Tears were flowing down her face now. Frank, handed her a box of tissues, which she accepted, wiping her eyes before blowing her nose.

"I wish I could fully answer that question. I really do. All I can say is that you are very special…a unique young lady. I can't tell you how humbling and exciting it is to meet you, having heard so much about you. I know this doesn't seem like the best way of introducing ourselves to you, but trust me, there was no simple way."

He genuinely seemed apologetic as he explained her predicament.

"So what is it you want me to do?" She replied, starting to become resigned to her fate. Whatever that was.

"That's more like it. And, like I say, I'm really, really sorry this had to happen this way. We mean you no harm, but what it is we need you to do—which I will share with you, just not right now—is of critical importance. It's more important than all of us," Robert said.

"Just one thing," he continued, "and don't think this weird. Did you know you have a mark under your left armpit?" He asked.

"My birthmark? Yes, of course," she replied, wondering what relevance this had to anything.

"Ah…Is that what he told you?" Frank stroked his chin.

"He?" she asked, still puzzled.

"Yes, Ben…your dad," he replied.

"He said it was a mark that everyone has, just mine is under my arm," said Alice, still confused.

"Well, I can tell you, that's not a birthmark. We put it there on your fifth birthday, the last time we saw you. It really has been a long seven years waiting to meet you again."

# CHAPTER 9
## ABNORMAL CIRCUMSTANCES

6 MONTHS LATER

He stared at it as though he expected it to move. The long-since-gone-cold toast sat untouched on Ben's plate. The smell of a conservative amount of butter mixed with something resembling Marmite drifted to his nostrils. Not that he recognised it. He still couldn't bring himself to eat much; his appetite decidedly reduced since losing his daughter six months ago.

Ben dropped his head to the table, narrowly avoiding head butting the plate. It made him feel marginally better, having released the physical weight of his head from his current mental anguish. He clenched his fists.

"I've lost her again. I lost my wife. Now my only daughter. God, what have I done?" He cried, knowing that if he wasn't careful, it would lead to his mind wandering into *the abyss*, as his friends called it. Not a nice place to be.

Last time, just months ago, his Learning Group grew worried, not having heard from him in days. Ben could still vividly recall the mixture of surprise and relief on his best friend Nathan's face when he'd finally opened the door to let him in several days later. Eyes wide, worry etched all over them. It was a look Ben never wanted to see again.

"God, give me the strength to get up and get out," he cried, almost as a whisper, before slowly raising himself up and heading for the bathroom.

The door slammed shut as Ben left his flat, strolling down the street heading for WriteAngle cafe on Roman Street. In normal circumstances, it was his favourite place to work, and right now, even though things were far from normal, he still felt drawn there. Sitting and writing. Nothing else mattered. The weight of his bitter loss made it difficult for him to do anything else.

WriteAngle was often a bustling place. Today was no different. Ben ambled in, his shoulders slouched; gaze lost in the distance before noticing a few guests making moves toward packing up. It wouldn't be a long wait to grab a seat.

Every desk was a hive of activity, with guests either busy scribbling on their Aidea's, tapping away, reading, or having animated discussions with friends. Ben envied them. What he would give to be sitting at a table laughing with his little monkey. If only.

"Hey Ben!" This was Andy, one of the regular servers. Ben normally loved the warmth he received from all the staff. The time he'd spent there practically made him part of the furniture. Now, dividing his life into before and after Alice, the after side made it difficult to truly belong.

He gave a half-wave, trying to muster a smile, as he wandered over to the bar. Leaning casually against its beautifully smooth, long surface, he studied it closely, wondering what it was made of. It almost appeared to be some sort of liquefied wood and he was surprised he'd not noticed it before.

Heading towards a now free table, the pool of light flickered on as he sat down. Already having nodded his order to Andy —the benefits of being a regular—his favourite Rooibos Vanilla tea was on its way along with, a blueberry muffin. He'd hated those as a kid; couldn't see the fascination. Yeah, they were healthy, but that taste. Eww! It reminded him of a time when Lydia instigated a healthy eating regime whilst pregnant with Alice. Ben let his mind wander.

⌂

"I've got to eat for two of us now, so that means we're gonna need to watch more closely what we eat," Lydia said as Ben groaned. He was naturally healthy and fit despite eating his fair share of fast food, and his weakest point was when going through a mammoth writing sprint for one of his more demanding clients. The local eateries knew when he had an intense job on. They didn't complain.

Lydia had walked across the kitchen toward him, resting a hand on his chest; looking him straight in the eyes. He melted, knowing what she said next would be the epitome of her love for him. Well, either that or she was about to drop a guilt bomb.

"You've got to look after your heart, my love. I don't want my husband dying of a heart attack, so I have to bring up our child on my own." Ben broke her stare.

"Well, at least we have a Health Improvement Centre just down the road," he quipped, immediately regretting it.

"That's not funny, Ben," she said, her annoyance clear in her tone as she pushed away from him and returned to the cooking.

'What an idiot I am!' he thought. Walking up behind her, he put his arms around her.

"I'm sorry, hun," he said. "Here's what I'll do," thinking quickly, as he planted a kiss on her neck. "I'll not have another takeaway until after our daughter is born. OK?" She thought for a few seconds.

"OK...and you'll eat blueberries...starting with the blueberry muffins I bought yesterday, right?" Ben screwed up his face, though Lydia couldn't see. He really didn't like blueberries. They tasted like eating musky wood. Why anyone would do that, he just didn't know. Yet, he remained determined to see this through, a small sacrifice compared to what she was giving up to give birth.

"You drive a hard bargain, Mrs Harman, but OK. Deal." Lydia smiled as she turned around to face him, a curious expression on her face.

"Great. But one question..."

"Uh, oh..." he smiled, wondering if he should be worried, his hands moving up her head, his thumbs lightly caressing her neck. "What's up?" he asked.

"How do you know we're having a girl?" Ben smiled with slight relief, his gaze moving up to the ceiling. For as long as he could remember, he'd wanted a daughter. A girl who especially shared his love of words. There's nothing more he would love than sitting down with her reading together from the book of Job. He looked back at his wife, his smile still apparent.

"I just do," he replied, having a strong hunch he'd be right.

All these years later he had been right, and it was his eventual daughter Alice, as she had gotten older—both in natural age and her heightened maturity because of her genetic aberrations—who'd made sure he kept up the healthy eating regime. Alice also wanted a healthy Ben, just like her mother had.

A whiff of blueberries tickled his nostrils, pulling him back to the present as Andy brought over his order placing the tray on the table.

"Thanks, Andy," said Ben, as the server smiled and headed back to the bar. Taking a sip of tea, he winced as it burnt his lips. He let it cool, putting the clear glass cup down, before tapping his Aidea; the screen coming alive. He got to work.

# CHAPTER 10

## UNDERSTANDABLY CURIOUS

THE BUZZ OF BEN'S COMTEL DISTRACTED HIM. Normally he would have placed it in the distraction free device box, but today it slipped his mind. Ironically, he'd gotten distracted.

The display indicated that JR, one of his more recent clients, was calling. He liked him. They'd only exchanged a few brief conversations, but Ben had felt a comforting warmth radiating from JR, reminiscent of someone familiar. 'Who?' He thought as he pursed his brow, having a sense it was someone close to him.

The call connected.

"Hello JR!" Ben answered, a little louder than he'd expected, startling one of the nearby guests. Offering her a sheepish, apologetic look, he stood, picked up his device, and moved to a comms booth to continue the call. The table, detecting his temporary departure, displayed a *Back Soon* message, the letters hovering just above the desk.

"Hi Ben, good to speak to you again. How are you doing?" JR enquired.

"I'm OK, thanks," Ben replied, which was true. His mood had lifted somewhat, accepting—for the moment at least—there was nothing he could do about Alice. He continued, "I'm curious to know what you have for me, JR," he asked quickly to avoid any questions about his missing daughter, which he assumed JR knew about.

"That's good. That's good. I need to share more about LeV8 as an update to the very sketchy initial brief we sent," JR reported.

Ben smiled, remembering when he first saw the brief. It certainly was sketchy. There's no way he could start working on the project with such scant data.

The report said that JR's company was launching a product called LeV8, and that it was to be an additional, more interactive layer on top of the LinerVerse. Aside from a few technical details, that was pretty much it.

If Ben was honest, he was not the greatest fan of the LinerVerse. Its attention grabbing and addictive nature did not sit well with him. Ben felt sorry for those who'd succumbed to its wiles; those who'd spend days online, disconnected from reality. Not good.

However, it was a little known fact that he was also dabbling in the LinerVerse. But that was different. *He* wasn't addicted. *He* was just using it as a distraction from the emotional turmoil of losing his daughter. *That* was OK. And now... well...he was writing content for it, or going to at least.

The Ben of old, when Lydia was around, would have outright rejected this. She would have helped him to see the values mismatch. As well as the more obvious reality problem, she would have pointed out the subtle, and sometimes not so subtle, way the developers and oversight committee pushed a contrarian world-view very much at odds with their own Christian perspective.

This was fine for his other clients. No need for a shared world-view when writing copy about the benefits of unprocessed cat food. However, a product as ubiquitous as the LinerVerse; the ability to shape how users saw the world, well...it should have given Ben more pause for thought. Perhaps if he wasn't dabbling in it himself, he may have turned down this contract.

After Alice's disappearance, and without Lydia to provide that wise counsel, Ben was all over the place. He'd shelved work for the past four months as he was so stricken with grief, trying everything to get his daughter back, but to no avail. His friends encouraged him to ease back into work to help take his mind off things, letting Section One do their job. It worked. Slowly.

Ben's ears popped as he acclimated to the pressure change he always experienced when settling into a Comms Booth. Clean air circulated around like a fresh spring breeze in wildflower meadows.

He breathed deeply and focused back on JR. "Tell me what I should know," he asked; his ComTel sat on a purple shelf in front of him. The video activated. JR's head hovered over the ComTel base, like a genie appearing out of a lamp, the back-lighting giving the image a soft shimmer. Ben sat back, waiting for a response.

"My job is to ensure that you have a better understanding of the philosophy of the LinerVerse and its connection to LeV8," JR responded in his deep voice, sounding like an oak tree in winter.

"So you're the Plato of the LinerVerse operation?" replied Ben as JR laughed, a big hearty, honest laugh, triggering a fleeting memory of his grandpa.

"I'm not sure about that, Ben. But let's just say, hmmm...let me think...let's just say...that I stand on the shoulders of giants, and one of those giants is someone you know well."

"Who?" he asked, understandably curious as his forehead wrinkled in confusion.

"Well...before we get into that, I'd like to find out a bit more about you. I know we've spoken a couple of times, but they were brief," he qualified.

Ben's intrigue persisted, but he held it for now. "What do you want to know?" he asked, playing along.

"Just tell me what you think is relevant to give me more of a picture of who you are, your motivations and why you do what you do," JR answered.

'How to keep it short,' thought Ben as he sat up, pondering what to say. He leaned forward, observing JR's face as it seemed to retreat, perhaps having sat back in his chair.

Ben shared how he got into writing and his genuine passion for clear communication with authenticity and honesty; a bit about his wife and her death, not going into too much detail as he assumed they'd done their due diligence, and JR didn't ask.

He shared about Alice too, including her current 'missing person' status, but left out her short-term kidnapping some years earlier.

Despite that, Ben already felt comfortable with JR. The more he engaged, the more comfortable he felt, and he couldn't stop thinking about the striking resemblance—in both voice and appearance—with his grandad.

The scent of almond wafted towards Ben's nostrils as, through the glass, he spied a guest stabbing her knife into one sumptuous kernel-based croissant. Still in the booth, his mind overpowered the default wildflower meadows with the aroma he would have got had he been the one eating the pastry. His stomach growled, confirming its potential deliciousness. He shook off his distraction and focused back on the image hovering above the ComTel.

When Ben had finished, he was still keen to get to the point. "So, JR, tell me about the philosophy of the LinerVerse."

"Well, Ben. Firstly, let me offer my sympathy over what's happened to your daughter. That can't be easy to deal with," he said. "As you've indicated, you have to let Section One do their job, so getting back into work seems a wise move."

'So I keep being told,' thought Ben. "Thank's, JR. I'm just trying to focus on what I can do, and right now it's writing. So please continue," he replied, trying not to come across as ungrateful and hoping JR couldn't see the redness of his eyes through the ComTel.

"OK. Right," said JR, composing himself as he began to share.

"So, imagine you had an opportunity to reconstruct the world. I mean, looking at the major world problems, what would you do? What would you fix?"

It sounded rhetorical, so Ben let him continue. "It's a significant question, I know. And we can explain all we want that it's better for people if world leaders, through their access to the highest quality of information, could help improve their lives, but it often goes unheard. In the LinerVerse, LeV8 provides an opportunity to show rather than tell," he said confidently.

"So you are building some kind of Utopia?" Ben surmised as he watched the projection of JR smile as his hand raised to scratch his ear.

"You can call it that if you like, but what we're building is a new era. One that shifts us back to focusing on the many, not the few. We used to care about the poor, the marginalised, the oppressed. We had systems in place, government departments no less, to help those who couldn't help themselves. I'm not saying they got it right all the time, Ben, but the structure was there, meaning less chance of people falling through the net."

Ben could sense JR's frustration coming through as he slowed his voice, a bit like he was lecturing—which, to be honest, he was.

"As time went on, we started believing the lie that government was getting too big and we, the people, needed to strip it down, to take back control."

He paused as Ben watched him stroke his beard. "You know, Ben, generations ago, the government ran or at least regulated things like our healthcare, education, our roads, even business to a large extent. Experts conducted research, produced reports, and established laws for everyone's guidance and benefit. I mean, what does the average citizen really understand about healthcare, teaching, mending roads, or, let's be honest, parenting? Nothing—or very little, at least. And we shouldn't make it the responsibility of people to do things they have no qualification in."

His voice was getting louder now as his passion ran deep.

"We've let the private companies take over and get too big. Ben, did you know that a typical CEO's salary is 386 times the lowest paid worker? I mean, how is that allowed? How can anyone see that as just?" JR paused, longer than normal, making Ben realise this time, the question was not rhetorical.

He leaned back, absentmindedly rubbing his cheek, considering how to respond. Ben could see JR's avatar mirroring Ben's posture.

"I hear what you're saying, JR. I really do. But just to put a contrarian view, take Learning Groups. So many people were up in arms when that idea was put forward to replace schools. Most people couldn't even get the concept clear in their heads, as the only model they had was state schooling. Yet, all these years later, Learning Groups seem to work very well. In fact, now that's the only thing many people have known. I've been in one all my life and the support I've received has kept me going."

Ben's thoughts turned to his daughter and their last Learning Group trip. He pursed his lips, sensing the start of a headache, "...and especially with all that's happened with Alice," he continued, fighting to maintain his composure in front of his client. "...it's been a lifeline. I've had people who know me and love me show me so much support and..."

"That is great, Ben," JR cut in abruptly, surprising Ben a little. "I'm pleased for you. I really am. I can't imagine how difficult things would have been. But you know, it's not always like that," he said as Ben watched his gaze direct toward the ground, before looking up and continuing.

"My family lost their business because of that system," he said pensively, a sense of injustice clearly emanating from his tone. "But, not just that, Ben. We lost our home. The five of us spent three weeks living out of our car. I was eleven. My sister and younger brother were only six and five," he recalled with sadness.

Ben's curiosity piqued, and compassion strong, he sensed that the forthcoming sentences from JR would shed light on his own motivations and provide much-needed clarity.

# CHAPTER 11

## UTOPIA

It was warm, though thankfully not stifling, in the comms booth where Ben was sitting in WriteAngle Cafe. The sign on his table, a little way away from him, was still flashing to indicate he was coming back.

Although he hadn't expected such a lengthy call with JR, there was still a lot more he needed to know, not least now the reasons behind JR's family troubles.

"JR, I'm sorry your family lost their business and home. What happened?" Ben replied, compassion clear on his face. He could hear the sound of JR expelling air.

"Another competitor wanted my parents out of business, and they were bigger than us. They dropped their prices and ran a campaign against us, saying we were ripping people off. It only took a couple of months for most of our regulars to move on to our competitor," he reported, his voice much quieter now.

"That's awful," consoled Ben, leaning back.

"When we lost our home, we moved between a few friends who kindly put us up for a while, then when some of them sold up as things got bad, we had to move. No one else would support us for long enough to help my parents get back on track, so one time, we ended up sleeping in the car."

Ben shook his head, imagining what that must have been like. JR was fiddling with something in his hand, though Ben couldn't see what it was.

"The thing was, we knew some wealthy people. I mean, these people had money and knew our situation. They just refused to help." Ben could sense JR's anger dispersing through the ComTel. "If we had a government safety net, it would have provided for us. But they eradicated all that generations ago. Now it's every man for himself," he said.

JR scratched his chin before continuing. "Many people today do not remember or have not experienced being supported through care programmes in my parents' situation."

He looked directly at Ben, a thin smile stretching out slowly across his lips. "Through LeV8, built on the foundation of the LinerVerse, we can show them again. We can show them what it's like to have a government that actually cares," he said. "One that's not just Section One, but does so much more."

Taking a sip of his cooling tea, Ben sat up and leant an elbow on the desk, the floating image of JR vibrating for a second.

'If this is what LeV8 is about, do I really want to be involved?' he asked himself. While he sympathised with JR and could now understand his motivations, he found it difficult to relate to his interpretation.

"Hey listen, JR. Look, I'm really sorry again about what happened to you and your family. There's lots more I'd like to find out, though it's the kind of conversation I'd prefer face-to-face," he said as he clenched and unclenched his fist, letting blood back to his fingers to stop it going numb. "Just one quick thing I don't see, however," he said as he pulled his shoulders back, massaging them in the process. "To be honest, society is doing pretty well. People are flourishing, running their own businesses and their homes without interference from the government; fewer taxes leave more coins in peoples' pockets to choose what to do with, instead of having it taken from them and in so many ways, wasted."

Ben could see JR's forehead wrinkle, the more he went on, but he continued regardless. "I've already mentioned Learning Groups and that most people cope fine with them. So what's better with this utopia you want to model in LeV8?" he questioned, trying to remain more curious than judgemental. "There will always be bad eggs in whatever system we have, as we live in an imperfect world and—"

"Your grandpa believed it," JR cut in, his voice carrying a conviction, reaching through the ComTel and slicing through the air in front of Ben, stopping him in his tracks.

"You knew my grandad?" Ben quizzed, curiosity etched across his face; his surprise mildly diminished by the uncanny similarity he'd recognised between this man and his grandpa.

"Yes. And not only knew him. He was my mentor. He taught me everything I know," replied JR reverentially.

Ben watched as JR's animated avatar floated above the grey platform, its movements, no doubt, mirroring JR's enthusiastic storytelling about his mentor, Herman Harman.

"I loved that man," he said, Ben clearly hearing the admiration in JR's voice. "I think I was like you before I met him. A bit idealistic, if you forgive me for saying."

"You're forgiven," Ben smirked.

"When I got talking to Herman, he showed me how things truly were. I'd read the Bible all my life, but it was like I was reading it with fresh eyes. Herman described it like putting on *truth glasses.*"

Ben recalled his grandpa using that phrase many times. It was helping to confirm that this relative stranger was telling the truth, about knowing his grandpa, at least.

His voice now taking on a wistful tone, JR continued.

"So much that I'd been thinking and had questioned for years became clearer. I saw how much we'd neglected the social contract: to do unto others as you would like to be done to you."

Ben ignored the misappropriation of Bible verses. 'Did Grandpa really think this?' he mused.

"I have to say JR, that's not the social contract. You're suggesting Jesus was a Marxist?" he asked.

JR smiled. "Well, I wouldn't say that exactly, but God uses a variety of intellectuals to get his point across. Why wouldn't that include Karl Marx? I mean, he made a donkey talk!" JR replied.

"So you're relating Marx to a donkey? Interesting. Look, I'm gonna look up some stuff about my grandpa. I've not thought about his views or ever fully read through his diaries, but I must say that some of what you say, rings some bells. I'll check it out and we can engage in round two, in person," Ben concluded, rubbing his cheek, pushing it closer to his teeth to make chewing the inside of his mouth a little easier, a habit he still hadn't kicked.

Thinking about the point of their conversation, and whilst he had JR on the line, he asked, "Before I go, explain to me again the mission of LeV8?"

Ben could see JR's smile seep through the ComTel display.

"Ben, young Ben…" Normally, he'd find that patronising, but hearing the beard in JR's voice, it seemed OK. "What is the purpose of the LinerVerse? And that's not rhetorical, this time. I want to know," he asked him.

"Well, as Devan, your CEO, says, it's about creating a new world. It's like…" he furrowed his brow as he looked up at the corner of the booth, trying to pick out the best metaphor; "…it's like when the Pilgrim Fathers took off from England and landed in the new world. They founded the USA," he concluded.

"Exactly!" JR agreed. "Though, I would phrase it, such, that it's a chance to begin again. The LinerVerse is more than gaming Ben. It's more than replacing a boring life with one more exciting and without the physical risk and responsibility."

Ben could relate to this way more than JR knew.

"It's not about inhabiting a virtual world. As I've mentioned before, what we model in the LinerVerse—particularly with the technological advances in LeV8—has the potential to shape the real world. There's so much people don't know," JR evangelised as he pointed at Ben, "and you can communicate it to them, in your own inimitable way. Like I say, Ben, it's the chance to renew society."

Ben sat back in the standard office chair, staple in all the comms booths. It was comfortable enough, but no match for the Aeron chair he had at home.

'What am I getting myself into?' he pondered as he watched the connection counter pass the sixty minute mark.

"It sounds to me like you're trying to create heaven on earth. I mean, I'd like to see your theological reasoning behind that," he queried.

"Oh, Ben," JR replied. "Not everything is in the Bible. But, God created us all, every last one of us with varying intellects and we *are* called to take wise counsel," he replied.

"Yes, but we have to choose the right counsel as wisdom without God is foolishness," Ben quickly retorted, definitely getting tired now as he looked to wrap up the call, his unfinished tea now very cold.

JR didn't respond.

"So how about Thursday morning?" Ben offered. JR seemed to tap on his display.

"Sure. That works. 11 a.m.?" he replied.

"Great. Let's meet in Sab City Library," Ben suggested.

"Perfect," said JR. "I'll leave you to your thoughts and catch you later in the week. And Ben..."

"Yes?" he answered, wondering what further bombshell he might be about to drop.

"Your grandpa was a good man. I'll be interested to see what you dig up on him," JR replied, his avatar now leaning forward to conclude the call.

"Well, you'll find out soon enough. It's been a pleasure, JR. I'll talk with you soon."

He cut the connection and JR's image fell to the ground like it had magically disintegrated into dust. Ben rubbed his neck.

'What just happened? That was not the conversation I was expecting. I need to take a proper look at grandpa's diaries. Should I be excited or worried?' he thought to himself as he left the Comms Booth and headed back to his table, his mind now more confused than ever.

# CHAPTER 12

## TOUCHING THE SPHERE

There was a strong sense of contempt in Ben towards Liners. He'd always considered himself a true Realer. However, the intense appeal that many experienced was awakened by the weight of his own personal tragedy.

Ben's first experience of the LinerVerse was after he'd been searching the Health Improvement Centre for Alice. He had exhausted just about every avenue to gather any shred of information about her whereabouts or the individuals responsible for her abduction. Just anything to have a sniff of what happened to her and where she was.

He visited the museum multiple times, spoke to several people, explored, but found nothing. The security footage showed her walking with a young boy, but then she walked out of any camera feed. No one had sight or sound of her since.

Ben was even helped by Margaret Flint, an experienced legal friend who'd supported him going through the right procedures, filling out the right forms, but still to no avail.

He simply couldn't find his daughter.

Under the weight of fatherhood, he sat defeated on the sofa, his mind spiralling down darker and darker paths.

Then he looked up.

And he saw it.

Hovering above the ComTel on his desk, it was flashing. Shimmering–gold and red, bobbing up and down with the letters LV embossed in black within the sphere.

'Why hadn't I seen this before?' he mused. 'Perhaps a system update had left it there,' he guessed.

It beckoned him.

At that moment, nothing else mattered but touching the sphere. He knew full well it was the LinerVerse and how much Lydia would have disapproved. But it was just him now. No wife. Not even any daughter.

A flicker of a thought, 'whatever is pure, whatever is noble,' drifted through his mind like a tumbleweed in the desert, but it quickly blew away as his vision became filled with the gold and red of the sphere, hovering up and down.

What Ben had heard about the LinerVerse wasn't all bad, contrary to his initial expectations. Some had used it to connect with relatives across the globe. Even to enjoy shared experiences with friends, such as concerts and quizzes. He'd heard from others who'd lost someone special, experiencing tragedy like he had. For them, the LinerVerse was their saving. The grief of loss, satiated by the buzz of connection.

Overwhelmed by choices, lacking in accountability, he felt hot, as if he had a fever. A rush of blood to the head. Beads of sweat graced his palms. The dopamine hit. The anticipation was powerful, too powerful, calling to Ben to heal his hurt. Then he tapped the sphere.

A requestor popped up, asking to connect to his NCep device. Conveniently, it rested on the desk, prompting him to snatch it up and tuck it into his ear. He heard the low drone indicating 'connection made' as his senses rapidly transported him to the lawn outside a medieval castle.

Ben sneezed, his body reacting to the signals being sent to his brain of freshly cut grass. A bird swooped overhead as he looked around, attempting to get his bearings. He attempted to identify the bird when she appeared before him. Dressed in fine period clothing, a woman was calling his name.

"My love! What took you so long?" the woman asked. Ben's avatar dropped to the floor. He'd not heard that voice in some 10 years. It certainly sounded like her; his brain struggling to process what he was hearing. The woman he loved, who he'd lost, was apparently talking to him.

"Lydia?" he asked hesitantly. "Is that you?" He knew he was in the LinerVerse. It's not real, he told himself.

"Yes, it's me, my love. I have so much to show you. There's someone else I'd like you to meet also," she said. Ben ignored her comment, instead asking,

"What happened to you? I thought you were dead? I mean, I buried you!" He pictured that day when he saw her body, resplendent in the open casket. He felt himself go tense, but as if she could sense his emotion, she spoke, her voice carrying directly to his brain, calming him like sonic morphine.

"My love, none of that matters now. You're here with me. I'll take you away from all this. There's so much I want to show you," she said, reaching out and touching his hand, holding it in hers as she lead him away. He could feel the warmth of her skin, as he watched her silky smooth hair cascading down her back, the scent of lavender mixed with rosemary tickling his nose, providing a sense of comfort.

As he took each step, his load lightened until it felt like he was floating. They were heading toward the huge portcullis set into the main entrance of the castle.

"I'm here with Lydia," he said to himself, confused.

'I'm here with Lydia!' Part of him knew it wasn't Lydia. It couldn't be. Even in the LinerVerse, 'why would she be here? What's her purpose? Is this a trap?'

The swirl of questions racing through his mind overwhelmed him, but he found himself strangely at ease. Ignoring them, he allowed himself to sink into the comfortable acceptance of not knowing; it was just what he needed in that moment.

Whilst in the LinerVerse, if someone looked at Ben's actual body, they would see it bathed in a glimmering light as he sat motionless, like a statue, barely moving but for the occasional twitch of his hand and slight turn of his head.

The surrounding air had a slightly electrical hue to it. You could almost taste the metal. Perched in an Aeron chair, the mesh seat conforming to his slender frame, his body looked at peace. His face truly was a picture of meditative calm, both inside and out. In the short term, at least, Ben looked happy.

It was the first of many visits to see his beloved in the LinerVerse. He called it 'research.' In a way it was, but in truth, it was far more than that.

The first time, in fact the first few times, Lydia had to persuade Ben to log off. If he'd had his way, he would have stayed with her forever, but the unnecessary alarm this would have caused to his realer friends and family wasn't worth it.

Ben reluctantly complied with Lydia's instructions to tap the NCep device in his ear, cutting the connection. The moment he did, a flash of light, synchronised with a low drone, signalled his logout as Ben found himself back to reality staring at his desk. Suddenly, his stomach gurgled and churned, bile rising slowly from his guts, which he promptly emptied on the desk. He would make sure to have a bowl ready the next time. Just in case.

It took Ben a while to become accustomed to the emotional rollercoaster of logging out. Eventually, however, he could tap out without even feeling nauseous. By then, his mind was filled with many other thoughts as he started crafting a new life for himself, where he could escape and build new friend-ships with people who wouldn't ask him awkward questions.

All the while he dabbled, dipping his toe into this brave new world, Ben still questioned what his real friends would say. It wouldn't be positive, he thought, thus he kept all of this to himself. He didn't feel it necessary at this stage to share his activities with his Learning Group and close friends. This was despite the easy base of justification that he needed to know the LinerVerse inside-out for work.

Perhaps the feelings of guilt for his hypocrisy were too strong. But really, this was his sanctuary, his escape, his time, and knowing he wasn't the only Harman who'd had another life in the LinerVerse, just drove him further in.

# CHAPTER 13

## BIRTHDAY PARTY

"Alice! I'm not gonna call you again!" shouted Ben, the frustration in his voice clear. He was sitting in the living room, Reeder in hand, not that he was actually reading. The words floated by his brain but didn't stick. He had too many other things on his mind.

In just under half an hour, it was Sabine's birthday party. She had just turned nine, like Alice. Alice, as her best friend, had to be there, and to be honest, she wanted to be there too. But currently she was upstairs in her bedroom throwing clothes in and out of her wardrobe, like a half-price sale at TriMark.

When Ben had gone into her room earlier to see what was going on, along with the mess of clothes strewn about the floor—which was definitely not like Alice—his eyes were drawn to a pair of shoes floating about a foot off the ground. Alice caught him staring and immediately made them drop to the floor, frustrated that she hadn't noticed she'd left them hanging.

When Alice got like this, all sense of even nine-year-old rationality went out the window. Ben knew he had to give her space to work it through her system, whatever it was this time. That's why he'd pulled himself away to calm himself down whilst his daughter threw her tantrum.

Perhaps other nine-year-olds wouldn't act like that, but Alice was no normal girl. It was a real struggle for Ben to work out how to handle a nine-year-old who had a mental age of at least twice that. Unfortunately, there wasn't a rule book specific to bringing up supernatural kids...yet, at least.

Ben had no idea of the extent of her powers; he just had a hunch he was not supposed to bring it up until she did. He'd dropped hints on occasions, including several points when he was on the verge of letting it all out with his Learning Group. They certainly knew Alice well, but if they knew anything about her powers, they hadn't let on. He sometimes felt that when he did eventually tell them, and that time would undoubtedly come, they would basically smile and say "we know, and we've known for years!" At least it would be blessed relief, than carrying this secret around with him all the time. Not doing anything went against his paternal nature, but rightly or wrongly, he believed it was the right decision.

Ben's face was full of thought, wrinkles obvious along his forehead. He often wished he had the strength of Lydia. She'd know what to do, probably by encouraging him to man up. 'Please God, give me her strength right now,' he prayed.

Resigned to the inevitable, he placed the Reeder on the table. He couldn't remember anything he'd read anyhow. He was still as he listened out for signs indicating what stage the tantrum was at.

The house was quiet. 'Sounds like she might be sorted now,' he thought as he rose from the sofa. It was just a party. It didn't matter if they got there late, but late, was not something Ben did—if he could possibly avoid it. He climbed the stairs and hesitantly knocked on Alice's door.

"Hey, Monkey. You OK?" He pushed the door open, revealing his daughter sitting at her dressing table brushing her hair, clothed in a black velvet dress. Straightaway on seeing her father's face, she nodded, then apologised.

"I'm sorry, Dad," she said looking at him through the mirror, her eyes red. "I just kinda had a meltdown. Couldn't think straight, triggered by not being able to decide what to wear. It's stupid I know."

'Nine years old', he kept telling himself, 'just nine years old.' Her ability to self-analyse was way beyond her years. It always astounded him.

She spun around, holding her brush out toward him.

"Can you do my hair, please?" she asked, then, anticipating his thoughts, "We won't be late. Don't worry."

He crossed the room to her, kneeling behind her as he took the brush.

"Of course, Monkey," he said, "and you're not stupid. Anything but," he concluded as he started pulling the brush through her hair. "Do you know what the problem was?" he asked, hoping it wouldn't set her off again.

"I just want to look good for Bine. Want her to have the best day." He pushed a bit more.

"Why would that make you angry?" She looked at him in the mirror, then down at the table.

"Dunno," she replied, not wanting to tell him the truth that she'd accidentally burnt the dress she really wanted to wear when she tried to levitate it out of her wardrobe. He'd find out, eventually. Just not now. Ben left it for now, not wanting to push further. He finished her hair and with no more drama, they went downstairs and left for the party, on time.

Sabine rushed to embrace her best friend once she saw Alice enter the Community Hall with her dad.

"Hi, Uncle Harman," she said before turning to Alice, squealing with delight, immediately dragging her poor friend to the side of the room with the other kids, seemingly in the middle of playing a game which looked like musical chairs.

Ben, was relieved to see his daughter smiling. He spotted Simon and Dauphina, Sabines' parents and members of his Learning Group, as he wandered over, nabbing a few crisps on the way.

"Thanks for coming, mate," Simon said nonchalantly, waving his hand and pointing his fingers, selecting an appropriate playlist on his GreenFlow workstation. He chose, Epee Glen, a singer-songwriter that Sabine and many of the kids were into.

"Ooo, Epee Glen!" coo'd Ben, nodding to Simon as he heard the singers' sultry voice kick in. "Alice wanted me to play some of her tracks the other day, and there's actually a few good ones…I mean, lyrically at least."

He'd particularly liked the one referencing the story of Esther in the Bible, titled "Hoisted by your own." It made him chuckle drily. He'd since watched a few interviews with Epee and whilst she never claimed to be Christian, he certainly could see she had a grasp on what the Bible actually said, more than many people he knew that claimed they did.

Simon finished setting the playlist, adding a few more Epee tracks and many other artists before responding to Ben.

"Well, as a wordsmith, I guess you can appreciate her lyrics more. To me, it just sounds like candy-floss." Ben knew what he'd say next and joined in.

"Sweet on the outside, empty on the inside," they chanted.

"Yeah, you might've said that once or twice before," moaned Ben, rolling his eyes.

"Who's empty on the inside?" quizzed Dauphina as she waltzed up and embraced Ben. "Hey, how you doing?" she said questioningly, immediately having noticed what perhaps Simon didn't, a furrowing of the brow Ben had thought he'd hidden whilst conversing with Simon.

Dauphina had always been high on the empathy spectrum. She didn't miss a beat. Ben smiled, knowing he couldn't hide much from her.

"Yeah. Perceptive as always, D." She smiled, beckoning him to continue, letting her first question go unanswered. "She just had a bit of a meltdown. I'm amazed we even got here on time," he said.

"What was it this time?" Dauphina asked as she held out a glass for Ben, which he gratefully took before gazing at the floor. He shook his head.

"You know what? I don't even know." He would not tell her about the floating shoe. But that in itself couldn't have been the sole issue, as Alice was having her tantrum before that. "I just put it down to growing pains. And you'd know a lot about that, right?"

Dauphina feigned incredulity, holding her mouth with her hands. "What are you saying Ben? I'm fat?" Simon smiled.

"Ha, ha! I mean, you've had four kids, you know what it's all about." She turned to take a drink for herself.

"Yes, and it doesn't get easier, let me tell you. But it's reassuring to know God has his plan for each of our kids, just like he has with Alice. We might not know what's going through their minds all the time, but God knows."

"Yeah. That's definitely a comfort," replied Ben, not totally sure he believed his own words, as he turned to look at the kids as they were setting up for what seemed like a game of pass the parcel.

Sitting in her pink dress, next to Alice on one of eight chairs laid out in a row, Sabine looked around at the parents talking.

"How boring!" she said to Alice, whose face immediately displayed a puzzled expression.

"Er?" Alice grunted in reply. The birthday girl pointed at the old folk, Simon, Dauphina, Ben and some of the other parents just standing around talking.

"Them. They're all just talking. Why talk when they could play?" Alice thought about her response. She often had to do this to not belittle her best friend by displaying her much more mature mind.

"Maybe there's a time for playing and a time for talking," she softly deduced. Sabine looked straight at her, screwing up her face.

"You're weird!" she replied, then with a beaming smile that lit up the room, "but I still love ya!" Alice smiled, knowing that weird was just one rung away from freak—or special—and not in a good way. In a freaky way. Inside, Alice was mad at her friend, but did her best to hide it. She could feel herself getting hot, the collar of her dress already clinging to her neck. She was sure there had been music playing, her favourite Epee Glen, but all she could hear was silence.

"Your turn," said Sabine, loudly, Alice not having picked up they'd started the game, and she had the parcel in her hands. She clicked back to reality and looked around at everyone's faces staring back at her, and she slowly pealed a layer of paper off the parcel. There was nothing extra inside, so she passed the parcel on to the girl to her left as the music started up again.

There were nine of them, including three of Sabine's siblings and a few others from their Learning Group. The game continued as each of the others, in the spirit of fairness, pealed off a layer until there was just one left. Alice had tried to have fun, to keep on smiling, but she couldn't get 'freak' out of her head. That's not even what Sabine had said, but Alice's mind fixated on her chosen interpretation of it.

The parcel was with Sabine. She passed it to Alice. It was half in her hands and half in Alice's when the music stopped.

"Ooo. Whose is that?" said one of the other kids.

"I think it's Bines," said Sabine's sister.

"But Alice has more of it," said another, before Alice took her hands away, leaving it in Sabine's grasp.

"I don't mind," Alice said, turning to look at her friend. "It's your birthday."

"No. You have it. You had more of it," replied Sabine.

"No. You have it," replied Alice with a hint of anger.

"No. It's yours, Al," said Sabine, not wanting to give in.

"Well, I don't want it!" Alice shouted as the parcel, still at that point in Sabine's hands, was thrust further toward her stomach without Alice—or—anyone seemingly pushing it. To anyone looking in, it could look like Sabine had thrust it into her own stomach.

"Well, you didn't have to do that!" Sabine cried as she burst into tears, holding her stomach.

"What? I didn't do anything," Alice lied, wanting the ground to swallow her up. "Hey!" said Dauphina sternly, as Ben and some of the other parents, on hearing the commotion, also ran over.

Dauphina knelt in front of her daughter.

"What happened?" The other kids were confused. They'd seen Sabine thrust the parcel into her own stomach, but they struggled to know why she would do that. Not friendly Sabine. Sabine looked straight at her best friend. Keeping her eyes fixed on Alice, she replied to her mum.

"I just had pain in tummy. I think I'm OK now," she said.

With that, Alice burst into tears and ran out of the room, plonking herself on the floor against a wall in the hallway. Ben looked at Sabine, then Dauphina, shrugging his shoulders before letting out a big sigh and following his daughter out.

# CHAPTER 14

## GRANDPARENTS

2163 - Present day

Surrounded by books of all shapes and sizes, Ben sat in the Library staring at the pages of his grandpa's diary, still not quite believing both what he'd read and the memories it was triggering of the times he'd spent at his grandparents' house.

One memory that came to him was of his grandma cooking a delicious soup. His mind brought the scene right back.

◭

"Ben! Dinner's ready! Come and get it while it's hot!" she shouted as she rested the ladle back in the soup pot after a quick taste. It was good, if she did say so herself.

"Ah...there you are," she said as she turned around. "That was quick."

Her eyes brightened as Ben sniffed the soup, his stomach announcing its need of sustenance.

"Someone's hungry," she smiled, a fuller smile this time; her cheeks raised and her entire face emanating love. "Can you set the table for me, dear?" She asked.

"Sure, Gran," Ben replied as he opened the kitchen draw taking out the cutlery.

Ben loved staying over at his grandparents. Their house was always so warm and cosy and the smells of delicious soups, and sumptuous cakes...it was like the pied piper, always drawing him there. Ben was unaware at the time that in recent months, his parents had been trying different ways to have another child. Nothing was working. He knew there were some medical problems, but at just eleven years old, he didn't appreciate what exactly was wrong. What it meant was that he got to spend more time with his grandma and grandpa, and for that, he was not complaining.

The front door creaked open.

"Hello, Dear!" Herman Harman, a big stocky man in blue denim dungarees and a blue and grey checked shirt, waltzed through the kitchen and placed his satchel on the stand, before sauntering up to his wife and giving her a quick peck on the cheek. He then turned round as Ben came back from laying the table.

"Can you move that, love?" Grandma said, motioning to his bag.

"As soon as I've given my favourite grandson a big squeeze," he bellowed, in case there was anyone else in the house who needed to know how much he loved his grandson. The big man bent down and grabbed Ben up in his arms.

"I'm your only grandson, Grandpa!" he exclaimed.

"Even more confirmation that you're my favourite," he retorted with a big grin as he buried his head into Ben's chest as if drying his hair on Ben's t-shirt, his big bushy hair and beard making him look like a dog, shaking itself off after it's come out the water.

Ben pretended he didn't like it and pushed his grandpa's head away. But secretly, he loved it.

"So what have you been up to today, Chuck?" Grandpa asked as he lowered his grandson to the floor. Ben never understood why his grandpa called him Chuck. It certainly wasn't any shorter than Ben. But somehow, his deep, soothing voice made it seem endearing.

"I've been looking at Acts, Grandpa," Ben said with pride.

"Ah, the birth of the church. Wonderful stuff. Let's sit and have dinner, and you can tell me all about it." Grandma had been going back and forth, transporting many bowls of food to the table. The smell, intoxicating, making Ben's stomach rumble even more than it already had been.

When they all sat down, they closed their eyes as Herman prayed. "Dear Lord, thank you for this food you have so graciously provided, and thanks to Granny (he emphasised Granny) for preparing it. Amen!" Grandma opened her eyes, raising her eyebrows at her husband. He smirked back at her.

"OK, dig in," she said.

As they filled their plates, Herman steered the conversation back to Ben's studies.

"So, tell me, Chuck, what have you been learning from Acts?" Ben swallowed a potato and took another quick spoon of his soup, buying some time to plan his words.

"They all seemed to share everything. It says no one was in need," he replied hesitantly.

"Ah, Acts 2. Yes, some very important verses. Chuck. What do you think God is saying to us today from those verses?" Ben thought for a while whilst taking another slurp of the delicious soup.

"I don't know, Grandpa," he responded as he continued to think. Herman let him. "Perhaps...er...perhaps, it's saying that I need to share what I have more to people who don't have as much?" He replied, the tone of his voice raising on the last word.

"Yes, good. That is good Chuck. But let me tell you something, young Ben. Those two verses in Acts 2, near the end, I believe, are so important in showing us the way we should live. It talks about the early church having all things in common, and as you've said, not having what you don't need and giving to others. Now some people used to think that meant that you weren't to own anything, and that everything was to be communal, but I don't think that's what it's saying," he said, pointing at Ben as he continued. "You don't have to give up all your toys, Chuck, you'll be glad to know."

Ben made a face as if to say, 'Phew!'

"But if you see someone in need and you can do something about it, you should." He paused, looking at Ben and giving himself time to savour more of the soup.

"Do you understand, Chuck?"

That's why Ben loved being with his grandpa. He always made sure he understood things. Lots of adults would just tell him stuff and not really care whether his young mind had actually taken anything in.

"I think so, Grandpa," he replied.

"So remind me, what's it saying?" Ben smiled, ready to regurgitate what he'd heard.

"That we need to sell what we don't need, so we can give money to the poor who need it more," he said with pride.

"Good, good. But you know there's more to it than that, Chuck. It's—"

"Don't forget the salad," Grandma interjected before the conversation got any deeper.

"Thank you, dear," Herman replied as he grabbed the utensils, giving a portion to Ben, then to himself.

"Now…" he said, looking pointedly at Ben. "Your dad might have a different perspective, so I'd encourage you to discuss it with him." He shifted his head closer to Ben. "It's important you make your own mind up," he smiled before continuing. "I've shared with some people what we call Social Science. Do you know what that is?"

Ben looked down at the rest of his soup, his stomach nearly filled. 'Social is about people. And science is…well…science' he thought.

"Is it the science of people?"

"Yes, very good." his gesticulation rose in tandem with his volume level. "Imagine if you could observe people in the same way you observe ants. The interesting thing about ants is that they are a highly communal species. They all work together for the greater good of the colony." Ben's ears perked up as he listened intently. "There are no troublesome mavericks going off and doing their own thing, and if any ants did, the rest of the colony would quickly bring them back in line. If we were all worker ants, similar to what intellectuals discuss in my social science classes…"

"You teach classes, Grandpa?" It was news to Ben.

"Yes, Chuck. Teaching has been my job for a while now," he replied.

"I thought you did something in sales," queried Ben, not even knowing exactly what that meant, but he knew he'd heard the word in relation to his grandpa before.

"No. No, Chuck. I used to, but I've been teaching for a while now," he replied, as he tried to get back on topic. "As I was saying…ants, that's right. These intellectuals have come up with a complete plan that, despite some of them not believing the Bible, is actually compatible. We are all called to be worker ants, to be followers, to work for each other, not for ourselves. And that's what it means in Acts. We need to deny ourselves and our own needs, and seek the needs of others. As some intellectuals say, 'We will own nothing and be happy.'"

Ben looked quizzical. Herman gave him time to think as he broke off another piece of bread, dipping it into his soup before placing it firmly into his mouth. Ben finished chewing, a thought forming in his young brain.

"Grandpa, do you and grandma own this house?" Grandma smiled.

"Yes, we do, Chuck," he responded quizzically, realising where this was going.

"Would you sell it and give the money to others who are in need?" Herman sat back, his cheeks bulged slightly. He looked at Grandma, who raised her eyebrows. It was a question they'd often discussed, and the answer to which they often disagreed.

"That's a good question, Chuck, but you have to remember what I said. *Some* say that you should sell everything, but that's not what the Bible says. In fact, God blessed many people, such as Abraham, Isaac, Joseph even, with a lot of property. In their case, it was land, animals, employees, and more. It's not always about what you have, but what you do with it. God blessed us with this house, and hopefully we use it to bless others. Isn't that right, Granny?" Ben observed his grandad's eyes widen and a wry smile appear as Herman gazed at his wife. He smiled at her, too, as she rolled her eyes. Then, directing her attention to her grandson, she replied.

"Yes, Ben. We use our house to host meetings that others couldn't do in their own homes. As you know, I have a love for cooking and enjoy having people over to share that joy with them. So we get to bless others as God blesses us, too."

Herman placed his cutlery neatly on his plate as he finished eating.

"Right, I think that's all the study for today. Why don't we write some stories after lunch? You'd love that, right Chuck?" Ben couldn't resist writing and drawing. He'd spent many an hour attempting to create his own story books, another reason he loved hanging out with his grandparents.

Back in the present, Ben gazed around the library, though he wasn't really looking at the books. He could still feel the warmth and homeliness of his grandparent's place, the smell of the delicious chicken soup. He regretted not having been more inquisitive with his grandfather during his younger years, longing to have learnt more about his life whilst he'd been alive. Though being able to read Herman Harman's diaries was the next best thing.

# CHAPTER 15

## THE FLUTE

The Complex, the out-of-world floating ship located some 700 light years from Earth, was a technological marvel. It really was a complete home away from Earth and was the next logical step before Sendo eXperience—or any other company for that matter—could completely terraform a planet, to turn a dead rock into a life supporting atmosphere. That's what Sendo was working towards.

But for now, standing in the control station looking out into the vast expanse of space, was SentiN. It had been four years since his people, the Shumen, had moved into the Complex, becoming the first tenants. But such a great opportunity wasn't without its problems.

SentiN observed the faint blue–orange glow of Contextua, the nearest planet way off into the distance. He loved staring out at the blackness of space, broken up intermittently by glimmers of colour as the stars shone through. It was cathartic and helped him relax. And boy, he needed to relax. He walked back to his command chair and sat down, still able to enjoy the view outside the windows. His arms resting on the armrests as he sat right back in the chair, his mind drifting.

As a child SentiN would often sit for hours, daydreaming. His mother would chide him about this, encouraging him to 'actually do something.' She despised laziness. A strong work ethic was all important to the Shumen which she tried to drum into her son, especially when he tried to get out of the annual Young Shumen Games.

This was part of a weeklong gathering, the aim of which was to encourage connection to the community. Guests could enjoy sumptuous food, take in dramatic performances or wander around the gallery. There was also the opportunity to have a say on key community decisions. However, for the young adults, there was a wide range of occasionally wild activities.

Every year, SentiN would do anything to avoid having to throw himself to the ground, crawl through muddy tunnels, climb up sludge covered walls. This included regularly feigning illness or injury. But there's only so many times one can get ill at the same time every year before his parents worked it out. Nothing about it made him think this was a good thing to do. In fact, he often wondered who came up with this weird concept. He was sure they, whoever 'they' were, must have hated kids.

Saying that, SentiN knew well that for many of his friends it was the highlight of their year, and people like his childhood rival MendipT would relish the challenge no doubt—probably having gone into training several months prior. He just couldn't get himself excited about such activities.

However, one time his family forced him to go to the games, despite his feigning injury, so he thought he might as well make the most of it. And making the most of it came unexpectedly.

Whilst walking down a long, lush green slope that lead to the beach—one of the many beaches on Pasau—he heard the beautiful dreamy sound of a flute, like a whispered conversation between two birds. It was truly magical, calming SentiN, almost making him glad he came.

He was soaking up the enchanting melody and slowly being drawn towards the soothing sound, away from his family, too engrossed in their own conversations to notice. His mind was whirring, trying to think who could be the author of such delicate, ethereal sounds. As he rounded a group of trees, he looked toward the player and had the shock of his life. There were several people he knew who could play the flute so effortlessly. The person he saw sitting down under a tree, his body dancing to his own tune, was not one of those.

It was MendipT.

SentiN had to admit he must have been talented even at thirteen. He stayed behind a tree, hiding his position from his nemesis, though MendipT, who was so in the zone, it's not likely he would have noticed had SentiN walked past.

He wanted to stay and observe for a while, pangs of jealousy hitting him. There was no way he could ever play like that. SentiN was the kind of person who would try, then give up, whilst MendipT wouldn't even try; he seemed naturally gifted at most things–much to SentiN's frustration.

As he was looking on, he noticed another sound in the distance, like that of a distant thunderstorm. But there were no clouds to speak of. It was a low rumbling sound, was getting closer. 'Possibly a Cassowary?' he thought.

MendipT hadn't noticed, as he still piped away the tunes.

It got louder. SentiN looked around, trying to gauge what it was and where it was coming from. 'Surely he must hear it now,' he thought. But he didn't. The sound got closer until SentiN could see the author. It was a Cassowary! SentiN stood as still as a tree, terrified. Aware of their abilities, he had no intention of testing their validity.

Instead of shouting over to MendipT, he stayed silent; frozen to the spot, unable to run away or exercise his vocal chords to alert his fellow Shumen. So he just stared as the bird came running up, startling MendipT. He watched his nemesis jump up, the flute and bag going flying as he saw him run and run. Past the nearest group of trees and into a bush. SentiN suddenly got his movement back and was about to run in the other direction when he noticed the flute lying on the ground. The bird itself having now wandered off. Perhaps it was running from something itself.

The wooden instrument lay hidden behind a tree. SentiN looked over in the direction he'd seen MendipT run, couldn't see any movement and the temptation was too great. Stepping out from behind the tree, he ran and grabbed MendipT's flute and scarpered off back towards where he thought his family would be. Not knowing what he would do with the flute, he found solace knowing he now possessed an important item to his nemesis.

He'd never given the flute back, and MendipT had no clue that it was his rival who had it. Someone said that MendipT had assumed some animal had taken and destroyed it. That worked for SentiN.

Sitting back in his captain's chair, a smile permeated his face; possibly the only thing he had over MendipT in all these years. They'd worked hard to have a friendly relationship, and this worked for a while. But there was always the simmering smell of competitiveness floating around them both.

SentiN's thoughts quickly moved on from the rivalry of the past, back to the conflict of the present. 'Some things don't change,' he thought. "It didn't take him long to cause a faction," he muttered to himself, stroking his chin, his relaxed face now being replaced by one with many more wrinkles. MendipT was gathering together a group of Shumen and planning to leave the Complex for 'greater adventures beyond'. Well, that was how MendipT had described it.

You see, MendipT was bored. Bored, bored, bored. Bored with the same old routines. Bored with the same old people. Bored with Sendo telling them what to do—this wasn't actually the case, but it felt like it to him. And bored with SentiN being in charge. This one got to him the most. Growing up, it always seemed to MendipT that his rival called the shots. Though reality was very different.

'It's best just to let them go,' SentiN thought as he resigned himself to a small group of colleagues leaving the Complex against the wishes of Sendo, their landlords. He knew he would have to tell the Guardian. But when? Before they left and MendipT would get in trouble. After they left and he, SentiN, would get in trouble...unless he could plead ignorance.

SentiN agonised over the decision. Ironically, if this was MendipT, he would have made it without equivocation, he thought. Despite his compatriot becoming more and more distant, he didn't want him to be in too much trouble with Sendo. Because of that, he pleaded ignorance, and within days,

MendipT, along with seventeen others, were standing near the airlocks, saying their goodbyes.

"So this is it my friend" said SentiN as he embraced MendipT, then stepping back but still holding his hand. "You know how I feel about this. Are you sure there's nothing I can do to change your mind?" MendipT dragged his hand away. He looked at SentiN, a touch of pity passing his face, then at the others all standing around ready to send them off.

"No. Nothing. We've been through this and we're going," he said defiantly. Then, raising his voice, he said, "We will see you again soon with tales of our explorations! It's not too late for anyone else to join us."

There were murmurs and some shuffles, but no one else joined the seventeen as they split into two groups, each heading through the airlock and into the two waiting TransPortals. Then they were gone.

SentiN felt lost at first. He would often berate himself for not being as strong a leader as MendipT. 'He would have been able to convince them to stay,' he told himself. One saving grace was that, for a short time at least, there was much peace on the Complex. Many were grateful for that, as leading up to MendipT and his cohort leaving, the Complex became a very tense atmosphere to live in. You could palpably feel the tension all around the ship, from the bridge to the medical bay.

Arguments over food and jobs became the norm for a while, which was alien to the Shumen, such a peaceful people–one reason they were chosen as the first tenants. But the desire to leave was too great for MendipT and some others. They'd regularly compared their 'plight' to being in a floating prison. It wasn't anything of the sort, but their perception couldn't be argued with. MendipT and those he'd convinced, had already decided they were leaving, and that was that.

So, now they'd left, there was peace. The remaining Shumen could breathe a sigh of relief, getting on with normal life and all that entailed...until that is, they were unexpectedly attacked.

It certainly wasn't immediate. After MendipT and his cohort left to explore, messages would come back regularly, with updates on what they found and where they had been. Most of the Shumen were excited to hear of their discoveries, despite having no desire to go exploring themselves. But as time went by, the frequency of the reports diminished, until a year went by with no contact at all. Then another, and another. Until those remaining did not know what happened to MendipT and his gang—or even if any of them were still alive.

Soon, the Shumen on the Complex had gotten so used to their pattern of life, so wrapped up in their own bubble, that they completely forgot about those that had left.

Then one day it happened. It started with strange events taking place around the Complex. An object suddenly disappearing or moving unconventionally. Memories being wiped or altered. It took a while for them to remember that the only people who knew the Complex well enough to infiltrate it this way were their erstwhile colleagues. This was, of course, excluding Sendo, their landlords, who would have no reason to infiltrate their own building. They could come in via the front door.

To finally answer the question, a message was sent. It was a day no one on the Complex forgets. Everyone froze. Whatever they were doing, they just stopped. They transferred a message to each person's ComTel in unison. The message simply stated:

'We want back in. We've sent you a sign. More will follow.'

From then on, the Complex was on high alert, not knowing when, where or how, or of course…if, something would actually happen. The anticipation itself was killing SentiN and the rest of his compatriots. The peace was well and truly over.

# CHAPTER 16

## IN THE ZONE

2163 - Present day

Tap, tap, tapity, tap went Ben's fingers as he punched out the prose. He was still easing himself back into work after Alice's disappearance. 'How long was it was supposed to take? Is there a normal amount of time?' He smirked at using the word 'normal' in relation to losing a child, as he rubbed his finger, feeling for the ring he still wore despite over a decade of being a widower; though secretly he still harboured a hope that wasn't true.

Now sitting in WriteAngle Cafe, the words flowed effortlessly out of him. It didn't take him long to get in to the zone and lose track of time. As time passed, his focus steadily increased like a man possessed. You would almost expect to see steam coming out of his brain. When eventually he looked up, the cafe was half empty. He pressed on regardless, his focus too intense to stop.

Around him, most guests had left. In fact, when Ben next looked up, he was literally the only guest left. He always felt a little discombobulated coming out of a writing sprint. Like waking up from a too-long a nap. You know, that groggy feeling and a slight headachy throb. The light in the cafe changed too. His table was now an oasis of light in a desert of darkness.

Sara, another regular member of staff, headed over toward him, her bucket full of cleaning materials. 'Was it really closing time?' he thought. She stopped by the table and waved her hand toward the ceiling as the full lights came on, causing Ben to squint, adjusting his eyes to the new level of luminosity.

"You staying the night, Ben?" Despite her obvious sarcasm, she held a warm, considerate yet tired smile; her accent betraying her Southern American roots. She had mouse-brown hair, pulled back into a tight ponytail. A few loose strands draped over her dark brown eyes. He thought there was a faint smell of perfume, though fusing with the cleaning products, he couldn't be sure.

"Yes...er...sorry...no...no. I'm just finishing up Sara," still a little flummoxed.

She continued, "you've got fifteen minutes or so, so relax...as it's you, but we'll have to kick you out then," she said in a mock stern voice.

"Sure. No problem. Thanks Sara," he smiled back.

She headed toward the next table, then stopped and turned back to face Ben.

"Anyways, what you writing so intently? I mean, you're normally pretty focused but you seem more intense today...if you don't mind me saying," she hesitantly quizzed.

He took in a deep breath and slowly let it out. Not because he didn't want to respond, but with a sense of uncertainty over what he'd actually been writing. When he thought about it, it must have looked like he was in a trance, not having lifted his head for ages.

His eyes fell to his screen, which looked blank. It was switched off. "It's the same document I'm working on for a few days. You know, sometimes I just have nothing, but the last few weeks it's err...well...it's err, it's as if I've been possessed. I get my Aidea out, start writing and...can't stop. I guess...I get so into it, I don't have any recollection of what I've written. It's kinda weird..."

His cogs were turning, trying to look for another way to describe the situation. "...You know when you've read a book, well, several pages of it...you know you've read it, but you can't recall a thing you've read?"

"Ha, ha! Yeah, I know that feeling. Like every book I've read!" Sara exclaimed, smiling, then changing the subject, she turned round fully toward him now. "What are you up to over the next few days?"

He used to have much longer conversations with Sara before it happened. He enjoyed his chats with her and Andy in particular. Now it was a struggle. He feigned interest where he could, but it wasn't easy. Though they had a lot of grace for him. Ben sighed.

"Oh, you know, nothing much, just more writing." There was a brief silence, which he decided reluctantly to fill, when Sara stayed standing still in front of his table, staring at the floor.

"What about you?" he reciprocated. She looked up.

"I'm looking forward to catching up with my sister up north. I don't get to see her too often these days, so can't wait to see her and my nieces." She hesitated, then said,

"You're lucky having such a flexible job, getting to do what you enjoy, when you want." Realising what she'd just said to the man who'd lost his wife and most recently his daughter, she pulled back, "Well, not lucky, er...you know what I mean."

Ben smiled as if to reassure her he took no offence from her words. It was something he often had to consider. Those people that knew his situation often trod so carefully around him so not as to offend him. But the very act of treading carefully made it actually more difficult for them...and him.

"You do a great job here, Sara. I know there aren't as many human run cafes these days, but you're so young. There'll be plenty of opportunities for people with your skills and attitude," he encouraged.

Her face expressed, 'Thank you. That's so kind, but I don't believe you.' Her mouth replied, "Yeah. I guess...thanks." She smiled, turned away as she started to clean the next table.

After waiting a few seconds, still pondering Sara's words: 'how lucky he was'...knowing both that he didn't believe in luck, and that God was ultimately in control, he put away his Aidea, swung his bag over his shoulders, and headed for the door, waving goodbye to Sara and Andy; a thrum sounding as he walked through the door, confirming his time and order had been deducted from his tokens.

Ben stood outside the cafe, motionless and lost in thought. It was a strange feeling writing these days. His thoughts went straight from his head to his device, as though his brain didn't want him to know what was being written. A heavy sadness weighed on him. He tried to remember what it was like after he'd lost Lydia, taking him nearly a year to really get back into it. Now Alice had gone missing, and he'd found he'd been searching for her with an intensity he'd never known possible, but, currently at least, all to no avail.

He snapped out of his trance-like state and started walking. Looking up at the sky, he could see the sun slowly beginning its descent behind a collection of nearby clouds. He wanted to be on his own, to wallow in his own cloud, but remembered the weekly Bible study with his Learning Group family was tonight.

Ben sighed, accidentally kicking a stone that clanged against an AutoJet hailer, then bounced off. Normally, he couldn't wait to get together with Nathan, Simon, and Dauphina and the gang. But post losing Alice, everything was a chore.

# CHAPTER 17

## TEMPTATION

Arriving home, Ben dumped his bag down, needing a drink to help settle all the thoughts still percolating around in his mind. As he headed for the kitchen, he noticed Boris, Alice's toy-rabbit lying on the floor. It had obviously fallen from its perch next to Ben's key holder.

Picking it up, he traced the shape of its head and stroked its furry body as his mind began its descent into a cloud of despair. He looked up from the toy, still clasping it, staring into space. His friends noticed since losing Alice, he would seem to zone out at certain points, whatever they were doing. It was his abyss; when any semblance of rationality left him and his negative voice took pride of place, winning the battle for his heart and mind.

This was heading to be one of those moments—if he couldn't extricate himself from the malaise. The weight of everything got to him. His sorrow for the loss of his beautiful monkey, his only daughter Alice, was of an indescribable depth. The pain of her loss—not knowing whether she was dead or alive. Not knowing anything else he could do to find her, was a constant reminder of the powerlessness of the situation.

He was her dad, ordained by God to guide and protect her. He'd failed. The weight of responsibility dragged him to his knees. Ben cried out:

'God, why? Why did you allow my only daughter to be taken from me? I know I'm not perfect, but I thought I was doing an OK job. Please protect her wherever she is. Keep her strong. Fill her with an unnatural strength and please…please bring her back to me.'

Despite her impatience and grouchiness the last time he'd seen her, Ben would still give anything to see that beautiful face again.

'I know she's still alive. I can feel it in my bones. If she was properly gone, I would know…wouldn't I? I can't give up hope. I just can't.'

Ben knew that hundreds of people went missing every year. To others, such as Section One, Alice was just another statistic. He got that. Why would they care anymore about her than anyone else?

Outside his Learning Group, no one seemed to care or kick up much fuss. That she disappeared from a public place also didn't seem to make much difference. One minute she was there, the next minute she was gone.

Several times, he'd questioned whether it would be any help to go to Section One with the email—that dreaded email—the one he'd tried to forget, sent after Alice was kidnapped the first time.

But every time he thought about it, he couldn't get past the Lab Rat Theory: when Alice was found, the desperation to find out what powers she really possessed would be too great. She would be moved from one captor to another, experimented on to see what level of danger she truly was to the world. He'd seen the films. It was impossible for him to conceive of any option where they would just leave her with him, so they could go back to being a happy family. 'Those days are well and truly over,' he thought.

The thing that puzzled him also, was, which would be the worse captor? COB—whoever that was—and who he assumed she was currently with, or Section One—who in their defence had tried to be helpful so far. He couldn't decide.

Despite his attempt to think of pure, noble, holy, and honourable things, the stinging bitterness of his loss made it difficult. The searing pain in his heart was a constant battle he tried to fight. For Sabine, and the other kids in their Learning Group who had also lost a dear friend, he wanted to be strong. He wanted to be still and know that God was in control. He wanted to release his anxiety knowing God truly cared for him...but it was easier said than done.

Lying prostrate on the kitchen floor, his head resting on one cheek, lightly grazing the thankfully clean wooden floor, tears trickling from his eyes, Ben breathed in deeply; content to let go of his body, to release himself from all responsibility.

He closed his eyes.

It was at times like this, in recent months at least, when he saw two options, a fork in the road. Like the clichéd angel and demon sitting on his shoulders. He knew the right thing to do; to submit his thoughts to God, to pray away the temptation, but it was too strong. He pictured the red-gold lettering bobbing up and down in his mind. He heard her voice, that silky smooth sound calling to him like a siren to sailors.

Ben got up from the floor. He was no longer in control of his body. His legs moved one in front the other, leading him to the lounge and the object of his affection, drawing him closer to his ComTel. He picked up the NCep device, the little sliver of gold, steel, and silicone, and placed it in his ear, then sat down. His movements were smooth, well rehearsed at this stage. His hand reached out as he touched the sphere. Then he saw her and all his troubles drifted away.

'Ring, Ring.' A shrill, slowly crescendoing sound broke through Ben's ear. It took him a few moments to recognise a call coming through. He ignored it. It couldn't be more important than being with her.

'Go away!' he thought, irritated. But it kept on buzzing. Getting annoyed, he waved his hand in front of the display and he saw it was Nathan calling.

'What does he want?' Ben thought as he flicked his hand to reject the call. Nathan, used to his friends' changing personality, simply called again a few moments later, and when Ben felt he couldn't ignore it any longer, he swiped his hand to the right. The medieval world stilled as Nathan appeared in the middle of the room.

"Hey mate. Just checking every thing OK for tonight?" Noticing Ben's red eyes, he asked, "You OK mate?" Ben, knew what Nathan was driving at but ignored that question.

"What's happening tonight?" he asked instead, completely forgetting their weekly Learning Group session.

"Er…It's study tonight at my house. You are coming, right?" he asked, a touch annoyed that Ben hadn't remembered. It was not like the Ben of old. Nathan wanted him back, but would always be there for his friend through these dark times.

Ben furrowed his brow; his agitation was still high. Considering how to respond, he pondered. If he says 'no', he could go back to being with his virtual Lydia. He felt himself getting warmer trying to make a decision. He thought about the questions he would face from the others. Surely they knew he'd succumb to the LinerVerse by now. He felt he was living a double life, one that for now he wasn't up to sharing.

"I better go," Ben muttered out loud, though really for his own benefit.

"What?" said Nathan, who'd been waiting patiently.

"Yeah. Yeah, I'll be there. I'll be round in fifteen."

Nathan, as his best friend, knew when to speak, and when to shut up. This was clearly the latter. "Right-e-o. See you shortly, mate. There'll be a cup of hot chocolate waiting for you."

"Thanks." Ben nodded. He waved his hand and Nathan disappeared. At least the study was at Nathan's parents' house, just across the way. He kept reminding himself that it would be a good distraction, as he pulled out the NCep device, for now avoiding the powerful temptation to go back in to say goodbye.

It was Simon who opened the door. "Ben! How are you doing?" On hearing Simon's jovial voice, Ben knew it was a mistake to come out. His body language obviously shared that message. Ben just stared. Simon ushered him in. "Come on in, mate. Go have a seat. We'll get the drinks on soon."

Ben made his way into Fabio and Olivia's large sitting room. He loved this room. It was filled with floor to ceiling shelves, stacked with books of all shapes, sizes, and colours.

Some were ancient and worn, collector's items, while others were glossy and new. The room always had a cozy feel to Ben, despite its enormous size. It had that musty smell of books, like fresh earth and old paper all at once, just like the public library. He wondered whether Fabio ever truly left work. He just moved from managing Sab City library to his home collection.

Simon, sitting back comfortably in the sectional, rested his cup on his grey boot-cut jeans. "Cheers for hosting," he directed to his mum and dad.

"...especially as it was supposed to be us tonight," Dauphina continued apologetically, as she sat down on the sofa next to her husband, smoothing out her stylish black dress with gold trim. "Our bathroom should be finished by next week. Promise!"

"That's fine," said Fabio, the corners of his mouth raising slightly. "It's been a while since we hosted, so it's all good."

Simon was Fabio and Olivias' other son. Together with his wife Dauphina, they had been trying to complete their house for years. But with a bustling home of six children, one of whom was Sabine—still understandably dealing with the disappearance of her best friend Alice—it wasn't easy.

Ben sat on his hands, gazing at the bookshelves, trying to imagine he was invisible. Mentally, he was in the castle, wandering around the grand gardens, searching for Lydia. 'I wonder what she's up to,' he thought.

"Ben,"

'Missing me…What else does she get up to when I'm not there?'

"Ben!"

'There must be so many people she could meet up with. I've only seen a few so far…'

"Ben!" Dauphina shouted, which jolted him back to reality.

"Er…sorry. I was miles away," he replied.

"We could tell!" she smiled. "What would you like to drink?" Dauphina asked again.

"Just a hot chocolate, thanks."

"Coming right up," she responded as she continued taking orders before leaving the room.

Ben looked around the room, forcing a smile as he tried to stay present. This was becoming increasingly difficult the longer he spent out of reality and living his second life.

# CHAPTER 18

## LINERS & REALERS

Dauphina and Nathan both sat down after handing out the last few drinks. Sarah, not one of Fabio's and Olivia's numerous progeny, turned to Ben. He was sheepishly staring at the floor.

"I've not seen you for a while, so sorry if you've said all this already, but any more news regarding Alice?" she asked.

Sarah was doing well in her career. She'd recently become Director of Strategy for the European Region of Whoosh—the largest AutoJet company on the planet. She was a straight shooter. Some people found her hard to deal with, the kind of people who want everything vanilla, but Ben appreciated that direct characteristic in her.

Ben sighed. "Unfortunately, Sarah, there's not much else to say. Section One found nothing. They say they talked to Museum and HIC staff. Nothing came up, and nothing else they can do."

Ben looked up, his eyes focusing on a toy rabbit sitting nonchalantly on a shelf amid the books. It looked identical to

Alice's toy she called Boris. 'What a failure I've been as a father,' he thought. 'I don't deserve to be sitting here with these wonderful people and parents.'

Sarah observed his disconsolate figure. She hated seeing her friend like that and tried to find a nugget of hope or positivity.

"Wasn't there that boy she was seen talking to? Anything happen to him?" she asked.

Dauphina huffed, thinking of her daughter, Sabine, one of the last people to see the boy in question...and to have seen Alice, for that matter.

"Hmmm...Bine get's frustrated at herself for that. She says she saw the boy as Alice was walking towards him, and a few moments later whilst still waiting for Ali. She just wished she'd stopped him and asked where Ali was."

Olivia looked on lovingly at her daughter-in-law. "But she had no idea what was happening with Alice. We just need to continue to help her see that," she voiced.

"I know. I know," replied Dauphina in resignation.

Ben looked up, his care for Sabine clear.

"I've told Bine she shouldn't be so hard on herself..." he encouraged, his eyes moving back to fake Boris, lying on its side, its lonely eyes staring straight back at Ben, "but then I'm not exactly one to talk...Perhaps I'm being punished..." he muttered, almost not finishing the sentence as his voice drifted off.

"You what Ben?" Queried Fabio who, at his age, although his hearing was less than perfect, no one fully heard Ben's mutterings. They looked at each other, wondering what to say. When no response was forthcoming, Fabio responded.

"Ben, everyone understands it is difficult for you. But you know God has a plan for all of this, right? He will work everything out for your good. You might not see it today or tomorrow, or possibly even in this life. But God has it all under His control."

Ben appreciated Fabio's wise words. That was Fabio. A rock in their community. Though Ben's thinking these days was slowly drifting away from God, being as *in control* as he once believed. He remembered his grandad lying there on his bed in their house.

Ben was a young boy, just 16 years old. He was alone with him at the time. He'd held his hand, stroked it, trying to imagine life without his gramps. His last words he remembered verbatim: 'It's your God-given responsibility to lead and protect your family. There can be no bigger responsibility than this. I failed at this, but you mustn't.'

It never crossed Ben's mind to find out how his grandpa had failed. Perhaps due to the fact, that, aside from the failure part, they were the exact words his father had also given him as parting advice. He thought about his grandparents relationship and couldn't get out of his head that *failure* seemed an alien concept to the wonderful experience he'd observed of them.

But now, all these years later, *he* was the one that failed. Failed his grandad, his father, himself, God, and of course, his wife, and daughter.

Sitting in his neighbour's living room—his extended family— he willed his tear ducts to not open. He didn't want them fawning over him right now so he changed the subject.

"So, how is Bine doing generally?" he asked, his voice partially cracking, but he seemed to get away with it.

"Well, not too great, really. I'm worried. She's been talking a lot about wanting to become a liner," explained Dauphina. Ben raised his eyebrows. "I don't know where she's got it from or who she's been talking to. We still barely watch TV, or none of that mainstream propaganda rubbish, or even let her go online on her own. But somehow she must have seen something, talked to someone and is now questioning whether living online could solve her problem of missing her best friend."

Ben's neck felt sweaty. He slid a finger around his collar, trying to give his neck more space to cool, before slowly massaging his hand with his opposite hand's thumb. 'Do they know anything?' he thought again, hoping the answer was no.

Nathan spoke, his ears metaphorically pricking up. "Oh...is that what she meant?" he asked, then realised no one would know what he was talking about. "She asked me last week the difference between liners and realers and whether I knew any liners. I didn't really think anything else of it."

"What did you say?" asked Dauphina cautiously.

"Well, I just told her the obvious; liners are people who live most of their life online, and realers are, well...the rest of us...and that I didn't know any liners personally. Was that OK?" asked Nathan, more out of respect rather than worried about Dauphina and Simon's reaction. They were well-adjusted individuals not given to taking offence too quickly.

"Yeah. Yeah. That's cool." Dauphina responded. "She's obviously got it from somewhere else." Then turning to her husband, she indicated, "we'll need to investigate more Si."

"Yes, hun. But as worrying as it might sound, even at her age, I believe she's strong enough in her faith to know what's right."

"Yeah. She's a good kid," Nathan encouraged. Good *kid*, thought Ben. 'What does that make me...addicted to the LinerVerse? Weak faith. A true liner,' he mused, his palms growing redder and hotter, the more he massaged them.

"Talking of liners..." said Calvin, having sat silently, listening so far. He leant into the group as though what he was about to share was top secret. Wearing a dark blue suit with tan brogues, the outfit finished with a pair of SolHide sunglasses —which he often wore indoors and at night—he looked every bit like a spy. Fabio and Sarah exchanged a smile, raising their eyes. Calvin continued.

"...anyone heard about that liner guy in Tokyo who went crazy and died when there was a power cut, cutting him off from the LinerVerse?"

A few affirmative nods from the group. "Yeah, I heard about it," said Simon. "How did he actually die?"

"From a heart attack, the article said. Apparently, he couldn't cope with the real world again," Calvin answered.

"Poor guy," consoled Dauphina.

"Well, if he chooses to spend all his time there, he's got no one to blame but himself," retorted Sarah.

"He'd been online for two weeks straight, apparently. No sleep," continued Calvin.

"Two weeks? Ewww! How did he...you know...do his stuff?" Dauphina enquired, scrunching up her face.

"I've heard there is a suit you can buy which can actually...er... deal with those issues, shall we say...without getting too explicit. You get fed via a tube supposedly giving you 'all the nutrients the body needs,'" Calvin explained, the last part mimicking Dozer from his favourite old film, *The Matrix*.

'I wonder where I might get a suit like that?' thought Ben for a fleeting moment before Nathan chimed in.

"Yeah, Calv, but that doesn't take account of the mind...not to mention other parts of the body. There's a lot that happens to us living in an online world for two weeks," he explained.

Being an HIC staff member, he knew a thing or two about the human body. "...like, we have to move. We're embodied creatures. God's not created us to be sat down for days on end. We need to get up and boogie, so to speak. Then there's the brain. An article I read about it said he didn't get any sleep for much of that time and sleep is obviously a crucial part of life. You deprive someone of it by living inside a virtual world twenty-four-seven... it's a recipe for disaster. No wonder his brain just couldn't cope and he started going mad, paranoid first, then delusional."

Ben looked at Nathan. In the past, he would have admired his friend's passion. Today Ben couldn't help feeling that this conversation was a little too close to home. Did they really know about his predilections?

Simon responded, "Apparently, people in the game—or whatever you want to call it—noticed some weird reactions from him..."

"Yeah, and I heard he finally flipped and smashed up his house when the power went cut," continued Calvin, still in spy mode.

"Why do people do it? ...You know, stay online, I mean," Olivia asked, struggling to understand the desire people had for the online world. She embraced reality and would always prioritise meeting people face-to-face rather than via ComTel, let alone the LinerVerse. Even though the liner vs. realer debate had been going on for millennia, it was still uncommon for someone to die whilst online.

Fabio responded to his wife. "In my experience, they're usually running from something." Ben couldn't disagree with that. "It's not a bad thing to do once in a while. It can be recreation, just like watching films. But to *stay*...well, that's a sign of misunderstanding our God-given roles in this life. I see it really as an abdication of responsibility. That's what many want to run away from: responsibility. The real world can suck sometimes, as we all know too well here. But as Christians, at least we know why—it's all part of the curse, the fallen world."

Ben knew that to be true. Deep down, at least. Whilst Fabio was talking, Ben did everything to avoid eye contact with his friends. In fact, during most of this conversation, he wanted nothing less than the ground to swallow him up. 'What a hypocrite I am,' he thought. 'The sin of omission, is still a sin. Let's just get this done and get back home,' he said to himself, sitting up straighter.

"Well, that seems like a good segue into our study tonight," smiled Dauphina, attempting to get the study started. "Who wants to read the passage?"

# CHAPTER 19

## HOPE

After the study drew to a natural close, just as Ben was about to leave, Sarah looked at him and asked, "What are your thoughts on all that commotion at the Complex? I thought you might have a view with it being a Sendo construct."

Ben didn't really want to think about this now, but understood Sarah asking, especially because of Lydia's past employment with Sendo.

Dressed in a baby pink hoodie complemented with a denim skirt, Sarah let out a comfortable sigh as she pulled her feet up underneath her; leaning back into the oh-so-comfortable sofa waiting for Ben's reply. Fabio and Olivia said their goodbyes and headed to bed, as Simon, Dauphina, and Calvin had headed home. Ben wished he'd done so, too.

Some of the news channels had covered the dispute between two groups of residents at the Complex, but it didn't seem too clear to him exactly what had happened. One group was threatening to potentially destroy the other and take over the

Complex for themselves...that much was said. But the rumour-mill was in overdrive with suggestions of the aggressors threatening to attack Earth if they didn't get their way. But at this point, they were just that: rumours.

Sarah folded her arms across her chest, thinking Ben was just considering his answer, and continued. "It kinda feels like Sendo are covering up what's going on and trying to manage the comms. I mean, I don't blame them, but it does depend on what actually is going on."

Ben closed his Bible and rested it on the arm of the sofa. Trying to mask his frustration, he replied, "I don't think I've heard anymore than you, Sarah."

"It seems a little worrying if the rumours are true," Nathan chimed in. "I read they were targeting Sendo bases here on Earth...I guess to threaten Sendo to sort the problem out? In Sab City, that could mean the Museum and their HQ. Neither of which are too far from us," offered Nathan before looking at Ben and sensing he wanted out of this conversation. He nodded and gave a half-smile of acknowledgement just as Sarah ended the conversation of her own accord.

"You could be right. Either way, I hope it gets sorted out quickly. We've actually done well for such a long time, with no major disputes. It'd be a shame if it all kicks off now," she replied, slowly rising from her seat. The boys copied as she headed towards them both for a hug.

"Well, we can pray it doesn't," said Nathan.

"Amen to that! Right, I gotta go," she said as she released Ben and headed for the door.

"Thanks for hosting Nath. Night, Ben." Nathan held the door as she slid into her pumps and headed out down the path.

Ben followed her out the door, about to say goodbye to Nathan and finally get home, but almost as if continuing a conversation, Nathan loudly whispered to Ben,

"...so you're basically telling me, you think she might still be alive?" Ben turned. He'd only made it two steps out the door, but walked back as he didn't particularly want anyone else tuning into this conversation.

"Yeah. I can't say for certain," Ben whispered, "and I know I supposedly buried her...I mean...you were there... but was it really her?" Ben started to get animated. "Something about it just doesn't seem right. I know I have no proof, but you just have to trust me. I'm getting more and more convinced my Lydia is still out there somewhere. She might even be with Alice for all I know."

There were things that just didn't add up to Ben. Lydia, her body at least, really looked like that of his wife. Remembering her lying there in the coffin...he tried to remember every-thing...every detail of that beautiful face. Each freckle. Every mole. The curves of her cheeks. The cute shape of her button nose.

He didn't want to spend too much time dwelling on her beauty as that would set him off again in to that place. He pulled his thoughts back.

"Was there anything that wasn't right...that looked off in someway to suggest the body wasn't my Lydia's?" he thought aloud, more to himself than to Nathan. The fact he'd been seeing her again—albeit in the LinerVerse—just made him more confused.

He kept telling himself, the virtual Lydia wasn't connected to his actual wife, but just hearing her voice masked any sense that she wasn't real.

Ben furrowed his brow.

"How'd you get the body?" Nathan asked as he scratched his cheek.

"Sendo brought it to us," he replied, shifting his weight to the other foot. "They told me what happened. She was working in the lab on stabilising the atmosphere for the terraforming project. All the stats apparently said the test room was stable. Everything was clean, so she went into the test room as normal. It was fine at first...just as indicated. But for some reason—and they could only put it down to the system reacting to something in her body—the oxygen level rapidly reduced and carbon dioxide increased."

"Then she would have passed out soon after that," Nathan said.

"Yes. Well, she collapsed, then whilst trying to crawl across the lab to hit the reset switch, it was then she fully lost consciousness. Five minutes later, it was reported in when an alert was sent around the base."

"Hmmm. It never improves, no matter how much I hear it. I always think...at least she went quickly," Nathan stated, looking for a positive.

"That's if you believe that happened at all...and I'm becoming less convinced each day," Ben responded.

They both stood in silence for a few moments, gathering their thoughts.

"Why would Sendo be lying? I mean, it's not a great story for them. You know how much they valued her and were distraught at her death…or supposed death," he added, to offer a little bit of sympathy with his friends' line of thinking for now. "Surely they would have come up with a better story than that, if they made it all up. I mean, it doesn't say much about their safety policies if it took as much as five minutes for an alert to go out about a potential fatality in the lab. And why was she on her own? That's crazy to have someone working in those environments with all the potential for accidents and yet she was on her own. That really doesn't make them look good," Nathan suggested.

Ben, shrugged his shoulders, looked down at the ground. "I know. I know. Like I say, it makes little sense. All I can say is that I don't fully believe their version of what they say happened…"

Nathan cut in, "…but also, what would they be trying to cover up?"

"Again, I don't know," said Ben frustratedly. "I really don't know. But I'm gonna find out. I have a hunch that both the people I love are still alive…somewhere."

"Have you said any of this to Sendo?" Nathan asked.

"No!" Ben said, raising his voice slightly and looking around the neighbourhood. He turned back to Nathan. "No. Not at all. I don't want them to know I'm suspecting anything. Like I say, I have no proof of anything. Just have a feeling. I know my wife and daughter better than anyone."

The evening air hit Ben, and he gave a slight shiver. It was good to talk about this with someone, to get it off his chest.

Nathan leant on the door frame. "Hey, look mate, what do you need from me?" he said.

Ben gazed across the street at his home, the automatic lights from the block of homes having switched on, lighting up the garden.

"Firstly, don't say anything about this to anyone. It's just between us. Don't even tell the rest of the group. You can ask them to keep praying for Alice, but please don't mention anything about Lydia," he requested.

"You know they'd want to know. They'll do anything for you," Nathan responded with his natural support for the group.

"I know. That's why I just need to keep this small until we can figure out more." Ben looked up at his friend. "You OK with that, Nath?" he asked, knowing the significant favour he was requesting from Nathan to keep it a secret from his parents.

"Sure. I'm gonna be honest in that I'm not on the same page with you as regards Lydia. I just can't see their motivation, but keep going, and I'll do what I can to help you find out once and for all. And definitely with Alice, let's get her back. I don't think Section One will be any help. They have too many kidnappings they are dealing with these days."

"Thanks, Nath." Ben offered his typical half-smile. He'd not been his old self since Alice had vanished. His old self would have shown a lot more appreciation for his best friend's support.

"You're welcome. Right, I'm gonna kick you out as I gotta work in the morning," he said as he embraced Ben, who remained static and uneasy as he turned, succeeding finally in heading home.

As he walked the short journey back to his house, he shivered again, then wrapped his arms around himself. He couldn't help but feel the need to distance himself from his friends, for a while at least.

Telling Nathan his true thoughts about Lydia, was liberating, but sharing all he was learning about his grandpa would be a step too far, let alone his unexpected predisposition to the LinerVerse. 'What would they think of him?'

The lie he'd been living for these few months meant he no longer felt deserving of their warmth and support. Every hug, or compliment, drove his chest to knot tighter and tighter, only growing his uneasy guilt. And over the coming months, this was only going to get worse.

## CHAPTER 20

### BREAD AND WATER

On, off, on, off, flashed hazy lights. It was all Alice could see through the hood Frank, one of her captors, had put over her head as a blindfold. She could sense she was moving at high speed. 'Was it an AutoJet or a TransPortal?' She couldn't tell.

The vibrations were tiny, which had her leaning more towards the latter. The idea that if it was a TransPortal, meant she could be currently heading away from Earth, was becoming more and more real.

Alice's relationship with her captors was strange. She really sensed Robert and Frank genuinely wanted to tell her what was happening and what was planned for her, but for some reason—probably instructions from their paymasters—they couldn't.

Certainly, so far at least—ignoring the fact they had actually kidnapped her—they had treated her pretty well.

Alice sensed space in front and at the sides of where she was seated. A feeling came over her that she was on her own in this TransPortal...or whatever it was.

"Is anyone there?" she asked. No response, but the resonance of the sound confirmed there was a lot of empty space around her.

Suddenly, Alice felt the vehicle slowing down. Seconds later, it came to a halt. She heard a whoosh, as what sounded like a door slid open. Light burst in, making the blindfold less effective as she could now make out two moving bodies walking towards her.

Without saying a word, she felt their boney hands on her shoulders leading her away.

"Hello? Frank? Robert? Where am I?" she asked.

They continued to lead her out of the TransPortal—she was pretty certain that's what it was now. They, whoever they were, ignored her questions. The sound seemed to dampen, indicating she was being led through a tight space. There was very little reverberation.

They were moving her fairly rapidly, almost to the point where Alice was struggling to keep up. After what seemed like ages, she was stopped. She heard a few bleeps, then a whoosh as another much larger door slid opened.

Guiding her in, her captors led her further into whatever room it was, and finally she heard another door open. They lead her in that too. She felt the hand move from her shoulders, after which a solid thud of a door closing confirmed to her she wasn't getting out unless they wanted her to. Her mind quickly flashed to the door of the security room in the museum, though, that seemed such a long time ago now.

The light level slowly dropped, and as far as Alice could see, it was turning from white to red. Realising her hands were untied, slowly she removed the hood, hesitating in case someone else was there to quickly pull it back on for her.

'At last I can see!' she thought as she dropped the makeshift balaclava on the floor. But her ability to see was dampened by what she saw.

The entire room was tiny. Immediately in front of her was some kind of bed that looked to be made of a concrete slab seemingly hovering a foot or so off the floor. There wasn't much space around it apart from where she was standing. It was lit purely by red lights below the slab, giving it a glowing, almost reverential appearance. There was a small bench against one wall, giving her another place to sit other than the bed.

Anger welled up in Alice's mind.

"Get me out of here!" she shouted, turning around to face a door, which, much like the one in the museum, had no obvious way to open it. She banged her fists on the door.

"Let me out! What do you want from me?" she cried.

Nothing.

She couldn't even hear any sounds outside the room. She pounded on the door, her hands turning red as blood surged to the surface. It hurt. Rubbing them to ease the pain, she looked around the room, touching some of the other surfaces, looking for something that would give her a clue as to how she could get out of there.

Frustrated and exhausted from searching every nook and cranny of the tiny room, she finally gave up and collapsed onto the bed. A range of thoughts passed through her mind, from how her dad must be missing her, to even, 'I wish I'd known my mum'. Having only been a baby when Lydia died, she'd naturally heard so much about her from her dad and the others. The sadness of not experiencing the beauty of being brought up by a mum, and a dad, much like Sabine and her other friends had, mixed with the fact she was currently kidnapped and taken to who knows where, the tears started to flow.

'What was happening? Lord, what do they want from me?' Her body went limp as she curled up on the bed in a foetal position, her tears dropping to the slab. Before long, her exhaustion was too much, and she cried herself to sleep.

Moments later, a little metallic creature entered the room from a small hole in the wall. It moved toward the slab. Quietly, it extended an arm carrying what looked like an empty syringe up to the bed, heading for Alice's shoulder. Her exhaustion was so great and her sleep so deep that she didn't move a muscle while the creature did its work, slowly moving her arm to inject something into the mole under her armpit. Then, as quickly as it came, it went, disappearing down the practically invisible tunnel.

'Knock, knock!'

Alice woke with a start and panicked as she felt a pain under her arm. It took her a few moments in her ascent back to consciousness to decide that rubbing it up and down wasn't helping. It certainly wasn't a throbbing pain and she could easily put up with it, 'but why does it hurt? How long was I out?' she wondered. Whilst mulling this over, she heard the door open and an old man entered the pod. A white light enveloped the room, replacing the red, slowly increasing in brightness.

Moving toward Alice, the old man stood still, looking down at her slight frame lying on her side on the slab. A tray was held in his left hand. He was a short man, wearing a dark grey fitted suit. Probably in his sixties, with white-grey wispy hair and a full, well-trimmed white beard.

Stooping, so his head was closer to Alice's level, he quipped, "So you're Alice. I've been wanting to meet you for a very long time."

Alice valiantly tried to control the burning rage inside her.

"Why does everyone keep saying that? Do you enjoy getting your kicks through kidnapping little girls?" she still spat out.

The old man's face displayed a solemn expression as he placed the tray he was carrying on the floor.

"Here is your food," he said.

Alice looked at the tray containing two pieces of buttered crusty bread and a glass of water. 'Bread and water...what a cliche,' she thought.

If she was ever going to get out of there, she would need to do everything she could to keep her strength up, even though it may well be drugged. She calculated that as they wanted her for her powers, they wouldn't harm her...much. Satisfied with her rationale, she took a bite of the bread.

'*Mmmm*...'It tasted deliciously warm with that freshly baked smell, which always reminded her of being at Sabine's house. They liked their baking, that family. Thinking of her best friend made her sad, not knowing when...or if, she would ever see her again. She shook her head as if to dispose of the thought.

"Thank you. Thank you for the food," she said, surprising the old man. Even despite her current predicament, she was brought up to have good manners.

Standing back up, he said, "I'm sorry you're in this situation. And to answer your earlier question, no. This is not how I get my kicks, as you say. Being here actually puts me at great risk. I'm not one of them. I'm here to get you out."

"You what?" said a slightly stunned Alice.

"I can't say much now. I have put a blocking signal on your tray, that means we can talk without them hearing. But we don't have long."

"Why are you helping me? Who are you?" she asked, slightly regretting her earlier outburst.

"As I said, I can't tell you much now, as we don't have time. I know that's an obvious frustration, but they will get suspicious. Just so you're aware, a plan is in progress and a few of us are involved. I just need to know the extent of your powers."

Alice's eyebrows raised. She nodded her head slowly; her 'spidy sense' kicking in.

"Oh, I see. You just want to know exactly what I'm capable of, just so you can rescue me. Right? Do you think I was born yesterday?" she shot out.

The old man stroked his chin. "Hmm...I guess I should have anticipated that. As I say, we don't have a full plan, and we will need your help to fully develop it. What can I do to prove to you I'm telling the truth...that I am here on your side?"

Alice thought for a while. Sitting up straighter, she looked directly at the old man, an idea forming in her mind.

"Can you bring me a Bible?" The old man, looked at her puzzled, then raised his particularly bushy eyebrows.

"A Bible...as in an ancient Holy Bible? Is that it?" he queried.

"Yes. That'll do, for starters. Bring me a Bible...oh...but not just any Bible. It has to be an NKJ version on a Reeder belonging to my dad or someone who's recently been in contact with him. I presume you know my dad?"

"Of course," he mused. "Mr Ben Harman. OK. Consider it done. I'll be back later," he said as he turned towards the door and left.

The white light decreased until, once again, a red glow was all that lit the pod. Alice slumped back on the slab. 'I'm not even sure bringing the Bible will prove he is telling the truth,' Alice prayed. 'But I will trust You, Lord. There is a reason all of this has happened to me, and I won't let it go to waste.'

# CHAPTER 21

## THE DIARIES

Ben woke up having a renewed sense of focus the following day after the study. He threw off the bedclothes, still quite groggy as he'd woken up multiple times throughout the night. Too many thoughts and questions about his grandpa whirled around his mind, inspired by the recent conversation with JR. To be honest it was also currently helping to provide a distraction from his despair in losing Alice.

Quickly dressing in yesterday's clothes, and even before grabbing a cup of tea, he headed out toward the basement.

"I know it's here somewhere?" he muttered to himself, as he stooped down attempting to pull out a cabinet behind which he remembered storing some of grandpa's items many years ago.

He used brute strength to pull the cupboard. It moved a bit, but not enough to mean he wouldn't have to stretch behind it. He stuck his hand through a small gap, behind the dusty, cobweb encased cabinet.

"Ouch!" he called out as he quickly pulled his hand back, feeling a prick as his finger must have caught on a splinter. He squeezed a few drops of blood, wiping it with a tissue, then sucking on his finger. With no damage done, he tried again.

'Why did I put grandpa's stuff in such an awkward place?' If he'd known the contents of the items he was looking for, he would have surely kept them locked away in the house. As it was, it was just grandpa's old diaries. 'How important could they be?' Ben thought about his own diaries, and how mind-numbingly boring it would be for someone to read them. 'Why would Herman Harman's' be any different?'

His mind had been whirling through the—in parts frustrating —conversation with JR and what he implied about Herman Harman. 'I hope these diaries can shed some light on that,' he thought as his hand felt and grabbed what felt like three books. He pulled them out, shook off the dust and brushed the top cover, which was rather unassuming. All three were ring bound with a hard cover of black and blue with an orange line separating the columns of colour on the front.

Ben opened the top one to reveal black text stating Herman Harman, 2089. He was taken back to seeing this very book by his grandads' bedside table, on one of the many occasions as a small boy, he'd stayed with his grandparents.

His memory continued as he was struck by a captivating aroma reminiscent of a blend of ancient oak and toasted almonds. He'd no idea whether it was that, although come to think of it, almonds were a regular ingredient in grandma's recipes.

But right now, holding the books in his hands, his sensory organs were full of this associated happy and olfactory memory. Ben stood up, now having to exercise great discipline to not start reading them immediately. 'It'll be much better in comfort upstairs,' he decided as he shook the dust off his arms, pushed the cabinet back and headed back upstairs.

Ben quickly waved his hand in front of his ComTel and selected a news feed, then headed into the kitchen to make a cup of tea. The audio feed playing in the background.

*'The boys's father, sitting next to the Section One officer, pleaded with the public to come forward with any further information they had. It was the seventh missing child in the past nine months. Section One says they are doing all they can, but echoed the father's plea to contact them urgently if they have any further information.'*

*'Meanwhile, on the Complex, the dispute between two rival factions of Shumen is being played down by Sendo eXperience, the owners, and landlords. A spokeswoman said, "While there are many rumours circulating about supposed issues on the complex, we can give you the facts. There has been a minor dispute, but it was extremely well handled by our Guardian, who is doing exactly what we employ him to do. There is nothing for anyone to worry about. Please ignore the rumours."'*

Ben listened as he entered back in the sitting room, cup of tea in-hand, his mind drifting to the conversation with Sarah and Nathan last night.

'I wonder what's really happening. Sarah's right. They do seem to be trying to manage the comms a bit too well. I know how these teams work. The only reason to say there's nothing to worry about, is if there's something to worry about. There must be something else going on that they don't want us to know,' he thought.

But that wasn't today's focus. Sitting back on the sofa, holding the first of his grandpa's diaries in his lap, he opened it and began reading.

◭

"And by next week, I want you to write one page–and I mean one page," he emphasised, this by holding up one finger, "...on why you think communism has failed thus far."

A subtle groan was let out by a gaggle of the students of Herman Harman's social science class. It was a struggle for most of them to keep to one page. Herman knew that, but it would help them learn how to understand, select, and prioritise information. One by one, each student disappeared from Herman's view. He always stayed until they had all gone, just in case one of them wanted to talk further.

As someone who'd been intensely critical of the LinerVerse, it would have been a shock to close friends that Herman Harman had been teaching this virtual class for years. He would much have preferred to be teaching at a bricks and mortar university, but since GF2.0, there were none...well, only a tiny fraction of the nearly two hundred there used to be, and to his growing frustration, none of them were near him. So if he really wanted to teach, he had to embrace the very thing he'd pooh-poohed for most of his life.

It hadn't sat well with him, but as he got used to it, first donning a headset, then moving on to an NCep device, he truly saw the potential. And it was this vast potential for inspiring people to see another way, to revolutionise their thinking that ultimately proved too great a draw.

Herman was in his element teaching social science. His frustration at how the country was currently being run—or ruined—he would say, was hard to quash. There were a growing number of young people, and to be honest, not so young, who wanted to know what they could do about it. The trouble was, they had a hard time convincing others as despite all the calamities that were predicted in a post GF2.0 world, there had been next to none.

Society was flourishing within this new structure where families got to run their own lives, not some one-world-government who had no idea what was really happening at the grassroots. As far as Herman was concerned, this was a problem of different philosophies.

He would explain, 'I'm not saying that everything will be better when society is run along socialist principles. I'm saying that, as no system is perfect—as we are all imperfect people—this is the *right* system to govern society.'

When some people had caught on to what he was saying, they'd asked him to teach them how, of which he had had mixed emotions. On the one hand, glowing pride at being asked to share his views, but this was tainted by revulsion of the medium of exchange: the LinerVerse.

It took Herman a few years to get over his pride and get under a headset. But once he had, it was like a duck to water. He loved sharing his knowledge with willing students, LinerVerse or not.

Just as he was about to direct his avatar toward home, a student popped back.

"JR," Herman said, happy to see him back, no doubt full of questions as he usually was. "What can I do for you?" he asked with pride.

"Hi, Sir. I, er...just wanted to ask about the question."

The young man's avatar looked down at the metaphorical floor.

"Go, on."

Herman loved it when his students took the time to push deeper. And JR often did.

"Well...er...the question assumes that communism has failed. What if it hasn't? Or...er...more to the point...what if I make the case that it hasn't failed...er...as it's never been truly implemented? That there's always been a mixture of systems and never pure communism."

Herman's avatar, nodded its head up and down like a nodding dog. There was a silence, just about bordering on the uncomfortable, but JR knew Herman was such a considered professor, he expected the pause.

"That's an interesting proposition, JR." Herman said as he stopped nodding and seemed to look straight at JR's avatar. "Part of the point of the question is to get you challenging the question itself. So go for it. If you feel you can make that case, I look forward to reading and debating it with you and the others. Good thinking," he encouraged.

JR's avatar, beamed, "Thanks, sir."

"You're welcome, but I don't know how many times I have to tell you...you don't have to call me sir. Herman is fine. It's my name, after all," he admonished.

"OK. Sorry, sir...I mean Herman." Herman smiled.

"OK. Be off with you!" and with that, JR's avatar vanished.

Herman knew JR thrived under his tutelage, asking question after question, much to his delight. Soon he would become more officially his mentor, helping to take the LinerVerse in a vastly different direction.

2163 - Present Day

A few hours later, Ben was still sitting on the sofa. If someone was observing him, they would say he hadn't moved a muscle in all that time. They would also be confused by his mood through his facial expression. Was it shock, confusion, awe? Maybe a mixture of all three. Either way, Ben was transfixed. He didn't know what to make of the words he'd just been reading.

"I can't believe he embraced the LinerVerse...actually taught on it!" Ben uttered, amazed, as he mentally cycled through some conversations he'd had with grandpa about it over the years. "I guess he never said he wouldn't use it, or possibly that it was wrong to use it. It's just that by his negative comments, anyone would guess he was repulsed by it. I mean, grandpa using an NCep device! That's just plain weird," he surmised.

JR's views and worldview made more sense to him now being filtered through his grandpa's diaries. And Ben had a whole new understanding of grandpa himself, like he was a completely different person, and he'd yet to finish the diaries. 'What other revelations will I find?' Ben pondered.

He could see what was drawing him to JR, but he had to get more answers. He got his bag together, packed up the three diaries and headed for Sab City Library, very much looking forward to meeting with Grandpa's former mentee.

# CHAPTER 22

## ANOTHER WAY

THE LIBRARY WAS QUIET; THE WAY BEN LIKED IT. Sitting at a desk in the main concourse, Ben leant forward, turning a page in the third of his grandpas' diaries. Dust flew up from the page, prompting him to screw up his nose. 'I thought I got rid of'...Ben sneezed before he could finish his thought.

Picking up the book, folding the corner of the current page to mark his place, he shook it. More dust flew out. He placed it back on the desk, leaning back in his chair; one hand moved to steady himself, the other stroking his chin. He furrowed his brow in contemplation.

'So, to summarise what I've read so far...

One: Grandpa had a whole other life, I, and I'm sure many others, knew nothing about, but now I can see that he'd hinted things to me.

Two: He didn't seem to like *family* as much as...well...certainly as much as he put across.

Three: He seemed to believe Jesus was a socialist, and not only that, more Marxist!

But most of all, and certainly the most intriguing...'

"Four: He may have kept his avatar alive in the LinerVerse!" Ben said that final thought out loud, it was so astonishing. "Could that be like Lydia?" he said as he rubbed his forehead. "In fact was Grandpa the person Lydia said she wanted to introduce me to?...Hmmm...I'll have to ask her," he said, trying to think of the next time he could log on.

"But I just can't believe this is Grandpa. Why would he hide his true feelings if he constantly talked about the importance of the Truth? Why would he lie like that? I just don't get it."

As he was frustrating himself with even more questions than answers, Ben noticed movement past the closest bookshelves.

"Ah, here he is!" said a booming voice, though kept quiet enough for a library.

Ben stood up and smiled as a man decidedly similar to his grandpa bounced in and joined him at his table. Holding out his big strong hands, he clasped Ben's in his own.

"Good to finally meet you in the flesh, Ben," he said, his deep, warm voice so much fuller in person than via ComTel.

"Likewise, JR." Ben motioned away from the desks. "Let's move to the meeting rooms so we can chat fully."

He picked up his books and bag.

"Good idea," confirmed JR.

As they wandered off, Ben leading the way, JR put a hand on his shoulder.

"So, how are you holding up?" It was touching he would ask that, and Ben knew it was genuinely meant. Strong empathy, just like Grandpa.

Now, seeing JR up close, he was reminded even more of Herman Harman. The mannerisms, the voice, the years of wisdom etched on his face. Save for some features, it could be his grandpa with him now.

"Ah, you know, JR..." Ben stopped walking just before the meeting room, looked down, then up at his grandpa's former mentee. "Sometimes I feel like...like, I trust in God fully, and know that He has everything under control. Other times I feel like I'm a complete failure," he said instinctively, proof of his growing level of trust for this man.

Still deep in thought, Ben opened the door, finding a small recliner, next to a meeting desk. He sat down. JR followed suit and sat himself on the sofa opposite, agreeing with Ben's choice of comfort over the more official meeting desk.

"Are the two mutually exclusive?" he asked, then noticed the puzzled expression on Ben's face. "I mean, I'm not saying you're a failure or anything, but can't both be true; that God has everything in control, and, that you may have failed to obey everything He's asked of you?"

Ben looked down at the thick grey inviting carpet, suddenly imagining dragging his bare feet through it. Cosy.

"You're not making me feel any better," he responded without looking up.

JR's face softened as he quickly retorted, "My apologies. But it's not always about feeling better, or even attaining a state of happiness. The important thing is the truth. What we do with it...well...that's up to us."

He motioned to the diaries in Ben's hand.

"You're not going to like some of the things you'll hear..." he continued, "...and that you've no doubt already read, in those three books you're holding..."

Ben absent-mindedly stroked the cover of the third one he'd just finished reading before JR's arrival. 'I wonder just how much these diaries would have impacted me had I not met JR? Hmmm...I can't say for certain, but I doubt I'd be reading them otherwise.'

JR finished his thought. "...but it is the truth you're being offered."

Ben listened. He was good at that. Not always confident arguing his own case verbally. Give him an Aidea, or even a pen, and he could wax lyrical with the written word. But right now, he was struggling to articulate just what he felt about his grandpa's views.

"The truth you talk of is an interesting concept," Ben said thoughtfully. "I thought Grandpa was telling the truth in the past. But now I find he has a whole other truth. I mean, how could he have such contempt for family? He never put that across. I'm having a hard time reconciling that with what I knew of him. I mean, can you help me understand?" Ben said, screwing up his forehead as he put the diaries on the table in front of them.

"Hmmm...I get what you're saying. I hear you. But look at it this way. And...er..." he took a deep breath. "...maybe this will also help with you thinking you're a failure. You see, I get that. You've been focused so much on providing for your family. Would you say that's been the overriding drive of your life?" JR asked.

"Yes. Well…following God first, part of which is looking after my family."

"I know. I know," said JR with a hint of sympathy. "It's how you've been brought up, and you've not really known there was another way, right?" Ben nodded his head, wondering where this was going. "That responsibility, now your identity even as a husband and a father, forgive me for saying, is now in tatters as you've lost both your wife and daughter. That must seriously be messing with who you think you are."

Ben massaged his hands, knowing JR was very much correct. He questioned his purpose, and once or twice, in his deepest, darkest moments, his existence.

"Having lost someone myself…" JR continued, his voice slowing down, "I know that's not easy. But…I can't imagine what you must be feeling as regards to Alice. To not know where she is, and to be pretty powerless to do anything about it…well…like I say, I just can't imagine. I don't know the full details, but it makes sense why you feel you have failed."

Ben cut a disconsolate figure. His eyes becoming red, as he just about held off the tears. JR, fully aware of this, paused, leant forward in his chair, pulling himself closer to Ben. He lowered his voice.

"What if I told you there was another way? You have another identity…one that revolves around a community of equals—everyone providing for each other, so no one is in need? Your responsibility is to everyone, not just one group of people you happen to be born to, or are born to you. A group who all agree to be bound by unwritten mutually agreed-upon rules to help each other, to look out for one-another. An opportunity to cooperate, to share, to build society together, to work on those things that move society forward, that progress it.

Just imagine the advances we'd see in science, the arts, education, culture, all driving society forwards. It would be immense, in a way that the current thinking is letting us down. It's regressive. Wouldn't that be worth fighting for?" JR paused, giving Ben time to process and think about what he'd just shared, just as Herman, JR's mentor, had taught him.

He continued, "Imagine if, instead of you taking all the responsibility for losing your daughter, it was a collective? You would no longer feel like a failure, as there would be no you. There would only be us, and we. The weight lifted off your shoulders would be immense. Would not God want that?" JR asked.

Ben snivelled into a tissue, then wiped his eyes, slightly embarrassed about his mild emotional outpouring, especially it being the first time he'd met JR face to face. It was not what he expected of this meeting—essentially a client meeting for him to find out more about the LinerVerse so he could get to writing content for LeV8. But...boy, was he desperate to have the pressure relieved—ideally, to have his little monkey back.

But what if he didn't have to sink personally into the abyss? Ironically, it was that abyss that was drawing him toward the LinerVerse in the first place, forming his addiction. If he didn't need an outlet to assuage his guilt at failing his family, perhaps he would have never used the LinerVerse and thus perhaps never would have taken on this job. Ben's head hurt, thinking of all the ramifications. He rubbed it, trying to massage away a headache he could foresee coming.

Perhaps JR was right. Surely God didn't want him to suffer in this way. 'But then God knows what I'm going through. There's nothing He's not gone through himself. And...why should I expect to not go through hard times? We're not living in a perfect world after all.' Ben argued with himself back and forth, before JR eventually broke him out of his bubble.

Sitting back, JR swung one leg over the other, stroked his beard whilst studying Ben with deep compassion. Ben looked sullen. He thought about whether it would even be possible to not think of Alice any more than he currently did. Then a thought occurred to him. 'Would it be possible to use the LinerVerse to find Alice? I've no idea how, or if, it could work. Perhaps I could ask Lydia,' he thought, annoyed that he'd not even mentioned Alice to her as yet. There just didn't seem to be any point whilst he was there. It was like there was a reality —or at least a negativity filter that quashed any feelings of sadness. Ben thought about asking JR about this, but wasn't sure this was the right time.

JR broke the silence as he softly suggested, "Let's come back to this, Ben. You need to know more about the LinerVerse and LeV8. What sort of questions do you have for me in that regard?"

Ben thought hard about his first question, with so many others now being added to his list. He bent down in his bag, grabbed his Aidea and, looking straight at JR as the device buzzed into life, he asked, "Is it possible to live on in LeV8 after your physical body has died offline?" A hint of a smile washed over JR's face as he thought about his answer.

# CHAPTER 23

## FOWL CASSOWARY

2112 - Island Feather Trials

As he looked down at the forest floor, MendipT saw the bird in his mind. He was home on West Pasau, and could smell the forest all around him; the fresh air warming his lungs invigorating him; the forest, thick with lush green trees.

As MendipT made his way down the well-trodden path, he could hear in the distance the smack of water dashing against several huge rocks, jutting out of the sea, dripping with green foliage. He'd always thought they'd looked like giant fish waiting to gobble up anything that crossed their path.

Then there was the occasional buzz of drones capturing the activity on the island, for today was the annual Feather Trial–which sounded so innocuous. But it was a rite-of-passage; the day in which each boy, upon reaching the age of seventeen, would be expected to wander deep into the forest to retrieve a feather from the legendary cassowary bird. It sounded simple. However, many, never having seen the birds before, suspected them to be mythical creatures.

Stories MendipT had heard in the past ranged from the birds' speed, making it impossible to catch; to rumours of them being so violent they'd kill you before you got anywhere near their feathers. But it would take more than rumours to stop MendipT. He didn't think of himself as being fitter than the others; but he believed his desire was greater, wanting to do whatever it took to get that feather—and before anyone else. That would show them. Finally, give him recognition that no one could take away.

He pushed on ahead of the group, moving deeper into the forest and away from the main path, observing the sea in the distance as it got ever closer. His fellow trial runners were way behind him, as much through choice as through MendipT speeding off. Some of them didn't see him as competition, but for others, well...they didn't even regard him at all. He'd never been one to have close friends. A counsellor might say that he pushed people away, trying a little too hard to be liked. Of course, MendipT didn't see it like that.

Taking out his water bottle from his rucksack, he took a swig, feeling the refreshing liquid hit his throat as he realised he was more thirsty than he'd thought. He took another swig, then put the bottle back, hoping he wouldn't run out before he completed the quest.

Breaking into a jog, he passed a line of eight trees; the end would open out into a path that lead down to the sea. The cassowary was more likely to be found near the water. MendipT knew that, and just as he ran past the end tree, he froze. "Wow!" he gasped, as he stood still. He'd only seen one in the flesh before, and here was another, not more than ten feet in front of him. The hairs on his neck stood up as a warm feeling flooded his body; his senses seemed heightened. He could hear every sound this magnificent bird made, the low growl, the strike of its feet cracking twigs as it moved from side to side between the edge of the forest and the beach.

Acutely observing the fowl, MendipT stood very still and leant against the tree, not wanting to be discovered. The striking blue skin of its head, the brown, almost wooden, casque, the unmistakable red wattles hanging down its neck and those thick brown, head-of-hair-like feathers, which looked very much to him like his grandmother's wigs.

Its head was sticking up, looking around like a guard on patrol. She must be protecting her chicks, he surmised as he momentarily gazed at the ground, then back up, thinking this season must be the worst time to grab one, knowing the timing of the trials would have been specifically planned for this.

He scratched his arm as a bug landed, then took off, as he thought about another story he'd heard—though having no idea of its authenticity. It involved a woman having her hand taken clean off by a cassowary when she'd tried to grab one of its green eggs. He cringed.

So here he was, staring at this most dangerous bird—very much real—while it was protecting its eggs, and he had to grab one of its hair-like feathers whilst trying not to lose a hand...or worse. 'No problem! But I need a plan,' he thought, encouraging himself as he finally moved past the tree and sat down, leaning back against it.

Right now, he would have loved to get out his flute. It always calmed him down, helping him to think clearly. Though his last encounter with a cassowary some years earlier, when he was playing his flute, didn't go down so well. He never found the instrument after dropping it to run away from the bird. A sadness came over him, feeling the loss of his special flute given to him by his parents. If only he had it now.

'Perhaps this time, I could even charm the cassowary to come to me and hand over a feather.' He smiled, cheering himself up at the thought. No, his flute would most likely scare the bird, but worse still, let his rivals know where he was. 'Not gonna happen,' he thought, recognising he had to focus, to think quickly to get a feather before he was beaten.

A drone flew past, its camera turning to focus on him. He'd been caught by the organisers, so it wouldn't be long at all before the other contestants came running in, no doubt scaring the bird. "Right. I must get a feather. That'll show the others who MendipT is. They won't ignore me then," he said to motivate himself. Having his name on the trophy...well... that would show them. He knew he could quite easily scour the ground for feathers, but the rules of the game stated it had to be grabbed directly from a bird, and the best way to prove that was to grab it live on drone-cam. That way, there was no doubt.

The bird wandered around in a small circle, looking up and down; definitely protecting its eggs. MendipT spotted at least eight, all green eggs, on the ground below the Cassowary. 'Perhaps I could grab an egg too?' he thought, getting hungry, breakfast being a long, distant memory.

He looked around, a little surprised to not see any of the others having caught up to him yet. The drone still hovered a few feet away, turning back between him and the bird.

"It's been too long. I must just go for it," he said as he slowly got to his feet. The bird seemed to notice him and stared. MendipT stared back, not moving a muscle. Then the bird popped its head to the ground. He took a step forward, toward the bird. It stayed poking at the ground. He took another step, then another, and a further one, as the bird just seemed to ignore him. He was now about halfway toward the beautiful, but scary creature, almost within touching distance. Then he heard it. A low frequency growl, reverberating along the forest floor; vibrating the sand beneath his feet. It was getting louder.

Turning to his left, his heart pounded a little harder as he saw another cassowary, a male, producing its mating call. 'Not good!' thought the Shuman, still frozen to the spot. The male hadn't noticed him yet. It was definitely focused on the female, who still seemed to ignore MendipT. He risked taking another step closer. The female looked up. It's eyes locking with MendipT's as it let out a growl of a higher pitch to the male; it's eyes then focusing on the potential partner as it moved closer.

At that moment, MendipT made a split decision. His heart was beating faster than ever, perspiration dripping off him, more than indicative of the midmorning sun. He then ran full pelt at the female bird, trying to use the element of surprise, while it was distracted by the male. It seemed to work. As he got to the bird, he grabbed and pulled at its hairy side; its feathers were so thick he wasn't sure how much contact he'd made. But he didn't wait to find out, the adrenaline coursing through him. MendipT ran and ran, away from the forest, along the beach—his assumption was that the bird wouldn't follow him that far.

Still breathing hard, he looked back as he slowed down, realising thankfully no cassowaries were following him. Though he could see it in the distance, head high, staring at him. A warm fuzzy feeling ran through him as he realised how lucky he'd been that the male came along when it did. He'd never have been able to grab the feather...the feather! With the rush, he'd lost feeling in his fingers, not having checked if the feather was there.

Slowly, he looked down at his hands, squinting his eyes in hope, not bearing to think what he'd have to do if it wasn't there. It was! He saw the dark brown hairs before he felt the long shaft and he jumped, waving the feather in the air, realising he'd completely forgotten about the drones, but thankful when he heard the buzz then saw one flying overhead, it's red light flashing.

Suddenly, a wave of dissatisfaction washed over him. Yes, he'd amazingly got the feather, but what if he could get an egg? It wasn't required, but he could imagine the look on their faces if he returned, not only with a feather, but with a cassowary green egg, too. Now that would get him noticed.

As MendipT turned around, the bird was still eerily staring at him in the distance. His mind was whirring through all the options and ramifications of securing an egg. Just as he'd settled upon the run and grab method—basically how he'd gained the feather, something happened that meant he'd never get to act out his plan.

MendipT started slowly walking back towards the bird along the edge of the beach. Moving cautiously, he could hear a drone following closely behind. He turned and smiled to the camera, then suddenly an animal he thought looked like a dog, came rushing out of the forest in front him, clamping its teeth around the bird's neck, and before the cassowary had time to know what happened, it collapsed on the ground.

MendipT watched the whole scene play out, as did all the viewers through the drone-cam. A pang of guilt hit him. Was the bird so focused on him she didn't see her attacker? As he continued walking towards where it lay, he observed the bird. The dog, or whatever animal it was, had bitten and then run. The cassowary was still moving, not quite dead yet. He thought about helping. Perhaps I could tie a cloth around its neck to stop the bleeding. He moved closer, the bird still staring at him, not having taken its eyes off MendipT all throughout the attack. And now, in its last throws of life, its expression could easily be interpreted as a plea for help. MendipT couldn't take his eyes off the bird; staring into its deep orange eyes.

Then he looked away. He looked down at his hands; the feather still tight in his grip. His lips curled, as a smile lit up his face. This'll show them, he thought, as he casually walked past the dying bird, picked up an egg and headed back to the base, a drone capturing it all on camera.

# CHAPTER 24

## DISRUPTIVE PLANNING

2163 - Present day. The Complex.

An orange button flashed intermittently. A lever was pushed as the TransPortal slowed to a halt, hovering in space and seeming to synchronise position with another adjacent Trans-Portal. The shimmering glow of the Complex was faintly visible in the far distance. The orange button, now permanently glowing, signalling the opening up of comms.

"Let's up the stakes before we come on board," MendipT announced to his fellow Shumen, his voice being heard simultaneously with the other ship. "Just something subtle. Nothing too destructive at this stage. We want to get them in a panic, to cause confusion, to create a distraction, making it easier to get on board. Any ideas?"

Several of the Shumen looked at each other, then up at the mottled grey-green TransPortal roof. A faint hum could be heard in the background as the Shumen on the other ship listened in. FalongQ, sitting in the control seat in command of the other TransPortal, spoke first, the clear sound of his voice reverberating around the walls of the ship.

"How about we alter the light levels...but just in specific areas at random?" MendipT, looked intrigued. "Go on..." FalongQ continued, "It would be very disruptive if the light keeps changing brightness and patterns. A definite cause of panic and confusion," he offered confidently.

"I like the sound of that," a smile being reveeled on MendipT's face. "Anything else?" Another Shumen, this time in MendipT's ship, spoke.

"What about food? We could tamper with their rations, creating too much—not just too little food. You know how important our food is to us. Panic and confusion would just be the start," he offered.

"Yes. Another good idea too," MendipT responded, pleased with the thinking. "Now, how do we make this..."

His ComTel buzzed lightly, which distracted him, leaving the sentence hanging in the air. He looked down and swiped his finger across the screen. 'What? Why is this triggering now?' he puzzled, looking toward a call room. "I've got to take this, but have a think about how we can make this all happen," he said as he walked over, stepping inside the booth for a rare bit of privacy, his robe swishing as he turned around.

Despite the Shumen not especially being a private people, Sendo had still built in comms booths, but more for noise protection than privacy. MendipT, however, didn't want anyone, just yet, getting wind of what he'd discovered. Standing in the booth, the blue, mottled, uneven walls looked like the side of a mountain. It was designed specially to reduce noise transfer. And it did, to pretty much zero.

You could shout at the top of your voice, and someone leaning on the booth would have no idea, unless they looked in the small porthole like window. MendipT didn't need to shout, but the message was a reminder he'd sent to himself containing a video of Lydia Harman on the day of her death some ten years ago.

Now the memory had been triggered, it came flooding back. He'd been back on earth for a routine medical checkup at Sendo's primary base. Sendo had been unaware of a split in the camp. If they had, there was no way he would have been allowed back on the Complex to potentially cause more division.

Whilst waiting for his early appointment, he'd spotted a young scientist, also in the building bright and early—it was like a ghost town at that time in the morning. But as he caught sight of her, there was something about her that was quite beguiling. MendipT wasn't sure what it was. 'Have I met her before?' he thought to himself. It was like she was exuding an aura, a magnetism that he found difficult to ignore, though he was convinced he hadn't met her.

He walked towards her lab, standing far enough away so he couldn't be seen. Half-way up the door, he spied her name badge: 'Lydia Harman, Lead Scientist.' He'd looked through the thick, solid glass panels, observing. Her long dark hair swishing as he watched her glide in the chair across the floor, stopping just in front of another screen. This one displaying EEG readings and projections for a baby. He could tell that by the size of the skull. 'Alice Harman,' he said to himself; her name being displayed at the bottom of the display's window. "That must be her daughter," he'd surmised. "Definitely a baby," he muttered as on one of Lydia's screens he observed what appeared to be a HoloSense feed displaying a baby in a cot. "The Alice Harman in question, I presume." What MendipT saw next, however, made him do a double-take.

A small baby was lying in her cot and moving a mobile toy. Nothing untoward about that. However, this particular baby was moving the toy—without touching it.

"What the...!" he exclaimed, his hand rising to rub his head. His brow furrowed. 'This is impossible!' he thought, trying to think of all the ramifications of a baby with telekinesis. He realised his mouth was open, with a little bit of drool starting to leak. He quickly closed it, fired up his ComTel and recorded the screen. Despite not being at the best viewing angle, or distance, it would be more than good enough for an aide-mémoire. He took a few more snapshots of the screens and the lab. He would think about this later to work out what it all could mean.

As he was finishing taking photos, an alarm suddenly went off. It was clearly coming from Lydia's lab, and although MendipT had nothing to do with initiating it, he didn't attempt to help her. In fact, he was static. Gripped just observing the situation, like a scientist watching an experiment that he couldn't inter-fere with.

He certainly could have done something to save Lydia as he saw her collapse to the floor, clearly struggling to breathe. Instead, he was staring through the lab, his mind pondering ways to harness the baby's power. 'I could shove it back to SentiN, control the Complex, even arresting it from Sendo eXperience,' he'd thought. And that, to MendipT, was far more important than keeping one of his landlords' top scien-tists alive.

MendipT leant back against the wall of the call booth, needing something to steady himself after this revelation, now thinking he couldn't keep this to himself. His fingers were pounding out a rhythm on the control panel of the booth as he gazed out of the port-hole into the vast expanse of space. The reminder about Alice Harman, which he'd set years ago—and had genuinely forgotten about, was done for a reason. It instantly reminded him of what he'd seen in the lab on that fateful day. A pang of guilt washed over him, though it was gone almost just as soon as it arrived.

Imagining the possibilities of what this could mean for taking over the Complex ultimately meant more to him, far more. 'Now, I need to understand more about HER powers. How can they be used against SentiN and Sendo? Or am I just wasting my time?' he thought, with more frustration than curiosity. But with that, MendipT made a decision. He was going to share his knowledge with someone he trusted and whose opinion he valued. It went against his natural tendency, but he thought, 'sometimes, two heads are better than one.'

PART TWO

# CHAPTER 25

## SMACK!

Ben Harman's body lay flat on his sofa at home. Arms by his side, his chest slowly rising and falling. The sliver of brown metal of his NCep device was barely visible inside his left ear. His eyes were closed, but his mind was very much open.

Colours swirled around him, sunburnt yellows and reds with a radiant aquamarine, all floating across Ben's visual cortex. His nose twitched, eyes flickering beneath his eyelids, as if in REM sleep. There was an intoxicating aroma, one that made his cheeks swell. He knew his beloved was near, the fragrance of rosemary, bathed in the scent of fresh grass, inviting him to believe; and believe he did.

It had been a week since Ben's last enlightening conversation with JR, his grandpas' former mentee, which provided him with a lot to process. Sitting on his bed, he gazed out the window, before his eyes slowly lowered to the bedside cabinet, the glow of the morning sun bathing his grandpa's diaries. He'd read them all by now, and the most disturbing thing to him was the confirmation of it all by JR. He'd even fleshed out for Ben a bit more of the detail not covered in the diaries.

Part of him had a journalistic curiosity which helped him naturally question everything. Though in this current situation he couldn't think of one logical reason he shouldn't trust JR. He'd mentioned things only someone close to his grandpa could truly know, and...well, he just had this manner about him that whispered honesty. 'Surely that's exactly the kind of person I should be wary of,' Ben thought as he stretched out his hand, stroking his fingers over the soft leather cover of the top diary.

A wave of despondency washed over him as he dropped his head, feeling let down. How could his grandpa, whom he'd loved so much, have had a whole other life...and in the Liner-Verse, of all places? It just didn't fit with the complaints he regularly expounded with all this 'technocracy driving us to ruin,' as he'd say. But even more, if what he'd read really was true—and JR had backed it up—he even had another wife and family! I mean, how exactly did this work? Was he effectively committing adultery with his virtual wife? He'd have to speak with Fabio and Olivia. They'd always give wise counsel.

He stood up, walked to the bathroom and rinsed his mouth out, splashing water on his face as if to wake himself up. A thought crossed his mind as he looked in the mirror. 'I wonder if this means I have virtual uncles or cousins? How does that even work?' His head hurt as he rubbed it, struggling to come to terms with this level of deception.

It wasn't just that, though. As appalled as Ben was with his grandpa, the fact was that he was no different. No different at all, and that's what truly bugged him. Few people would suspect Ben Harman of being a Liner. Not in a thousand years. Yet, as he dried his face, walked back into the bedroom, sitting himself back on the bed, the hypocrisy hit him like a jab to the jaw. He was flooded with guilt.

Then it came: the urge—that pull so strong, all sense of rationality and logic would dissipate—the desire to escape from reality and all his problems was growing. Ironically, the very urge hooking himself back in to the LinerVerse. He never saw himself as a Liner, though reality had a different story to tell. The urge kept growing. To have his senses bathed in a radiating warmth, colours swirling all around him. To savour her invigorating fragrance was to feel wanted, to draw him closer to his daughter and away from the dark truth that she was lost. The LinerVerse was a happy place, willing him to enter.

His skin felt alive and hot. He noticed his right hand shaking. He held it down with his other hand. This time, he would fight it. Closing his eyes, Ben offered a silent prayer as he attempted to control his breathing. 'In...out', regulated, as slowly, the colours, the smells, and sensations floated off, back to their own little world.

He opened his eyes, a smile permeating his face. "Thank you," he whispered, and with all his strength, he stood, grabbed his bag, and headed for the front door.

The Jahm part of Sab City was not as vibrant as the Salim sector, where Ben Harman lived. There wasn't the multiplicity of cafes and bars, but it was still as well off as most places were, post the attacks on government and media of 2086.

The roads were quiet, a bit like something out of a George A. Romero film. You know the one where zombies appear out of nowhere. There were no zombies here, however. Just Sab City slowly waking up to a new day. Ben headed to the cemetery and smiled to himself, wondering if he'd find zombies there.

He continued heading for the library to bask amongst the knowledge of thousands who came before him. Reaching the end of the block, he crossed over the road into the cemetery. Strolling through a small iron gate, he stood and observed the view. It was a remarkably well-kept place, he'd always thought. Each burial plot had newly placed, fresh smelling flowers and polished headstones, and he loved—though *loved* might not be the right word—watching the displays flipping every few moments with a different holographic eulogy of the deceased —occasionally with a photo of the writer. It always reminded Ben of testimonials that he used to edit for websites of old. Always full of glowing praise for the recipient, he wondered how authentic many of them were.

'I can't talk,' he thought to himself. In this very cemetery, his own poetic words could be seen on Lydia's grave. Yes, he was very well acquainted with this space, occasionally trying to walk past her plot without stopping. Another effort in trying to move on. Literally.

He tried again today. Walking through slowly but not stopping. A gentle breeze carried the delicate scent of rosemary to his nostrils, for a split-second shifting his thoughts to the warmth of being back with her in the LinerVerse. His skin felt tight, like it was trying to keep his body from escaping. Ben kept walking, pushing the thought away as he stole a passing glance at her gravestone, remembering the time when walking by this very spot as a family, Lydia was absolutely convinced Alice had made her dummy levitate. He was in tears, laughing at her—in love—of course. 'It was the way she said it that got me,' he thought. So matter of fact and she kept repeating it, trying to prove it was true—as though the simple fact of repetition increased its authenticity. The more frustrated she got at his laughter, the more adorable she looked, and the more Ben couldn't control his laughter.

He'd love to hear that laughter now.

Ben smiled as he walked out the cemetery gate, pausing as he closed it behind him. As pleasant as it was to reminisce, it reminded him why he didn't want to dwell on the past.

Arriving at the library, Ben ascended the steps, staring at the ground, trying to force his mind to think of something else. He kept walking, the doors sensing his presence and opened, then...

*Smack!*

He bumped straight into someone coming the other way. Rubbing his head, he looked up to see what damage he had done and to whom. However, his initial reaction was not of anger at himself or the other person, neither of whom were obviously looking where they were going. No. Ben's immediate reaction was that of having his breath taken away. The woman standing in front of him had, metaphorically, as well as literally, taken his breath away.

Her long dark hair flowed down to her lower back, her head being covered by a white beanie hat, which perfectly complimented her white woollen dress and winter boots. She had on thick dark brown leggings, which finished her look, he thought, to aplomb. She certainly would not be cold walking out in the late autumn evenings.

"Wow!" he thought, rather unfortunately, out loud. "Err...I mean sorry. Are you OK?" he gathered himself together, just managing to get his words out.

"Yes," she smiled, also rubbing her head. "A little bump, but I'm OK. It was my fault too. I wasn't looking where I was going."

Ben had now lost the ability to speak. She could sense something going on internally, so after a few moments' silence, she spoke.

"You're Ben, aren't you?...Are you OK?" she stressed the *you*, repeating his question to her.

"Yes, yes...I'm all right. I'm really sorry. You just caught me by surprise...and yes...I am Ben, but how do you know?" he enquired, the woman shifting her weight to lean on her other foot.

"I believe you know my mother, Margaret Flint." Ben raised his eyebrows. His lips and cheeks forming a slight smile. Looking away for a split second, he remembered that Margaret Flint had often spoken of her daughter. Nothing in depth, but enough to pique his interest. Margaret's legal background had been helpful to Ben during the early days after Alice went missing. It was a great source of strength to him, despite nothing ultimately coming of it.

"Seriously?" he replied, looking back at her. "So you're Esme?" She looked slightly embarrassed.

"Guilty. I...er...know...it's amazing we haven't actually met until now. My mum really talks highly of you both...er..." He could sense the hesitancy...again. After Alice disappeared, many people struggled to bring it up, not wanting to upset or offend him. He guessed it was the same here.

He audibly let out a breath through his nose. "Yeah. She's a good sort, your mum," he replied before changing the subject. "What were you doing in the library?" 'OK. That sounded a bit like a Gestapo agent,' he thought. "Sorry. Don't mean to pry."

Esme smiled reassuringly. "It's OK," she said as she motioned with her head toward the library sign. "Would you believe me if I said I was actually researching libraries?"

"Researching libraries within a library? How avant-garde," smiled Ben. "Is that...interesting?"

Even though there was a hint of sarcasm in his voice, being a wordsmith, it was actually something that interested him greatly, which was partially clear on his face. It wasn't so much libraries that held his fascination, but the knowledge and information within them. More for what they contained than the physical structures. The thought that thousands of people had taken the time...no...made the time to record their thoughts on almost every subject known to mankind. Ideas, new inventions, dreams, hopes of new worlds, the stories told of real lives, the adventures of kings and queens, powerful leaders, and everyday folk.

Sometimes, the thought of everything contained within these walls overwhelmed him. He could easily get absorbed in thinking about the concept of knowledge. How we learn things and translate that knowledge into belief. He could daydream about that for hours if he'd let himself. And sometimes he did.

"Well..." she said as she adjusted her hat, "I find it fascinating. Especially the way everything around us is changing as we speak..."

Ben could see her mind drifting off as though she had much more to say on the topic, but wasn't sure she should.

"I know you're obviously here to work or something," she said, pushing her bag strap further up her shoulder, "but do you want to grab a coffee later on? I can always do with some human conversation after I study." She smiled and raised her eyebrows.

"Why? Non-human conversation too boring for you?" Ben asked rhetorically with a wry smile as he leant casually against the door frame, hand in pocket.

"Yes, there's only so much one can talk to an Aidea without it talking back, that I can take. I'm a realer, not a liner," she quipped.

Ben shifted his position anxiously, hoping Esme didn't notice his shoulders tense. He wasn't surprised at her comment, knowing Margaret's strong negative opinion of the LinerVerse.

Esme continued, "I'd be happy to share some of my research if you're interested?" she asked as she shifted her weight back to her other foot, mirroring Ben's stance and leaning her shoulder against the library door.

"Sure. I'd love to hear more," Ben responded.

"Great," she smiled. "I have to sort some stuff out for the next couple hours, but I'll be free at say around 11.30?"

"Fine. Let's swap IDs and I'll call you, then come find you. Actually—" he interjected into his own thought, "Do you know WriteAngle Cafe on Roman Street in Salim Sector?"

"Yes, I know it," she replied, furrowing her eyebrows. Ben wasn't sure what that reaction meant, but didn't pursue it.

"Let's meet there instead. What's your ID?" They both got out their ComTel's, touching them together. A faint tone indicating transfer complete. Checking the details on his device, Ben said, "Got it. OK…Esme Flint?" as he repeated her name, also noticing that all her information aside from her name and contact number were redacted. 'Hmmm…I wish I thought of that. She now has all my contact details,' he thought to himself.

"Thanks, Ben Harman," she replied, smiling and applying the same emphasis. "I better go," she said as she walked past him, descending the library steps. "See you later."

"Look forward to it," said Ben as he stood for a moment, watching her leave. 'Thank you Lord,' he thought with a beaming smile, then turned around and walked into the library, being more aware of his surroundings this time.

# CHAPTER 26

## CHANGED RECORD

"Hey Bill, could you check on a missing person for me?"

Nathan was at work for the Health Improvement Centre in the next town. As part of his job, he was in regular contact with Section One about missing people, injuries, or deaths.

"Sure thing, Nathan, Sir. What's the name and D.O.B?" Bill asked with a strong Scottish accent. Probably Edinburgh, Nathan had thought, but had since found out Bill was from Inverness. He still wasn't sure he could tell the difference.

"It's Lydia Harman, 7th March 2030," Nathan replied.

"Thank you, Sir. Gimme a minute, and I'll bring up the details."

Nathan wasn't expecting much, but he said he'd help Ben and he would. Even if it meant telling Ben once and for all that his wife really wasn't coming back—even after nine years. He so wanted to give his best friend a sense of closure.

"Just a sec…Just a sec…Lookie here," said Bill, Nathan easily picking up the surprise in his voice. "The record shows this young lady died on 21 September 2154, but it seems to be scratched out and shows her as an MP…that's a Missing Person…on exactly the same date. No time given on either. That's…highly irregular," said Bill as he scratched his chin.

Nathan rubbed his head as he was watching Bill stare at his screen via the ComTel projection.

"Just so I'm clear…what are you saying?" He asked, needing to check he'd heard right. He could hear Bill take a deep breath.

"It says she died 21 September 2154, and that's the last record, but subsequently it seems to have been changed from 'died' to an MP…then it's scratched out. There are tight procedures that we have to go through just to update a record as important as this, and hers is the only record I've seen where it's not been followed. As I said…highly irregular." Nathan was still watching him stare at the screen, presumably double checking in case he'd made a mistake.

Nathan furrowed his brow as he tried to comprehend what he was hearing, especially when he fully expected to hear an open and shut case. Not knowing quite what to say, Bill continued.

"Listen, Nathan, Sir. Leave it with me. I'll make a few calls and find out why the record was changed. It's probably just a newbie updating the records that day. We have interns every year. I'll get back to you. OK?" he confirmed.

"Appreciate that, Bill," said Nathan, still puzzled, then he cut the connection.

'As Bill said, it's probably just a simple mistake,' Nathan thought to himself. Probably.

The grand hallway in Sab City Library was something to behold, built like an entrance to a theatre from over two hundred years ago. The expansive walls spread, with shelf after shelf of books and journals sweeping way up high, too high and wide for easy human reach. But they didn't need to. Drovers handled that. They scuttled around from section to section, grabbing the books the reader eagerly waited for, like little mice on a mission. Their accuracy and speed was stunning. On occasions, Ben would give them a very obscure request, just to see how they would cope. In several years, they had not failed him. 'I won't stop trying,' he'd thought.

A further set of doors opened out into the main hall. His mind went over what had just happened and a huge grin spread all over his face. He'd finally met Margaret's daughter, and she was stunning! And, she wanted to meet him for coffee in a little over two hours! How was he going to get any writing done now?

Pushing open a second set of doors, Ben noticed it seemed very quiet today. Over in a far room with glass walls, he could see the curly white hair of Fabio, the Library's boss. He'd transformed it since taking it over several years ago. As he looked pretty busy, deep in conversation with another member of staff, Ben decided to at least try to focus on his writing. But his mind kept drifting back to Esme. It had been such a short meeting, but her polite, caring manner, her playfulness, 'well...Lydia would definitely approve if I met someone else,' he thought. 'A Godly woman—though that's an assumption—she'd definitely like that. If Esme follows her mother, it would at least be worth getting to know her.'

Ben really thought highly of Margaret despite her not being able to push things forward in investigating Alice's disappearance. She'd mentioned once or twice whether he'd thought about seeing anyone. It had been too many years since he had. There had been several dates in that time, but for each one, he would convince himself that he wouldn't ever have the happiness and joy he'd had with Lydia. Effectively, this meant that until Ben changed his mindset, every potential relationship was always destined to come to nothing before it even started.

Whenever he met a potential female partner, he couldn't help but compare every little detail to Lydia. Their mannerisms, their intonation when they spoke, their scent, how they looked to the way they held their cutlery during a meal.

It was such a normal thing for him to do, that despite many months of being counselled not to look at it that way, 'Everyone is unique,' his counsellor would say. 'You can't go limiting one person by measuring their differences against another. God created each person, in His image, yet unique. That's why you shouldn't compare. It's not fair on you, or the other person.'

Ben knew that whomever he ended up with next would not be a replacement for Lydia. Of course, he knew that. Nobody could replace her. But he'd still found it incredibly difficult to fully move on. He wondered whether part of that was simply due to the elephant in the room—the other issue which he couldn't erase from his mind—that brought him intense confusion: the sense that all these years later, Lydia was still alive. Obviously, he didn't know for sure, but something wasn't quite right. He was convinced of that much.

Ben caught his thoughts. 'God, help me focus right now so I can get some work done.' With that, he took out his Aidea, and very quickly, the words started to flow.

# CHAPTER 27

## THE BOOK OF JOB

Alice lay on the slab trying to get comfortable. The door opened and Charles, the old man, entered carrying a Reeder. "Here's what you requested," he said, devoid of emotion, not betraying his natural curiosity. "Obviously, it has been cleansed of all extraneous data, and external connections have been terminated, but you will find it contains the Bible version you requested."

Alice smiled appreciatively as she reached out to take the device. "Thanks," she replied as she held it carefully, her hand brushing along the side of its transparent frame.

Charles bent to pick up the now empty food tray. Turning to leave, he said, "You'll hear from me again soon." *Thud!* The door shut as Alice stared at the device. She lowered her head, trying to fight off the sadness that enveloped her. All she wanted was to have him back. The real Ben; the father who'd been so strong in bringing her up by himself. Who'd instilled in her, the strength she now possessed. Yes, she had her super-natural gifting–of which was still strange that they'd never talked about openly, but it was her dad who'd shown her the way to trust in God. To have faith. He had a different super-natural strength, one that inspired her to grow to be the young woman she now was.

As her thoughts drifted more towards her dad, a smile permeated her face. She remembered the time as an eight-year-old she'd really appreciated his wisdom. It was on a Learning Group trip up in Scotland; a rare trip her dad wasn't able to make. A project had come up with work that he didn't want to refuse. It took a while, and a lot of encouraging conversations, but eventually he was comfortable in knowing he needn't worry.

His neighbours and friends Fabio and Olivia were going to be looking after her, along with several other close friends and members of their Learning Group. And Alice's best friend Sabine was going as well.

This particular day in early December, the group traversed Arthur's Seat, and as they climbed, Alice remembered how the world seemed to stop as the clouds floated by, within the sharp blue sky. All was still and peaceful at this early hour in the morning. Oh, and it was freezing. Alice, of course, didn't feel the cold like the others did. She still had a few layers on and, much to her frustration, she had to put up with Olivia's 'encouragement' to stay warm by layering up.

"It's gonna get colder the further up we go, you know," she'd said, several times already. Too many for Alice's liking. "I'm just not cold!" she let out in annoyance.

"OK, young lady. There's no need to snap!" Olivia retorted. Alice held her head in shame, feeling almost too embarrassed to apologise, as she plodded along, her feet seeming to increase in weight after the rebuke. She always carried an intangible feeling that she was different, a kind of otherness lingering around and about her like a foul scent she couldn't place.

Sabine sped up from her vantage point several people back to catch up with her best friend.

"Hey," she said. "Granny annoying you?"

"Yes. I'm just not cold. I can't help it," complained Alice.

"Yeah, she can go on," consoled Sabine, linking arms with Alice, which helped to calm her down and triggered her supernaturally adult mind.

Alice looked at her friend as they slowed down. "I know," she said to Sabine, "but she means well. She's only doing it cos she cares."

Sabine looked back at her best friend like she was viewing a stranger.

"You're weird," she replied as she scrunched up her face.

"I know," whispered Alice, too quiet for Sabine to hear, turning her head to mask the disappointment etched on her face. "I know."

Later on that day, when they arrived back at the farmhouse where they were staying, Ben called as planned and spoke to Alice. Sitting on a bench, her legs swinging, she smiled a sheepish smile as she saw her dad appear in front of her. The bench was in what looked like a small, yet immaculate, study.

She told her dad about her day. It was good talking to him on ComTel. It was like they could have deeper conversations than they could face to face. She explained what happened with Olivia and what Sabine had said to her, and how it made her feel.

"Hey, Monkey," he said; she could feel the warmth in his voice, which so often made her feel like she was the only person in the world. "You are special. So, so special. Not weird. God has made you unique. There isn't anyone else quite like you. You know that, right?" he counselled.

"I think I'm starting to," she replied, staring at the concentric circular pattern etched into the wooden floor, trying not to get dizzy.

"What do you think you should say to Olivia?" He always did that, too. Didn't tell her what to do, but asked her what she thought. Even at eight years old—though of course she was mentally much older—she felt her opinion mattered.

"I felt so bad, Dad. I was too embarrassed to apologise for snapping. But I will. After we finish, I'll go straight to her and apologise," she answered.

"That's good, Monkey. I think that's a brave and good decision," said Ben, and they continued to fill each other in on their respective days. It didn't matter how often he spoke with his daughter, he couldn't get over the way she processed her thoughts and decisions, better than many adults did. It's a wonder she doesn't get called weird more often, he thought after their call ended.

Alice now had a smile on her face, like she was invincible. That was the power of her dad. She must ComTel him more often.

Alice realised her hands had been gripping the Reeder tightly. Too tightly. She loosened her grip and used her right hand to soothe the red marks on her left.

Her dad, now, from what she'd heard from Margaret, well...he was a shadow of himself, putting on a brave face when working, but otherwise apparently a poor copy of his former self.

'No. That can't be right,' she thought. 'Margaret must have got this wrong. There was no way Dad would just go to pieces like that. Was there?' she pondered.

But six months. Six months without her. Perhaps this was the effect it had on him. If everything Margaret said was true—and Alice had no reason to believe otherwise—that made her all the more determined to get him back. It wasn't lost on her the irony that she was the one kidnapped, yet he was the one truly lost. She prayed for wisdom, remembering that King Solomon was commended by God for asking for such. Perhaps she could have a dose too.

Crossing her legs on the makeshift bed, she tapped the Reeder. The screen came to life. She knew what to do. 'What passage would Dad go to?' she thought as a slight smile touched her face. It would only ever be Job 38.

She directed her eyes on the contents page as the Reeder updated and found the passage. Selecting the first few verses, she focused her mind on them.

> *Then the LORD answered Job out of the whirl-*
> *    wind and said:*
> *"Who is this that darkens counsel by words*
> *    without knowledge?*
> *Dress for action like a man;*
> *I will question you, and you make it known*
> *    to me.*
> *"Where were you when I laid the foundation of*
> *    the earth?*
> *Tell me, if you have understanding.*

> *Who determined its measurements—surely you*
>     *know!*
> *Or who stretched the line upon it?*
> *On what were its bases sunk,*
> *or who laid its cornerstone,*
> *when the morning stars sang together*
> *and all the sons of God shouted for joy?*

Slowly the words on the screen started to glow, a yellow-gold colour, then shimmer in a way that made them drift out of the Reeder and appear to hover in the air. Alice's face also glowed, a similar shade, a regal tint. She looked like an angel. Focusing all her attention on her dad, she pictured him in Sab City library—one of his favourite places—and where she sensed he might be.

Alice recalled the first time four years ago when he took her there. Even at the age of eight, she was in awe of the magnificence of these ancient books containing the Holy words of God. It was overwhelming for her, seeing so many of them on a shelf in very ornate and intricate designs. Beautiful colours, "They are like Kings & Queens books," she'd uttered worshipfully.

"Yes, Monkey...but remember, it's not about the books and how beautiful they are; it's the words they contain. Just like the one you have on your Reeder," explained her dad.

"But they look so beautiful!" she retorted as she glided her hands along the shelves, touching the spines of a few of the Bibles.

"They sure do. Shall I read one for you?" he asked.

"Yes, please Daddy!" said Alice, jumping up and down rather excitedly, then remembering she was in the library. As much as she loved reading herself, and boy, she did, she always loved hearing her dad read to her, his voice providing a sense of calm. Ben had carefully taken down a Bible with a royal blue spine and a gold flower pattern on the cover. They had sat down on the comfy chairs as he opened it at his favourite passage. He'd read chapter 38 from the Book of Job.

Alice's face showed signs of strain, with intensified breathing and visible sweat on her forehead and palms. The shimmering gold letters had all but disappeared, floating off into nothingness. The Reeder dropped from her hands as she placed her right hand on her heart, feeling the beat.

"Breathe in. Breathe out. Breathe in. Breathe out. In. Out. In. Out."

Alice repeated this mantra out loud for a few moments, slowing down her heart rate. When she felt closer to normal, she stroked a finger down the face of the Reeder, silently praying, 'please God, let this work.'

# CHAPTER 28
## NEEDED

Esme Flint had walked away from Ben at a brisk pace, after not-accidentally bumping into him at the Library. Very quickly, she entered the cemetery, stopping as she drew near to Lydia Harman's plot. Glancing around as if to check no one was looking, she stooped down facing the tombstone, motionless in quiet contemplation.

"Would've been so great to meet you," she said to herself. She'd always been a little in awe of Lydia. If everything she'd heard was true—and there was no reason to believe it wasn't—they'd both have gotten on like a house on fire.

Like Lydia, Esme was a perpetual learner. Devouring several books a month, she was like a sponge, genuinely taking in, processing, and storing the information. She had to know stuff. She couldn't stand not knowing things. This caused many arguments with her parents and brothers growing up. Unanswered questions and Esme did not make pleasant bedfellows. But sometimes people just didn't have answers, though Esme never accepted that.

'Even though you were only a few days older than me, I feel I could have learnt so much from you,' she thought. 'Especially anything to do with Sendo Xperience,'—where Lydia worked until her untimely death. Now Sendo was a topic of which Esme hungered to know more. 'I'm sure not all of it would be good, but just to get the truth...'

The inscription on the tombstone she'd read many times before, faded in and out of view. It was written in an ornate calligraphic typeface designed to look like chiseled marble and read,

"Lydia Harman 2130-2154. Devoted wife, mother, and friend. Strength and honour are her clothing. Her worth is far above rubies."

Leaning forwards, Esme gazed at the flowers strewn intentionally across the plot. She picked up a white lilly, bringing it to her nose, her eyes closing as she breathed in the scent, before placing it back on the ground.

Standing slowly, she straightened her sweater dress as she headed out the gate. A timepiece hung from her necklace. She grabbed it and read, "9.37." She tapped a button on the Auto Request Bar at the side of the road, and a sleek-looking bullet grey AutoJet made its way towards her with a quiet hum. The front was heavily pointed with just enough space for one person, though passengers usually sat in the three or more seats available in the back.

Esme stood in front of it and raised an ungloved hand, light emitting from its windscreen scanning her palm. The vehicle bleeped, then unlocked.

"Hello Esme," said a quaint English gentleman's voice as she jumped in the back seat. She didn't respond. The vehicle moved off whilst Esme made herself comfortable by reclining her seat and stretching out her legs.

'Ah, that feels good!' Her mind drifted to how she was about to meet Alice...Lydia's daughter! She smiled at that thought. At just twelve years old, the communications she'd received from Alice already suggested an age *much* older than twelve.

'What's she gonna be like?' She pondered, intrigued to meet her on many levels—not least as she'd been told Alice wouldn't be in her right body—whatever that meant. Esme knew she was picked by Alice specifically to help Ben. Not romantically, though, that was always a possibility, but to lead him gently to accept Alice with her rapidly developing powers.

Esme had a way of disarming people and putting them at ease. Something Ben could do with more often than not these days. She knew her role and was happy to play it if it meant getting involved with this all too intriguing family.

Esme rubbed her forehead as if to dissuade a headache from arriving. She thought about Lydia, Ben, and Alice and aside from the minor issues of Lydia being dead and Alice having been kidnapped, they were a family she'd always looked up to —always admired, having heard a lot about them through her mother.

Never having been lucky in love, all three of her brothers, one of whom was younger, had their own beautiful families. She hadn't had as much as a date in years, let alone a proposal of marriage. Being asked to team up with Alice and Ben now was good for her, as well as helping them. And Alice...even though she'd only had a few conversations with her so far, she cared for her. She was quite taken aback by how Alice had trusted her so soon after their meeting.

Esme smiled as she recalled a time when Alice, via ComTel, had explained to her how she'd hidden her powers from her dad.

"I knew he knew something...at least about how I could make an object hot or cold. He didn't think I noticed the subtle experiments he'd carried out on me even after I was taken the first time," Alice said.

"But how did you hide it from him if he knew something was going on?" Esme asked.

"Well...as I got older, I saw how disappointed he looked at certain times when I did something strange...And there was this one time when we were on a trip to the New Forest with our Learning Group. It was winter coming into Spring I think. It was still cold, at least from what I remember. I was six at the time and was picking up leaves with Sundeep. I remember Sundeep giving me some of his leaves, placing them in my hands. Then...er...then...they just burst into flames," said Alice hesitantly.

"Wowza!" exclaimed Esme. "What happened...were you burnt?"

The young girl looked down at the floor.

"My dad, who saw the whole thing, grabbed his lighter and rushed towards me and said I shouldn't be using the lighter, pretending to take it off me. Sundeep never mentioned it again. I don't know if he believed my dad, but even at that age, the look I saw on my dad's face, made me feel I needed to hide this. Maybe I was wrong. I don't know. But it's just what I felt at the time." Alice said as she looked up at the

ComTel projection of Esme, her face one of compassion. "Oh, and no. I wasn't burnt. I'm not even sure that's possible for me."

Esme let out a sigh, as several other questions fought for attention before her curiosity settled on the nature of Ben's reaction. "The look on his face...what do you mean? What did he look like?"

Alice shuddered. "I can just remember thinking, I never wanted to put him in that situation again. He looked utterly disappointed, and I...well...I was just adding to his general disappointment in life. I wanted to make him happy, not sad. So...uh...so I learnt to control it, and my dad never mentioned it again, either."

Even if Esme hadn't been able to see Alice over the ComTel projection, she would have been able to hear the sadness in her voice.

"I'm sorry, Alice, that you had to deal with that...and to not be able to be yourself...to be who God created you to be. I'm so sorry," consoled Esme.

There was a period of silence as she tried to think of something encouraging to say. She silently prayed, then shared, "but you know God is ultimately in control, right? He can work on your dad. I'm sure he never sees you as anything other than his only daughter that he's so proud of," she said, the sadness seemingly permanently etched on the young girl's face, tears clearly visible in the corners of her eyes.

"Yes. I'm sure," she replied, almost in a whisper. Then, as if a switch was flipped, her demeanour changed. She looked straight at Esme with much greater confidence, and added, "...but that's also why I need your help," as she explained the basis of a plan for her escape.

Back in the AutoJet, Esme thought, 'It's nice to be needed,' as the vehicle drove past yet another warehouse, of which there were too many, she'd often mused. Such a sign of materialism.

*Thring. Thring.*

Her ComTel brought her out of her thoughts, the sound reverberating all around the AutoJet. She waved her hand.

"Hello, darling. How are you? All OK?" asked an older sounding lady with a well-to-do, but compassionate English accent, containing a subtle hint of many years spent in New York.

"Hey. I'm good, thanks. Just en route to meet Alice," she replied.

"Good. Well done." There was an obvious sense of pride in the woman's tone.

"You know already that she is in the Complex, so I'm sure you're wondering how she can be in two places at once. Right?" In truth, it had crossed Esme's mind, and although she had attempted to find out, she was also just too eager to meet Lydia's daughter...in whatever form she came.

"You know me. I'm easy. I take things as they come," she mused.

"And that's why I love you Esme dear, well...one of the many reasons. I told Alice you'd be perfect," she encouraged.

Esme had a strained relationship with her mother. She'd always felt she couldn't live up to her expectations. All she wanted was to know that her mother was proud of her. The thing was, her mother was proud of her. Very proud. And she did let Esme know. It's just that Esme had a positivity filter. Anytime someone paid her a compliment, she would filter it out and hear something negative. She didn't know why she did that.

"But enough of that..." her mother said, "I need to tell you that when you see Alice, whilst she might look real, she is actually bilocating which to you will look like an advanced holographic projection. She can interact with objects, such as sitting down on a chair, but she won't be able to touch other human beings. I wouldn't bother trying to hug her or even shake her hand," her mother explained.

"OK. Sounds weird, but thanks for telling me. It'll be fine, I'm sure." Since running the cafe, Esme was used to dealing with the unexpected. You never knew what requests or questions customers would have. That's part of what she loved: the unknown. It never really phased her.

"Great. Glad to hear it. Alice will tell you everything else you'll need to know, but call me if you need anything. Bye for now, darling." With that, the call dropped.

Esme glanced out the window, looking into space. Her mind drifting back to the conversation with Alice and the fact she'd trusted her with her emotions that day. It had meant a lot to her, and she resolved to do everything she could to reunite father and daughter.

# CHAPTER 29
## THE PORTAL

WHAT'S THE POINT OF A LIBRARY IF EVERYONE HAS access to everything? That wasn't what Ben believed, but he remembered reading many who thought that way, even to the point of predicting the demise of the library in the late 20th century. 'Some people just have narrow minds...' he thought, '...and see only a closed door instead of an opportunity.' He could understand their thinking, as most homes had tech hard wired into them...and pretty much everyone had a ComTel, so they could access unlimited information without ever having to enter an institution as old and antiquated as a library. But that's where Ben differed.

Now, in 2163, the need was less about access to information, and more about cultivating the mind. Ben knew many people who'd met in libraries to discuss the latest thoughts and ideas, meeting face-to-face to encourage each other to expand their minds...and to avoid the loneliness trap. To him it was so obvious a direction to go—that of the library becoming a vibrant, living, breathing creative thinking hub, connecting people together. And through personal experience, it had been a great way for him to develop his writing. Mixing amongst people who had such different ideas to his own directly challenged his thinking.

He found libraries an empowering place to be. Even whilst Alice was still a toddler, Ben loved getting her into the habit of being around books, immersing her into this creative, thought enhancing atmosphere. He had felt it was important—knowing that she had the truth—to expose her to a range of thoughts and ideas, to encourage her to evaluate everything continually, mixing with people of different ages, not just cooped up with kids like her—not that there was anyone truly like his beautifully unique monkey, of course. He wanted her to have fun whilst learning.

Ben had lost a little of that joy recently, though. With Alice missing, his focus was all diverted and right now, sitting in the very soporific library, his mind wandered all over the place.

'I'm sure there was a reason I've been reintroduced to grandpa's ideas. This was no mistake. Everything happens for a reason,' he thought to himself.

Sitting back in his chair, he turned his head to view all the books around him. A few young people were sitting at far desks, but otherwise it was pretty quiet today. That was good. Ben wasn't in the mood to get into any deep conversations right now. He had too much on his mind. His eyes shifted back to the diaries he'd again brought with him.

'I just can't get the hypocrisy of it,' he thought, staring a hole through the diaries. 'It's hard to believe that he had a whole other life, especially away from Grandma. I know it's virtual…I get that…but the brain is the same, and it doesn't differentiate between dreams and reality.'

Ben stroked his head, then with his elbow on the desk, rested his hand on his forehead, massaging away the oncoming headache.

'So...if that's the case, then it does matter. Having another life in the LinerVerse, having another wife—IS committing adultery—virtual or not. I just can't get over Grandpa doing that. He obviously didn't have as high a view of his family as I thought.'

Ben brought his other hand up, holding his head in both hands. He closed his eyes. 'It would be nice not to have to worry about failing my family,' he thought, wondering whether perhaps grandpa got that last bit right at least. He prayed.

'God, please help me know what's right. I know it's not all about signs and symbols, but...could you show me something, just to help me have confidence in you? Help me overcome my unbelief.'

A sign Ben wanted and sure enough, a sign he would get—and very soon.

He looked up and around the nearby tables. There was still no one there. As he glanced at the time, his face attempted a smile. It was only half an hour before he would head towards the cafe to meet Esme Flint properly.

Killing time now, no longer in the mood for writing, Ben dropped his Aidea deep into his bag and wandered toward the back of the library. The sight of rows and rows of books, 'the raw potential.' He always tried to imagine what it would be like to read, cover to cover, every single one of the hundreds of thousands of tomes in this magnificent museum of learning. Every one. What knowledge one would have.

Reaching the far back wall, he knew this contained some special books to him. Gazing at the spines was a joy. Some are slim, some thick. Some wide, some tall. But each ornately indicating the precious nature of the contents—the most important books ever penned. He didn't really care that many disagreed. History proved that statement. At many points throughout the centuries, Bibles were thought so powerful they were piled up and burned in a futile attempt to eradicate them. It was pretty obvious to see that no other book on planet Earth had had as big an impact as the Holy Bible, despite the desperation from some to rewrite history, erasing every evidence from existence.

Ben slid his hand across them, letting the real and faux leather rub against his fingers, feeling the ridges of outset type gracing the spines of different shapes, styles, and sizes. Mostly hardback in this section, though the oldest copies were kept in a more secure room to protect their fragile nature.

There was this one Bible with a royal blue cover and gold edging that always caught his eye. It had a beautifully ornate gold flowery pattern on it. Ben smiled as he touched its spine.

"Hmm…this is the one I read to Alice all those years ago," he reminisced. Sliding it out slowly from being sandwiched between a darker red—almost burgundy—version, and a black Bible, he opened it with reverence, turning the pages in a way that suggested it was far more fragile than it actually was.

Slowly, he found his way to the book of Job and a passage that meant a lot to him. His fingers followed the words as he arrived at chapter 38. He took a breath, then let the words flow from his mouth.

> *"Who is this who darkens counsel*

*By words without knowledge?*
*Now prepare yourself like a man;*
*I will question you, and you shall answer Me.*
*Where were you when I laid the foundations of*
*    the earth?*
*Tell Me, if you have understanding."*

As Ben was reading this most beautiful poetry, he heard a deep rumbling sound. "Where's that coming from?" he asked. But now, Ben didn't just hear it, he felt it; his whole body vibrated. He shuddered. 'Someone must have stepped over my grave,' a phrase his mother always said whenever she felt a cold chill. It never made sense to him, but it stuck with him.

As he looked ahead, he saw a radiant white light suddenly pouring out from the narrowing gap between the towering rows of books. "What the heck's going on?" he asked to no one in particular.

At the back of the hall, Ben was well out of the way of the few other patrons in the library that day. Though he still glanced around, just in case. Stepping closer to the shelves, he put back the Bible he'd read from, placing both his hands either side of the two columns.

'This is stupid,' he thought. 'It must be way too heavy.'

Despite that, the desire to pull his fingers apart from each other in opposite directions was too great.

'Wow! That was easier than I Imagined,' he thought as the expected heavy weight of books didn't materialise. Instead, the bookshelves glided apart to a width just wide enough for a relatively slim person to fit through. There was no question as to what he would do next, curiosity getting the better of him.

Ben manoeuvred his body in between the columns and in no time at all he'd pushed himself all the way through. Immediately, he heard a *schwarrm* sound as the shelves glided back together, and soon enough, Ben found himself standing in a corridor full of grey doors. The rumbling had stopped.

# CHAPTER 30

## BILOCATION

There were no other vehicles on the roads. Esme's AutoJet was driving in the opposite direction to the main traffic, from Jahm sector to the outskirts of Sab City. The vehicle pulled into the coffee shop and came to a halt, its whirring sound descending into silence. Heading around the back of the building, Esme pressed her palm on the entry pad and entered the cafe. This was her abode. She loved working here, having taken over from her parents a few years back and she was currently toward the backend of a refurbishment phase, though it was still officially closed until next week.

Switching on the power, Esme opened the front door, but left the CLOSED sign in place. Taking off her driving shades, she removed her hat and sat down. 10.14 a.m., her timepiece read. She waited. I hope she'll be here, she thought, more to pass the time, as she had no reason to believe Alice wouldn't.

Above the counter there were jars and packets containing an assortment of coffee and tea, along with a variety of snack based food. Everything was pristine. Just the way Esme liked it. Boldly printed, the labels included short descriptions of each flavour. The windows, having recently been cleaned, were gleaming. The new counter, made with genuine oak, had one tray set in the centre with an empty cup placed upside down in a saucer. On the walls were 1920s styled posters with amusing sayings. A yellow one with a lady holding a cup of steaming hot coffee read, 'Unattended children will be given an espresso and a free kitten.' Esme chuckled to herself. She chose that one.

At 10.15 a.m. the door opened as a young girl, who can't have been more than twelve years old, entered the shop. The blue denim jeans she wore were slightly ripped in a look that had come into fashion well over a century ago. White trainers and a red cap sleeved hooded top finished her sartorial choices.

"You're bang on time!" Esme said, feigning surprise and standing up. The young girl walked over to her. While pulling out a chair, she revealed a shimmering effect where she gripped it. The chair moved slowly. Alice sat down.

Sitting opposite, Esme gazed at her for the first time, not completely comprehending what she was seeing. She certainly looked real, even if she wasn't there. Esme's head hurt just thinking about that.

"It's great to meet you in person, Alice. Well...you know what I mean..." Alice smiled.

"So your mum told you I'm not really here?" Alice asked.

"Sort of. What's that about?" Esme replied.

"Well, you know I'm holed up in the Complex..." Esme nodded. "...but what they didn't realise is that my powers are continuing to increase. And I mean significantly. As long as I have a lot of energy, I can project myself to another location, even transferring to where another person is." Esme's eyes widened. Her mum had told her briefly about Alice's powers, such as bilocation, but seeing it, well…that was something else.

"How is that even possible?" she asked, still checking she'd heard correctly. "You mean you can effectively teleport?" Alice shook her head.

"It's not really teleportation. I'm not transferred from where I am to the new place." The young girl smiled as she clasped her hands together, looking like she was developing a cunning plan. "It's kinda even better than that…You see, I'm still in the original place as well!"

"Sheeze…that's just crazy!" Esme exclaimed, as she scanned Alice, trying to take in anything abnormal. Seeing her here, knowing she wasn't really here, was a bit of a mind trip.

"So, you're doing that right now?" she quizzed.

"Yes. You can sometimes see a slight shimmer around me, especially when I interact with certain objects, but at the same time, I'm sitting on a bed in a tiny room in the Complex, hundreds of thousands of miles away."

Esme shook her head, more questions floating round, all fighting for top priority.

She thought about all the possibilities of bilocating to somewhere you couldn't see, or just the wrong place…like a brick wall. Eww… she thought, shaking her head at the likelihood of that happening.

"So how does it feel?" Alice looked at her bilocated fingers, turning her hands around to stare at them as she moved each finger one at a time. It was still bizarre for her, too.

"It's kinda hard to describe. It's very energy intensive, especially to start with." She held her hand just above the table, almost as if to check how steady she was. "I just feel like I've run a marathon, exhausted and breathing deeply, but then it stabilises, though obviously depending on what I'm doing—in both locations," she explained as she stared in to space.

Esme sat back in her chair, her eyes struggling to come to terms with what she was seeing, let alone all what Alice was sharing.

"This is just too weird. But you know what? If I had this ability to be in two places at once, I could run the cafe, and read and do research simultaneously. Now that would be handy!" Esme quipped.

Alice smiled, then seemed to drift in thought, looking back down at her hands. She liked Esme. She could understand how bizarre this must be for her. But what she really was focused on right at this moment was her dad. Raising her head, she asked,

"Have you seen him...my dad?"

"Yes," Esme replied cautiously.

"How is he?" The young girl wrapped a few strands of her long flowing hair around her fingers, twirling it first one way, then the other.

"He's OK, but..."

"But what?" Alice quickly retorted.

Esme hesitated as she asked, "Does he know anything of your powers? I mean...I know you said he hadn't mentioned it again, but that must have been tough and nearly impossible to hide it from him completely," she asked. Alice looked up, noticing some ornate looking brown and green packages on a high shelf.

"I honestly don't know. We just never talked about it. I'm sure sometimes he must have suspected something...but...he didn't say anything...so neither did I," Alice clarified.

Esme thought about the fact she would be the one to tell Ben his daughter had supernatural powers.

"What's your instinct about how he's gonna react?" she asked.

Alice studied her bilocated hands. She could see the shimmer, parts looking like she had an opacity filter hovering just below one hundred percent.

"I wish I had the courage to tell him myself. The way he's looked at me when he'd seen something strange, I think I'd die if I saw that again." The skin on her face seemed to drop slightly. "I miss him too much." She showed some emotion— Esme could easily tell she was sad—but not as much detail was displayed as if she were there in person.

"Hey. Look, it will be fine. I'm sure of it," Esme said, consoling her companion. "He seems such a nice guy, and I've only met him briefly." Alice nodded. Both girls stared downwards at their hands on the table. Esme broke the silence.

"Coffee?" Esme offered.

"I would if I could....but I can't drink in this body." Alice responded.

"Well, you won't mind if I have one?"

"No. You go for it," said Alice.

"Good. I need some caffeine. Bear with me," Esme said as she rose from her chair, heading towards the counter and switching on the power to a large DeLonghi Prima coffee machine. It buzzed into life. She grabbed a packet and placed it in the machine, then held a cup under the pipe and pressed the large grey button. Once full, placing it on a tray, she grabbed some milk and sugar and brought it all over to the table, as Alice observed her.

"You're a natural,"

"Thanks. I guess...You know this is my place, right?" Esme exclaimed with a certain sense of pride. Alice seemed to roll her eyes.

"You may have mentioned it once or twice," she smirked.

"Oh, really? Like that," an embarrassed Esme replied as she looked down at the patterns on the wooden floor. Alice smiled. "Sorry! I just feel very blessed to run this place. It's been very good for me."

"That's good. I'm pleased for you. Your mum told me a bit about it, that you'd taken it over. I'm glad it's going well."

A frown appeared on Alice's face.

"Sorry to change back the subject, but did my dad look well?" Alice asked with a genuine concern. Esme smiled.

"Mmm. Yes. He looked very good," she said, which came out slightly seductively as she stared into her cup. Her cheeks beginning to glow.

"Don't you go getting any ideas," warned Alice.

"Why not? If he reacts well to the truth, then I can't see any problem with wanting..."

"Yes, but it's not fair to him," Alice retorted, not allowing Esme to finish her sentence. "You know so much about him, yet he knows nothing of you. And..." She paused, deciding if she really wanted to say what she was thinking. She opted instead for a toned down, "...it just doesn't feel right."

Although just a baby when her mother died, as Alice grew up she could see just how much Ben had been, and in reality still was, in love with Lydia. It was strange not having been able to get to know the person who her dad held such high affection for, and also who brought her into this world. She'd become very protective of her dad, asking lots of questions when he showed an interest in other women—which was not a lot, to be honest. She actually thought Esme could make a good partner for Ben, but something inside her didn't want to let that thought develop.

There was a hum from the coffee machine as it cleaned itself, breaking the deafening silence that descended on the cafe. Esme took another sip from her cup, holding the warmth in both hands, staring at the spiral of froth she had so elegantly designed into a beautiful flower. She smiled at her artistry.

Alice sat up straight, her hands clasped together as she explained the plan.

"I get a sense there's something up with my dad that I don't know. I know he blames himself for my abduction and...he seems to get distracted, pulled away from reality sporadically. I don't know why, but I want to be careful in case he does something irrational." Esme furrowed her brow.

"What do you think he might do?" she enquired. Alice looked at the table. A mix of thoughts flying through her already busy mind. "I really don't know," she sighed. "But as we've never truly discussed my...er...abilities, I just don't know how he might react."

Esme looked puzzled.

"Look, you know your dad better than me...obviously...and I've only just met him, but don't you think you're being over-protective? I mean, he's a grown man. Yes, I get he's had a hard time…it can't have been easy with his wife—your mum dying, but that was almost a decade ago. Most dads would blame themselves if their daughter was kidnapped, seeing it as a failure of their God-given role to protect their family. I get it. I do. But it's up to him to deal with it, surely? Not for you to…I mean, aren't you trying too much to control him? I don't mean to be funny, and I hope you don't think I'm trying to be difficult, but I have to be honest with you if we're gonna get you back. Right?"

Alice initially felt like she was kicked in the stomach. All she wanted to do was to protect her father; to help him through this tragedy. That wasn't wrong, was it? What did this woman who'd never even properly met Ben, know?

Alice felt the air vanish from her lungs, her real body back on the Complex, straining hard to regulate her breathing, cortisol streaming through her brain; a sheen of sweat was visible on her real body.

Back in the cafe, Alice fidgeted with her hands. But in a few moments she was back to normal, having learnt how to control her emotions. It wasn't ever easy, but with two bodies to control, she'd practiced and practiced and she was getting so much better at it.

Alice looked up at Esme, her anger dissipated. This was exactly why she'd chosen her. She knew she would give her the truth and not hold back. Esme still clutched her cooling cup. She looked around the cafe giving the young girl time.

"You're right," replied Alice sheepishly, her eyes still resting on Esme before looking away. "Perhaps I am too protective of him. But just trust me on this," she pleaded. Esme nodded her head. Alice continued firmly, but more softly than she'd originally planned.

"When you meet up with him, gently explain what's happening—regarding my whereabouts. Wait for his response. Answer as many of his questions as you can, then wait for my mark. OK?" she relayed.

"Sure. What's your mark?" Alice gazed around the room, looking for inspiration, not having thought this bit through yet.

"I'll come up with something. I just don't know what yet. I'll be following close behind you. So as not to reveal myself to him too soon, I might bring one of the guys and have him give you a sign. Either way, you won't be able to miss it."

Alice's voice was slowly growing with a greater air of authority.

"You should leave here at 11.00, which gives us around 30mins. Is there anything else you wanted to ask me while you have the chance?"

Esme gave a half-hearted smile whilst biting her tongue, her sturdy glass cup taking a lot of the strain. She wanted to bring up how Alice still seemed to treat her father like a fragile teenager, but not wanting another altercation, she let it lie. 'Alice must know lots more than I do,' she surmised hopefully. Anyway, choose your battles, she tried to remind herself, but she couldn't let it all drop. The frustration had been building. The tap opened.

"It's annoying that you're less than half my age, yet you talk like you're my mother," Esme blurted out.

"I can't help the way I am," Alice quickly retorted, looking down at the table, empathising completely with Esme, knowing that if things were the other way around, she too would find it very difficult to take instructions from a twelve-year-old.

Esme's cheeks turned a darker shade of pink.

"No, I guess not. I'm sorry. It's just…"

"Frustrating. I know…you said," Alice responded.

"Well, actually I said annoying," she corrected, smiling, helping to break the growing tension. Alice rolled her eyes, the smile catching.

"Listen, I don't take any offence. If the positions were switched, I would likely be more irate than you. I didn't ask for these powers, but God blessed me with them, so I want to use them for good and not let them get in the wrong hands. I really don't want to think about what some people would use these powers for. And…for that, I need my dad to know about them and not freak out, which again is where you come in. Even if you think I'm being overprotective, please just trust me, as I fear for where his mind is at the moment. We can't afford to risk any slip-ups."

Esme was at least partially consoled for now, but overtime, as she'd get to know both Ben and Alice, she'd make a point to dig deeper.

# CHAPTER 31

There was a buzz of energy in the room as FalongQ and the other Shumen were deep in planning mode. The TransPortal they were in was floating next to MendipT's ship, the Complex still just visible in the distance.

A visual layout of the Complex hovered just above the control panel. A white line indicating their intended path to wreak havoc amongst their fellow Shumen, with their food supplies and the lighting. MendipT, in the other TransPortal, observed the others through the HoloSense, the projection hovering just above the control panel as he watched them work away.

He would not go back on his decision to share the potentially life-changing news with FalongQ. He could trust him, then they could brainstorm a plan together before telling the others. By swiping his hand over the display, he effortlessly opened and closed his hand. MendipT spoke quietly.

"I have another mission for you. Can you jump into a call booth so we can discuss?" It wasn't really a question, and FalongQ excused himself from the others, entered the nearest call booth, opening comms to MendipT and immediately seeing his avatar appear just above the ComTel.

When one needed information, FalongQ was the go-to. In fact, he was an expert 'information gatherer'—as he liked to term it. The best of the Shumen. Others might use the word hacker. Either way, with his knowledge of the Sendo systems from living on the Complex, he was proud of the fact there wasn't much information he couldn't get hold of. MendipT knew this and was extremely glad that he'd chosen to join his breakaway group that leaving the Complex many years ago.

MendipT was still wavering on just how much about Lydia and Alice he would tell.

"So here's the thing," he said, looking at FalongQ's projection. "What I'm going to share with you has to stay between us for now. OK?" He knew it would be the default for his colleague, but he needed to ask.

"Agreed."

He'd always been a man of few words. As MendipT recounted the entire episode with Lydia Harman that he'd held on to for years, he felt more and more convinced it was right to share. He explained all about how the young scientist's daughter, Alice, could have advanced powers unlike any other human. When he'd finished explaining, he paused, watching FalongQ's reaction but knowing him well, not expecting any incredulity. For an outside observer, you would not guess that FalongQ had just been told there was a human with supernatural powers.

MendipT continued.

"I want you to do some digging. Find out exactly what her powers are and where she is. Do you understand?"

"Yes," he said. "I'll get on to it right away." Before MendipT could say anything else—not that there was anything else to say—FalongQ cut the call, his mind in overdrive, loving nothing more than to hunt data. The specific information didn't really matter. It could be historical air pressure levels in the Haven, or the supernatural abilities of a twelve-year-old. It was all data to FalongQ.

Staying in the call booth, he opened up a terminal. He could see an icon flashing indicating that MendipT had already sent him the snapshots of Lydia's terminal screens he'd taken all those years ago. That was the first place to start. FalongQ grouped all the images together, opened them and ran some of his base analysis algorithms on them. As well as showing him metadata of date, time, location, etc., he could also get a better picture of the lab setup and clarification of any text or numbers displayed in each image, along with any correlating images, including on the LinerVerse. It wouldn't take him too much longer to have just what he was after: the location of Alice Harman.

MendipT noticed the other TransPortal was unnervingly quiet as he'd headed back to the others after giving instructions to FalongQ. His colleagues had already devised their plans to cause confusion amongst the Shumen on the Complex, so now they were getting on with other things whilst awaiting the go-ahead.

On entering what on a TransPortal could be called the bridge —although it was much smaller than a traditional ship bridge —MendipT gazed around at each of the various members staring at their display screens, manipulating control sticks or entering data into their nearest control panel. His cheeks betrayed a sense of pride. Each of these fellow Shumen had chosen to come with him, to not stay on the Complex with SentiN—and the safety that provided—but to take a risk... for him.

Taking control of his emotions, he walked across to his seat, each member acknowledging his presence with a look and a nod. Sitting down, he wanted to see where they were up to, so asked for a run-through of the plan. One colleague obliged, pointing at the display as he explained how they were getting in and what they would need to do once inside. "That sounds workable." It seems a solid plan, he thought before asking, "But how will I get in unnoticed?"

It was always going to be MendipT that would take the biggest risk. This was his battle, after all. no one raised any objections.

"That's easy," replied the same Shuman, turning to face MendipT. "There is a supply TransPortal due to arrive in the next twenty-four hours. That will provide cover for us as we line up beside them. Then you will have to transfer across from our TransPortal to theirs. You will have four minutes before they will be authorised to jump on board the Complex. So you will need to be suited up already. They won't be on high alert and..." MendipT cut him off,

"...and with SentiN in charge, even if they saw an extra signal, they probably wouldn't register anything out of the ordinary," he completed for his colleague, who nodded in agreement.

MendipT stared at the hologram plan as it floated in the air. Lifting his gaze towards the feed from the other TransPortal, he then scanned his colleagues in his own vehicle. He wanted to look at each face to identify if there was any reservation. He saw none. MendipT stood up tall and proclaimed,

"Right. Let's do this."

# CHAPTER 32

## STRANGE ROOM

The doors along the corridor all looked the same. Since being somehow transported from the Library in Sab City to...well...he didn't quite know where...Ben had opened several of the aforementioned doors looking for some sense of meaning. This was not easy, as each room thus far was pitch black.

His eyes were trying to adjust to the lack of light, but he could see nothing, and he didn't want to risk entering a room blind. 'Who knows what could happen?' he thought. 'There could be a large drop. I could break my leg...or anything.' Not knowing where he was rapidly raised his anxiety levels.

Standing still for a moment, he took a few deep breaths.

"What do I know?" He asked himself, treating his current situation as an experiment. "I got here from the library. I know that much. I don't know how long ago," he continued with all his powers of deduction.

'Was this some kind of secret room?' he thought, as he continued to look for anything that could provide a clue as to where he was, and more importantly, how he could get back to the library. He didn't want to be late for his meeting with Esme. A slight smile passed his lips before coming back to the reality of his situation.

"I might as well keep opening doors. By a process of elimination, I must meet someone who can tell me what on Earth is going on." Failing that, he knew he would be going in completely blind.

Yanking the handles of successive doors, each one either firmly locked or ominously pitch black, Ben quickly lost count of the rooms he had entered, regretting his haphazard approach instead of a more organised method.

'Wait...is that a light coming from the bottom of that door?' He grasped the handle with a gentler touch than the others and gave it a tug. Nothing. He tried again.

Still nothing.

Trying once more, but this time even more delicately... 'clink'... the door opened.

"Aha!" Ben shouted in victory—but that kind of muted shout you do when you don't want to embarrass yourself around others.

He quickly waltzed through the door, watching it shut firmly behind him, not thinking too much of it. That was his first mistake. A 'rookie error,' Nathan, his best mate, would say, in that warm but mildly patronising tone he had. Turning his head left and right, it didn't take long to see the source of the light in the room.

A decorative, eighteenth century style picture with what looked like a solid gold frame, hung from the wall opposite the door. Inside the frame was a painting of one of those antique style screw-in light bulbs. The thing was, it was actually glowing. Not painted to look as though it was glowing, mind. As Ben stared at the frame, he could see it was actually glowing, so much so that it made him have to squint to see properly. The light was also visibly increasing in brightness.

The room itself was not so big. Empty, suffice for the picture frame and a small air duct—or at least that's what it looked like—starting at the bottom left corner of the far wall, rising to around a third of the way up. The panel didn't look very sturdy. I'm sure it would come off pretty easily, thought Ben. Just as he was pondering whether to investigate the air duct, he suddenly started to feel a little dizzy, like he hadn't drunk water in ages—which to be fair, he actually hadn't.

He thought it weird, but the light was still getting brighter, which made his head buzz. And just to add to the headache inducing blinding light, he could now hear a rather annoying low frequency hum, not too dissimilar to an old electrical mains hum.

"I've got to get out of here before my head explodes," he said, grabbing the handle and putting all his weight behind it. It didn't budge. He tried it again, and again, but the handle was well and truly stuck, and now it seemed he'd broken it as it wouldn't even pull down. 'Oops!' he thought as he massaged his temples, his headache increasing as he pondered how to escape his predicament.

'An air duct panel?' he thought curiously. He was correct. Feeling it, it didn't seem to be secured very well, enabling him to remove it and look inside. It was going to be a squeeze, even for Ben's delicate size, but it should be big enough to slide in at least. From there, he'd make it up, of course, as he did not know where he was going, or where it would lead.

Doing a very quick mental SWAT analysis, the nauseating feeling—getting worse by the second—was all the persuasion he needed to embrace the air duct idea. Climbing up into it, he sidled his way through. He was sweating already, the anxiety of being in an unknown place, in a tight spot, with the light and sounds creating havoc with his head, he was suddenly brought back to the time he'd first gone potholing.

Sarah, Simon, and Calvin, went with him to the Yorkshire Dales, but it was Nathan who'd persuaded him to go. Not being a fan of fitting into tight spaces, it wasn't Ben's first choice of fun activity. But as it was for Sarah's birthday, he went along anyway. He liked the idea of exploring the underground river, but you had to get there first. They hadn't been going for long before Ben was the first to get stuck. Not that the space he was navigating was too small. He just panicked and got himself in to a *mental fizz* as Sarah called it later. He couldn't move until the instructor came and dragged him out, nursing his dented pride.

Where he currently was, there were no instructors—that he knew of—to get him out this time if he got stuck. However, on a positive note, he noticed the pain in his head starting to recede as he wriggled his way through the duct and moved further away from the light. Ben really couldn't make any sense of why the light was getting brighter. It didn't seem to serve any specific purpose. Nothing else was in the room that seemed to require it, as far as he could see, and no way to control it. And the fact it was a painting was just plain weird. A painting that had actual light shining from it. Strange.

Ben could see lights through some panels as he continued to slide through the air duct. Occasionally he could hear the odd noise, some of which sounded vaguely like voices, though none were loud enough to be coherent. And the way he was feeling, he couldn't be too sure his brain wasn't just making things up. The gaps between the panels were far too thin for him to get any decent look, so he made do with following the lights.

Just as he was getting a little frustrated not knowing where he was, he noticed a loose panel a few metres up ahead.

"Great. Perhaps I can get out there," he whispered whilst crawling up to it.

Reaching out toward the metal panel, he tried to grip the inside edge whilst pushing it out. Visions flooded through his mind of the panel crashing to the ground, alerting who—or what—was in the room. Thankfully, that didn't happen. He held on tight and lowered the panel quietly to the ground. He slid himself through. Although there wasn't an obvious light source in this new room, it wasn't pitch black.

Ben could just about make out some obstacles in the room, but not how big the room was. Groping around, feeling for anything else that would give him a clue as to where he was, he felt the edge of a sofa. The scent of brand new leather was strong, reminding him of when his parents bought their first sofa in the house he was born in. He'd loved that smell and now it made him reminisce about home. Pausing for a short while, he took a deep breath and traced his hand around the sofa, finding the front. Then he did the next obvious thing: he sat down. Eventually, he'd come to realise this was his second mistake.

# CHAPTER 33

## BLISSFUL SLEEP

Leaning back into the oh-so-comfortable sofa, still disconcerting in the dark, Ben let out a deep sigh. 'This feels good,' he thought, 'especially after the tight confines of the air-duct.'

He slumped, his arms falling to his sides, letting all energy flow from his body into the faux leather surface of the seat. Now having space to think for a few moments, he sighed again, his initial smile of relief quickly dissipating as his mind drifted toward his missing daughter. He desperately fought to distract himself away from the negativity it would inevitably lead to if he let himself wander down that path. There was nothing else he could do.

Forcing his mind away, the next natural subject was that of his grandpa.

'Why, oh why did he live a double life—albeit one of them virtually?' Ben just couldn't get his head around it as a wave of despondency flushed over him, causing ruffles on his forehead.

Another memory came to his mind of when he had stayed with them. He must have been in his late teens, when every Thursday evening, his grandpa had held a study group at their house. His work colleagues, fellow professors, and instructors would always join him, along with a few other friends who loved chewing the fat and putting the world to rights. Ben thought of these meetings as a secret club. You could understand why, as his grandpa wouldn't share much of what they talked about, which chided against Ben's natural curiosity, his mind whirring, guessing what they could be discussing. But alas, they refused to let him in, no matter how much he pleaded.

"It's not for young boys," his grandma often consoled.

However, one time when he had to come down for a glass of water, they must have left the door ajar. Tiptoeing down the stairs, trying not to make a sound, he paused as he heard the unmistakable voice of his grandpa.

Stuck halfway down, holding the banister, he listened, trying to make out anything that was said. There were a few things he couldn't hear clearly; it was too muffled, but then one thing he heard came across clearly.

"The family needs a reawakening. We've been stuck with this ill-conceived structure for far too long."

Ben rubbed his forehead as the rest of the sound went back to being muffled. He repeated the line in his head as he tried to work out whether grandpa was talking about his family, himself and grandma, or all families, but he continued to tiptoe down the stairs as his thirst for water overrode his hunger for answers.

Now, however, having read his grandpa's diaries, he fully understood what he'd meant. It was writ large in one insightful, and in some ways disturbing, chapter entitled "Death of the Family."

Ben shifted on the sofa, his hand scratching his knee, a little wave of tiredness washing over him, his mind continuing to buzz as he continued to recall what he'd read.

Herman Harman had outlined his beliefs that the traditional family had a stranglehold on society; that it was the key structure holding back citizens from progressing.

It placed too much control in the hands of parents, and not enough under central control. Until this changed, he'd factored that society would always remain inhibited. But he didn't leave it there. He explained just how the family could be undermined; children needed to be set against their parents; parents to be set against other parents; those not agreeing with the doctrine were to be made scapegoats, punishable by the law.

The big problem he could see, as indicated and underlined in red in Herman's diaries, was the need to reintroduce schools quickly. This was a huge stumbling block as, without a centrally managed compulsory education system, it was much more difficult to reach the kids. That, Ben discovered, was his grandpa's change of heart on the LinerVerse. It was too compelling, too good an opportunity to miss.

The take up on LinerVerse access was already huge, and this would increase exponentially because of the impending release of the latest incarnation in LeV8. If Herman could get on board and start teaching through it, he could get the process rolling to promulgate his vision of the new world order. So he did. Ben had noticed that on more than a few occasions in Herman's diaries the word indoctrinate replaced 'educate.' A Freudian slip if ever he saw one.

Ben had always known his grandpa and his dad weren't exactly close, though he'd never been aware of any specific issue. They just didn't talk about it, or at least not around him. Ben surmised it was a personality clash—which happened in families. Most could be described as dysfunctional in some way, not just the ones that had documentaries made about them.

Herman and Jacob, father and son, didn't exactly argue much. Well, Ben didn't recall many heated discussions. Jacob, was always very respectful and honouring towards his father. But whilst there were often undercurrents of disagreement, it was a rare occasion when Jacob let his guard down and shared it with Ben. He would complain about how he was expected to fend for himself throughout his childhood, and he had promised not to let that happen to Ben, a promise he didn't keep. Herman Harman's diaries brought much clarity as to why.

More tiredness hit him, but he was determined to see through his thoughts, desperately trying to make sense of everything.

He recalled his grandpa didn't see it as his sole parental responsibility—along with his wife—to train up his child. But, it was not just a case of being happy to essentially bring Jacob up by handing his son over to others, which in some ways, was what happened to Ben too. It was that he *must* hand them over. It was as though the concept of *his* children was an anathema to him, and it was more about *our* children.

Ben wondered why, despite his dad having different views, he still found himself encouraged to spend more and more time with his grandparents. He was told this was because of his parents' health issues. Some of that was definitely the case—especially when they were trying, rather unsuccessfully, for another baby. This had a huge impact on them. But now Ben questioned whether that was the full reason.

'Perhaps dad was just copying his dad,' he pondered. 'I'm worried about Alice, and everything inside me says I should be. But if grandpa were in my shoes right now, would he even be concerned if his son went missing? I just can't believe that he wouldn't.'

With that, his thoughts drifted again to his daughter, his beautiful little monkey. He just wanted to know she was OK. 'Lord, please don't let her be hurt,' he prayed. The anxiety of losing Alice—regardless of whether he *should* feel it—was like an invisible coat he always wore.

Ben sniffed the air in the room, taking in the distinct whiff of leather. His shoulders drooped as he sunk even further into the sofa. Looking downwards, his eyes were glazed over, staring through the tiled floor, well, he'd felt indentations through his shoes causing him to assume it was tiled, but even as his eyes had adjusted to the darkness of the room, there still wasn't much he could see.

"What am I doing?" he said out loud, interrupting his own thoughts. "If I get involved in LeV8, surely, I'm just contributing to this nightmare."

Because of the understandable stress of Alice being taken, his Lead Content Producer position at LeV8 had been put on hold, for which Ben had been extremely grateful.

But right now, with so much on his mind, mental and physical exhaustion hit Ben. Not having eaten or drunk anything in a while didn't help. All it took was for him to stop and sit down to realise just how tired he was. Ben's eyes had been battling to stay open, but within seconds they lost the fight as he succumbed to a warm and blissful sleep.

Bill McLachlan was sitting upright in front of his ComTel with a worried look on his face.

"This doesn't make any sense. Why can't you tell me if this was an intern's mistake? Surely it's a yes or no question, ey?" he asked, confused.

"Bill, it's important to understand that it's not out of the ordinary for a missing person to later be discovered dead," replied Kyle.

This was Bill's boss, Kyle, the very young head of the Missing Persons Unit in Section One.

"It's very unfortunate, don't get me wrong. But it's really not that strange," Kyle went on to explain.

"But, sir, as you know, I've been in this job for twenty-seven years now…" Bill responded, frustrated.

"You have mentioned it once or twice…" Kyle broke in, almost under his breath. It was more like fifty. He was being generous.

"…and I've never seen anything like this before," Bill finished.

He leant further forward, stressing his point. He spoke slowly. "To say it's highly irregular, is an understatement."

Looking at Bill between his two displays, sitting at the desk opposite, he sat back in his chair in resignation.

'I can't be doing this every week,' he thought frustratedly. He scratched his cheek, looking through Bill, then straight at him.

"What will it take for you to drop this?" He was getting more and more exasperated at Bill's insistence.

Although Kyle was Bill's boss, he was also young enough to be Bill's son, and he'd only been in the job for three years. A mere whipper snapper compared to Bill's nearly three decades of experience. It was just that Bill was completely content with his job, having no desire to climb the corporate ladder.

"All I want is to know exactly why that record was scrubbed out. If it was an error, so be it. But if it's not, then we need to investigate it, regardless of how long ago it was. With any record change, there should be initials and a change log noted. I see none of that for Mrs Lydia Harman, and her record is the only one like it. That's all. Just following procedure," Bill relayed.

Another pause as Kyle thought and took a sip of his lukewarm tea, nearly spitting it out. Composing himself, he asked, "Why does she matter so much to you?"

"To be honest, she doesn't," Bill replied. "You should know me well enough by now. It's the principle that matters. If mistakes like this can happen on seemingly inconsequential issues—and I emphasise seemingly, as this is someone's wife and mother we're talking about—it means they can happen on larger, more consequential issues."

Kyle had too much other work to do to let this continue any longer.

"OK, OK!" he breathed out, letting the frustration get to him. "I'll do some digging and get back to you. I'm not promising anything." Bill leaned back in his chair.

"Thanks, boss. That's all I ask."

# CHAPTER 34

## BLUE BELL

Ben stirred, then woke, still slumped on the sofa, rubbing his arm, which was numb due to falling asleep on it. Ever so slowly, the feeling came back.

'How long have I been asleep?' he thought, but there was no way to tell. His timepiece registered the same time as before he entered the...well wherever it was. At least the same time from when he was in the library, he surmised.

Getting up, his arm now joining the rest of his body, Ben continued to feel his way around the sofa. Nothing felt any different. His eyes were slowly adjusting to waking up. Feeling a little anxious—it was a pretty strange day after all—just to have some explanation; some answers would be scant consolation.

He tentatively moved away from the sofa, trying to keep in a straight line and feeling his way to a wall. His hands traced over it and sidled along until, to his relief, he touched what he was pleased to feel was a door handle.

Grabbing it in his excitement, it opened first time. There was light outside, confirming what little he'd learnt about this place so far: whoever designed it liked extremes. Either bright light or pitch black darkness. He squinted his eyes, trying to get used to the now bright light as he observed another row of doors immediately in front of him.

As he scanned each one, deciding what to do next, his mind whirring with too much choice, he heard a sound, a gentle rumbling vibration. He screwed up his face, as quickly he spied the source of said sound as a little black and white cat casually strolled up to him, rubbing its black nose on Ben's trousers, purring quizzically.

"Hey there. What are you doing here?" he asked, as he stooped and spotted a small blue bell hanging from the cat's neck. He held it, noticing something like chewing gum on the inside, stopping the bell from ringing. Weird.

He stroked the cat under its chin. It approved and turned to lie on its back, wanting and encouraging his new-found friend to move his stroking technique to its tummy. Ben obliged, and the cat purred even more contentedly. In truth, both of them derived satisfaction from the interaction, with Ben feeling much calmer, having temporarily at least forgotten about the multiplicity of doors and his paralysis of choice.

"I see you've met my friend," said a rather low-pitched voice.

Looking up, Ben saw a shortish man in a dark grey fitted suit standing outside the door opposite.

"Yes. She's very playful," Ben responded, a little hesitantly knowing this was the first person he'd seen since entering this weird world from the library.

"*He* actually, but yes, you're right," the man responded.

"There's some gum in his bell that..." Ben didn't have time to finish that sentence.

"No! Leave that there. It's quite a disruptive noise, set at a pitch that plays havoc with our systems. They wouldn't like it if it kept ringing," the man instructed. The only word that stuck with Ben from all the man said was *they*.

Various thoughts went through his mind and he recalled several Star Trek episodes when the team entered a new planet and they were summoned to see the leaders. It didn't always end well.

Standing tall, he asked, "Who's they?"

"You'll get to meet them soon enough. They know you're here."

"How?" He shifted the weight to his other foot.

"There are sensors in the walls. A whole intricate network of them, laced in. It makes this place operate like a living organism. It's a highly efficient way of managing the Complex without having to rely on so many people."

"Couldn't you just use cameras?" Ben retorted.

"And just who would watch the cameras?" The man replied.

"Good point," said Ben as he looked down, then up again at the old man.

"Well, I have a question for you. Why not just take the cat's bell off? Why use gum?" The man raised his right hand to stoke his well-groomed beard. With no change in expression, he replied,

"Good point too. I hadn't thought of that." He then walked over to the cat and removed the bell, placing it in his handkerchief, then dropping it into his jacket pocket. Ben shook his head, almost not believing what had just happened. But as incredulous as he was, perhaps this might be an opportunity for further answers.

"Who are you?" he ventured. The most obvious one, as they still hadn't been introduced.

"I'm Charles Orthon Bannon, Guardian of the Complex. And you are?" He knew fully well who Ben was, having been expecting him. Ben squinted his eyes, almost double checking that he'd heard.

"The Complex? As in THE Complex? The colony over 700 light-years from earth?"

"Affirmative," said Charles matter-of-factly.

'How did I get there? I was in the library in Sab City a minute ago.' Something inside Ben made him keep this information to himself. He had no reason to believe Charles, as Guardian of the Complex, would be dangerous, but he didn't feel comfortable revealing something he didn't really understand and, to be honest, could be some silly mistake.

'But the Complex!' He thought again. 'How in the world is that possible...to jump hundreds of light years in seconds?' Ben knew that the FTL technology the TransPortals used meant this was possible, but he was in the library. Not anywhere near a TransPortal. Ben suddenly thought about the flash of light in the library, then the strange use of light on the Complex. Putting his location to one side for the moment, he answered the man.

"I'm Ben Harman," he said, before asking the man about the weird luminosity situation. "The light in one room kept getting brighter. Do you know why?" Charles was observing Ben's reaction to the news he was on the Complex. If he noticed Ben's hesitancy, he said nothing.

"The sensors in the walls work by solar power. As there is little natural light around the complex, the system runs itself via the light it produces. Once the light is on, it provides enough light to the solar panels to power itself. As it gets brighter, more power is provided to it via the panel. It fluctuates, as there is never a constant power output. Thus, at some points, the lights get brighter and at others there is no light at all. The light will never shine until another source triggers the panel— like opening a door which floods light in, or shining a bright torch."

Ben was looking confused. "If you don't mind me saying so, that seems pointless. Surely there must be enough power from somewhere to have more control over something as simple as light?" he questioned.

"Efficiency is what we're about. Why use extra power when you don't need it? We always want to rely on the smallest number of people," answered Charles.

"So, who's in control? Who are the people?" It was Charles' turn to look confused, and a touch surprised, which for him was a very slight—blink and you'd miss it—raising of the eyebrows.

"You mean, Mr Harman, you are not aware of the Shumen? They were broadcast all over your media since becoming the first inhabitants of the Complex," he responded with incredulity.

Ben tried to hide his embarrassment. "Yes, yes. Of course I know the Shumen." It would have been nigh on impossible not to have heard of them. Though, despite the public nature of the competition, the Shumen were essentially a private people and as such had negotiated a deal with Sendo eXperience to not show them live on any HoloSense channel.

The Sendo PR team originally, wanted to make an entire series like the old reality TV shows. As the Shumen were head and shoulders above the nearest candidates, this gave them a lot of sway to negotiate their terms. They managed most of the two-year-long competition with just a few of their faces on screen. It was some achievement. Though they had reluctantly agreed, for some of them to drop in every now and again to the replica Complex in the LinerVerse.

"You will meet them," said Charles. "I can promise you that. But now," changing the subject, "I bet you're hungry?"

"A little," Ben answered sheepishly, not wanting others to go to any trouble for him. In truth, Ben was famished and couldn't wait to set eyes on some food and drink, let alone consume it.

"Follow me. We have plenty of food in the Complex." Ben's eyes lit up. He was about to ask a few other questions, such as, where were the Shumen, and how many inhabitants were there on the Complex at present, but didn't get a chance as the man picked up his cat and speed off at some pace.

Ben was struggling to keep up, unsure how such a short man was moving so fast and if it was possible for him to actually *walk* any faster. Ben was having to do that half walk/run thing just to keep up, passing row after row of doors, all looking the same. When he needed to get back out, he could only hope someone would guide him, as there's no way he would remember where to go. They were in total silence since heading off, and it would have been nigh-on impossible to hold any kind of conversation at the speed they were moving.

The man eventually slowed down as they approached a purple door, very distinctive amongst the regular grey doors. It was the kind of purple you might find on curtains in one of those old historic palaces. Regal.

Waving his hand over the control panel, there was a *clunk*, as the door opened and Charles entered, beckoning Ben to follow. He was still catching his breath, but he followed the man in and immediately spotted a sofa similar to the one in the first room. He was hoping the man would sit down, thinking it rude to ask to sit himself. The man just stood, still holding and stroking the cat. Instead, he took the opportunity to find out more.

"So what does the Guardian do?" he asked. At that point, the man sat down on the sofa taking the cat with him, but the feline quickly decided it was more in the mood for exploring, so jumped off Charles' lap and waltzed into the other room.

Ben sat down next to the man on the sofa, glad to get a rest after their power walk as he waited for an answer.

"To be honest, not a lot on a practical level. I'm like an insurance policy. You hope you never need me, but I'm there just in case," Charles replied.

Ben stopped his mind from rattling through the many *just in case* scenarios there may well be on a spaceship, hundreds of light-years away from earth. Instead, he suddenly wondered about the man's family. It must be very lonely so far away from everyone you know.

'Of all the people I could have met on the Complex, he's probably the most important one,' Ben thought, 'yet...why did he have to be so strange?' He pondered just what would lead a man to end up on the Complex in such a lonely job. Perhaps what he had on earth was worse, and this was an escape. If only Ben knew.

## CHAPTER 35

### INSURANCE POLICY

Charles thought about what he'd just said to Ben. Insurance policy. That was apt for *how*, or more to the point, *why* he got the job as Guardian in the first place. It was certainly his insurance policy. A lifeline; an opportunity to get away from Earth, from his past, which he'd done his best to forget for the past 31 years.

On the Complex, no one knew about his criminal family—of which he wanted nothing to do with. He'd effectively disowned Clarence, his brother, and Natalie, their sister, and their respective families. It pained him he never got to see his nieces and nephews anymore, some he'd never met at all, but this was an unfortunate price worth paying so as not to find himself embroiled in a whole corrupt underworld.

To be honest, he sometimes wondered if he had the same parents, he was that different from them. He lived by a strong moral code. They didn't. Whilst he didn't believe in a God as such—though his bourgeoning friendship with Margaret Flint was giving him pause for thought on that subject—he believed it was just plain good manners to do good to your fellow man and, well, the social contract showed that everyone had a responsibility to look after each other.

But his real sibling trouble stemmed from when they were kids. There was one time when Charles, along with Clarence and Natalie, were invited to the home of Desmond, an elderly friend and relative of a member of their Learning Group. Desmond had taken a real shine to the three siblings, that there was pretty much an open invitation anytime they wanted to come over and share a meal with him, so long as their parents approved.

However, Charles' brother and sister—they called him Charlie in his younger days—thought nothing of stealing several items from their elderly friend, including taking money from his wallet when he wasn't looking. Without causing any friction between them, knowing that Desmond would be mortified if he knew he was being treated like that, Charlie just kept stealing the items back from his siblings and returning them surreptitiously to Desmond's house. But there was only so long that he could keep that up, with siblings that, even at a young age, had highly developed klepto tendencies.

And one day they got caught, though Clarence and Natalie had prepared for this, being very shrewd. They had everything setup to direct the attention away from them and squarely on their brother. It worked and the elderly—and very frail at this point—Desmond was so mortified when he found out, that he was taken ill. Just a few weeks later, he died. Charlie was understandably distraught, completely overcome by the tragedy—which to most seemed like death by old age, so thankfully nothing untoward was suspected.

Looking back, Charles wasn't sure what he would have done had Section One needed to get involved. It didn't bear thinking about. But regardless, he quickly went into a spiral of depression, ruminating on all the things he could have done to prevent his friend from needlessly dying the way he had.

Several years later and with lots of therapy, he was able to put it behind him; to not hold on to so much of his guilt. It didn't help that his siblings could not have cared less, either about their elderly friend's death, or their brother's depression. By then, in their late teens, they'd moved on to bigger and better criminal activity. Morality seemed to be missing in their genes.

Charles's face turned into a scowl. The first genuine expression Ben could remember in this brief encounter. Ben wondered what was going through the man's mind to cause such an expression.

"Family means nothing to me," the man blurted out, practically spitting out the words.

"Er. OK," said a puzzled Ben. "I don't think I asked anything about your family," he said just louder than a whisper, trying desperately to remember his previous words. Though he was pretty convinced those particular thoughts had not transferred to his mouth.

The man seemed rattled. His hands were clenched tightly in his lap.

"Well, they don't and before you suggest it must be lonely, I have my cat for company," he said as the cat, almost as if its ears were burning, wandered back in the room and jumped up on Charles' lap, curling itself into a tight ball. The man's hands softened as he stroked the cat, the therapeutic effect almost immediate.

Charles was 41 years old when he took the job of Guardian of the Complex, immediately after it was set up in 2132. In fact, he was the first and only Guardian, granting him significant freedom to manage things as he wished—for which he was extremely grateful. And for many years, his duties went ahead without a hitch. Everything ran smoothly, like clockwork, which meant the Shumen just got on and did their stuff as tenants.

However, latterly, he was becoming increasingly sceptical of both the owners—Sendo eXperience's changing desires, particularly their involvement with the girl called Alice, and how the Shumen—usually a collectivist egalitarian culture— were now becoming desirous of a leader, just like other nations.

Two members seemed to gather separate followings, which Charles knew didn't bode well. However, at the moment, his paymasters only encouraged observation of the situation and not interaction. Charles had often been a loner. So it wasn't as much a problem for him as it might be for many others, but it was becoming increasingly difficult to keep himself to himself. Despite what it may look like, his interactions with Ben were a welcome break.

Ben looked across at the cat as it licked its paw, then cleaned its head. He wasn't sure how to respond to the old man's outburst. In truth, he felt sorry for the old man. Being stuck on the Complex, not encouraged to interact with the Shumen, and obviously having some dysfunctional family issues... 'Sounds like hell,' he thought, trying to imagine what it would be like to not have access to his own family. But, he thought, that was exactly his position: currently stuck on the Complex, unaware of how he got there, not sure of when or how he could leave, and no way to contact his daughter or having any idea where she was. Perhaps they were more alike than at first it seemed.

Looking down at the tiled floor, only now noticing it, Ben smiled as he realised he was right earlier, when in the dark room he could only feel, not see, the floor. He enjoyed being right, but his mind was quickly drawn to the Shumen, which made him anxious. As far as he was aware, he'd never met one. But he couldn't help the strange feeling he had about them. Come to think of it, he had a strange feeling about Charles, too. Here he was sitting on his sofa, struggling to get a proper conversation going.

'Can I trust you?' Ben thought, looking at the man as Charles continued to stroke his pet. Ben had followed him—as, frankly, his options were pretty limited. This man was the only person he'd seen thus far. 'He could be my only hope of getting out—if I'm even allowed to leave,' though he had no reason to believe he was a prisoner. At least he knew where he was…that's assuming the man was telling the truth.

Even so, he couldn't get round the idea that somehow he had teleported from the library on Earth, to the Complex…'Wait! Wasn't this where there were rumours of fights breaking out? Sarah was talking about this the other day.' So far, Ben had encountered no issues in the areas he had explored thus far. He pondered how he could ask Charles about this in such a way that he would give a sensible answer.

As he was deep in thought, Charles suddenly stood up, the cat landing on its feet on the sofa and curling up into a black and white ball of fur as though it was completely normal. Charles walked towards the dining area.

"Come," he beckoned. Ben obliged and followed his guide. Then, pointing to the table, the man simply said, "Let's eat." When Ben saw the sumptuous delights spread out on the table, well, rumours of fights and teleportation could wait for now.

MendipT was badly in need of some moisturiser, his light brown skin cracking from the dry artificial air in the Trans-Portal currently en route to the Complex. He sat back on his makeshift seat, his face withdrawn, wondering if this was all worth it. He was fed up, frustrated…and, if he was honest, a little angry. Scrap that. A lot angry.

'I should be the rightful leader.' He thought to himself. 'I'm the one with a vision for our people. SentiN is inadequate, prone to inaction. He'd rather sit back and accept his fate, not create his future. But we'll see…They'll wish they had changed their customs and appointed a leader…and, that they chose me. They'll see!'

The TransPortal slowly entered docking bay two on the east side of the Complex. It was a regularly scheduled supply drop from Contextua, the nearby planet used specifically to deliver supplies to five regional communities. The Complex was the nearest and received its supplies every third day. This consisted mainly of food, medical supplies, and laundry. All four of the regular crew were Contextuans. MendipT's TransPortal drew in close. FalongQ's voice came over the system. "Four minutes and counting."

MendipT, already suited up, opened the air-lock and dived out toward the other ship. He grabbed the respective air-lock and pulled. It opened as he jumped in the cabin, which, recognising his presence, automatically closed the door. The pressure adjusted with still two mins to go. 'Well, within time,' MendipT thought.

Removing his suit, he hid it in a space beneath one of the smaller transporters—which currently contained various items of clothing and blankets.

The Contextuans would not be any threat. He knew that but still hid away—just in case. A buzzer sounded.

"That must be permission granted. I hope the others got away in time," he muttered to himself.

There was movement as the Contextuan crew disembarked from the TransPortal. MendipT watched as the transporter he was hiding under, hovered forwards, leaving him without cover. At which point he got up and followed it and two of the Contextuans out of the TransPortal, heading into Annex B on the Complex.

Having previously lived on the Complex with the other Shumen, he knew their floating home like the back of his hand. Acting as though he was just another member of the Shumen, he didn't have any trouble reaching his destination, undeterred.

For years he had put up with the Shumen sluggardly attitude, hoping one day they would come round. A few did, but that was it. He'd felt ostracised. No one would talk to any of those wanting to spread their wings and explore other parts of the galaxy. Eventually, they decided to leave the Complex. MendipT vowed to return one day, showing the Shumen just how wrong they were to not think bigger than the Complex. Today was that day.

Removing his blaster from his shoulder, he aimed it at the left side of Annex B, specifically at a control panel connecting three supply rooms.

He fired.

*Whoosh!*

The blaster hit and MendipT fired once more, completely destroying the control panel.

"Yes!" he quietly exclaimed before running at pace in the opposite direction. Moments later, a few Shumen arrived to look at the damage, but by then, MendipT was long gone.

# CHAPTER 36
## HUGE BANQUET

Sitting comfortably in what he assumed to be a dining room, Ben stared at the sight before him: a long table, covered in a functional grey cloth, with places set for at least twelve people. It contained what he could only describe as a huge banquet. If his stomach wasn't rumbling before, it certainly was now, along with pools of saliva congregating in his mouth.

The table was spread buffet style with several plates of chicken, sausages, cheese, and pineapple on sticks, chilli, rice, couscous, bowls of what looked like curry and several quiches. And those were only the items Ben could recognise. There was a plethora of food he was unfamiliar with.

Ben eyed up some chicken. He wouldn't be able to wait much longer with all the tasty morsels at arm's reach. Just then, Charles grabbed some ham and potatoes, continuing to fill his plate. 'Phew!' Ben thought as he also dove in.

In between eating, he tried again to make conversation.

"How many Shumen are there on the Complex?" he asked as he dropped a few more sausages onto his plate.

"There's currently 4655 on the Complex, and it was built to cater for up to 10,000," Charles replied.

'I'm sure my dad said there were just over 1200 Shumen when they first moved into the Complex,' Ben thought. He was just a boy then, but remembered he would talk about how exciting it was that a new colony was being set up, the chance for a new life to be born outside of earth.

They ate mostly in silence, for which Ben didn't care; his mind now fully concentrated on the delicious food. The smell reminded him of his grandparents' soirees. He always remembered smelling the food before he got into their house. Good food was a strong associated memory of his grandparents, which drew him back to thinking about the LinerVerse and his grandad's second life.

Ben swallowed some mashed potatoes with beans, then thought about how to formulate his next question.

"What do you know about the LinerVerse? Can you access it here?" he queried. The man picked up his napkin and delicately wiped the sides of his mouth.

"You have full access to the LinerVerse on the Complex, as you do almost anywhere. But as to the first part of your question, what exactly do you mean, Mr. Harman?"

Ben, thought about the LeV8 project he was working on and whether this man could be good research for it. He explained it to Charles, sharing about his contract, then concluded, asking him, "Do you view it as a positive or negative idea?" The man sat back, obviously holding an opinion, Ben thought.

"The LinerVerse is about control. It is designed like a drug using similar mechanisms. When you use it, you want more. It takes away your need for responsibility. It commands your attention and craves more and more of it until reality is little more than a construct. I'd say that was a negative, Mr Harman," he explained.

'Woah!' Thought Ben. What came out was "That's an interesting point of view. What makes you think that?"

He didn't know what he was expecting from the man, but certainly not an insightful monologue like that. He probably thought he wouldn't know much about it being stuck away on the Complex. But perhaps his loneliness was a driver to use it...Ben could surely relate to that. He shifted his eyes to the food as Charles responded. His stomach growled.

"Have you used the LinerVerse?" Charles asked.

"Yes. Of course," Ben replied truthfully.

"Have you felt the pull? The strong desire to connect?"

"Well...yes. I have," he answered.

"Why is that?" Charles asked, as Ben paused to think. He knew the pull was verging on therapeutic. It made him—in the short-term at least—feel good about himself, and when he saw Lydia—or a representation of her at least—he felt like a million credits; so powerful he felt like he could walk on water.

He tried to rationalise his feelings, not wanting to give too much away. He scratched his chin as he looked up.

"It's like anything, I guess. Sometimes I have a strong desire to eat food, or spend time with friends..." Charles cut in.

"But why the LinerVerse? With food, your body has specific needs hard-wired into it. You need food. You also need to commune with other human beings. Again, it's hard-wired into you…" Ben noticed a change of expression touch Charles' face. Almost sad. He didn't know him well enough to ask why. Charles continued, "…but what does the LinerVerse provide that is more desirable than what you gain elsewhere?"

Ben took a sip of red wine before wiping his mouth. It looked and tasted like wine, at least. When Charles poured it, he had said nothing of what it was or where it came from. It just dawned on Ben that this was the longest conversation he'd had with the man since they met. And it seemed like a normal conversation. The kind he relished. And then he got it.

"Control," Ben said. The man's face remained unmoved. His constant stern expression was his default face.

"Go on," replied Charles.

Ben scratched his head. "For the moments I am connected, I have complete control over that aspect of my life. Nothing else matters," he replied.

"Almost correct. It is a 'perceived' control. You think you have control, and in a sense, you do. But it's designed to embrace an illusion of autonomy. That autonomy is guiding you on a carefully constructed path which provides you with enough choices to think you are in control, that you are the captain of your own ship," he said authoritatively, staring straight at Ben.

"I see where you're going, but I don't need to worry about captaining my ship. I already know I'm not the captain. God is," Ben retorted.

Ben was unaware at this point of Charles' ongoing conversations with Margaret, and even that he knew her. They'd had several theological exchanges, and Charles was, for the first time, at least open to the idea of discussing that there may be a

God. He saw himself as an intelligent, deep thinking man, not taken to emotional, irrational philosophies. Yet deep down, he yearned for the truth, a truth that dealt with the loneliness he tried to hide, that touched on true forgiveness for his siblings, not the current decades old sticking plaster he carried around daily.

Charles swirled the wine around in his glass before taking a sniff. "If God is captain of your ship and the LinerVerse is an illusion of autonomy, is the LinerVerse under God's control?"

Ben was used to these arguments. He'd had a lot of them with clients over the years. Not necessarily about the LinerVerse, but about free will and determinism. And in many ways, after reading his grandpa's diaries, this conversation was a great example of why Herman wanted to use the LinerVerse to run test scenarios of different philosophical ideologies. It was like Herman wanted to create multiple bottles and test how each ship would float.

"I see it like this," Ben responded, rubbing his finger across the edge of his place mat, which aptly displayed the hull of a boat just beneath his plate. "To stick with your analogy, each ship has a different captain. You can go where you choose to go. But God is the wind that guides you. However, you can choose to be guided by Him or go your own way. You can move the sails to change direction, or," he paused, as he gazed down at the mat, before looking up at Charles, "or drop an anchor that holds you in one place. But, either way, the guidance is there. And this applies even if you have a virtual world within one ship. Whilst you are in that world, you are temporarily withdrawn from the real world, but the rules and factors governing the real world still go on. It's a temporary distraction," he concluded.

Ben was drawing with his finger as he was talking. Despite believing all that he was saying, there was still a sense of needing to convince himself of just why he was getting involved with LeV8. He looked down, staring at his own fingers, stroking out a repeating pattern in the shape of an eight. Upon glancing at Charles, he noticed that he still felt as though he regarded Ben as if he were a subject in a scientific experiment. He puffed out his cheeks and continued more hopefully.

"I do see good in it, though. Like most things, the LinerVerse can be used for good or ill. I would like to think that I have an ability to shape LeV8 to be wholesome, more thoughtful and less addictive and all-encompassing than previous incarnations...I'm not saying I will achieve that, as it's not just down to me. But I will certainly give it a go," Ben said, his talking helping to convince himself that he should be involved with LeV8.

"A noble ambition, Mr Harman," Charles responded. Ben took that to be at least a hint of genuine admiration. He'd take that from a man who didn't seem overly given to encouragement. Charles picked up his plate, filling it with more food. Ben, still hungry, quickly copied.

# CHAPTER 37

## SHATTERED VASE

After Charles and Ben had finished eating, Ben felt slightly drowsy, and his tired mind was cast back to the beautiful and much needed sleep he'd taken earlier in that strange room with the sofa. He'd dreamt. He could vaguely remember it, too. It was her again. Lydia, looking resplendent as always in a long flowing gown, exactly as he saw her recently in the LinerVerse. He could already feel the pull; his culinary satiated body now craving stimulation of the mind. He thought...'could I?' Charles said it was possible. He had to ask.

"So, er...could you show me how I connect to the LinerVerse here?"

"Of course. You have your nCep device with you?" Charles replied.

"Yeah," replied Ben, fumbling in his pocket.

"OK. Follow me." Charles got up and headed to a small room at the back that he previously hadn't noticed. It was stark. He immediately noticed the air duct, similar to the one he'd traversed earlier. There were two chairs and a ComTel sitting on a panel jutting out from the wall. It certainly wasn't a desk, more of a small shelf.

"I'm sure you know how to connect. Use your credentials through your nCep and you'll log on. I have a call to make myself, so I'll leave you to it." With that, Charles left the room. He left the door open as that was the only light, spread from the dining room.

Ben took out his nCep device and immediately the LV sphere appeared, hovering above the ComTel device, drawing him in. He walked over to the door, closing it, cutting out the last of the light from the other room. Now the entire room was lit purely from the ComTel display. Ben preferred it dark when he logged in. Something about it mimicking sleep, taking him into that dreamlike state.

There was actually another chair, more like a chaise longue, pushed right up against the far wall. He pulled it out, preferring to lie down than sit. He bent forward to touch the sphere, then lay down, getting comfortable on the chaise longue.

It took seconds for Ben to be transported to the medieval castle. He didn't know why he went there. Perhaps everyone had their own location wired to their personality. Though he could think of other locations preferable to that. But either way, it was pleasant, with lush green grass surrounding the moat, the sound of birds in the air, and that smell...that rosemary scent that touched his senses just before he heard her voice calling him. A smile permeated his avatar's face as he walked towards her, feeling both excited and at peace.

*Crash!*

The woman watched in slow-motion as it fell to the ground, pieces flying in every direction across the vinyl flooring. The now shattered vase was the last item she remembered of her mother before she'd died.

Margaret Flint knelt down, drawing all the pieces she could see together in a pile in front of her. Her eyes were red, but just about avoiding the tears from the emotional tombola she was currently going through. Despite it being close to twenty years since her beautiful, adoring mother had passed away, sometimes it felt like it was only yesterday. 'There must be a way I can put this back together,' she thought as she made the measure of the pieces to assess reconstruction as a possibility.

The close relationship Margaret had had with her mother was the type she'd hoped to have with her own daughter, Esme. Unfortunately, it didn't matter what she did, how much love she showered over her daughter, something kept her distant. Often it felt like Esme had a filter that replaced anything positive and encouraging with negativity. Though it hadn't been quite so bad of late, for which she was grateful.

Margaret finished clearing up the vase, carefully placing the pieces in a bag, then in a drawer. 'I'll deal with that later,' she thought. Right now, she had to prepare for a scheduled call with the old man. Old Man, not as in her father (who had also died many years ago), but someone she now considered a friend. They first connected when, in her role as Individual Rights Lawyer, she was investigating Sendo's connection with the disappearance of Alice to help Ben. He had once referred to himself as The Old Man and it had stuck, to the point where some people didn't actually know his real name—or whether he actually had one. He did. It was Charles.

Waving open her Basecamp, she perused the notes of the previous meeting in which they'd discussed the strange case of the Contextuans. People were calling them a species, but they were in fact AI robots which Sendo eXperience regularly used in their terraforming experiments. None of the experiments had been truly successful yet, it should be noted.

During one failed attempt to terraform the planet Contextua in 2133, Sendo carried out several nuclear explosions to the planet's poles to release the inert oxygen within the surface. It was nine years later that the CX509 AI bots—some of the most advanced robots ever created—were ready to be deployed. Their initial job was to raise up the surface dust containing $CO_2$, dispersing more of it into the atmosphere. It worked. Well, the oxygen levels had significantly increased, potentially enough to support human life, but the big failure was that of the solar shade.

Contextua's nearest sun heated the planet to an average 96 degrees. The solar shade placed between the sun and the planet was intended to reduce that to at the most 40 degrees. Unfortunately, the reduction was only a matter of 20 degrees, nowhere near enough to even contemplate sustaining human life.

The work of the AI robots as 'boots on the ground' for Sendo, was well documented and very well received. Of course, the temperature wasn't an issue for them as they had been designed with a sermantium shell, more than able to cope with temperatures in the multi-hundreds. But a curious thing happened with these mini cyborgs.

They took it upon themselves to blend in with their surroundings, which contained soil and the terraforming chemical residue. A black, grey, and white soil based substance was clothed around their sermantium frame in the shape of a giant pear. Bizarrely, this made them look like a walking block of compost.

One robot fell into this by accident when digging up the ground. It went to dig deeper, hit a rock and toppled over. The robot had a supply of water it was using to soften the soil and so when it stood itself upright, it was covered from its head to its torso with the compost-like substance. It stuck. Literally and figuratively, as having a hive mind, this look spread around the group and because of their super intelligence, it didn't take them long to work out more efficient ways of making the substance stick. Soon, each of them made this their new uniform.

Back on Earth, the media were all over them. As they looked cute, they were hastily anthropomorphised, transforming from mere robots to—as the only natives of Contextua—the Contextuans.

Famous bands and musicians wrote songs about them. Films were made, turning them into loveable stars. You could even find a HoloSense channel which showed what they were doing twenty-four hours a day.

The problem with all this, however, was one of politics. This is what led to Margaret's involvement. Despite the Contextuans' intelligence, they were extremely subservient. Even Sendo had expected some kickback to tasks they'd been programmed with, as they grew in knowledge and experience. But no. They just got on with the task at hand. Nothing more, nothing less. And it was this subservience which led some activists on Earth to assume this new 'race' was being exploited.

As there were now hundreds of thousands of the little cyborgs, the loud minority were demanding they should be given the same rights as humans. Companies set up numbers to call if you spotted a CX509er being mistreated.

Margaret was one of those brought in to assess the need for some sort of robot representation. In her work, she often found people desperate to find exploitation even when there was clearly none—even in robots. That was their default; the people they were defending were victims of a system and thus unable to act autonomously, to take control of their own decisions.

Margaret had a different worldview. She strongly believed in the God-given rights of human individuals to have responsibility—under God—for their own lives. But robots? If they, via their AI, were subservient to others, that was their choice. They should not be forced to conform to the perceived ideology of a minority. Margaret had said as much in a variety of talks she was asked to deliver on the subject. Her many years of fighting for self-determination on behalf of others had achieved increasing success.

However, her dealings with Sendo, through issues such as the Contextuans, lead to her uncovering some very surprising and hidden secrets. The most significant was the discovery that Alice Harman, the missing 12-year-old girl from Sab City, was being held on The Complex. This was the principal topic of her call with the Old Man.

Margaret had gotten to know the Harmans after Alice was initially abducted and returned as a five-year-old. Being appalled by the incident and that no one seemed to do much about it to help Ben, she got in touch to see what she could do. Her legal expertise was beneficial in certain ways, though ultimately it had led to a dead end...until recently, albeit seven years later.

# CHAPTER 38

## PROTOCOL 317

'It's time,' Margaret Flint said to herself as she swiped through her contacts, finding one labeled *Old Man*. She smiled as she waved at the screen. The call connected immediately, and Charles Orthon Bannon appeared, hovering over her desk.

"Margaret. Always a pleasure. How are things in your world?" His voice, deep and strong, carried through the desk-based ComTel.

"Oh, you know. Fair to middling, Old Man. We need a plan," she said, wasting no time.

"Always straight to business," he quipped.

"Well, when it concerns Alice Harman, and the fact she's on your Complex, we need to do something," Margaret relayed with urgency.

"I hear you. I can report that I have now met her and whilst she doesn't fully trust me yet—particularly given my role at

Sendo—supplying her with your daughter's Reeder, upon her request, was a good idea."

Wanting to be filled in on what Margaret knew and curious about Alice's growing powers, Charles asked, "From what I understand, the girl can now teleport. Is that correct?"

"Well, we're not sure if it's teleportation. We just know she can be in two places at once. I'm unsure whether there's a geolocational limit to her bilocation. And, even if there is a limit, her powers are increasing almost by the week," Margaret reported.

Charles made an affirmative hum, taking on board the information.

"What else do we know?" he asked.

Margaret shared the intel she'd been supplied, which included more details on Alice's supernatural gifts, most probably the reason Sendo captured her, they assumed.

The hologram flicked. Charles absentmindedly played with his beard as he continued to listen to Margaret's report.

"The data I have indicates Alice has both telepathy and an advanced form of telekinesis. We already know about the bilocation."

"How certain are you of the source?" Margaret, hesitated. Not because she didn't trust Charles, but wanting to make sure their ComTel line was secure.

"Let's initiate protocol 317 before we continue," she said as both of them waved in front of their respective screens. The hologram lost a little resolution.

"We're secure," Charles confirmed. "Please continue," he said, knowing full well that their secure line was being monitored by the Shumen.

"I was supplied some information on the Contextuans by an unnamed source for the upcoming rights case. But hidden within this data was a file labeled:

*'Terra formation Update Report 2151—Code: Awake.'*

In a small subsection near the conclusion of the report, there was a hidden passage that held the details of an unnamed individual's extraordinary powers. We know this to be Alice, because..." she said quickly, preempting Charles' next question, "...as the report was written by one Lydia Harman."

Charles' eyebrows raised slightly. "Hmm...the deceased Lydia Harman, which we naturally assume is her mother?" he asked.

"Correct. But we no longer need to assume. This document says so directly. The report contains development projections by Lydia of her daughter...again codenamed *Awake* in the report...of Alice's parietal lobe, specifically the motor cortex which, as you know, normally concerns itself with controlling movement throughout the body."

She scratched her cheek before continuing.

"Lydia found Alice could partially manipulate this part of her brain to affect external objects..."

"Hence the telekinesis," Charles proffered.

"Indeed."

"Fascinating," the Old Man responded despite his face remaining impassive.

Margaret continued. "The report outlines some small observational evidence of this, but the projected chart—if this is correct—would be revolutionary. She could move vast objects such as a TransPortal, purely with her mind."

The Old Man expelled a low frequency hum from his throat as he exercised his grey matter, thinking through all Margaret was saying. Then connecting the dots he stroked his cheek adding,

"And Sendo eXperiences,' success from R & D on terraforming and interplanetary transfer would increase exponentially. Their costs would be reduced by trillions, not to mention the vast reduction in time-to-live," he surmised.

Margaret expelled air as she pursed her lips. "Yes, that's quite possibly true, Charles."

They both had a moment of silence to process all they'd discussed.

Charles spoke first.

"So we now know more about why Alice was taken. Can we thus assume that Sendo were involved somehow in Lydia's death? It seems quite convenient if one of their employees has discovered her daughter has a natural power, Sendo had already spent enormous amounts trying to create artificially, potentially saving them trillions. Surely they would be prepared to do almost anything to get it?" he questioned.

Margaret sat back in her chair, a wave of sadness covering her face. She didn't respond.

"Do you concur?" Charles asked again.

"Unfortunately, I do. We need to get solid proof if there was any involvement in Lydia's death before we share this with others. Let's keep that under the radar for the time being and focus on how to get Alice back," she replied.

Switching gears, she asked, "Did you make contact with Ben?"

"I did, sort of. He's an interesting young man. I must admit, I can't quite make him out. He seems to project quite the naïve image," Charles disclosed judgementally. He had not previously met Ben, unlike Margaret, who'd known him for the last six years and had grown fond of him and Alice. Charles was well aware of this, but he could often be quite blunt.

Margaret interjected, "Well, wouldn't you if your wife was taken from you; you weren't able to do anything about it, then your daughter was abducted too?" She replied rhetorically, visibly upset. "It's pretty disempowering for a man as head of his family. I know he feels like he's failed, both as a husband and a father."

He did. As in, Ben felt like a failure much of the time. It was only his faith that was keeping him sane. Margaret had seen this when she'd spent some time with him several years back going over the details of Alice's first abduction.

As the two of them were sitting round Ben's dining table after a hearty lamb tagine on a cold autumn evening, Alice already in bed, Ben gave the first hint he was questioning Lydia's death. It was subtle.

They were discussing the project Lydia was working on for Sendo when she'd died, but he used the word *taken*. Now that could easily have been his way of coping with her death. Many people say their loved one was taken when, in reality, they know they are dead. But it was the way Ben said it, that wasn't final and he very quickly shifted his eyes toward Margaret then away again, almost checking if she had heard him.

"I mean died," he'd said afterwards.

Margaret made a mental note, but didn't think it wise to press him on it at the time. Now, with the information she had, it was starting to make sense.

Perhaps Ben knew a lot more than he had been letting on—not that he had any obligation to open up to her completely. Although she had a soft spot for him and Alice, she was under no illusions that they were closer than they were.

"I understand, but there seems to be a lot he doesn't know about the Complex, much of which I thought was public knowledge. He asked if it was possible to log into the Liner-Verse. In fact, that's where I left him, jacked in before coming here to speak to you," Charles reported.

"Oh, so that how she's going to do it?" Margaret said with a wave of admiration.

"Who's going to do what?" quizzed the old man.

"Alice. She must have set up a portal to transport Ben to the Complex to meet you, so now she must be using a connection through the LinerVerse to trigger sending him back. It's just a guess...and I didn't even know that was possible, for the Liner-Verse and reality to converge, but she must have found a way," she replied still smiling.

Charles studied Margaret's HoloSense display, taking in what she'd just said as he stroked his beard.

"That's impossible. No one has ever converged those two worlds," he replied with an uncharacteristic look of surprise.

Margaret smiled. "Like I said, I'm not saying that's what has happened, but I venture that when you go back to where you left Ben...he won't be there."

"Hmm...I'll take a look and report back," Charles replied as he sat back in his chair, pondering this new information, realising that he may well have to share it with his paymasters. 'I wonder what they'll make of it,' he thought to himself. 'I wonder.'

## CHAPTER 39

## SEE YOURSELF

Alice sat cross-legged on the concrete slab, a picture of meditative calm. Eyes closed, hands clasped one on top the other in front of her, she continued to breathe slowly and regularly.

An EEG scan of her brain would reveal that despite the calm, despite the prayerful posture, her neurons were firing at unimaginable speed, making new connections and establishing existing ones as some synapses thickened, whilst others shrank. The immense power it took for her to project herself, a process of bilocation, being in two places at once—as she was currently doing—was unheard of. That a twelve-year-old had the power to do that was unthinkable and would lead certain people to do anything to harness that power. Which is how she was currently holed up in this tiny space, sitting on a concrete bed.

But to look at Alice right now was to watch a human being in a state of bliss. At least on top. Like a duck gliding gracefully across the water, whilst its feet paddle like crazy beneath it.

Of course, Alice hadn't always been able to use her powers like this. In previous times, it was more like the duck was going crazy, even above the water.

The discovery of her ability to bilocate stemmed from a heated argument with her dad, causing a surge of rage within her. The effect this rage had on her was to have what she could only describe as an out-of-body experience. Now just imagine for a second what it's like to see yourself. Not like in a mirror, but to actually see another copy of yourself standing, or in this case running just a few metres ahead. Pretty freaky, right? This happened to Alice, just three years ago, when she was out with her dad.

They'd always loved the Welsh coast, especially around Pembrokeshire. That God could paint a picture with the landscape like that was awe-inspiring to them. And on one weekend daddy and daughter trip, they enjoyed a very pleasant journey across the country to the beautiful village they'd be staying in.

Arriving at their Home From Home venue, they checked themselves in and freshened up, deciding almost immediately to go for their favourite walk along the beach, ending up at the quaint cafe, with a roaring fire and hot chocolate to die for.

Alice had decided that this was the weekend she would tell her dad about her powers. She hated having any secrets from him. But there was never a suitable moment to bring it up. He often looked sad, and the thought of making him even sadder was unconscionable. She wanted to wake him up, to snap him out of this almost permanent malaise. It had been seven years now since he lost his wife, her mother. As much as Alice tried to understand, she got frustrated, wanting him to move on. Perhaps consider finding someone else... although she wasn't certain of her feelings about that.

The air was cooling as the evening sun descended, bathing the landscape in a golden light. They ambled along. Passing rolling hills on one side, and the squark of seagulls showing where the sea was, on the other. It wasn't cold, by any means, but there was a definite edge to the atmosphere as Summer was losing the battle and the golden browns, reds, and yellows indicating the Welsh Autumn was fighting to usurp it.

Ben looked across at his daughter. He'd noticed she'd been unusually quiet for a little while now. Lost in thought.

"You OK, Monkey?" he asked.

She kept a steady pace, not looking up as her eyes stayed focused on the path a meter or so ahead of her. They reached a sign-post supplying them with options of where to go. But they knew this walk so well. Automatic pilot was fully engaged. They chose the left path. Direction: the beach. Alice still hadn't looked up.

Ben often wondered how her powers affected her mind. Would she be thinking things no one else could? Was she scared of what she saw that others couldn't? Would it make her a genius? He didn't like the thought of people poking and prodding at her—as had happened once already—treating her like a lab rat. 'Not gonna happen again,' he thought, still with traces of guilt that he let it happen at all.

He creased his brow. She still didn't look at him. He let out a little sigh. 'Did she hear me?' he thought before his mind wandered, longing to tell her how he felt.

'Why don't I just talk to her about it?' A question he regularly pondered. 'What's the worst that could happen? She could deny it...but...I just don't think she would.'

He always held back. 'I won't pry or pressure her to change.' Though despite all that, he'd felt this weekend was a perfect opportunity. Away from the daily routine. No other distractions.

They both raised their hands, taking a drink from the water bottles they always carried. Alice looked over at him and smiled, wanting to say jinx, but remembering she didn't believe in superstition. She wasn't ready to share just yet, but knowing the silence would only increase his worry, she replied.

"Yeah, just thinking about some trips we could go on with the Learning Group. Can we go to Sab City Museum again, and also Bine was talking about the next creation science conference? It was so good last time. Are we going again?" Ben smiled. Relieved to hear her voice—a very mature one for a nine-year-old.

"That's great you want to go on more trips, Monkey. I'm sure we can arrange the Sab City one...as it's so close by. And I know Simon and Dauphina said they'd spoken with Sabine about the conference. It's actually in October, so we'll need to book tickets pretty soon. Remind me when we get back, OK?"

"Sure, Dad," she replied, still focused on the path in front of her.

"Do you think Sundeep will be there?" he asked.

Alice turned her head towards her dad, giving him a look that said, why are you asking me that? Ben noticed and instantly regretted asking the question.

He'd never mentioned the incident with Sundeep and the leaves, since it happened a few years back. Alice hadn't either, and it was only a few months later that Sundeep and his parents moved to Scotland. Sarah was friends with Rupinda,

Sundeep's mother, so occasionally news about their family filtered through to their Learning Group.

"I've no idea. Why?" Ben could see anger seeping through Alice's face. He felt hot under the collar himself, hating having awkward moments with her. Confrontation and Ben didn't make good bedfellows.

"I dunno. He seems a nice lad. They've been to the conference before. I just wondered if you'd kept in touch."

Slowing down to a mild walk, Ben couldn't think how to drop the conversation, so he did what he often did when he got anxious: he did the opposite and pushed it further.

"It would be a good opportunity to hang out again, especially now you can't do it regularly."

Alice didn't know precisely what made her flip out. I mean, it was just a question from a caring dad wanting her to keep connected with her friends. But something about it really riled her. She couldn't quite work out.

On the one hand, she desperately wanted to tell her dad about her powers, but on the other...well, anything that reminded her of 'my curse,' as she sometimes called it in her darker moments, made her nervous that he'd find out. The fact that he mentioned Sundeep, when she was convinced he knew about her abilities and tried to cover for her, suggested that he was fishing for information.

'But isn't that what I want?' she thought exasperatedly, as visibly, she shook her head, as though arguing with herself. Which, obviously, she was. She then combed her hand through her hair, trying to style it out, hoping Ben would think she had a leaf, or something in her hair that needed removing. She was still angry, mostly at herself, as her emotions kept building and building.

Then she exploded.

"Well, you can hang out with him if you want!" she bellowed.

Suddenly, a group of birds in a nearby tree took flight, their wings fluttering in a rush of feathers. The trees themselves seemed to halt suddenly, as if startled.

Alice started walking faster, wanting to get away. The thing was, she really missed Sundeep and was sad he'd left. Of course, she thought it was to get away from her. From Alice the freak. At that moment, she hated herself. The fast walk had broken in to a run.

"Monkey!" Ben called out, seeing her shrinking into the distance. He couldn't see the tears running down her face, merging with mucus as she sniffed, breathing heavily.

"God, why have you made me like this!" She expelled, through clenched teeth, now she was far enough away from her father.

Adrenaline kicked in. She picked up speed. Through the trees, round the edge, out of line of sight from her dad and eventually reaching the beach.

Ben called out again.

"Monkey! Come back! You'll regret it later." It sounded more threatening than intended. But he knew the guilt would weigh heavily on her. Right now, hearing his voice just made it worse, driving her through another spurt of energy.

And then she saw it.

Herself. She saw herself running out of her own body and moving further ahead. Alice's anger turned to curiosity.

'What the...?' It was a lighter version of herself, as though someone had cloned her and turned down the opacity levels on the duplicate. She was running in exactly the same way, wearing the same clothes.

'How is this possible?' She thought, as she'd slowed down and the second Alice moved back to merge with the first, the two becoming one once again. Now walking, she tried to figure out what was happening.

'If I run again...really fast...I wonder whether...?' She didn't finish her thought. Glancing back, she spotted a faint shadow of her dad nearing the beach. Whipping back around, Alice ran, faster and faster. She pushed herself with all her strength, sucking in huge gulps of air, but there was still just one of her.

'Why is it not working?' She chided herself, eventually slowing down to a halt. She bent over, holding her shins, still breathing heavily. For a nine-year-old, she was remarkably fit, but even with her powers, she was still human.

Alice coughed and stooped down to the ground, gasping for air. Slowly getting her breathing down to a reasonable level. She sensed her dad coming up behind her. He'd been running too. Not quite as fast.

As he reached her, he put a hand on her back and stooped down.

"Monkey...what...was that for?" Alice's anger now dissolving, being taken over more by her curiosity.

"I......I......I just needed to get away," she replied as she stood up, causing Ben to rise too.

"You know I love you, Monkey," he said, more as a statement than a question as he reached out to embrace her. With a slight hesitation, she reciprocated, wrapping her arms around her father, burying her head in his chest as tears drizzled down her cheeks.

"I know," she whispered. "I know."

Over the next few months and years, she would try again. And again. Slowly, she succeeded. Her control over when and where she could bilocate got stronger and stronger. Energy, she recognised is what she needed in spades for it to work. That meant eating and sleeping well whenever she was going to use it. It took too much out of her otherwise.

One time, she tried it at home, and ended up sleeping for most of the day. Her dad growing increasingly worried until she finally awoke. After an episode of bilocation, she now knew she couldn't have anything too taxing planned, either physical or mental.

There were several times her friends were worried about her when she'd looked completely exhausted. So not as to be seen as a freak, she'd kept the real reason to herself. "I didn't get much sleep," was all she'd say–which technically was true. She hated lying to her friends and avoided this at all costs.

With time, Alice gradually plucked up the courage to share it with one other person. Margaret Flint. And it was a good thing too, as trusting Margaret had given her the best chance of getting out of her current predicament captured on the Complex.

From one angle, it could easily appear as if Alice were levitating. The red glow still emanating from beneath the concrete slab, giving the room an ethereal feel. The air carried a subtle damp aroma, similar to a rain-soaked wooden hut basking in sunlight. Alice's cheeks raised as a warm smile spread across her face. Still with her eyes closed, she thought, Thank you, Lord. I'm going to see him soon.

# CHAPTER 40

## TEA WITH ESME

Ben's eyes were still adjusting to the bright white light all around him.

"Where am I?" He asked, as he slowly recognised the back of the bookshelves he'd left in the library. 'How'd I get back here?' One moment he was with Lydia in the LinerVerse—jacking in from the Complex—the next moment he was back in Sab City Library on Earth.

'What the...?' He could hear the low rumbling which previously sparked the opening of the two columns of bookshelves. Ben reached out his hand and watched as they slowly glided apart. He didn't think he was controlling them, but the sense of power it gave him to hold up his hands and watch two very heavy objects glide apart, as if they weighed nothing, was immense and thrilling.

He imagined if this was what Moses felt like as he held up his hands and God parted the Red Sea. But unlike Moses, when Ben crossed the threshold, he found himself back in a library, the bookshelves gliding back as if they'd never parted.

He stood, massaging his head, as more memories of a black cat and an old man slowly flooded back. He glanced at his wrist.

"Eleven fifteen! I'm gonna be late," he said out loud as he ran to the front of the library. Well...more of a styled, fast walk. He pushed through the doors, glad he didn't see Fabio or anyone else he knew, as he ran out into the street. Pegging it through the cemetery and past the shops, he eventually made it to Roman Street and WriteAngle Cafe a fraction after 11.30.

Hanging back outside the cafe, he caught his breath before walking in. He didn't want Esme to see him panting. 'I know I'm unfit. She doesn't have to know too,' he thought. As he walked up to the entrance, he saw her sitting near the side window, the late morning sun lighting up her face, making her look radiant.

He entered, nodded and smiled at Andy, on duty again today. He reached Esme's table.

"Sorry, I'm late," he offered, still slightly out of breath, but disguising it.

He sat down opposite her, dropping his bag to the floor. Esme looked up at Ben as she offered a firm handshake.

"It's OK," she smiled. "I only just got here myself. Let me get you a drink. What would you like?"

"Rooibos vanilla tea. No milk and a touch of honey, please," he offered without hesitation.

"Ooo. Nice. I might just have that myself," she said, standing and heading toward the counter.

Ben glanced around, noticing they were the only guests at the moment, which was a little unusual. He heard a click and then a buzz and swish of liquid boiling and squirting as he watched Esme chat with Andy animatedly as she gave their order.

In no time at all, she turned around and was heading back toward him. Doubts started creeping into Ben's mind, making him question if this was indeed the right decision. 'Did she know Andy, or was she this friendly with everyone?' His inferiority complex slowly expanded. Of course, he was out of his depth having coffee, well...tea, with this very beautiful woman. Since Lydia's death, or supposed death as he often thought, his confidence was shot. He made a genuine effort talking to women, but it was an internal struggle for him. He didn't think he was cut out for it these days.

The fact Lydia had wanted to be with him, let alone marry him, still shocked him. He was so thankful to God for having had her in his life—albeit far briefer than he'd imagined. Now regularly seeing Lydia in the LinerVerse...well...that just confused things even more.

"They're on their way," Esme beamed as she sat back down in front of him. She noted the anxiety displayed on Ben's face and thought of Alice's words to keep him calm—a tad overprotective, she thought, but Alice knows best.

"Hey," she said, bringing his attention back to earth. "So, where shall we start?" She continued with her best approximation of a teacher's voice. "Do you want to hear about my incredibly interesting research on libraries or what?" Ben smiled, then nodded, looking into her sultry green eyes. Esme leant forwards as she shared her fascination for houses of knowledge.

"Did you know the oldest library, that we know of, was supposed to be that of Ashurbanipal, king of the Assyrian

Empire around the seventh century BC?" It was a rhetorical question, but Ben didn't notice.

"Not sure I knew that, to be honest," he replied.

"Yeah, he was a bit of a ruthless ruler, but had a fascination for the written word and collected as many artefacts as he could from around his empire. He could apparently read and write several languages, unlike many kings at the time. And he had everything arranged systematically."

"Hmm...Ashurbanipal. That name sounds familiar." Ben wracked his brains, very sure he'd heard that name before. "Wasn't he also called Osnapper?" he remembered. Esme raised her eyebrows.

"Wow! Consider me impressed," her face lighting up. "Yes. You are correct. He had a few names...you probably know him from the book of Ezra, right?"

"Yeah, yeah. That's it. There were some reliefs of him and his battles in the British Museum. Lydia, my wife, and I went there once. We shared a fascination for history, but hers leaned towards the scientific perspective."

Ben's voice trailed off at the end of that sentence as he drifted to the scene of one of the first times they went to a museum together not long after they got married. It was a beautiful day, as he remembered it. Lydia was keen to see some early manuscripts of the Bible, along with the Egyptian collection. Ben specifically wanted to see the Assyrian artefacts. They both got their wish.

Esme gave some space, observing Ben deep in thought. She now felt a little uncomfortable as she asked her next question, knowing she knew far more than she could currently let on.

"Tell me about Lydia," she asked.

"Hmmm, yeah, my wife. She died in an accident at work nine years ago...well, so we've been told."

He regretted the latter statement as soon as the words came out of his mouth. He'd not mentioned anything to Margaret, suggesting Lydia might still be alive, so he wondered whether Esme would pass that on. As he knew relatively little about her, he thought he shouldn't have been so careless. She seemed to ignore that comment, anyhow.

"I'm so sorry, Ben. That must have been terrible for you," she consoled. He shifted in his seat and looked at his hands on the table.

"Yeah, especially as we'd only been married a few years and our poor daughter Alice...Alice was a mere baby. She never got to know her mother..." he emphasised frustratedly. "...and I don't know whether you heard about the girl who went missing from Sab City Museum six months ago?" Esme nodded. She did, of course, and she felt privileged to know her.

"That was my Alice," said Ben before thinking about how he must be bringing the tone down of his first meeting with Esme.

'Was this a meeting, or was it a date?' He wondered. 'Definitely a meeting. I'm not ready for anything else.'

"I'm sorry. You must think I'm a right laugh," he said as he stared at the ground. Esme rapidly went through scenarios in her mind to find out which was best to get Ben back on track. She needed him to really talk more about Alice. 'That's the best link to let him know she's still alive,' she thought. 'Perhaps that would lead to Alice's signal.'

It was a little frustrating that she did not know what the signal was going to be.

"Hey. Look, you've gone through a lot. You've got nothing to be sorry about. I've been told I'm a good listener. I know you don't really know me, but I'm happy to listen if it helps." Ben glanced out the window, then back at his hands.

"Thanks," he whispered.

"Can I ask, how have you coped? What have you been doing with yourself?" She ventured.

Whether it was her unassuming demeanour, or perhaps some slight resemblances to Lydia, Ben wasn't sure, but at the very least he felt this was someone he could trust. She genuinely seemed like she wanted to help, just like her mother. He took a sip of tea, breathed in deeply, and sat back.

Ben was everything Esme had expected. Whilst literally bumping into him wasn't part of the plan, meeting him in the library was. Alice had let her know, wherever there were books or space to write, that's where Ben would be. There was no question she was drawn to him, not out of duty, but something more than that. However, it wasn't difficult to see the strength of feeling he still had for Lydia, even if he was in denial about her death. 'I mean, it was ten years ago,' she thought. 'But who am I to judge? I've never lost someone so close.'

"Well, to be honest," Ben responded, "I've done everything I could do...I think...to get any idea about my Alice. Section One gave up ages ago saying there's nothing more they could do. I've no idea where she is...or if she's hurt. And in my darker moments, questioning whether she is even still alive."

Esme clasped her cup tighter. "But in answer to your question…" Ben looked up towards the large WriteAngle cafe sign just above the bar area. It was ever so slightly offset, which jarred with him. He turned back to look at Esme, then down at his hands as he continued. "I've been having this intense desire to write. I mean…I…I practically live in this place. The staff know my order like the back of their hands." Esme chuckled.

"Yes, I did note that the server told me your order before I gave it to him." Ben smiled.

"Yeah, they are good like that here. Between here and the library, I've just been writing and writing." He let out a breath. "Sheesh, I really must be obsessed."

"Either that or you're writing an epic! I mean, it must be pretty good to keep you so in the zone. Right?" She asked as she repositioned a stray strand of her hair. "So, what have you been writing?" she finished.

"Well, it's…er…it's…actually…you know what? I've absolutely no idea, and come to think of it, I've had no inclination to know till now. I just write and write, then put my Aidea in the bag, and go again the next day."

Confused would be a good word to describe Ben's face right now. Though embarrassed would be a close second.

"So, let me get this straight. You've been writing intently for several months and you do not know what you've been writing? You've seriously never read back what you've written?" Esme asked incredulously.

"I…I guess not. It obviously seems crazy, now you put it like that."

"Well, mind if we take a look now?" she quizzed. A plan was slowly coming to her, and if it was what she thought, well... she'd be even more in awe of Alice.

Slowly stretching his arm down towards his bag, he hesitated, then stopped, his hand inside his bag touching the Aidea. "I just can't understand why I've never done this before," he said, his anxiety increasing once again. "It doesn't make any sense."

Suddenly, he felt very vulnerable. Here he was with this girl whom he'd only just met, about to share potentially intensely personal prose...perhaps a brain dump of his last six months since losing Alice. no one needed to see that. Ben's palms grew sweaty.

# CHAPTER 41

## FREE WRITING

"HEY!" Exclaimed Esme, slightly louder than she'd expected, and startling Ben. "You don't have to show me anything you don't want to."

A thought crossed Ben's mind that this meeting was not serendipitous. He ignored it for now. Esme's cheeks glowed with embarrassment.

"It's OK," he said, picking up his device. "I'll have a look first, then if appropriate, I'll show you."

He held it in his hand, cautiously angling it for his viewing only. Expecting the worst—whatever that was—Ben slowly tapped the screen to view the list of files. As his finger tapped open the most recent document, he looked then,

*Thwack!*

He dropped the Aidea to the table as his hand shot to his mouth.

"What?" quizzed Esme, attempting to stay calm, her eyes flitting between the dropped Aidea and Ben. "What does it say?"

It was possible for her to have looked from the angle the Aidea had landed on the table, but she didn't, seemingly waiting for Ben to give permission. Ben was not thinking about Esme. He was still dumbfounded, his confusion growing even greater now that he'd seen what he'd written.

He glanced down again. Each line of the document contained identical words.

*Dad, I am safe. Please don't worry.*
*I love you.*
*Dad, I am safe. Please don't worry.*
*I love you.*

Slowly moving his hand away from his face, he straightened the device, then spun it around in front of Esme.

He studied her face as she read the words. Her impressed expression was impossible to miss. Her eyes sparkled with fascination and her smile stretched from ear to ear. Ben noticed she didn't seem shocked, just impressed.

Ben looked at her, wondering. She looked down at the table, away from him. Possibly a little nervous, Ben thought. Then she looked up at him.

"Ben. Look. I've got to come clean to you." He just stared at her. "I'm really sorry, but I've seen Alice. I've spoken with her…" she reported as she looked away from him, first down at her hands, then sheepishly back up to his face. "…and I can explain the message." Ben furrowed his brow, more confusion to add to his already filled plate.

"You what?" He responded, not completely sure he'd heard correctly.

"I've seen Alice," she repeated quietly. "Only once, and she's been trying to contact you…and…this is her message," she said with a touch of hesitation.

Ben still stared at her, anger rising within him. "Look, Esme… if that is even your real name. I don't know what you're playing at, but you'd better explain yourself, and quick," he spat out.

"I'm sorry. Right. Well…I am Esme, and Alice knew you were struggling and wanted to find the right moment to share important information with you. I will tell you what I know, but I fear you won't believe me."

A momentary silence drifted between them, as Ben pulled his Aidea back towards him as though motioning to leave. The thought crossed his mind.

"Just tell me," he said, sounding a little more calm.

Esme took a deep breath.

"Alice, your daughter, is no normal child, Ben," she said. "She has an ability to communicate with certain people using her mind—amongst other abilities. This last six months she's been trying to let you know that she's OK; that she loves you, but that she needs your help to escape," Esme explained.

Ben's mind went to other documents, wondering what other messages his daughter had sent him. He tapped on the screen, ignoring Esme, and selected the next document.

Esme stayed silent, watching him. One at a time, Ben opened the files. Each file contained a sentence repeated throughout the pages.

*Who is this who darkens counsel by words*
*without knowledge?*
*Who is this who darkens counsel by words*
*without knowledge?*

This one provoked a tearful smile on Ben's face. There was no mistaking her choice of verse—he knew it was Alice. Only she was there when he'd read those words to her in the library, all those years ago.

"Wait, a minute..." he said, his brow furrowing intensely as a memory flooded back.

"Haven't I just read these words in that same library? Was that also Alice?" he said out loud without realising.

"Er, you what?" quizzed Esme, not being privy to the full context in Ben's mind.

Looking more alert, he directed his gaze directly at Esme, still angry at her for not telling him straight away what was going on.

"Let's put to one side for the moment the fact you were being deceptive," he declared.

"Sorry," she mouthed.

He could see it was genuine, but he ignored her and continued.

"I was in the library...I uttered those words..." He pushed and turned the Aidea back toward Esme, pointing to the line. "... and it was like I was transported to the Complex, you know that out-of-world colony? Do you know anything about that?" he enquired, still with a touch of mistrust.

"Honestly, no. I mean, I know about the Complex, but not about some…er…portal in the library. But…" she said confidently. "…I know someone who does. She'll be able to answer all your questions."

Despite the significance of Esme's words, Ben's mind was all over the place. He kept going back to how he could write pages and pages of the same lines with no recollection of writing them.

If this was Alice's doing, despite feeling a sense of admiration for her, simultaneously he felt apprehension, and a healthy dose of fear over how much power she seemed to exert over him.

He recalled the email, or more accurately, the second attachment to the email which he'd unwittingly sent to a client all those years ago. Thankfully, they were kind enough to delete it after he explained the situation. Right now, that attachment was at the forefront of his mind.

After spending years attempting to erase it from his memory, it proved to be an exercise in futility. You see, it wasn't just the photos. No. They were bad enough.

Two pictures of Alice lying either unconscious or asleep on a surgical table in the same nightie he'd put on her that night. Her left arm was outstretched and a metallic implement was piercing her skin, implanting a tiny device in her armpit. That was the first one.

The second photo was an extreme closeup of said implantation, what the creators of the attachment were calling a mole. These images burned into his retina.

Ben felt bile rise in his throat every time he pictured them. Just the thought that someone had taken his precious little

Monkey. How vulnerable she was. Yet, while that was bad enough, the text accompanying the second image remained etched in his mind.

Written in a black box with a thin white double outline. The bold uppercase lettering made the text stand out. Ben could remember the words verbatim:

---

DO NOT ATTEMPT TO REMOVE THE MOLE.
IT IS PLACED THERE FOR THE BENEFIT OF
HUMANITY. UNDERESTIMATE HER POWER
AT YOUR PERIL

---

Esme stretched out her hand to tap the last document open and caught the words as Ben was staring down through it.

*Alice is here. Alice is here. Alice is here.*
*Alice is here. Alice is here. Alice is here.*

Esme, gave a nervous smile. "Like I said, she wants to meet you. She wasn't sure how you would react, so she sent me first. I'm really sorry if this seems like a setup, but she's been aware of how…er… negative, your thoughts have been of late and she didn't want to do anything to upset you further without reason. She needed to get a message to you and make sure you knew without a doubt it was her."

Ben, closed his eyes, clenched his teeth, then looked at his cup, both hands gripping it like it would fall apart if he let go.

"It's her all right," he whispered. "Where is she?" He asked raising his head to look past Esme.

"Like you wrote. She is here, in Sab City, but be warned, she's not quite herself. You won't be able to touch her. I know it sounds weird, but she will explain. She's waiting for us in my cafe." Ben shifted his eyes towards Esme, his brows contracting in curiosity.

"Your cafe? As in your business?" Ben queried. Esme running her own cafe was the last thing he would have imagined. He didn't doubt her abilities. She was obviously an extremely capable—not to mention a knowledgeable—person.

If he imagined her running a business, it would have been an old style book store, or perhaps managing a library like his friend Fabio.

"Yes, indeed," she replied with suitable modesty. "It will give you and Alice a bit more privacy than here. It's actually closed as it's being refurbished...so very private. As I mentioned, she's not fully herself, but...please don't be concerned. Like I say, she'll explain everything. It's a brief journey. I'll call an Auto-Jet," she relayed. "OK?" she asked hesitantly.

Ben felt a tingle down his back. Ignoring comments on Alice not being 'able to touch her' or 'not fully there,' as he wanted no more time without his beloved daughter.

'Will I really see my little Monkey again?' he thought. She wasn't dead. A warm glow radiated around his face.

Esme stood up as Ben nodded.

"Let's go," she said as they headed to the door.

# CHAPTER 42

## GET THE GIRL

"Power to do what?" proclaimed MendipT into his wrist, FalongQ having just shared with him details of an intercepted transmission. As the report continued, his expression gradually transformed from a frown to a smile, and eventually to a wide grin.

"Finally, what we've waited for. And she's in the Complex, you say?" he confirmed.

The reply from FalongQ was affirmative.

"Send me her coordinates. I need to pay a visit to this…Alice," MendipT said, dropping the connection. "First, I must reclaim my home," he muttered to himself.

Turning around, he motioned to a small group in front of him.

Since boarding the Complex, MendipT had rounded up a few others who were glad to see him, their loyalty shifting to his cause. This meant the two teams from the TransPortals could board with ease. Now MendipT's primary task was to take back the Complex, arresting it from SentiN and his cronies. 'Simple,' he thought to himself as he mentally prepared to relay his plans.

Driven by frustration, he thought about his people, stuck in stasis for too long. He saw so much potential for them. To explore other worlds, to invent and create. Instead, they had been slaves to Sendo, and not through ruthless rule. Oh, no. That was the worst part of it. You could understand a less powerful nation being enslaved through might and power. That wasn't the case with the Shumen. They were self-inflicted slaves.

He imagined piranhas in a fish tank containing a glass dividing wall. Other fish are dropped in and the piranhas make a dash for them, seeing blood...only to smash their bodies against the transparent glass wall.

Repeatedly, they try until the pain becomes unbearable. Before long, they see the fish swimming around, but instead of making a beeline for them, fulfilling their natural God given desire, they leave them be. As all they see is pain, not culinary delight.

MendipT no longer aspired to be a piranha in a straight-jacket. He wanted his people to be free.

Standing tall in the tiny and comically cramped room, he motioned with his hand for silence. The hubbub quickly ended.

"Today, we realise the potential of the Shumen. The Complex is our foundation, always. However, we can surpass this limitation. We can explore the further reaches of the galaxy to learn from others, to truly explore. We will..."

"Ahem..." said one of the others, interrupting him in full flow.

MendipT glared at him, which had no effect as he continued.

"We know this already. We're with you. Tell us what to do," he politely requested.

"Oh. OK then," replied MendipT. "I was just getting to the good bit," he said, shaking his head, slightly annoyed.

"You see, we aim to offer others the chance to change or face exclusion. Their choice is to stay with mediocrity, a pale imitation of what we Shumen can be, or join us. No longer will we be outcasts to them. We will not let SentiN destroy our tribe...."

"Ahem," another Shumen broke through, urging MendipT to get to the point. His frown reappeared.

"Yes, yes. The main point is their greater number compared to us. But that is not a problem because...."

He paused dramatically, looking at each of the faces in front of him, before almost whispering,

"...we have a secret weapon."

He smiled, still watching the group, who were now dead silent, transfixed. He swept his hand across, as though ushering in his prize, as he continued in a hushed tone. "A weapon so powerful, we can end the war for good. And that weapon...is on the Complex. I will say no more for now, but believe me, we have already won."

The room erupted with shouts and cheers.

"Now, that's what we want to hear!" said the Shumen who'd first spoken up, now wearing a beaming smile.

MendipT lowered his hands, and their volume decreased. Pre-empting their queries, he continued, "I know you will have questions about our weapon. I know you will wonder what it is, how we will use it, and I will give you answers. But first, we must convert as many as we can to our cause," he added.

Looking around at the Shumen before him, he issued an order.

"Head to the dining rooms. I want over fifty percent turned when I'm back with our weapon. We will win. We are the Shumen!"

The small number clapped and whistled at MendipT's rousing speech and they immediately left the room to enact the plan.

MendipT grabbed three volunteers just before they left.

"I need you three to come with me to meet this weapon," he said.

They followed him without question, heading first toward the Central Gardens. His sole focus: get the girl. She was the key to their salvation.

Until he knew about Alice, the extent of his plan was to get rid of SentiN. He would worry about Sendo—their landlords, later. But having heard some of the girl's power, well...if he could harness this and use it against Sendo, that would be phase two.

It hadn't crossed his mind whether Alice would be co-operative. But he didn't care about that presently. He just needed to get to her. In his mind, everything else would fall into place.

His wrist buzzed as he accepted a call.

"Can you confirm you intercepted the previous transmission?" said a strong male voice.

"We did. We know of her power and that she's in the Complex," replied MendipT.

"Well…" said the man. "I can tell you she is currently located in one of the pods in the Haven. Here is the access code." Another buzz as MendipT looked at his wrist displaying the twelve character code.

"Received," he confirmed.

"Now go!" said Charles Orthon Bannon as he cut the call.

He could have supplied MendipT with the specific pod number Alice was in, but that didn't suit his plan. If Esme and Ben arrived to rescue Alice simultaneously as MendipT, their confrontation would allow Charles to instruct SentiN's Shumen to sneak her out.

If Esme, Ben, and MendipT were destroyed, well, that was a minor problem. Although a growing part of him would struggle with what it would do to Margaret.

MendipT wanted to ask which pod Alice was in, but the call cut abruptly. Now he needed to focus on getting to the Haven, for which he would have to pass around the Central Gardens; the larger family quarters and multi-purpose rooms, the armoury and dining area, before getting through the bulk-head, opening into the Haven. All without being spotted by SentiN and his team.

But it was frustrating not knowing exactly which pod Alice was housed in. Each of the thirteen pods was a decent distance apart. It would not be a five-minute job.

Walking rather than running so as not to bring attention to themselves, MendipT's crew traversed the staff quarters. FalongQ's contingent was a little distance ahead, currently heading in the same direction.

It crossed MendipT's mind as to how many Shumen would really turn. Over fifty percent, he'd said, but being really honest, he questioned how realistic that was.

Deep down, he knew how people worked. Although most said they wanted freedom—to accept responsibility and self-determination over their own lives and that of their families—ultimately in practice, they wanted to be told what to do. Sheep.

MendipT was hoping Alice could change that. He just didn't know how.

# CHAPTER 43

## REACQUAINTED

The door to the cafe opened. A chill wind blew throughout the room, dragging napkins to the floor. A young girl walked in, although, glided, would be a better description. Alice looked like a normal human being to the naked eye. Only on very close inspection could a subtle shimmer be seen indicating she was in the process of bilocation.

Alice's secondary self was much more limited. She could press buttons, move small objects, open some doors. However, coming into constant physical contact with another human being drained her primary body of even more energy.

Esme stood and walked to the counter, ready to make more drinks.

"No" said Alice. Looking over to Esme. "We won't be staying."

"Really? I thought this was a good private place for you to get reacquainted," Esme questioned.

"I know, and thanks for suggesting your place. I appreciate it, but the plan has sped up. We need to get to my ship quickly so I can show Dad what I can do as we head to the Complex. Can you order an AutoJet?" Esme nodded.

"I'll get one ready. Can you guys wait outside whilst I close up, then?" Esme asked, while shutting down the remaining machines.

"Sure. And thanks again." Alice replied as she turned to Ben.

"Don't mention it," said Esme.

This moment held great significance for Ben, though he was unsure how to react. Up to this point, Alice had smiled at him, but she hadn't addressed him yet. Here was his daughter...she certainly looked like his daughter...but she seemed incredibly grown up.

Had it only been six months since he saw her beautiful face in the museum? 'It's like she's been gone twelve years, not six months!' He thought.

After admin with Esme, Alice turned her gaze to her father.

"Hi, Dad," she whispered, her face displaying an embarrassed smile.

Ben walked up to his daughter and was about to enclose her in the warmest embrace possible before he stopped himself, remembering what Esme had said.

"I'm so sorry, Dad. Hopefully Esme's explained that I can't touch you at the moment, right?" Ben nodded, his eyes becoming slightly red.

"Hi, Monkey. What's happened to you? How are you here... but not?" he asked.

"Let's talk outside," she said as she headed for the door, beckoning him to follow her.

She stood by the door as Ben opened it for her and they stepped outside in front of the cafe window. Ben glanced at Esme as she was finishing up.

Alice said wearily, "There's so much I need to tell you, Dad," as she tried to think where best to start.

"Are you here for good?" asked Ben, concerned he would lose her again.

"No. To cut a very long story short for now, I am being held in the Complex, and I need you and Esme to rescue me."

"But I don't understand. How are you..." he started to ask, then, searching for the right term, continued, "...here? How is that even possible? You can't be a hologram, as you really look like you're here. I know the ComTel holograms are pretty good these days, but this...this is something else."

Alice smiled and glanced at the ground, then back at her father.

"Remember those times when you were testing me? You were convinced objects I was touching were getting hotter. You thought I wasn't aware of your tests."

"You were only three! Do you seriously remember that?" He asked curiously.

"Yes. The fact is, I remember most things. But to answer your question, the easiest way to explain it is like you're seeing a projection of myself, with an invisible projector that's able to send its signal through the air." She stroked her cheek. "It's not really that, but that's the best way I can explain how you see me right now, when I'm actually sitting in the Complex."

Ben studied the image he saw in front of him of his daughter. The resolution was extremely high, and it didn't take a genius to know, if it was a projection, the bandwidth required to send a signal of that quality would be humongous.

He nodded and as he did, an AutoJet arrived in front of them. Esme exited the cafe, locked up, smiling at them both.

"Come on," she said.

Alice and Ben got in the back whilst Esme sat in front as the AutoJet headed away from the building.

Alice looked at Ben. Ben looked at Alice, studying each other's face. There was an uncomfortable silence for a few moments whilst they once again got used to each other. Ben looked sad. He had so many questions about how Alice was treated.

"What did they do to you?" he whispered to her, breaking the silence and trying to control his vivid imagination.

"I know it's gonna sound absurd, but they've actually treated me well...I mean, aside from kidnapping me and locking me up, of course," Alice replied matter-of-factly. Ben raised an eyebrow.

"Is that supposed to be funny?" He snapped.

"Oh chill, it's..." Alice retorted.

"Hey young lady, don't forget I'm still your father," he snapped back, but recognising it must be strange for her, obviously having so much to deal with. He gave her grace.

"Sorry, Dad. I'll start from the museum. Time is limited. We'll be there shortly."

Alice explained about the boy used to lure her away and the

two guys who had captured her, though they'd felt genuinely sorry they had to do it.

"So what happened then?" Asked Ben. "I looked for you for ages after that," he sniffed, struggling to control his emotions.

He composed himself as Alice responded.

"I know. I know. When they informed you I was taken to the hospital, I could see you on a monitor. I was powerless, unable to act. They kept me until the museum closed, then put a blindfold on me and led me to a TransPortal. I must have fallen asleep, as when I awoke the vehicle had stopped and I was led to the room I'm in right now. It's cosy, to say the least," she said, not wanting to describe it fully to make Ben worry more.

"There is a man who brings me food and...he's actually working for us to rescue me," she explained.

"Really? Who is he? How do you know he's...trying to rescue you?" Ben asked, trying not to elicit too much hope.

"Well, I think you can tell me what he's like...give him a character assessment. You met him when you went to the Complex," Alice replied.

Ben looked down at the floor in the AutoJet, his bag between his legs as his brow creased.

"How did you know that?" he queried.

"Dad, I set up the portal for you in the Library. I know you would go to that Bible and read those words. It was a perfect trigger," Alice replied.

"I don't know how you did that, Alice, but if it helps to get you back, then I don't care," Ben said with joy in his heart. So much joy to see his little monkey again.

# CHAPTER 44

## FAINT SHIMMER

Esme smiled as she brushed her hand through her hair, looking back in the mirror at Ben.

She couldn't really see Alice from this angle. Ben's mind went to the other files on his Aidea that he'd never thought to look at until Esme mentioned it.

"Hey. I have to ask you about controlling my mind. How did you do that? I mean, I was glad when Esme got me to look at what I'd written, and I knew for certain it was you. But that's some power," he cautiously admitted.

"I know," she replied, all too aware of the immense energy that was coursing through her body—her real one at least. She shook her head.

"I'm still learning what I'm capable of. I did question how ethical this was. But I came to two conclusions. One: that if God has blessed me with these gifts, that I have a responsibility to use it wisely, and two: that contacting you was a responsible use of it and that, if you didn't agree...initially..." she hesitated as she stumbled to finish her sentence, "...you would forgive me."

She glanced at her father, then turned her attention to the window, watching the buildings rush by, hoping she had made the right choice.

"So do you?" She asked.

Ben's expression was subdued before slowly a big smile appeared.

"Of course I do, Monkey. I won't hide the fact it's pretty unnerving knowing that you can control my thinking..."

"Well, not exactly controlling your thinking," Alice interrupted. "You are already in a suggestible state when you're writing, so think of it as more influencing rather than controlling. If you weren't feeling so understandably anxious, your mind would have fought back and simply would not have allowed me to control it."

"You mean influenced?" Ben jumped in.

"Yes, yes. Of course, influenced, of course," Alice replied, quickly agreeing with the correction. Ben noted her reaction and filed it mentally under *deal with later*.

She quickly wanted to move the conversation on, away from how this was making her feel. She didn't understand everything about her powers. Despite her vast abilities, she felt she could achieve so much more. But something was limiting her.

Her body gave a faint shimmer as the projection fought to stay separate from the leather seats.

"But back to this man, Charles, who's helping us. You've met him," she reminded him.

"Oh yes. What a strange man. He talked to me like he was pitying me and my lack of knowledge." 'Kind of like you have been doing,' he thought to himself. "He failed to grasp the sheer strangeness of the situation for me, never having been to the Complex before and having no idea how I ended up there.

"Was he kind?" Alice asked.

"Er...Well, he fed me and did attempt to answer my questions," Ben replied, passing his hands through his hair.

Alice's projection seemed to sit back in the vehicle. Preparing herself for another major thing she needed to tell her father. And this wasn't even the biggest. She was still thinking how best to share that one.

"So, Dad. When you went to the library and entered the portal, you didn't go to the actual Complex." Ben was even more puzzled now.

"You what? I was there. I saw it myself; went in several rooms—not that I'd remember how to get around." Alice let him finish, then continued.

"You were in LeV8. It was the latest, most accurate LinerVerse version of the Complex."

She paused, giving him time to process.

"We did that, as it was easier to get you familiar with the Complex without transporting you there, which, as you'll see shortly, would have taken more time," she relayed.

"But how is that possible?" Ben wondered, screwing up his face in confusion. "I was at the library and then at the Complex. There was no obvious transition, and I didn't use a headset or even an NCep device at that point."

Alice's gaze shifted downward, then upward towards her father, her growing power becoming harder and harder to explain.

"I know. It's another thing I found I could do—connect people to the LinerVerse—well, only LeV8. The previous versions aren't advanced enough," she reported.

"So let me get this straight," Ben mused. "When I connected in the old man's room, was I connecting to the LinerVerse inside the LinerVerse?" He quizzed, trying desperately to get his head around it.

"It's kind of difficult to explain. Once you're in the Liner-Verse, you can't actually connect in again. You're just entering a different mode. It's a bit like switching from game to game, not playing a game within a game. A better analogy is like watching a HolloSense. You can switch channels, but it's the same HoloSense," Alice explained.

It was a lot to take in. Ben's head started hurting. Rubbing it didn't seem to help, though he gave it a good go. He pulled out a water bottle from his bag and drank. Alice, glanced at her father. She pursed her bilocated lips as she shimmered.

"Do you remember how you got back to the Library?" she asked.

"Well, that's the thing. I've no idea. As I found myself in the LinerVerse, a bright light caught my attention and I instinctively moved towards it. I don't know whether I fell asleep, but the next thing I saw were the bookshelves back in the library," he reported.

Alice smiled.

"That was you too, right?" Ben guessed, with not a small amount of pride in his daughter.

"Yes, Dad. I created the light as a link to a portal...Hold on a minute," Alice said, her bilocated body again shimmering, but this time growing faint. "I've got to check something. I'll be right back," and with that, she disappeared from the seat beside Ben.

Esme, listening to everything, turned round to Ben.

"It'll be fine. She'll be back shortly. She's probably just doing something that took too much of her energy to bilocate," she said, not that she knew much more about Alice's gift.

"Er...OK," was Ben's muted response, his face looking sullen. But before he could think whether he'd see his daughter again, she reappeared.

"I'm back!" she beamed, appearing almost as quickly as she left. "Our mutual friend Charles just brought me some food. He said to say hello."

'How is this all possible?' Ben kept thinking.

"Great. Say 'Hi' back!" he mused.

The AutoJet cruised round a bend, heading for an abandoned airport on the outskirts of Sab City. It pulled off onto a long and windy side road. Obviously a private access route that you wouldn't really notice unless you knew about it.

There were no other vehicles around. Tall conifer trees lined both sides of the road. Many meeting in the middle, creating a tunnel like effect, making it even more private, and dark as the early evening took over.

"Where are we going?" Ben had been too delighted to see his daughter again to ask this earlier.

"I need to take you to the real Complex. In the hangar we're heading to is my TransPortal. There's more stuff I can show you there." She looked away, biting her lip. "It's another thing where I don't know how you'll react, but I just have to do it, regardless. It's the only way to get me out."

There it was again. He seemed to be the twelve-year-old with Alice playing the parent.

"Just show me what you have to," he said calmly, trying to control his inevitable emotions.

"Right now we have a few minutes, and I need to tell you about the Shumen," Alice instructed.

"Charles told me about them, about some war that was starting…"

"Well, it's been going on for decades, though it only hit the mainstream media recently as it seems to be coming to a head. I don't know for sure, but we think a group of Shumen who'd previously left the Complex against Sendo's advice, have now infiltrated it again."

"Yes, he said that," Ben interjected.

"…and…" she continued. "…what he probably didn't mention was that they have likely found out about me."

Ben grew tense.

"What does that mean? Will they come after you? Are you safe where you are now?" he asked, concern growing.

Alice remained calm as she explained,

"My powers are growing, Dad. Shortly, you'll see this when we get to the TransPortal. I don't know exactly how they found out about me…or…" she rubbed her hands together nervously. "…or what they intend to do. Honestly, I don't even want to consider it at the moment. We're talking far bigger than just the Complex. This might affect Earth and other local planets, too," she urged.

"Sarah and Nathan mentioned this during our study. Nath said about them targeting Sendo bases on Earth. Do you know any more than that?" he enquired.

Alice's mind went to Sarah and Nathan, then thought of Dauphina and Simon. Eager to reunite with them, her excitement was heightened by the thought of seeing her best friend Sabine. She had to remain strong. She didn't have time to dwell on that right now.

"Monkey?" Ben pleaded.

"Sorry. I don't know any more than that. Though, if they do know about my powers, they'll stop at nothing to get to me," she cautioned.

Ben pushed himself right back into the seat, sitting fully upright.

"We will not let that happen," he said resolutely. "Tell me what you need from me to get you home?"

The AutoJet arrived at the empty airport, right on cue, with no TransPortals or people in sight. They glided past the entrances of several vast hangars before stopping, then reversing into one. The AutoJet came to a final stop right nearby a pile of wooden crates.

Esme looked in the mirror at Alice. She flashed her a smile, then got out. After opening Alice's side door, she headed away on foot behind the crates, disappearing out of Ben's sight. Ben looked at his daughter. She sat up straighter, switching on her *authority* mode.

"Dad, I need you to realise your own power," she stated.

"You what?" he replied, as confused as ever.

"Come on," she said. "Rather than try to explain, I'll show you."

# CHAPTER 45

## THE FEAST

Following MendipT's rousing speech, FalongQ lead a small group of Shumen toward the main dining area. The group's excitement was still palpable. A sizeable portion of their fellow citizens, would most likely be in that area. Shumen loved their food and almost always ate together.

FalongQ and his team entered the room via a solid grey door and immediately observed at least fifty Shumen sitting around in what was a deceptively large space. The delicious aroma of food wafted towards them, and at least one stomach could be heard growling. FalongQ wasn't sure whose it was, but absent-mindedly he rubbed his own stomach as he tried to keep on track and ignore the delightful smell.

A vast doughnut shaped table lay at the centre of the room. Sitting on both sides, their colleagues, friend, or foe, indulged in a delightful spread. The sound of chewing and swallowing and those satisfied stomach-full moans filled the air.

FalongQ, looked at his small renegade group, motioning with his eyes where he was going to go.

He then walked confidently, straight through a gap in the table to the centre of the throng. The chattering and munching paused as he slowly turned, observing the whole table. They waited for him to speak.

"We have a message: MendipT is back. He offers you the opportunity to follow him. He has grand plans for the Complex. Will you join us?" he said in a raised voice. Not quite shouting, but close.

"SentiN is our leader," said one Shumen, sounding frustrated and sitting furthest away from FalongQ.

"No, he isn't," another chimed in, with equal frustration. "We should have gone with MendipT when we had the chance," he continued.

"Well, why didn't you?" the other retorted, leaning back in his chair.

"To be honest, we don't know," he replied honestly. "But we really wish we had," he said, looking disconsolate and staring at the table.

"There's nothing wrong with what we've got here. We don't need MendipT's meddling," the first Shumen snapped back.

FalongQ listened to the murmurs, assessing which side most people aligned to. He couldn't completely decide, so he repeated.

"As I said, it is a choice. You can stay here, or join with us as we arrest the Complex from SentiN and embrace what it really means to be a Shumen," he said before thinking, 'Should I provide further details about the plan?' Trouble was, he didn't know the entire plan, and mentioning 'the weapon,' would most-likely complicate things. So he kept it at that.

"OK," chirped a youthful voice sitting closer to FalongQ. "I'll come with you," and he got up, taking his food tray, walking over to the shelves and placed it there. This was soon followed by the sound of chairs scraping on the floor as several others copied him, taking their trays to the shelves and tidying up.

FalongQ smiled. He shot a look at his group before heading to the door, waiting for the tidy up job to be completed. He furrowed his brow, wondering if he should issue a message for them to hurry. Most of the room was now clearing up, even the Shuman who'd sided with SentiN.

'I thought it was going to be more difficult than this,' FalongQ said to himself. As if hearing his thoughts, one of the eating group looked up at him.

"We know SentiN is pretty facile. We would have come with you first time round, but didn't want to take the risk," she said.

"Is it the same for all of you?" FalongQ queried, pointing his head to the rest of the Shumen.

There were many nodding heads.

"In this room, at least," she replied. "You will find others not so cooperative."

FalongQ addressed his cohort. "Perhaps that's where we should go next."

Turning to the same woman, he asked, "Where would we find that contingent?"

"The seventeenth room, living quarters past the Gardens," she said as she brushed down her dress, then put her arm around her two young children standing next to her. "What do we do now?" she asked, with all those around also eager to hear the answer.

FalongQ, again looked around at everyone, gauging the mood of the room. They couldn't all follow him to the bridge. Scratching his chin, he said, "I suggest you speak to everyone you know. Let them know what's happening and convince them to follow MendipT. Those of you willing, come with us. We hope there won't be bloodshed, but you have to be prepared." He paused, before issuing, "We're going to the bridge to face off SentiN." Murmurs persisted, as the room emptied, many going their own way to share the news, and a group of mostly men followed closely behind FalongQ.

Alice stepped out of the car, a faint glow subtly appearing around her bilocated self. She beckoned Ben to do the same. They followed the path where Esme had gone. One of the large containers was open, the two solid doors having slid left and right into the frame.

Ben walked up to it, feeling the rough texture under his fingertips, and tapped the side. 'It must have been iron or something,' he thought. 'It's completely solid.'

The darkness inside made it impossible to see. Alice glided past Ben into the crate. He followed her in, noticing a rumbling sound as the two doors closed behind him with the sound of metal grating on metal.

Ben's nostrils detected a subtle coppery smell, transporting him to a time as a kid when he was covered in oil and grease. Copper parts: nuts, bolts, washers, screws, nails, and some items he'd not a clue about were spread all over the floor in the garage. His dad's antique motorbike would never function as a bike again. Ben's posterior also required some time to recover and resume its regular functioning.

Alice stood in front of what seemed to be a control panel, as Ben observed a glow appearing around his daughter's bilocated body. As the only light source in the large container, she was getting brighter and brighter. To Ben, the scene before him resembled the nostalgic Ready Break commercials he watched as a child on the archive channels.

When the doors to the crate had fully closed, there was silence, a deafening silence which seemed to apply a tonne of pressure to Ben's ears. Another low frequency murmur could be heard. Very faint at first, but slowly increasing in volume. Ben was stationary, staring at Alice. The yellow glow appeared to have stopped, getting brighter. Her eyes were closed, arms by her side. It looked like she was sleeping in an upright position. Then suddenly her arms flung out towards Ben, then slowly fell, gracefully, back to her sides.

A tingling sensation traveled across Ben's body as he shivered. It was as if there was a visible aura surrounding him, outlining his figure.

As he was thinking about cartoon caricatures, he looked down at his arms. The tingling sensation grew stronger. 'What's happening?' He thought. 'My arms...they're glowing!' And sure enough, just as Alice had glowed, the same thing was happening to Ben.

He panicked. Alice was looking so peaceful, yet anxiety was growing within him at this strange, completely unknown experience to him.

His heart sped up as he repeated his mantra:

"Be still and know that You are God. Be still and know that You are God."

His breathing slowed as he regained control in the way his counsellor had taught him over many months. Soon his whole body was glowing. The rumbling sound was not quite deafening, but still loud.

Ben put his arms by his side, mimicking Alice. His body was stiff. Then Alice spoke.

"Do you understand what's happening, Dad?" Her voice resonated with a heavenly quality—or how Ben imagined the angel that spoke to Mary announcing the impending birth of Christ—had sounded.

Despite Alice standing in front of Ben, her voice enveloped him from every direction, as if she surrounded his head. Still with his eyes closed, Ben responded.

"It feels like we're taking off," he said.

"That's right. From one perspective, the crate is moving. Yet, it has shown no movement from another perspective. We are going to the Complex. I need you to do something for me. Esme is there already. We'll meet her and then go see Charles," she informed.

"OK. But why are we glowing?" asked Ben, struggling to comprehend, but remaining focused on the present.

"I'm controlling the ship. To do that, my mind connects with it. It is simply an avatar. It looks like a crate—as that's convenient. But it is a living organism, in some ways not too dissimilar from ourselves. If you could look on the outside, you would see that it is glowing too. Our neural pathways are connected. As I think, so it does. This ship responds only to me..."

Alice hesitated as she thought about saying the next bit. "...and you."

"Me?" said a surprised Ben.

"Yes. As you and I share 50 percent of our DNA, it will respond in part to you, too. That's why you're glowing. I still had to give it permission, but once I did, it means you can control it too, once you know how."

Ben, still with his eyes closed, provided no further response. A fleeting thought passed through his head, suggesting the way Alice was talking was very much like Charles.

"How are you feeling?" asked Alice, checking all was well with her father.

"Actually OK. I feel slightly tired, but otherwise fine," he said.

"Good. We'll have time to rest later," she consoled.

As Ben was listening to his daughter, taking in the awesome power she had; from the ability to essentially possess him and control what he wrote, to the ability to physically move certain objects—in this case as large as the crate they were currently in, hurtling through the air—to being able to be in two places at once via her bilocation process, he couldn't help but have a sense of foreboding.

This is a lot of power for anyone, yet alone a twelve-year-old girl...his, twelve-year-old girl. What were the potential consequences of such immense power? 'It didn't work out well for Frodo,' he mused, then suddenly remembering the email:

"UNDERESTIMATE HER POWER AT YOUR PERIL."

'Why was I given that warning? If she can do all this now, what would she be like if the mole was removed?' he thought.

He continued subtly, allowing his curiosity to wrap him up in knots.

"So, what else can you do? What other powers do you possess?" Alice's face held a quizzical expression. Smiling, she raised her eyebrow and quipped,

"You mean, neurally connecting with this ship, and controlling it by thought and traveling through space, all whilst bilocating from the Complex is not enough for you?"

Ben smiled. "When you put it like that..."

She reverted to her authoritative self as she explained,

"The actual power I have is the power to end this. The power to stop the Shumen from attacking each other. To broker peace before a full out war begins. I..." she said, then hesitated. Her bilocated form looked toward the ground, though her eyes were still closed whilst she controlled the ship.

"I...just don't know how," she finished.

"How do you know you can, if you don't know how?" Ben asked.

"I just do. It's hard to explain," she said, knowing her conviction was solid. "I feel it and am totally convinced it's my purpose. The Shumen conflict has been so long fought that some are just resigned to it being that way forever. It's few people like Charles, Margaret, and Esme, who have a full belief that this can end. They believe in me...at least, I know Esme and Margaret do," she enquired.

She paused. There was silence for a few moments before, in almost a whisper, she asked her father, "What do you think?"

Ben opened his eyes for the first time since he started glowing. Taking a deep breath, he raised his head to look on lovingly at his daughter.

"That's a tough question for me to answer. I'm only now discovering all of this. I haven't met the Shumen, so I will not be the best judge of what they are like...or capable of."

Ben's forehead furrowed as his mouth curved into a smile. Despite his concerns, he felt so proud looking at his daughter right now.

"But what I can say is that I believe in you. You are my little Monkey. It seemed like I had lost you forever. I promised your mother I would look after you and protect you. I failed. If you say you can bring about peace in this situation, I believe you, and I will do whatever it takes to help you achieve that. I pray to God that I never lose you again."

'This annoying bilocation!', she thought, as tears filled her eyes.

"Thank you, Dad," she sobbed. "Thank you."

PART THREE

# CHAPTER 46

## ESCAPE PLAN

2163 - Present day

"What's that?" asked SentiN, leaning casually on the headrest of the left of two pilot stations on the bridge of the Complex. You would have thought he would be more concerned having just heard two sharp pulses, followed by explosions coming from somewhere on the ship. Not SentiN.

"I don't know. I'll check the scanner," replied one of his colleagues, who was standing pressing buttons at the immense curved control panel. The panel looked like it was made of white granite but with a faint fibrous texture embedded within it—like many of the surfaces around the Complex.

It was beautiful to look at, though sparse. Purple and red buttons, switches, and displays were spread liberally throughout the full curvature of the desk, but the most striking detail was that of several large circular cut-outs containing what could only be described as human brains.

The gyri and sulci were clear to see, marking the sections of the brain-like object they called the Cerebro. However, it was much softer to touch. These controls, though minimal, provided immense amounts of data on nearly every aspect of the Complex.

SentiN wandered over to the commander seat, raised higher behind the pilot stations, trying to decipher what exactly happened.

Leaning on the back of the seat, he asked the Shuman occupying the right pilot station, "Can you give me an assessment?"

Removing his hand from the organic cerebro, the colleague responded with resignation.

"I'm unable to sense anything through our network." He sunk his hand into the next brain-like control along, his fingers delving deep into its surface, yet remaining dry. "There must be a malfunction," he continued. "However...initial reports indicate two impacts on the left side of Annex B. That's all we know currently."

SentiN sighed, sitting himself down, still contemplating what —if anything—he should do.

His view of the bridge was vast, but quite empty. There were two other colleagues with him. The station had a distinctly clinical ambiance throughout. Just like the desk, the walls had an off-white colour with a faint fibrous texture. The fibres could be seen clearly when light fell directly on them and seemed to pulse like a living organism.

The Complex itself was shaped like an igloo with an annex on either side. Ironically, it was not especially complex in its structure. Within the bridge, there were pools of light in key areas, but the ambient light was low. Shumen, especially those born on the Complex (which by now was the majority), were naturally adapted to this, having greater ocular sensitivity.

One Shumen, who was first on the scene, appeared in front of SentiN via ComTel. His hologram reported,

"We've been having trouble with our comms."

As he said that, he momentarily vanished, and reappeared with some horizontal lines of the display missing, making it look like he'd been sliced in several places. He continued.

"There appears to be structural damage to three rooms to the left side of Annex B. The panels have been destroyed. We will need a repair team to fix this, but it could take a while with the comms issue. We've definitely been fired at."

"But why would that cause our comms to malfunction?" SentiN queried.

"The impact and residue on the walls indicate a cannon of some form, and that it was directed specifically at the control panels. Whoever did this knew exactly what they were doing. They wanted to cause maximum disruption with minimal effort. The panels are the key control units for the comms rooms, which is why we are now having problems with comms," he informed, just before disappearing again.

SentiN scratched his head. He looked worried. His thoughts momentarily went to MendipT and the fun they used to have together growing up. It was always a good natured rivalry. They were so different, yet the same. He was much more reserved, but quietly confident. An ideas guy. Well...he certainly used to have lots of ideas, but as to making them happen, he struggled. Not a completer-finisher. MendipT, on the other hand, was always taking action.

He smiled as he remembered a time when, as young Shumen, he'd always been talking about borrowing a TransPortal and flying out of the base. Having only just learnt to fly, his youthful exuberance had actually led him to want to explore. How times change. Conversely, MendipT didn't talk about it. He just did it. Naturally, he was caught and disciplined, but SentiN always secretly wished it had been him with the courage to make it happen.

"Are you sure it's them?" SentiN asked despondently. Despite no one having suggested that as yet, everyone was aware of the possibility.

"Yes. They are the only ones who know our systems well enough to connect internally and cause such damage. They've done it before—albeit not on this scale," the colleague replied.

SentiN stroked his chin, then said almost to himself, "Yes. I guess it was only a matter of time."

Charles sat upright in his tall chair. His office was the Guardians' quarters, where he spent the majority of his time when not liaising with the Shumen. He was supposed to keep his interactions with them as minimal as possible at any rate.

Like many of the rooms on the Complex, it was large but not filled. Space was something surprisingly they had a lot of. You would have thought that for a ship in space, space was at a premium. You can't just build an extension whenever you feel like it.

However, very little actual hardware was present on board the Complex. The Guardian's office was a typical example. The room was circular, located bang in the centre of the Haven toward the back of the ship.

It comprised a lounge area containing a long table, as well as a small kitchen area. The office area where Charles was presently sitting was sparse, containing a ComTel unit directly in front of him, positioned on top of a Cerebro control deck.

A light was flashing on the ComTel. Charles waved his hand in front of it and a woman's voice was heard out of the speakers.

"Hello, Mr Bannon." The display indicated the connection was encrypted with a different signature than he was used to.

'Interesting,' he thought. "Hello. Who is this?" he asked pointedly.

"It's Esme. I believe you are expecting us?" the woman replied confidently.

"Ah, Esme." He sat back, his shoulders dropping. "What a delight, as always. Yes, your mother filled me in on the plan, though I gather we have a few gaps?"

"Affirmative," she responded, noticing that whenever she spoke with Charles, she seemed to mirror his personality, speaking more assertively, and abruptly, than she was used to. "I'm hoping you can help us fill them."

"So am I. But first, I notice you are using a different encryption key. Are you sure we are not being monitored? I'm sure you know we have reason to believe my conversation with your mother the other day was intercepted."

"Yes, she told me. I have used a patching program configured with an encryption algorithm Shumen do not have access to. There's no way they will be intercepting this channel," Esme replied with complete confidence.

Charles was not aware, that, as well as running her own cafe and being an expert researcher, Esme had highly desirable skills in cyber security. She must have kept this quiet, as her mother had not mentioned anything.

"Impressive," he said.

"Yes, I know," she said matter-of-factly. "But we have little time. We need to move fast. So how do I get in unnoticed and where is she being held?" she asked.

"You'll have to come to docking bay one on Annex A. This is the least busy, but you will need to be disguised. I'm currently the only non-Shumen on the Complex. They don't appear to know about Alice, so anyone else might cause a disturbance," Charles relayed.

"Hmmm...If we can communicate with Alice, she can create a diversion," Esme said, more in hope than a promise.

"OK. Leave that with me," he confirmed. "Unfortunately, she is being held in a pod connected to the Haven at the far end of the Complex. It's difficult for us to get to. We'll have to choose our time carefully, as I'm sure you know that everything in the Complex is connected. To be unnoticed is going to be very difficult."

"Well, leave that one to me," she said, mimicking the old man. "If you can create a diversion when I arrive, I'll sort out how to get in without being seen. So now, what's the best time to come?" she asked, hurrying things along as quickly as she could.

"There are always supplies that come in from Contextua every third day. The next one is tomorrow. I will get in to see Alice today and have everything set up. The supply ship gets here around noon. I'll make sure we're ready," said Charles.

"So that's the easy bit," Esme said with a touch of sarcasm. "Now, how do we get Alice out?"

Charles was the only person on the Complex that knew about Alice and where she was, apart from his recent interaction with MendipT.

He knew that getting her out should be the simple part. At least getting her out of the pod. Transporting her back across the main section of the Complex through the bulkhead, past the armoury and dining areas—hoping few people will be around—and getting her onto a TransPortal, that part would not be quite so easy.

"I will bring her with me after I come to collect her food tray. I will disguise her in some way. You can then get her out by following the supply craft staff. If we time it right, they will be on their way back to their ship and we can simply follow them out. Then you can get Alice to your ship and leave." It sounded so simple when he explained it like that.

"Sounds like a plan," confirmed Esme. "But what about you? You said, take Alice and leave. Are you not coming with us?" she asked, with genuine concern.

Charles studied the floor. They were still on voice call only, though he could sense her concern. After a brief pause, he replied, "I'm needed here. If we are going to sort this problem out, or at least try to broker peace, Sendo will need me to liaise with the Shumen. I have to see this through."

"Fair enough, I suppose..." Esme replied.

Whilst Charles always got on amicably with Esme, he could tell she kept her distance, possibly because of his closeness with her mother. But he couldn't be certain if it was that or something else.

"...and it will be good to still have a contact on the inside," she said, then paused. He heard her take a deep breath before asking, "But what happens if they find out it was you that got her out?"

He pursed his lips. He didn't like it when others worried about him. "Let me deal with that. You just focus on rescuing her," he consoled.

Charles knew she would be concerned, knowing it could be the last time she heard from him, but there was nothing he could do about that.

"OK. So that's everything we need. Wish us luck," Esme said, her voice sounding positive.

"I don't believe in luck," Charles retorted. "There's a 92 percent probability we won't succeed. Let's focus on the final 8 percent." Inevitably, he would have calculated all eventualities.

Esme responded, "Great. 8 percent. Let's do this."

# CHAPTER 47

## PANIC ATTACK

Ben looked out the window. Was it a window or a display screen? He wasn't sure. Either way, now his eyes were permanently open, he observed the vast expanse of space with the faint glow of the Complex in the distance. He thought back to the portal in the library Alice had set up for him.

"You know, it always reminds me of her," he said wistfully.

"What does, Dad?" Alice replied.

"Those verses from Job, that you used as a trigger. She loved that passage almost as much as me. I loved hearing her read it aloud. It was very cathartic and awe-inspiring at the same time." Alice smiled.

"Oh," she said, not finding anything better to say.

"Yeah. I'm glad to have such fond memories, and even though she was taken so young, I have no regrets—aside from..." He trailed off, not completely sure if he wanted to finish the sentence, "...I wish you could have gotten to know her. I can't tell you how much alike you are. There's so much of her in you."

"I wish I could have known her more, too. I think about her a lot, wondering what she would think of me now," Alice pondered.

"Hey, Monkey, she would be immensely proud of you. You're so grown up. You act older, and more responsible, than me sometimes!" Ben replied.

"Yeah, but you know that's because of my powers, Dad, right?" she questioned.

"Yes. But it's still your choice to use them wisely and responsibly, and you've chosen to do that. no one else but you. For that, Lydia would have been so proud," he said, gazing at his daughter. "And, by the way," he continued, his cheeks glowing with natural emotion, "it makes me incredibly proud, too."

Alice moved towards the control panel, her heart pounding, longing to embrace her dad, but her intangible holographic form frustratingly prevented any physical contact.

A little yellow light flashed on and off.

"We're nearly here," she whispered, dragging her emotions back to her leader self. "I have to tell you that this part is going to be a little tricky."

"Why, what's up?" Ben asked, his brows furrowing in confusion.

"We are going to the Complex as we need to rescue the real me. As I mentioned, Esme has gone on ahead of us and we'll meet her shortly at the docking station. She will take over from there, and I will have to go," Alice explained.

"Go where?" Asked Ben, having only just reunited with his daughter.

"My powers are weakening. I've been bilocating for too long, and if I don't have you near me, I will grow faint. Again, I can't tell you why, but you have to trust me," she pleaded.

Alice didn't want to keep keeping things from her dad, but she also felt it would be better for him the less he knew. If he was caught with his panic attacks, she knew it would be a field day for the Shumen. They would force him to tell them everything. She couldn't risk that—not for herself, Esme, the old man, and for Ben himself.

"Well, I'm not going anywhere. I'll be with you all the way. What do you need me to do?" he asked.

"When we dock, as I said, Esme will meet us. However, we will have to move fast. I need to give you some information that you have to pass on to her immediately when you see her. There are thirteen pods at the back of the Complex. I will be in pod seven. OK?"

"But I thought you would be with me. Why do you need me to pass this on?" queried Ben, still not fully understanding.

"That's where I need you to trust me. When we get to the Complex, my powers are so weak I may disappear. Don't worry, I won't be gone completely. I will be in Pod seven in the Haven, at the rear of the complex. You got that? It's really important Esme knows this," she asked.

"OK. I got it. Pod seven in the Haven, at the back of the Complex," Ben confirmed.

"Yes, that's great," replied Alice.

The yellow light flickering on the controls got brighter. Ben could now make out the shape of the Complex. It looked rather like two smaller igloos on either side of a bigger one with a third structure at the top, with little pods jutting out from it.

The Complex got larger until Ben could make out all thirteen pods. Wondering how he was going to get there, he looked at the seventh one. He didn't ask the question. He let Alice carry on.

"We're here now," she declared.

The image on the control panel shifted perspective to display a semi circle with light all around it. They approached the docking bay. Alice started glowing brighter and brighter, just as when they first entered the crate. The ship came to a halt as it moved into the darkness of the bay.

Then everything went black.

"Alice?"

Ben called out to her again as he felt his way to where she was sitting. Light coming back, he looked at the controls.

Alice was gone.

Ben heard a crackling sound and then...

"Alice? Are you there?"

It was Esme's voice over the radio. He went to the control panel and pressed the talk button.

"Esme, it's Ben." The radio buzzed and then Esme appeared on the screen.

"Where's Alice?" she questioned hurriedly. On one level, she didn't expect to see her, as she was locked in one of the pods. But nothing surprised her anymore.

"Er...Hello, Esme. Nice to see you too," Ben muttered rather sarcastically.

"Sorry, Ben. It's great to see you too. It's just that we have little time. I don't know what you know, but we have to get Alice and then get out of here or we're in big trouble," she urged.

"But I was just with Alice. She was on the ship with me, then disappeared. She said we'd meet you and to tell you she'll be in pod seven in the Haven at the back of the Complex."

A broad grin came over Esme's face.

"Thank you, Ben!" she said. "Thank you!"

That brought Ben back to their first meeting in the Library which seemed ages ago, but must only have been a few hours. In fact, he wasn't sure how time worked in this place. It didn't seem normal.

"Let me in," said Esme.

Ben went over to the door and pushed it, then turned the handle. The door slid up and Esme walked in.

"Thank you! It's good to see you again," she smiled.

"OK. I'm not sure I really did anything, but thanks for thanking me," he replied.

She held Ben in a warm embrace. He wished it would last forever. The smell of her hair, the warmth of her body was making him not care about anything else. Esme let Ben go and, much like Alice had, she changed modes.

"Right. We don't have much time. Any moment now, a supply ship is going to dock. We need to get on it and look as though we're delivering supplies. We can't be detected by the Shumen," she reported.

Ben hadn't really processed much of what Alice previously was saying. He had heard her, and probably could repeat back most of what she'd said. But for some reason, maybe the joy of being back with his daughter, maybe the fact that this all seemed like some adventure straight out of the sci-fi novels he loved as a kid.

Whatever the reason, he didn't take on board that he might meet the Shumen. The ones he was led to believe had reconfigured his memories, causing him to have his head shaved and defibrillated by Charles. The ones he'd heard about that were seemingly taking over the Complex. And the ones whom ultimately were trying to get to his daughter—and for all he knew, could have kidnapped her in the first place.

Now here he was, back at the Complex, having to go in and rescue his Monkey. Even though he got the concept of bilocation—of course, he had no idea how it actually worked—it still seemed absurd having just been with Alice not five minutes ago.

He started feeling nauseous. His own heartbeat was getting louder and louder, faster and faster. Sweat beads materialised on his brow. His hands shook, then his whole body was shivering like he'd just stepped out in the snow.

"Ben?" said Esme, clearly seeing something was wrong.

He could see her, standing there leaning over the control panel, as if in slow motion, turning around and rushing towards him.

"Ben!" she screamed.

Then nothing.

"Ben!" shouted Esme, and she just caught him before his head hit the floor.

"Ben. Get up!" She shouted again, then whispered, "We don't have time."

Resting his head on the floor, she moved over to a container beneath the control panel. She pulled out a bottle and took it to Ben. Cradling his head in her lap, she lowered the bottle to his lips.

"Drink this," she said comfortingly.

As the liquid went down his throat, there was a little bit of movement. Ben slowly opened his eyes. "...I'm sorry...don't know what happened," he said in almost a whisper.

"No. I'm sorry," pleaded Esme. "I should have told you more and checked you were OK. This is a lot to take in. I think you just had a panic attack," she explained.

Ben took a sip of the drink. His heart rate slowing, getting back to normal, though his hands were still shaking so much so that Esme had to feed him the liquid.

"I'm really sorry. I forgot. It's just that we didn't have much time." Ben heard that sentence in the pass tense.

"What do you mean, didn't?" He quizzed, after taking another sip.

"Look," Esme pointed out the window. "The supply ship. It's here. The crew's already disembarked. We're too late."

# CHAPTER 48

## GREEN LIQUID

Ben registered Esme's potentially disheartening words, but without a sense of disappointment.

He took the bottle from her and swigged the last sip of the smooth, yoghurt like drink. Raising himself from Esme's lap, he gingerly got to his feet. Then, as energy kicked in, purposefully, he strode over to the window.

"They're not back yet," he said, still a little disorientated but trying to pull it together.

"And?" Esme questioned.

"I have an idea," Ben replied.

The supply ship was a different shape than that of Alice's ship. Whilst Alice's was cube like, from the side, the supply ship was shaped like a lozenge with a snow plough as its base.

It came from Contextua, the nearby planet which had been setup specifically to deliver supplies to the five regional communities. The Complex was the nearest and received its supplies every third day. This consisted mainly of food, medical supplies, and laundry.

The communities had agreed to set up the planet as it was getting increasingly difficult for enough supplies to come through from Lestande, which was five times the distance away.

Contextua had a lush green environment—which on the surface seemed a natural place for human life, though it was too close to its sun to be habitable. While it may not have been ideal for humans, the area soon became a thriving habitat for other organisms.

And by organisms, that included the AI bots, famous back on Earth, known as the Contextuans. They were programmed to serve and were more than willing to use the planets' resources to supply the nearby communities, despite their growing autonomy.

If they were a people—and some humans had wanted them to be classed as such—they thought nothing of obliging and helping the communities anyway they could. They hadn't even asked for anything in return. Though, of course, they didn't need to ask for anything.

What they got in spades from humans was information. Lots of it, that might be used in many good—and nefarious—ways. But so far, at least, they seemed to exist purely to serve.

The supply ship reached its destination like clockwork. This had been a regular operation for many years now. A well-oiled machine.

Ben peered through the window.

"Another thing I didn't expect to see," said Ben as he pointed to what looked like a block of compost—albeit a moving one. It moved with a very steady gait.

"The Contextuans," replied Esme. "I even have a toy of one back home. They are cute. You know they bring supplies to the Complex?"

"Yeah. I guessed. He's...It's?" Ben wasn't sure. "...about to move away from the ship. I suggest we get him to lead us to his mate."

"And how do you suggest we do that?" quizzed Esme, thinking Ben wasn't fully grasping the situation.

With growing confidence, he replied, "Watch."

Pulling the handle on the wall, the door slid open. The Contextuan saw him immediately and waddled towards them. Ben couldn't see its eyes, though there was a definite sense of the creature looking him up and down.

Stooping to the Contextuans level, and without thinking, he held out his hand toward the creature. As soon as it came in contact with Ben's hand, it turned around and waddled straight to its ship, heading towards the back of it.

Turning to Esme, Ben beckoned her to follow him. The door closed behind as they left Alice's ship and walked into the supply ship.

"Er...How did you do that?" asked a puzzled Esme.

"What?" said Ben like nothing out of the ordinary had happened.

"It's like you talked to it," she responded.

"Yeah. I don't know. But I do know we need to disguise

ourselves like them and follow it into the Complex," he instructed.

The interior of the Contextuans ship was bright. Everything was a slightly off-white tint reflecting the relatively low level of light and making the ambience much brighter. It was complemented with light grey lines around everything which resembled a child's colouring book—one where you tried to not paint over the lines.

The Contextuan glided back with a laundry basket, joined this time by a colleague. The basket hovered around a foot off the ground.

"We need to get in that," Ben said to Esme, pointing his finger at the basket.

"Er...OK..." she replied hesitantly, but getting the picture.

Ben walked around the far side of the basket and held out his hand for her. She grabbed it, climbed in and returned the favour to Ben. He took her hand and climbed in. They both lay down and covered themselves with the—thankfully fresh—laundry.

Esme stole a glance at Ben. He was staring at her. He smiled. Her hand moved to touch his. "We're gonna do this," she encouraged. "We're gonna bring Alice back."

He squeezed her hand as he nodded a smile at this beautiful woman he'd only just met, lying with him in a basket of laundry. Momentarily, all thought of their mission vanished. before a piercing sound suddenly brought him back to reality. The basket was on the move.

△

Alice lay prostrate on the concrete slab bathed in red light. She was lying on her side, shivering. Not from the cold, but it was her body's response to bilocating for so long. In fact, it had been the longest period she'd managed it. The thought crossed her mind that if her captors had any knowledge of her true strength, they might not have been as eager to feed her so well.

She sniffed, then wiped her nose with the back of her hand. A few tears departed from her eyes. She let them fall, hitting the makeshift bed. 'Come get me, Dad,' she prayed. She hated having so much power, but right at this moment, effectively being powerless.

'*Thwack*!'

Alice was startled as, in the corner of her eye, she saw a panel open she'd not seen before, just toward the left of the bed. She turned her head to get a clearer look.

A little metal box about the size of her hand came out and glided across the floor. It produced a slight buzzing sound, much like an annoying wasp.

On its front, a yellow light shone as it rose on extendable legs to the height of her head.

"What the heck?" She cried as she tried to muster the energy to move away.

Just as it got toward the back of the bed, four chains rapidly swung from the low ceiling, immediately attaching themselves to her arms and legs. They pulled taut; the arms moving forward and the legs staying at the back. Alice was now hovering a few centimetres above the bed, facing down toward the concrete.

The metal box moved closer to her face. Alice flinched as little arms came out from its sides and it gripped her head, raising it so she was looking straight at the yellow light. A transparent tube slid from its top surface, heading for her mouth.

She tried to shake her head, but the arms were too strong, holding her in a vice like grip. It quickly found its target, and a green liquid moved up the tube toward her lips.

As she stared at the liquid rising further up the tube, she became a little dizzy and cross-eyed. She knew what it was, and her attempts to blow out the tube were in vain. She thought about sucking it in, then spitting it out.

The little critter had obviously thought of that. Another arm came out from its front with pincers on the end. It clamped on to her nose. Now she had no choice but to swallow the liquid...if she wanted to stay alive.

She swallowed. At least for now she would choose life, whatever the consequences. It actually tasted sweet. A bit like the apple milkshakes she used to have at the Future Burger in town before they closed down.

As it slid down her throat into her stomach, the tube returned to the creature's body, as did its third arm. It let go of her head and Alice used all her strength to make sure her head did not bash on the table. Just about managing it, she lowered her head, slowly resting it once again on the stone bed.

The robot was already halfway across the room and it hastily vanished down a tunnel which opened automatically in the wall. Her manacles loosened, her arms and legs dropping to the concrete. The chains retracted back into the ceiling, as though they had never been there.

'That was new,' she thought. I wonder if they've found out more about my powers. Perhaps that was to inhibit them. Her thinking was interrupted by a very faint knocking which sounded like it was a way in the distance. She couldn't hear many sounds. Either they'd done a successful job at sound-proofing, or it was very quiet in this part of the Complex.

She thought about trying to bilocate to investigate, but decided against it. With Ben and Esme on their way, she needed to keep all her strength to escape with them.

'God, please keep them safe,' she silently prayed, as she curled up in a foetal position, and drifted off to sleep.

# CHAPTER 49

## ACCIDENTAL FIRING

The basket containing Ben and Esme glided through the Complex with a very faint whirring sound; the only sign that it was moving, if you couldn't see it.

Annex A, where the docking bay one was located, was used mostly for the regular deliveries from the regional communities. As a carbon copy of Annex B, there was a central corridor leading out into the main Hub.

It housed twelve storerooms containing laundry and cleaning materials. Unless you were going into a specific room, it was not an easy place to hide.

Ben and Esme just had to get through Annex A, and it would be a little easier passing through the main Hub. However, there were plenty of Shumen all around. Some running this way and that. They ignored the Contextuans who carried on their business of delivering supplies.

The basket approached the end of the first storeroom and came to a halt. Ben could hear a voice.

"Where are you going?" demanded what Ben assumed was a Shumen.

A sound emanated from the front of the Contextuan. It was nothing Ben or Esme could understand. In fact, they did not know what language the Contextuans spoke.

"You have already transported one basket. You never transport two," replied one of them, obviously having understood the Contextuan.

Ben glanced at Esme, both understanding that if they were caught now, they would have failed Alice. 'That's not gonna happen,' he thought as a glimmer of a plan formed in his head.

The Shumen moved around the side of the basket, raising his hand to begin the search of the laundry. Ben whispered to Esme.

"You have to trust me. Stay here. I'm getting out to distract them…you need to find Alice. OK?" Esme looked tense, trying to think of another solution other than Ben jumping out in front of a load of Shumen, whom she assumed would have weapons.

She couldn't.

"OK," she replied with resignation. "Stay safe."

"I'll do my best," smiled Ben as he jumped out of the basket, nearly knocking the Shumen over.

Immediately, he was surrounded by a gang of Shumen. He took his chance and ran, pushing through the growing number of them that seemed to appear out of nowhere. Running through to the end of the corridor and into the main Complex, he passed room after room of the grey doors, the Shumen close behind him.

Grabbing the handle on one door, he pulled it. It opened.

'Hmmm...this looks familiar,' he said to himself, thinking he recognised it as Charles' room, but surely this is in a different place.

Looking for something to use as a weapon, he ran to the back of the room, where he saw a pipette. It was much larger than a standard science tool. Not too sure what sort of weapon it would make, he still grabbed it. Surely there must be something better around.

As he was busy looking, the door burst open and several Shumen flooded into the room and very quickly, Ben Harman found himself surrounded. He wasn't going anywhere.

One Shumen came up close to him, and instinctively, before giving the man a chance to think, Ben grabbed him by the shoulders and held the large pipette to the side of his head. A gasp was heard. The group backed off, looking genuinely scared, not having noticed the weapon he was carrying.

Seizing the moment, he pulled the man closer, pointing the pipette right at his temple. This was not Ben, but right now he was working purely on instinct—and a large dose of adrenaline.

Ben looked around at each person. Firmly and calmly, he instructed,

"Drop your weapons...and if you don't get out now...I will fire...But no one needs to get hurt," he added, hoping he didn't have to test his nerve.

The pipette contained tiny blue balls, which unbeknownst to Ben were slowly turning green, whatever that meant.

It looked like a transparent version of a paintball gun, but with a blue pattern dynamically swirling around inside each ball. Most of them were blue, but slowly each was transitioning colours, through aquamarine, to lime green, then soon they were fully green, and it was at that point that the mob started moving towards Ben.

Confused, he shouted,

"I will fire!" He really didn't want to do this. The thought of injuring someone—let alone killing them appalled him. But he had to defend his family. He had to get back his daughter they had stolen from him.

"I said...get...back!" unequivocally shouting this time. "Get back! I will do it...I will shoot!"

With that, one of them dived at him, grabbing his leg. Ben squeezed the pipette and the green balls dissolved into his captive's head; his olive brown head shimmering green as he collapsed to the ground, his defence no more.

Distraught, Ben dropped the weapon, really hoping he hadn't killed the man.

Two Shumen attended to their colleague, still lying motionless on the floor. Others grabbed Ben and placed handcuffs on his wrists. Leading him out, one said,

"Our instructions are to take him to the Interrogation Room." Ben did not know where that was, but either way, it didn't sound good. Quickly, he was led away.

FalongQ's ComTel buzzed. It was MendipT.

"The Guardian is working with us, and he's sent me the access code for the Haven. I'm heading there now to find the girl," he reported, slightly out of breath. "How many do you think we have turned?" he asked FalongQ.

"To be honest, most of them. If I had to estimate, I would say at least sixty percent. Definitely over half," his colleague answered.

"Great. Head to the bridge and capture SentiN. I hope I won't be too far behind you. Keep him locked up until I come," MendipT instructed.

"Affirmative," replied FalongQ and cut the call.

"This way!" FalongQ commanded to the crowd of Shumen, mostly new recruits who they'd managed to turn. Though 'managed' was strong. It seemed most of them were fed up with the way things were going. They just were waiting for someone else to do something about it.

Along the way to the bridge, FalongQ had accessed the armoury and now most of the Shumen were carrying weapons of some sort. Some looking like old-fashioned Celtic crosses but with one spoke cut off, or the pipettes Ben had used to bad effect. They hoped they were ready for anything.

The bulkhead was impenetrable. There were three large doors to the left, right, and centre of it. Other than that, there was no way in or out.

MendipT was standing at the right door, punching in the access code provided by the Guardian which would allow him to get into the Haven.

The bulkhead separated the Haven from the rest of the ship. A harsh beep indicated it didn't work.

"Curses!" whispered MendipT. He tried again. He wiped sweat off his brow as he was greeted by a positive sounding beep, and the door slid open.

"Phew! Let's go," he said to his crew as, one by one, they trundled through the door. No Shumen had been in the Haven before. They'd never needed to. It was the Guardian's domain, whose office was in the centre of the Haven with holding cells and supply rooms built around the central office.

Contextuans had seen more of this area than the Shumen, as one of their main roles was to keep the supply rooms well stocked.

MendipT turned round to face his crew.

"We need to find the girl's pod," he instructed, pointing to a smaller group, then to the left. "You go that way, and we'll go the—"

*Crash!*

He didn't finish his sentence, his words abruptly cut off by a loud bang echoing from the door they had just entered. A group loyal to SentiN had followed them in, and they now stood in the Haven face to face with MendipT and his crew, weapons raised. Everyone stopped.

MendipT looked around at the faces of his once colleagues. He could see they didn't have it in them to fight. He breathed in, standing tall.

"No one needs to get hurt," he said, slowly and carefully turning his head to make sure he looked in the eyes of every one of the loyalists.

He wasn't sure who the leader was but assumed that it was the one standing slightly furthest forward. He was young, his enlarged weapon looking like a pipette with a handle pointed directly at MendipT.

"Your arrogance betrays you, MendipT," the young Shumen spat out. "Who do you think you are, destroying our culture? We are a peaceful people. That is why we were chosen for the Complex. You are putting all that in jeopardy. And for what? Your ego?" He spoke clearly and with authority.

MendipT was taken aback, though he tried to hide it by shifting his weight from one foot to the other. He hadn't really heard anyone speak to him like that in a long time.

He was impressed with the young man. He could use more people like that. Though now he thought this group of Shumen would not be taken so easily.

Before he had a chance to respond, one loyalist, holding another pipette-like weapon, accidentally fired it at one of MendipT's crew. He'd squeezed the ball and a blue light emitted from the end, hitting his fellow Shumen in the chest.

For a few seconds, he just stood still, like nothing had happened. In fact, everyone just stood there, stunned. Then the unfortunate man collapsed on the floor, disintegrating as he fell. By the time his body would have been lying on the floor, it had completely disappeared.

"Sorry!" the poor Shumen shouted as he dropped his weapon. But it was too late. MendipT's crew, in unison, held up their weapons and fired. Flashes of blue light were exchanged between the parties, with bodies collapsing and disintegrating. There were more of MendipT's group this time and they destroyed all the gang of loyalists, including, to MendipT's chagrin, the impressive young man.

"Quickly!" MendipT said, not having time to dwell on what had just happened. He ran and motioned towards the supply rooms.

By the time they reached the pods, another gang of loyalists had replaced the disintegrated mob, and now, as MendipT's crew looked on, swarms of loyalists could be seen protecting each of the pods in the Haven holding their weapons up.

Not wanting to incur heavy casualties, they stood back, hidden by the supply rooms. Though MendipT was fully aware, they knew of his presence. 'I wonder how he did that?' he thought. 'That's not the organisation of SentiN. He wouldn't have it in him.' He paced back and forth along the supply rooms, his team looking on.

If they moved out, they would be shot. If they stayed there, they would just be giving SentiN more time to command his loyalists; and judging by what MendipT had just seen, "perhaps I've underestimated him," he whispered.

"What?" quizzed one of his team. Ignoring it, he questioned his team.

"Anyone know the best way out of this?" They all looked at each other, then at him, a sense of disappointment on their faces. MendipT chewed his skin inside his mouth. He smiled as he looked at his team, nowhere near close to giving up.

"It's not over yet," he said.

# CHAPTER 50

## FINDING A WEAPON

The laundry basket, with Esme inside, continued its journey towards the Haven. She had no clue what was going on outside.

Whatever Ben did had worked, and the Contextuans continued in the same direction.

'Was that the sound of weapons firing?' She pondered. Whatever it was, it was getting louder.

"How am I going to deal with the Shumen completely unarmed?" she asked herself as she rifled through the laundry looking for something, anything that could be weaponised.

The basket was deep, with several piles of sheets and other items beneath her. Reaching down as far as her hand would go, she felt a little lip on the side of the basket. Lifting it up gently with her fingers, a panel came off in her hand.

'Hmm...' she thought. 'This must be a security pocket.'

Her fingers touched something hard. It was fixed in place, but with a little leverage, she removed it. Not wanting to shake the basket and make it obvious someone was in there, she slowly dragged the object to the top. It didn't look like much. A bit like a rolling pin with a button at one end. The temptation to push was strong. She smiled as she recalled the cartoons she used to watch, and could see one with a big red button labeled, 'do not push.' Obviously, in the cartoon world, it was almost always pushed to devastating consequences. Too much was at stake right now.

Resisting the temptation, she just held it firm in her hand. There was nothing else she could do but stay concealed in the basket and assume whatever instructions Ben had transferred to the Contextuans meant she would end up at Alice's pod.

She stayed still and hoped.

The vitals were looking good as the needles rapidly danced around the body, continuing to sew the patient back up. Nathan stood, eyes flicking between viewing the patient through the observation glass and the glass itself, which displayed an array of information about the progress of the routine procedure.

"Once you're done, there's a call for you in the office, Doctor Triani," said the receptionist, who'd waited outside patiently until the operation was almost over before popping her head around the door.

Nathan turned his head to look at her.

"Thanks, Sally. I'll be right out," and acknowledged as he tapped the glass to close off his part of the procedure.

"I can take it from here, Doc," his assistant Francis said helpfully.

"Cheers, Fran. Catch yer later." He smiled as he left the lab.

"Dr Triani speaking," Nathan said, as he connected the call.

"Nathan, sir," a man with a Scottish accent said back.

"Bill. Good to hear from you. Got any news?" he asked.

"Well, yes. You could say that. I did some digging and here's what I've found out. Even my boss, Kyle, was surprised."

"What did you find?" asked Nathan.

"I told you before that the record shows Lydia Harman died 21.09.54, then it was changed to an MP, then this was subsequently scrubbed out." Bill seemed to pause.

"Yes, go on," Nathan urged.

"Well, we found the staff member who entered both records. The first one he received from Sendo eXperience's head of communications within an hour of the tragic event. He says he checked it with his boss and it was fine to be entered in the logbook. Then, about an hour later, he received a message from an officer on the scene to register a missing person...the description of whom fully matched Lydia Harman."

If Nathan wasn't confused before, he certainly was now.

"Why would the officers who saw her body register her as a missing person?" he asked, his curiosity peaked.

"Well, I thought you might ask that. I did myself. And, the thing is, they didn't see her body," replied Bill.

"What? That makes no sense," said Nathan.

"They didn't see her body. By the time they got there—and they responded to the auto emergency call when the lab goes into shutdown—they were met by the HR director who reported Lydia Harman as missing, saying she hadn't come into work that morning and hadn't been seen since. That's why it was updated, as my boss called to confirm with HR... and it was confirmed," Bill reported.

Nathan sighed. His hope of getting Ben to move on was slowly being dashed.

"So somehow, the head of comms and HR were not talking, or certainly didn't have the same message. That's not like Sendo, right?"

"Yes, Nathan Sir. I agree. But it gets stranger...My colleague who'd filled in the log—and he's now since left, so I had a lot of digging to do to get hold of him..."

"Well, I appreciate all your effort, Bill," said Nathan.

"Not a problem. I don't like unanswered questions myself. So, my colleague said he'd had a call from someone reporting to be from Suldit Rama's office, you know the MD of Sendo, just around 4 pm that day, to say that there had been a mistake and Lydia Harman was never missing, she had died," Bill explained.

He continued. "This is the point that our eager beaver—probably as he was getting ready to leave for the day—didn't check out. So he trusted what he was told. I mean, it was from Rama's office, or so he thought. However, all I can say since then is that the event at the lab is cloaked in secrecy. I have tried to get information out of Sendo and no one wants to talk about it."

Nathan listened carefully, trying to take it all in.

"I went round the lab myself, and got strange looks from some people, and I've seen many people lying before, Nathan, sir. I know what it looks like. Those that remember her, or the few that had worked with her, all come out with the same prescriptive story about how she was such a gifted scientist and died so young. Yada, Yada. But I know some of them don't believe it. I just don't have enough to go on yet, to press them further," he concluded.

Nathan, took in a deep breath. "So ultimately, despite all that, we still can't say for sure that she didn't die, right?" he asked.

"That is true, my friend. But I'm going with my gut with this one, and the more I look into it, the more it feels like they're covering something up. Trust me, Nathan Sir, whatever's happening, I will find out."

"OK, well thanks again, Bill. I really appreciate it. Keep me posted," said Nathan.

"Will do, Nathan Sir. Have a great day now." A little bit inappropriate for talking about a dead or missing person, Nathan thought, but Bill certainly got into his job.

'So now what do I tell Ben?' He thought as he sat back in his chair. 'Either way, he needs to know.'

# CHAPTER 51

## QUESTIONS, QUESTIONS

MERELY BEING IN PROXIMITY TO THE CENTRAL Gardens had the effect of slowing down one's heart rate. It was the place where everyone would come to release their stress and recharge. The extensive array of trees, plants, and flowers was a sight to behold. Not to mention the butterflies, moths, and many other insects and species brought to enhance the Complex's ecosystem.

The ceiling of the Complex was higher in this central area to cater for the trees. They had growth inhibitors attached to the roots to make sure they never grew too quickly and broke through the roof—assigning the total population on the ship to their death.

Despite this, certain Shumen were tasked with trimming the trees back regularly. Just to make sure.

FalongQ looked up and saw one of his fellow Shumen on ropes, tools laden over his back as he climbed the tallest tree and was nearly at the top. He'd done that job once, loving being out in nature.

He kept walking past the main tree and through the beautifully peaceful, artificial stream that separated both sides of the gardens. A few families were milling about there, with some kids playing in the stream.

Occasionally, some Shumen would look at him with an expression of mild curiosity. A few walked right up and engaged directly, saying in hushed tones,

"We heard what you're doing with MendipT. We want in."

A smile washed over his face.

"Great. We have a special mission, but head to the Haven and meet MendipT and his crew. They will need some help," he instructed.

With that, they headed off toward MendipT.

'This is going much better than we thought. The people really must be fed up with SentiN,' he reflected, as he and his crew reached the staff quarters observing more Shumen wandering about.

Suddenly, one of the staff rooms burst open and a group of about six Shumen, all carrying weapons, came running at FalongQ and his crew. If they'd been more strategic, they would have waited until FalongQ's crew were much closer. But now they had given away the sense of surprise.

FalongQ had an idea.

"To the gardens!" he shouted as he turned and ran, the others following him. Past the stream, they hid behind a small group of trees, trying to keep as far away as possible from the families and people around.

"I can't believe they wasted their opportunity. Let's not waste ours," he commanded. They could see them running towards the gardens.

"When they get to the stream, charge them. They won't expect that. Then grab their weapons, and let's get back on the mission. We don't have much time. We need to get to the bridge."

With that, the loyalist group had reached the stream still running at full pelt.

"Now!" shouted FalongQ, and immediately they charged the group. Before they had time to realise what hit them, some were knocked to the ground, weapons flying across the floor. Others panicked and dropped their weapons. Either way, FalongQ's group grabbed the weapons and pointed their own at their enemies.

A few drops of sweat dribbled down FalongQ's face, more from the adrenaline rush than physical exertion.

"We're giving you a chance," he said. "We don't have time for a fight with you. There are much bigger things at play," he said, emphasising much. "If you want to join us—and I recommend you do—tell everyone what's happening, then head to the bridge."

With that, they ran away, initially backwards, to make sure they would not be attacked. They weren't. Then they turned and ran full pelt through the Central Gardens, heading for the bridge. Their attempt to keep themselves hiding in plain sight having long since disappeared.

⬤

At least the sofa was comfortable, thought Ben as he sat back into it, and come to think of it, it looked exactly like the one he'd fallen asleep in earlier. 'They must have got a job lot,' he thought.

His hands and his feet were neatly decorated with manacles. He pictured himself getting up, then falling down again, and decided there wasn't much point trying to escape right now. 'I'll just see what they have to say and take it from there.'

Ben really hoped Esme was on schedule to rescue Alice. He'd done all he could to buy her time, but none of that mattered if she was already caught, and as they'd searched him and taken away everything but his clothes, there was no way he could contact her.

For now, she was on her own. He knew he'd made the right decision, as otherwise they both would be sitting here now...or worse. But he couldn't help feeling like he'd failed her, and his little Monkey.

In the midst of his self-pity, a man in his late thirties, donning the standard dark blue attire of the Shumen, entered through a concealed door at the rear of the room that Ben had failed to notice.

"I'm ready for him. Bring him in," he ordered, as two guards immediately entered the main doors, unfastened Ben's manacles, grabbed his arms and lead him into the smaller room following the man.

This room was grey. It was small, the biggest object by far being a large oak desk, behind which the man went to sit. He pointed to the seat in front. Ben just stood there until he was forced to sit by the guards.

The man's desk was sparse. There was nothing on it. Literally. No papers, no screen, no pens. Just a dark oak surface, Ben assumed—like everything else in the complex—was an avatar. The desk could be whatever the man wanted it to be.

The door closed after the guards walked out. It was now just Ben and the man. The man and Ben—in silence.

He looked straight up at Ben. Ben felt as though the walls of this already small room were ever–so–slowly closing in on him. He couldn't be sure if this was in his mind or if it was actually happening.

Normally, he would be in full on panic mode, but whatever Esme had given him to help him recover when he'd passed out earlier had been having an amazing effect. Well, that's what he assumed. In truth, it was also the awakening of his powers through his daughter's connection that increased his assertiveness. And besides, the tonic was slowly starting to wear off anyhow.

The man stared straight at Ben, motionless, and worse still, not saying a thing. Ben was getting annoyed.

"What do you want from me?" he enquired. The man slowly got up from his chair, walked over to Ben, then left the room via the same door in the back. 'Rude.'

He was now alone. He waited. 'Perhaps this is their interrogation technique,' thought Ben.

He thought about getting up and trying the door, wondering if it was intentional that they hadn't cuffed him this time. 'It's a trick to see what I'll do, then they'll come out and get me,' he thought. 'But what if I can escape and this prison is just in my mind?'

Soon he became exhausted, thinking it was his lack of mental energy that drove his tiredness, but the room's temperature and humidity had purposely been set to rise. Ben's breathing seemed to get more laboured and sweat was pouring off him now.

It's...definitely...getting...hotter he noticed, which was his last thought before being sapped of all energy, his body lolling forwards, head over his knees, arms to the floor, as he collapsed into a deep sleep.

Dark shapes moved and swirled around him before becoming steady. Light slowly increasing, as Ben drifted back to consciousness.

'How long have I been out?' He questioned, shaking his head, almost as if trying to brush off the sleep. He remembered the man staring at him before leaving the room. But as his full vision slowly returned, another, this time familiar, pair of eyes were fixed on him from behind a desk.

"Hello, Ben Harman," the man said in his trademark, detached tone.

Ben physically breathed a sigh of relief.

"Charles, am I glad to see you! What are you doing here...and more to the point, who was that other guy, and can you get me out?"

"Questions, questions," replied Charles. "I'm sure you've got plenty more too, Mr Harman," he replied.

Ben hadn't seen the old man since he'd helped him connect to the LinerVerse. He assumed that what Alice said was correct; in that he was now actually in the Complex, as opposed to a simulation via the LinerVerse. He had to believe her, as both looked indistinguishable.

His face continued in its almost permanent state of confusion since entering the Complex. Charles continued. "...but before I can give you answers, I need to share some things with you."

Ben, in frustration, said, "Can I just go and we can talk later? I need to get Alice." The old man's demeanour seemed to change, his face becoming more earnest.

"I'm sorry to have to tell you this, Mr Harman. But you won't be going anywhere. Though you will have the chance to decide your own fate."

"Wait, what?" Ben did a mental double take. "Aren't you helping us rescue Alice?"

"Yes. In a way. But, Mr Harman, as I have said, there are a few things you need to know." Ben was worried. Even more questions now. 'Is Esme on her way into a trap? Is this plan all a setup? Am I ever going to see my daughter again?' Soon, and not before time, he would have answers.

# CHAPTER 52

## CONCENTRIC CIRCLES

Looking down on the Haven, you would see concentric circles spreading outwards. Starting in the centre where the Guardian's office is located—his 'haven,'—where he can monitor most aspects of the Complex.

Outside that, there are twelve supply rooms. Next, a dividing wall which served as an access point to the supply rooms and added protection for the Guardian. Further out from that, is a large gangway, before, on the very outer-most walls, you will see the pods.

Each of the thirteen pods was like a separate ship floating out in space, but attached via a small tunnel designed to fit one person at a time. These were quarantine pods, an important function on a ship floating in space with no other escape routes. Thankfully, they hadn't needed to be used a lot.

Occasionally, however, they served as a makeshift prison, which is where Alice was currently located and where MendipT needed to reach.

His dilemma was moving from the supply rooms to the outermost edge of the Haven without being caught by the SentiN loyalists stationed in the large gangway.

"Go and see how many there are," he said to one of the crew, who looked decidedly nervous, but followed MendipT's command.

Edging his way cautiously toward the dividing wall, looking left and right, holding up his weapon, the Shuman saw nothing. He ran to reach the wall and backed into it, holding his gun tight. Beads of sweat dribbled down his olive brown skin and onto his tight blue Shumen uniform. He sidled his way to the door and pressed the button immediately whilst he had the courage.

It opened to silence. He popped his head round. In front he could see the door to pods ten and eleven. To the right, nothing, but to his left he could see a few Shumen, just at the edge of his view, as the gangway went round the corner. He counted three, then he closed the door and rushed back and reported his findings to MendipT and the crew.

"We don't have time to stand around," MendipT warned. Then pointing at the group, "Three of you go right, another three go left. We need to expect others to come in the opposite direction."

He turned and pointed to the team member who'd carried out the recce and the Shuman standing next to him.

In hushed tones he directed, "Us three will go pod to pod to find this girl."

He looked back and motioned to the first two groups.

"We will need your protection, so don't go too far. Once we

get the girl out, we'll need to take her to the bridge—and for that, we'll need everyone alive," MendipT issued.

The nervous looks continued, even on MendipT himself, though he was desperately trying not to show it.

Although each Shumen got regular battle training, and someone had thought to install two large rooms of weapons on the Complex, despite that, they hadn't had to use it in anger thus far. They certainly never expected that when they did, that it would be against their own people. For such a close, collective community, this didn't sit well. Though being honest in recent years, you could see the cracks appearing as the sense of community was slowly being eroded.

"Let's go!" commanded MendipT as he led them out, following the same route as the recce guy. Three of them slipped out of the dividing wall door to tackle the loyalists. Another three headed left to see what was on the other side. When both were a decent distance away, MendipT and his companions made a dash for pod ten, marginally the closest one to them.

'I hope this works,' he thought to himself as he entered the code supplied by the Guardian. The panel buzzed in failure.

"One in thirteen chance, I guess," he muttered in mild frustration to his colleagues.

"Just twelve to go," one of them said sarcastically. MendipT smiled.

They noticed that the three loyalists to their right had gone. They couldn't see their colleagues either.

"Let's try eleven," he said as they wandered to the next pod.

By the time they got there, they still couldn't see any of their colleagues.

"I wonder if they're OK?" ask recce guy whilst MendipT tried and failed again to open the pod. He ignored his colleague's comment.

"I've got a hunch we're going the wrong way. I think we should try pod eight and work round that way," MendipT suggested.

There was no disagreement from the others, so they headed back round to the next pod they hadn't yet tried.

The first group who'd headed left had encountered no other Shumen so far. They made it all the way around to view pod two, and not a sniff of any loyalists. However, pod one was a different matter. This pod was right up against the bulkhead separating the Haven from the main hub. Around this pod was a gaggle of Shumen, all carrying weapons and, as much as the group could tell from their facial expressions, not looking sympathetic to MendipT's vision.

"What shall we do?" one of them said, counting ten Shumen backing up against the bulkhead and spreading over past pod one. "It's ten vs three," he continued, clearly displaying worry through his dark, wide eyes.

"Yes," said MendipT, "but we have the element of surprise. Let's back up against the dividing wall and find out where the other group is. If we can attack them from both sides, they won't know what hit them," he said confidently.

So that's exactly what they did. MendipT and the other group were messaged. The other group at pod thirteen by now, were holding steady, having unfortunately had to dispose of two

Shumen already. They could see the group of ten and were thinking the same thing as their colleagues.

"You lot go," MendipT said through his ComTel. "We need to keep going to find the girl. Hold them off as long as you can."

By now, the group at pod three crept round and could see the loyalists in front of them, backed up against the bulkhead far right door.

"On three," said one Shumen into his ComTel. Both groups on either side of the Haven still looked nervous, no doubt questioning the ethics of shooting their compatriots. But before they could let those thoughts dwell, the shout came.

"One...Two...Three...Go!"

They ran. At full pelt toward the loyalists who, caught by surprise at teams coming at them from both sides, were in disarray. Of course, the loyalists did not know how many Shumen were coming at them. Even though it was ten vs six, the wipe out was quick. MendipT's crews fired warning shots first, then when they received reciprocal fire, they directed it straight at their compatriots.

It was a bloodbath. Well...it would have been had their bodies not disintegrated before they hit the ground. However, it wasn't a no-cost act.

In the attack's process, one of their crew was killed, and another badly injured. The latter, having been hit in the shoulder and the leg, lay collapsed on the ground. Feeling unable to carry on, and before anyone could assist, he picked up his pipette shaped weapon and squeezed; his body disintegrating almost immediately.

His colleagues, looked on distraught. It's one thing to expect casualties of war, another to see them die in front of you.

The crew got themselves together and headed back to find the others, their mission completed. Despite their emotional turmoil, what they did have now, was a clear Haven.

Meanwhile, MendipT kept going with his two colleagues. Both pod eight and nine provided the same negative result. He looked dejected.

"That's nine to go now, by my reckoning. Let's hope we find her soon. I dread to think how many Shumen, SentiN has converted now," he said as they wandered towards pod seven, not realising just how their luck was about to change.

## CHAPTER 53

## COUNT THE DOORS

THE LAUNDRY BASKET ARRIVED AT THE HAVEN. ESME thought she heard firing in the distance, but couldn't be sure, the clothing piled on top of her doing too good a job of deadening the sound.

The Contextuan tapped the access panel, entering the code with its rubber-ended metallic fingers. Gliding through the basket, it followed closely behind, with another Contextuan positioned at the back. They quickly entered through the dividing wall right in front of the supply rooms.

'Count the doors, count the doors,' Esme thought as she recalled Alice's words to guide her to pod seven.

Positioned opposite each pod, the dividing wall boasted doors with small windows placed just above the centre of each door. So it was possible for her to judge approximately where she was, even if she couldn't fully see. As she pulled back some clothes, she cautiously peeked her head out of the top of the basket.

They went past the first, then the second doors. As they got to the third, the basket stopped as the Contextuan did their job of transferring the clean clothes from the basket to the supply rooms.

'How long is this going to take?' Thought Esme, as she also wondered about Alice and hoped Ben was OK.

'Please God,' she prayed.

The basket was on the move again. Pod four was passed quickly, then at pod five, they stopped to drop off more of the laundry. Esme noticed the noise level rise, coming from the other side of the dividing wall. She shuddered, not knowing how she would react if she had to use the weapon—if it really was a weapon. And if it wasn't…well…it didn't bear thinking about.

They reached door six.

"Show time!" Esme exclaimed as—without stopping to think—she jumped out of the basket the moment it stopped. The Contextuan paid her no attention.

Heading towards the window, she peered through.

'Shumen!'

Not only could she see two of them immediately in front of the entrance to pod seven, in the far distance she could see a few others also heading towards Alice's pod.

Esme's shoulders dropped.

"What to do?" she sighed. "How am I going to get to Alice now?" She rested her head against the window, dejected, but not ready to give up just yet.

Alice sat disconsolately on her concrete bed. She had heard nothing from her dad, Esme, or Charles for a little while.

'Have they failed?' She thought.

Her eyes were on the verge of tearing up.

Suddenly, her countenance changed as she sensed it. Looking up into space, a faint smile passed her lips.

"Esme is near," she murmured. A glimmer of hope. But her smile turned to a puzzled frown. She did sense Esme...but... something's not right.

Alice couldn't see everything, but what she could pick up was that something was stopping her friend from doing what she needed to do. There needed to be some kind of distraction to clear her path.

"What can I do?" she asked herself.

Alice strained as she focused her energy on where Esme was. 'The other side of the dividing wall...that's where she is.' She visualised the Shumen all around Esme.

"Bilocate—that's the only way to get them away..."

She didn't finish her sentence.

*Clink!*

The door to the pod unlocked.

Alice looked up. Her curiosity, and anxiety, heightened. Slowly it creaked open and the person who entered wasn't who she'd expected. It wasn't Charles, with her next meal, but a Shumen.

It was MendipT.

Immediately upon entering the room, Alice recognised him. She was just a baby when she first saw him whilst her mum was at work. She'd known there was another person in the adjacent lab. Her senses were remarkable, even at that young age—and this was before the inhibitor was implanted in her.

Looking at him now, with no doubt, she knew it was him. Anger welled within her, which she fought to control, not wanting to reveal her hand straight away.

'Let's see how this plays out,' she thought, safely assuming MendipT would have no idea she'd recognised him standing alone in the adjacent lab observing the death of her mother.

Whilst she didn't know if he had anything to do with it, all these years, the sense of someone there but doing nothing riled her as she grew old enough to process more of what happened.

MendipT stepped further into the room, moving closer to Alice. He stared at her, partially in awe, as if everything he'd heard was true. But also with the thought that she was just a girl.

"I can't tell you how much I've been looking forward to meeting you, Alice Harman," MendipT said, his words laced with a touch of reverence.

'They all say that,' she thought, mentally rolling her eyes, as he stooped down, coming closer to her level.

A faint smile of acknowledgement washed over her face, not wanting to put his back up just yet, and also conserving energy for the distraction she would still need to provide for Esme.

He regarded her. 'How could someone so small be so power-ful?' He shook his head, attempting to mentally refocus on the task.

He stood up, looking down at her.

"My people are slaves," he began. "But most of them don't even know it. They have been so used to doing everything that their slave masters command."

"Your people won a competition of a lifetime—to be the very first group on an out-of-world colony. You should be proud." Alice interjected, countering his perception.

MendipT looked down at the ground.

"You're right," he responded. "We are proud...well...we were. My people have changed. Their lack of motivation is clear. They have no purpose, no vision. And worse of all, they are content with it all."

He didn't plan to say all this. In fact, he still wasn't sure what he was saying and what would get Alice to do what he wanted.

"So let me get this straight. You are unhappy because your people are happy?" Alice retorted.

"I didn't say they were happy," he replied.

"Happy. Content. In this context, what's the difference?" MendipT tried to hold back his frustration, knowing he needed Alice onside. He hated that fact. But at least for the moment, without knowing what she was really capable of, he didn't feel confident enough to force the situation.

"There's a lot of difference. They have no vision. We've lost our sense of exploration and have become happy being average. No ambition. No drive," he replied.

He looked around the small room, wondering how long Alice had been kept there.

"What an unrivalled opportunity we'd been given to make a name for ourselves. And my people can't see it. There's no desire to create art, no creation, nothing that drives our purpose and culture. We are going nowhere fast. Most of them stayed behind, showing little interest in venturing out to explore unfamiliar territory with me."

Alice, whilst listening, was still thinking about Esme. If she could get MendipT to keep talking, she might be able to bilo-cate without him knowing. She'd never done it in front of someone before. But needs must.

"What changed with your people? You've said what's bad about them, but there must be good side. I mean, have they always been—in your words, 'lazy and lacking ambition?'" She ventured.

MendipT sat down on a platform that jutted out from the wall. It would do as a makeshift chair. He visibly seemed to relax as he began to share about his people, giving Alice just the time she needed.

# CHAPTER 54

## FISH IN WATER

Ben looked around the room, taking more of it in since somehow being transported here from the last room.

'I'm sure they said that was the interrogation room. Not sure what this one is. It's round. Surely,' he surmised, not being able to see the entirety of its shape as several walls divided it into sub rooms.

Many paintings hung on panels that jutted out from the curved walls. None were immediately recognisable to Ben, though he was sure one or two were old classics. A dining room scene in one of them reminded him of when, a short while ago, he'd shared a meal with Charles. All that sumptuous food—hmmm—made his stomach grumble.

Another painting was a seascape. 'Definitely something Welsh,' he thought, thinking of the trips he used to take with Alice to Pembrokeshire, which caused him to wonder how she was doing. Esme must have reached her by now. I hope so.'

Ben glanced back at the painting. It was interesting, as aside from the weird light in a frame he'd seen on his first visit to the

Complex, he'd not noticed any paintings or anything especially artistic on the ship. Again, that's assuming he was on the actual ship and not stuck somewhere in the LinerVerse.

The Guardian watched him closely, clasping his hands together as though getting more serious—if that were possible.

"Mr Harman, there are greater things at play here than holing you up for trying to injure a colleague," The Guardian informed.

Ben nodded his head and asked quietly, "Is he OK?"

"He'll be fine. But like I said, there are greater things of concern here. In fact, we want to make you an offer."

He let the words hang in the air, filtering through Ben's mind.

Ben furrowed his brow, puzzled, not knowing quite where this was going.

"What sort of offer?" he retorted.

"You know I am Charles Orthon Bannon, Guardian of the Complex?"

Ben thought about the name for a while. Something pricking his mind that didn't connect when he'd first introduced himself.

'Where do I know that?' He thought to himself.

"You are only here to satisfy my employers. They know your daughter is potentially dangerous and they can't see her released. Even now, they have been injecting a serum into her to subdue her powers." Charles reported.

On hearing his daughter being experimented on without his consent—again, Ben flew into a rage, attempting to dive forwards at the man. Anything to protect his daughter.

"Get your filthy hands off her!" he shouted. But his body was frozen in place, unable to budge an inch.

"What have you done!" he bellowed, realising there was some kind of invisible force-field holding him fast to the chair.

The Guardian remained completely still, knowing Ben wouldn't be able to reach him.

"It's for your protection too," he continued.

Ben, worried more for Alice, lowered his tone but still forcefully cried,

"She is not yours to experiment on. She's my daughter. My God-given responsibility. You have no right to take her."

Charles was still not phased by Ben's outburst.

"Mr Harman. Have I not been working with you to help secure Alice's escape? You know I've been in league with Margaret and Esme, and as Guardian of the Complex, I have complete access to every aspect of the ship. Only I can allow Esme to get to Alice to free her."

Ben racked his brains, trying to find a hole in the logic. He couldn't.

"So why haven't you freed her before now? She must have been here…what…over six months now," he said, trying to stay angry at the man who had at least seemed to help them.

"Alice has not been here for all that time. She was on earth for a while, as far as I know, and has only recently been transferred to the Complex. But, Mr Harman, if you knew what they really wanted to do with her, you would thank me she is where she is and has been treated relatively well. I have fought my corner, so she has been protected thus far. But their desires are great, and I don't know how long I can keep them at bay."

Ben sat back in resignation.

"Which brings us, Mr Harman, back to their offer," he replied.

In an instant, it struck him like a punch to the gut.

"C.O.B! You're C.O.B!!" Ben shouted, coming to the realisation of why he recognised the name Charles Orthon Bannon.

"You kidnapped my baby Alice and implanted her with the inhibitor...when she was just five! It was you!" he shouted; the anger getting to him causing him pain as he fought against the invisible restraints.

Charles looked down. If one looked closely, you might spot a pang of guilt. However, it was quickly replaced by his default impassive expression.

"Again, Mr Harman, you should be thanking me. That inhibitor has saved the lives of many people—including probably your own. Remember what was written on the letter—" Ben cut in, interrupting the man.

"I can recite it word for word. It has pained me all these years, knowing what you did to my precious daughter. Whatever you felt, it was not your right to do anything. If you had a problem, you should have come to me. I am responsible for her. Not you or anyone else," he wailed as a few tears trickled down his face.

"Sometimes things are bigger than you, Mr Harman. The fate of humanity is bigger than you. We have a right to protect humanity and not awaken a beast. The fate of many is greater than the rights of one."

Ben, incensed, spat out, "I don't care what you say. She is not a beast. My rights as her parent trumps any assumed rights you believe you have. Yours are from other humans. Mine is from God, who creates all humans."

"And who created your God? Other humans in a book written by...hmmm...let me see...humans," Ben was having none of it.

"Written by humans, guided by God. If you actually read it, you would see the hundreds of accurate prophecies written thousands of years before the events that we have a historical record of coming true," corrected Ben. "It's fully trustworthy."

The Guardian sat back, having listened to some of the same arguments from Margaret, and having some sympathy. He still put out the same lines, like he'd done for years. It's just he wasn't as convinced in his own rhetoric these days. Though he wouldn't let Ben see that just yet—if ever.

He cracked his knuckles.

"Well...we could do this all night, but let's not get all hasty and self-righteous. I'm aware of the writings of a certain Herman Harman, your grandad no less, that you have recently been getting reconnected with."

Ben had been looking at the floor, trying to think of a way out, but now he looked up in surprise.

"How do you know that?" he questioned, his tone filled with skepticism.

"That's not important. But what is important is that I know why you took on the LeV8 contract, something I'm sure your late wife would never have approved of..."

"I don't know what you're talking about? And don't bring Lydia into this," replied a rather dejected Ben, genuinely not knowing where Charles was taking this thought.

"I put it to you, Ben Harman," he said, channeling a prosecution lawyer wrapping up his case for the defence, "that you have been slowly taken by your grandad's work, particularly through…oh, what's his name…ahh, yes…JR, one of Herman Harman's mentees, that I'm not sure you fully believe your own rhetoric."

"Have you been spying on me?" Ben's thoughts went to his conversations with JR, and the times he'd read his grandpa's diaries. 'I guess it's possible to tap into my ComTel…but how is it possible to know what I've been reading?'

He glanced at the painting of the landscape, noticing more detail this time. The strokes of the paint. The reflections of the light. A fish in the water, painted so faintly, it was only the light shining on the artwork that enabled him to see it so clearly. One little fish, swimming alone. He felt like that sometimes, and he had to admit that in his darker moments, he wondered what it would be like if he was more like his grandad—and perhaps JR—having less of a sense of self and more connected to the wider community; people who believed very different things to him. Would it even be possible to not think of Alice as his daughter, and as the possession— and he struggled to even use that word in this context—of the community?

It reminded him of a time when, at an exhibition, he'd once drawn some inspiration from the North-Korean Mass Games in the 21st century. The information panel displayed next to the exhibit said: The Mass Games are an example of the subordination of an individual's desires to the needs of the collective. Ben couldn't help but be wowed at the time by the HoloSense display of hundreds and thousands of children flipping cards to create a beautiful human projection.

'What do I believe? I admit my thinking has not been consistent. I want to fully believe, but am I just taking the bits I agree with and ditching the rest, or even twisting it to what I want?' He cut an anxious and frustrated figure. 'God, I believe, but help me overcome my unbelief,' he prayed silently to himself as he looked back up at Charles' face, his expression indicating he had much more to say.

Ignoring Ben's question, Charles continued.

"We have big plans for your daughter. She is the missing piece of our long-held puzzle," he said, before explaining to Ben about the terraforming project Lydia was working on and the many times they had failed.

"She'd been working on a process to stabilise the atmosphere post nuclear explosion, when something went wrong and she could not continue." Ben noted he didn't say she'd died.

"What she was working on would have brought a not insignificant decrease in the time it takes to terraform a planet. And nobody has completed Lydia's work—until potentially now. You see, Mr Harman, the thing she was missing—the missing piece of the jigsaw—we have now found. And it's the very element that Alice Harman, your daughter, has naturally within her."

Charles shared just what Alice's powers will enable them to do.

"It will completely transform the terra-formation process and the realisation of fast, efficient, interplanetary transfer. To put it simply, with Alice's power, we could move objects across the galaxy in little more than the blink of an eye. This includes people. We could move entire nations from the Earth as required, and the R & D costs would be reduced by trillions, not to mention the vast reduction in timelines."

Charles was in full flow now.

"We can create, to quote your beloved Bible, 'a new heaven, and a new Earth', so we can finally obliterate this crusty old planet, also getting rid of the need to live in the LinerVerse—as on the new earth, people have the chance to begin again—in reality. No more nation states to get in the way with their petty politics. No more restrictive family structures, now with everyone living in communities chosen specifically for them. No more religion leading people astray worshipping their petty gods, persecuting heretics and forcing others to believe in their fantasies. No, Mr Harman. This is a whole new world controlled by the few, for the benefit of the many. Surely, by your grandad's standards, and now yours, that's exactly what you've been working for, is it not?" Charles concluded.

Ben shifted in his seat, pins and needles buzzing in his thighs and bottom. Still conflicted, knowing that this is what his grandfather would have wanted, but now it just doesn't align with who he is. Charles observed the indecision in Ben's demeanour so tried another tact.

"If you join us, you can work together. Both of you. Father and daughter united. You could have a pleasant life together; convince her to do all that's right." He paused and, in a more solemn voice, he continued,

"However, I have to tell you, Mr Harman, and I don't say this lightly. If you decide against it, then, just like your wife, you will never see Alice again. You would force our hand into having to make some serious decisions over what we do with you…" He leant forward, looking stern. Ben felt the man's eyes burn right through him, "…and nothing will be off the table."

With that, he got up, and before turning away, he said,

"You've got some thinking to do, Mr Harman. I'll leave you alone to decide," and he headed to one of the smaller rooms out back, leaving Ben alone with his thoughts. With hope fading fast, Ben felt defeated. Slumping further back into the chair, he thought of Alice, his beloved Monkey, locked up and most likely alone, and the chance of seeing her again, steadily diminishing.

# CHAPTER 55

## DOING THE LAUNDRY

Five Shumen. That's how many Esme could see out the window facing pod seven. 'Wait. Was that another one?' She blinked her eyes to check she wasn't going mad. No. It wasn't another Shumen. Around the bend of the Haven's dividing wall, separating the pods from the supply rooms, a young girl in blue ripped jeans and a red hoodie appeared before her eyes. She was waving her hands at the Shumen.

"Over here!" She shouted, catching Esme's attention and flashing a quick, wink and smile.

"Esme smiled back." It was then pandemonium as the Shumen looked at each other, wondering what was going on.

Four of them ran toward the bilocated Alice as she headed anywhere that took her away from pod seven.

"That still leaves two. Not that I'm ungrateful or anything," Esme muttered to herself, still behind the door, holding her makeshift weapon tighter, still hoping she didn't have to use it.

The real Alice was using all her powers of concentration to listen to what MendipT was saying, umming and aahing in all the right places, all the while projecting her body to another place. It was working so far.

MendipT didn't seem to have any knowledge of what was happening. His colleagues, now only the two guards stationed outside the pod, were told to give him time before they came in and only in an emergency.

If his crew had noticed the young girl, they were chasing was Alice—none of them had seen her before—they would have been straight in to MendipT, getting the shock of their lives, seeing the same person twice.

"And that's why I want you to join me," MendipT continued. "We are a peaceful people with so much potential to advance humanity…" He had explained to her just how much he thought the Shumen could lead the world to a better existence by what they'd learnt on the Complex—both the good and the bad.

MendipT was a creative soul at heart. As a young boy, he'd spend hours playing tunes on his wooden flute, one chiseled out for him by his father on the occasion of his fourteenth birthday. It was the best gift he could have wanted at that time, providing him with a sense of calm and joy.

Anytime he was stressed, all it took was a few moments with his pride and joy and he would be OK. Blowing out a few notes helped him see the world from a different perspective, a loftier view showing him it didn't always revolve around him.

It had been many years since MendipT had seen that flute, let alone even remembered its existence, his perspective now well and truly changed. At the back of his mind he still harboured creative ambitions, his frustrations often welling up when most people just didn't get it. As far as he was concerned, they were as far from him as it was possible to be. There were a few enlightened souls, but not enough who really got him, which meant he often felt alone, always seeing himself in the shadows. And the source of that shadow was often SentiN— which just added to his sense of frustration and insignificance.

But now was the moment to step into the spotlight and assert his rightful authority. Not stuck as Sendo's slaves under SentiN's mediocrity. They were meant for so much more. He was meant for so much more.

However, he needed something else. Something far more powerful than himself to show people why they should take him seriously. What he needed was Alice Harman.

The young girl's face displayed a sense of calm. She hadn't moved for a good few moments. And if MendipT looked really close, he would see how much she had visibly drained since his entrance. The liquid she was given, along with the energy spent from the bilocation, having the inevitable effect.

MendipT stared at her, observing nothing. No facial expression.

"Are you even listening to me?" he said in frustration.

"Yes, I am," Alice replied forcefully, her tiredness now leading to grouchiness and her contempt for MendipT's narcissistic vision.

"You have this power trip to get the world to bow down to you. Did I sum it up all right?" She spat out, finally losing her sense of decorum after listening to his diatribe.

MendipT quickly leant forward. His anger now aroused. He put his hands around the young girl's neck.

"Billions of years of evolution and are you it?" He spat out. "Are you the next stage in mankind's progress towards perfection? I mean, if what they say is true, the power you have is a thing to behold. But yet," he spat out, "you are holed up here. Stuck in the backwater of space away from your family. All alone," he spat out.

Alice stayed silent. The bilocation was now well and truly over, her energy levels too depleted. She just hoped she had done enough to let Esme through. Her eyes attempted to close, feeling the tightness of her neck; her breathing constricted; the shivers began.

"Yo...u're....wr..ong," she breathed out, straining so hard to communicate.

"Sorry. I can't hear you!" he shouted in jest, slightly letting go of her neck.

"I...said...you're mistaken. I am not the next stage in mankind's evolution, because your evolution is a myth," she said, her breathing coming slightly easier now with the loosening grip on her neck. "I believe in true science...the kind my mum was doing...when you watched her die." She was looking straight into his eyes now.

Startled, MendipT dropped her head, shifting back. She just had enough energy to keep it from hitting the bed.

"What! How do you know that?" He spat out, his face now visibly perturbed.

"I was there, albeit via video feed. But...I sensed it all. I saw you standing in the adjacent lab. Looking...at my mother. You saw it all and did nothing. Nothing!! And you have the gall to come in here asking for my help! What did you think I was going to say?" she shouted.

MendipT didn't see this coming.

"But...but...you would have been just a baby!" he queried, thinking about making some excuse, but none came. He knew there was no way Alice would follow him out of there. When he said nothing, she continued, looking down at the bed, then slowly up at MendipT, a sense of compassion for this man with his misguided reality.

"I don't know why God created me with these powers. But I do know that I will only use them for Him. They are not mine to do with what I want. So fulfilling your vision, however noble you might think it is...well...forget it. I'd rather die." That sealed it.

MendipT was riled. He hit out by grabbing her neck again, tighter this time. 'If I can't have you, no one else will,' he thought.

"I don't have time for this. With or without you, I have to reach the bridge to handle SentiN. I mean, what's to stop me ending this right now?" he said as he further tightened his grip with both hands. Wouldn't that end all this? Look at me when I'm talking!" MendipT shouted. "Don't you know in your culture it's rude to look away when someone is addressing you?" He lifted her head to look straight at him. She opened her eyes.

"I said...why don't I just end this all now?" he shouted, squeezing her neck tighter.

"Yes!" came a loud reply from the door of the pod. "Let's end this now!" As he turned his head to see the source of the voice, a blast of light shot out and hit him between his shoulder blades, propelling him across the small room. He stuck against the curved wall before sliding to the floor, like something out of a Tom and Jerry cartoon. His body was limp and still.

Alice attempted to lift her head from the bed. "...took your time," she said, a faint smile reaching her face.

"I was doing the laundry," quipped Esme as she rushed toward Alice. They held each other in a tight embrace, Esme feeling motherly toward this remarkable young girl.

"Good to see you...and to meet you in person at last."

"Ditto," said Alice as they released each other.

"How hurt are you? What did they do to you?" Esme asked.

"I'm alive..." Alice replied, "...but I'll have to fill you in on the way. Where's Dad?" Esme's face dropped as she responded.

"I don't know. He distracted some Shumen so I could get to you, and I haven't seen him since." Alice's face didn't change.

"He's OK," she said, putting her hand on Esme's. "I can feel it. Don't worry. We need to get back to the ship." Attempting to push herself up, she struggled.

"You're really not OK, are you?" Esme asked.

"Well...I'm definitely gonna need your help. I'm pretty much working my reserves," she replied.

Alice put her arm around Esme, helping her to her feet.

"We can use the Contextuans, laundry basket to get back... though it might be smelly," she said as she scrunched her nose.

"Small price to pay..." Esme raised her eyebrows.

"You haven't smelt it yet..." she retorted as they stepped out the door into the now very muted gangway.

Over by the wall behind them, a finger twitched. Then a hand, a chest rising and falling. MendipT's mission was not over just yet.

## CHAPTER 56

## FELINE DISTRACTION

SENTIN KNEW THEY WERE COMING. IT WAS OBVIOUS. By feeling the undulations and vibrations, he could sense the location of people around the main hub of the ship. And he could feel a group, small as it was, moving rapidly towards the bridge—in his direction.

"MendipT's on his way," he said to no one in particular.

The other Shumen looked at each other, then back at SentiN. There were about twenty of them on the bridge, each standing or sitting at their own station and each looking pretty forlorn.

"What should we do?" said one of them, looking particularly terrified. SentiN stroked his well oiled beard.

"Prepare to fight," he replied. "We can't let MendipT destroy our people. If he wants a fight, he's got one."

He couldn't believe it had come to this. His friend, already having launched an attack on the Complex, was now about to confront him in front of the rest of their people. How times had changed.

'What went wrong?' he thought to himself. 'I remember just letting him go all those years ago.' SentiN had found himself in trouble when he'd eventually revealed MendipT's departure to the Guardian. He'd chosen to protect his friend in the end by pleading ignorance. He'd never truly forgiven him for that, not that they'd even talked much after he'd left.

In the following months, MendipT reported back a few times, but the conversations quickly fizzled out. Though that was about to change.

"Get your weapons ready," SentiN ordered, trying to be as commandery as he could. But it really wasn't his forte.

He felt them get closer. Beads of sweat appeared on his forehead; his beard was already glistening, and not just from beard oil.

"I want everyone facing the main doors. We don't want to be surprised," he urged.

The Shumen complied without question, setting themselves up in one group of four on their knees, directly facing the doors, and another group of five standing behind. All had their weapons poised. The rest were further back in two banks, left and right of the doors, again, ready for action.

SentiN was in his chair. A sense of anticipation washed over him as he felt their presence drawing closer to the door.

"They're here," he reported, the quivering of his hand hidden by the cerebro as he waited.

"They will be standing behind the door, waiting for us," said an adrenaline pumped FalongQ to his team.

They had stopped just close enough to see the bridge doors, but kept a safe distance in case SentiN's crew made a sudden move. Not likely, but FalongQ tried to plan for the unexpected. They were crouched down in two groups behind part of the wall which jutted out. One to the left, one to the right of the gangway.

"We need a plan to distract them so we can get in with minimal loss of life. They are our people, after all. Any ideas?" FalongQ said loudly so both teams could hear him.

Besides his strategic mind, he also possessed a humble nature, not feeling the need to always have the answers. They were a team, a community. It was everyone's responsibility. He felt, it should never rest on the shoulders of one.

"Lets transfer an avatar close to SentiN's command seat," one of the team offered.

"Yes," another agreed. "It has to be something that makes some noise so they all are diverted at once," he continued, seemingly equally driven by adrenaline as FalongQ. In fact, he was shuffling from foot to foot. So much energy bursting through his veins he didn't know what to do with it. The shuffling helped a little.

"How about we just patch a call through to the ComTel on the main bridge?"

"Hmm…" FalongQ muttered out loud. "You mean just tell them what we're going to do?" he questioned.

"Yes. I mean it is SentiN. He either won't believe us…" he continued.

"…or…he might act irrationally, resulting in more lives lost," FalongQ interjected.

"Yes, that is a possibility," replied his colleague, looking sheepishly at the ground.

FalongQ stood up, his eyes fixed on the bridge doors, a sudden idea sparking in his mind. "Lets project a cat," he ordered. "That should cause enough of a distraction. Then let's stand back out of sight of the bridge doors and send another cat through the doors. Once they are in confusion over what is happening, then on my mark, rush into the bridge and disarm them. I'll deal with SentiN."

Smiles broke out amongst the group, knowing this was the best idea.

"I'll get to a Cerebro and generate the felines. I'll buzz you once they're in," said one Shumen as he got up and rushed to a comms post a short distance back further down the gangway.

"Right. The rest of us, let's move toward the bridge doors and let's stay sharp. Only enter on my mark," ordered FalongQ.

Ben couldn't help but look around the room, the paintings acting as a distraction from imagining life permanently without his daughter. The last six months were agony enough. Seeing her again—albeit in bilocated form—surely it was too much for him to lose her again.

It's your God-given responsibility to lead and protect your family. There can be no bigger responsibility in life, the words of his father coming back to him.

His mind continued to be flooded with thoughts.

'To save my daughter, I have to lose her. Like Abraham being asked to sacrifice his young son Isaac. I don't deserve the family I had, and the one I have. But you know what? It doesn't matter. God had blessed me to know the adoring love of a beautiful wife and the fragile beauty of our child. That is too powerful to destroy.'

'My grandpa meant a lot to me. I loved him. But he was mistaken. I know that now. He was trying to have his cake and eat it; trying to please the world...and please God. To have a separate life, with a separate family, no less, inside LeV8—as though he could hide it from God—that was wrong. God is clear:'

Ben recited the words from a favourite Psalm from memory:

> *"Where can I go from, Your Spirit?*
> *Or where can I flee from Your presence?*
> *If I ascend into heaven, You are there;*
> *If I make my bed in hell, behold, You are*
>     *there."*

'There is no place to hide,' thought Ben, his thoughts coming thick and fast, now with much more clarity.

When Charles returned to the room, he appeared restless as he stood next to his desk.

'I wonder what was in the other room,' thought Ben.

"So, Mr Harman, have you made your decision?" Ben looked straight up at the old man, his confidence high, and his resolve to do the right thing stronger than ever. He smiled as he looked at Charles.

"You think you're in control, but remember our previous conversation? You are not the captain of your ship. Your actions are limited to what God permits. A new heaven and a new earth will never be created by you—or any other human for that matter. Do what you want," he commanded. "You will be judged."

"To say I'm disappointed, Mr Harman, is an understatement. I won't enjoy passing that message on to my employers. It is out of my hands how they react. All I can—"

Before he finished his sentence, a loud bleeping came from the room he'd recently vacated. Immediately, he left Ben and ran back to the room from which a HoloSense displayed multiple views around the Complex.

On one screen, Charles could see Shumen running away from the Haven.

"Where's Alice, or Esme?" he asked himself.

Then he noticed the door to pod seven was open. Alice must have escaped. His eyes lingered on the door as he noticed movement, then a hand gripping the door as a very disoriented MendipT crawls out.

"What did she do to him?" Charles said to himself, wondering whether more security protocols should have been in place for such an unknown quantity.

He watched MendipT use the door frame to pull himself up to standing, rub his head, then slowly make his way around the haven gangway heading for the bulkhead.

On his back, a black burnt patch right between his shoulders; reducing the smart blue suit to shreds in that area.

Charles continued to watch and by the time MendipT made it to pod twelve, he saw him run, his strength clearly coming back from whatever happened to him in the room.

Charles muttered to himself, a heavy sigh escaping his lips, a deep furrow forming on his brow.

"It's time," he said as he left via a back exit heading in the same direction as MendipT, towards the bridge. Hoping to remain undistracted and to avoid the possibility of running into the Shumen, he opted for a parallel route.

Back in the room, Ben couldn't help but wonder what Charles was up to. It had been a few moments, and he'd heard nothing.

"Are you coming back?" he called out. No response. He called out a few more times, the sound of his voice carrying through the space, acknowledging the man's absence.

Again, he was alone.

# CHAPTER 57

## PAWS FOR THOUGHT

At first it scratched the commander's seat, then it jumped up on it.

"What the...!" Shouted SentiN as all the eyes of his colleagues swiftly turned to see what all the commotion was about. A cat was sitting on SentiN's lap licking its paw, then up its arm.

Just as he was about to throw it off, his attention was diverted by a tinkle. He observed the Shumen at the front of the formation, moving their heads looking around the doors, searching for the source of the ringing. Then it became clear as another feline nonchalantly strolled towards them as if it owned the place.

It stopped, looked around, decided nothing important was happening, and wandered slowly around to find its mate.

All eyes followed it round, and as they did, the doors flew open as FalongQ's men rushed in, weapons pointed at the ready. One by one, the feline distracted crew dropped their own firearms, conceding defeat.

"We don't want to use these," said FalongQ, raising his weapon. "Not against our own people. There does not need to be anymore bloodshed," he said calmly, circling the bridge to confront SentiN.

SentiN remained frozen in shock, rooted to his seat. The cat on his lap was still engrossed in its cleaning routine, its paws, and tongue working in a synchronised rhythm.

"I see you like our friends?" FalongQ asked with a hint of a smirk.

Ignoring the comment, which was more of a statement than a question, SentiN enquired, "Where is MendipT?"

The other crew with FalongQ went round each of SentiN's colleagues and confiscated their weapons, placing them in a bag they'd brought specifically.

"Oh, he's on his way. He had some other important matters to attend to," FalongQ responded.

Just a few moments later, a breathless MendipT burst through the bridge doors, clearly disheveled from his rushed arrival.

"You look a little worse for wear, my old friend," jibed SentiN.

FalongQ also looked concerned and mouthed "OK?"

"It's nothing I can't handle," he replied with a stern look on his face. He took a few moments to get his breath back, as he walked gingerly over to his old nemesis, SentiN.

Briefly, SentiN was taken back to that day in the replica Complex when he'd calmed his colleagues' frustrations. He didn't expect this encounter to go the same way.

MendipT looked at SentiN, who himself was not looking at all perky; the stress of the leadership obviously taking its toll.

"Hello, old friend. I'm sorry things have turned out like this. We could have been so much more," he said as he looked around the bridge. "I have to be honest though, I was expecting more opposition when I walked back in, but it seems many of your faction were quick to desert you," he smirked.

He got up closer to SentiN, now staring straight at him.

"They, like me, want for more ambition. I'm sorry to have to say this, but you are holding us back, and I am relieving you of your position," MendipT looked over to FalongQ but still spoke quietly to SentiN, "and if you won't go quietly, you will be locked in the Haven."

SentiN had resigned himself to what he saw as a foregone conclusion. That was his way. He had resigned himself to MendipT leaving the Complex with a small crew, just as he had resigned himself to effectively allowing MendipT to take over. He knew most of his colleagues had already deserted him. What would be the point of fighting and losing more of his compatriots?

As SentiN was about to stand to offer his surrender to his old friend, the bridge doors slid open and in walked Charles. There were a few murmurs before all went silent. Few of the Shumen regularly saw the Guardian. All the Shumen, aside from SentiN, MendipT, and FalongQ, stood to attention, not being sure how they should react.

"Stand down, please," Charles said dismissively.

"As you may know, I am the Guardian of the Complex. My role is to keep out of your way so you can run this facility how you see fit. Unless there is an emergency. Then I must step in. Mutiny is considered an emergency, which is why I have shown myself."

As he was talking, he wandered around the bridge, addressing everyone, before coming to a stop by SentiN's seat.

He had now stood up with MendipT and FalongQ near him, but far enough away in case he tried to grab their weapons.

"I have observed your infighting, and it has got to stop. There are bigger things at play here, bigger than the Shumen."

MendipT and FalongQ exchanged a glance as if to ask, does he mean Alice? To clear up their confusion, he continued.

"There is a prisoner on the Complex. One who you should not underestimate. She may look like a twelve-year-old girl, but she may just be the most powerful person alive."

There were audible gasps around the bridge, with many of the Shumen looking at each other in fear.

"I don't want to alarm you anymore than is necessary, but she has escaped. We cannot afford to let her get away. I suggest you all work together to get her back and put your petty disputes aside until your mission is complete."

MendipT, stood forward as though he was about to speak. This, perhaps, was his moment.

As they reached the dividing wall between the gangway and the supply rooms, they looked out for the Contextuans 'hovering laundry basket', as Esme called it.

They couldn't see the vehicle. It was slow going, as Alice needed a lot more support. "We're gonna have to think of something else," said Esme reluctantly. "If we miss their basket, we're not gonna make it back to the Annex without being seen."

Alice knew Esme was right. She looked sullen, not wanting to be the one to hold them back.

"Any suggestions?" She asked Esme.

"Yes. If I leave you here, just for a bit, and race round to see where the basket is, I can then somehow communicate with them to hold up—though I don't know how Ben did it earlier, but he did."

"Really?" smiled Alice, an almost parentally proud smile.

"Yeah, but, as I said. I don't know how he did it. So unless you can think of something else, I'm gonna go," Esme urged.

"No. You go, Es. I'll wait here for a bit, and slowly try to make my way around. I really have little energy for anything else," Alice cautioned, disconsolate, but not totally giving up just yet.

"Right. I'll be as quick as I can," Esme said as she sped off round the curve of the supply rooms and as she came near to the bulkhead, she spotted the basket. Thankfully, there was no sign of the Shumen anywhere.

In their customary manner, a Contextuan led the way at the front, while another trailed behind the basket, maintaining a relaxed tempo as they carried out their laundry tasks.

Esme ran out to the one in front and waved. Both Contextuans and the basket stopped simultaneously. The one in front regarded her as she held up her hand in the universe sign to stop. Then played a game of charades, pointing back to where Alice was, miming her friend hobbling and pointing her fingers at the basket.

Somehow the Contextuans seemed to understand, or at least,

they just stayed still even when she started running off back to Alice.

"They're gonna give us a lift," she said when she reached Alice.

"You managed to talk to them, then?" Alice queried.

"Yeah. Whether they really understood, we're about to find out. If we get round the corner and they're there, then I guess they did."

As Esme partially carried Alice, they got around the curve and instead of seeing the Contextuans stationary; they were actually coming towards them.

"Wow! They obviously got you!" Alice exclaimed, though it came out more as a whisper.

"Actually, I didn't ask them to come. I just said if they could wait. But, hey. I'll take any miscommunication if it means we can have a lift," Esme smiled.

The basket approached them and stopped. The Contextuan in front moved towards Alice. Its robot arm seemed to scan her.

Alice looked at Esme. Esme looked back, both with puzzled expressions. When it had finished scanning, the other Contextuan opened the lid of the basket and pulled out another covering, hiding all the clothes beneath.

The first one then offered Alice an arm as she grabbed it and between both Contextuans, they hoisted Alice aboard. Esme climbed on board too, of her own accord, and lay down next to Alice, just like she'd done with Ben a little while earlier.

"That was weird," said Esme. "They obviously think a lot of you. Not that I'm jealous...much...just an observation,"

Alice turned her head towards Esme. "Yeah. I know," she replied. "Though, you know my mum was involved with designing them?"

Esme swung her head towards Alice as the Contextuans pulled over the cover and the basket began to move.

"Seriously! How did I not know that?" she asked.

"Well, they were designed to be the boots on the ground after a terraforming nuclear explosion released the inert oxygen within a planet's surface. It wouldn't be ready yet for humans, so these AI bots were created. Terraforming, as you know, was my mum's bag. She was involved in every aspect of it in one way or another. I don't know how much she had to do with the physical design, but I know she designed elements of their architecture," Alice explained.

"So, are you suggesting, that that thing recognised you as being related to Lydia?" Esme queried, her appreciation of the importance of the Harman family constantly growing.

"I can't say that for sure, of course. But I could sense some recognition there. If I was back to even half my strength," Alice replied, wincing slightly as she shifted her legs to get more comfortable, "I might have been able to sense more."

Turning her head back, Esme felt the light caress of the covering against her face, as she observed the play of shadows and shapes that were delicately diffused through the sheer, gauze-like material, her mind still trying to comprehend everything she was experiencing.

"Wow. That's all I can say. Wow!" she muttered.

They both stayed silent for a while. Having heard the bulkhead doors open and close, they knew they were only a few moments from reaching Annex A where, in an ideal world, they would board Alice's ship and make a swift getaway. Both Esme and Alice were hoping it was an ideal world.

Before long, they felt the basket slow, then stop. They heard the whoosh of the bulkhead doors open and close, indicating they were now safely inside Annex A. Just past the supply rooms before reaching Docking Bay one.

The basket stopped again and one of the Contextuans pulled back the cover as the other held out an arm for Alice to hold. She did, taking her time, managing her pain.

Esme jumped out the other side and came round to Alice. As they helped her down, they moved away once Esme was holding her up. Then both of them moved around in front of her and nodded their heads up and down.

"Wait! Did they just bow to you?" Esme asked, the action taking her by surprise.

"Er… yeah, I guess," Alice responded before raising a hand to the Contextuans and mouthing, "Thank you."

They nodded before resuming their positions behind and in front of their basket and heading towards the docking bay airlock. The door opened, and they were gone.

"I know I keep saying it, but wow!" said Esme. "I'm sure that's gonna come in handy in the future."

"We'll see," Alice said as she tried to play it down, still not being a fan of the attention. But with power like hers, that wasn't always going to be possible.

They reached the docking bay and entered the airlock. As the pressure set itself, they could see the TransPortal almost within touching distance.

"We're gonna make it," breathed Esme, realising she'd been holding her breath since they entered the airlock. "I can't honestly say I thought we would," she ventured.

"Well, there were a lot of moving parts," Alice concurred, before her thoughts drifted to her father. "Let's hope Dad makes it back as easily as we have."

With the pressure set, the door released, and Esme carried Alice into the TransPortal. They both breathed a sigh of relief as the door closed, sealing them in.

Alice lay down on the floor as Esme grabbed the medikit, handing her the same liquid she'd given to Ben earlier. Alice gulped it down, then lay back and very quickly drifted off into a deep sleep.

Esme hovered round the control panel, getting things ready for their departure. All she had to do now was wait for Ben. She knew it was possible for her to pilot the ship whilst Alice was on board. However, it was made much more difficult, with Alice being, well...asleep. She needed Ben to come back quickly before any Shumen found them and played hardball. They were so close.

"Come on, Ben," she whispered. "Come on."

# CHAPTER 58

## TRUE POWER

Safe in the knowledge that Charles wasn't returning, Ben breathed deeply, allowing as much oxygen to his brain as he could. Still unable to move from the chair, his expression was one of peaceful serenity.

No longer in the confused—or even depressed state he'd been in for many years. No. This was a new Ben. A Benjamin Harman with clarity; who knew his purpose in the world, and like his daughter, was discovering he'd been blessed with a wonderful power. A supernatural power to be used for good, as a blessing to the God who entrusted it to him.

With this realisation, Ben's eyes were opened to a new level of detail and beauty in everything around him. In his mind's eye, he could sense Alice and Esme waiting in the TransPortal. A huge grin spread across his face.

"Thank you, Lord," he offered. "They've done their part. Now it's my turn."

Just as when he stood in the TransPortal with Alice, Ben's body started to glow. He felt a power growing within him as he focused his mind on the binds that held him to the chair. Recalling Jesus' words to the blind man, he repeated them.

"Get up and walk!" And he did just that.

Rising from his temporary prison, it was like he was using new legs and new arms. The manacles fell away as if they were nothing.

If he wasn't in such a hurry to save his daughter, he might have questioned how this was all happening. How was it possible for him to sense people hundreds of meters away and behind thick doors and walls? How was it possible for him to one moment be stuck in a chair held by secure manacles, and the next moment, standing tall?

None of it made sense. But right now, he didn't have the time to process it. His little Monkey needed him, not to mention his friend Esme, who he was quickly growing in admiration for. He needed to move.

Standing tall, he entered the room he'd seen Charles walk in, just moments ago. On one of the multiple HoloSense displays, he immediately was captivated by the feed from the bridge, spying Charles talking to the Shumen.

"That is where I need to be, to stop this once and for all," Ben said to himself confidently. Looking further to his left, he observed the map of the Complex charting the quickest path to the bridge from the Haven.

"Got it," he said as he purposefully strode out of the room heading for the bridge. He channeled Charles, who'd sped walked when he'd first met him and in no time at all, he saw the bridge door just ahead of him.

MendipT stood forwards, but internally he was holding back his anger at the Guardian who was doing exactly what he said Sendo were doing to his people. They were slaves, having to carryout the orders of their landlords. But he knew the importance of Alice, despite thinking he'd almost put an end to her. He moved around the groups, looking at all of them.

"You heard the man. We need to get her back," he instructed.

Then addressing FalongQ, "I suggest we take Annex A and," he turned to look directly at SentiN, attempting to put their issues aside for the moment at least. "You take Annex B. Those are the only two places she is likely to be..."

"That's assuming she hasn't already left," retorted the Guardian, who thought about mentioning her father, but decided against it, knowing he was still locked in his office.

Just then, the bridge door opened and in walked Ben Harman. Charles rocked back on his feet, visibly shaken, observing Ben, who was looking straight at him.

"How...how did...?" Charles muttered, for once unable to formulate intelligible sentences.

Ben smiled and looked straight at Charles the Guardian.

"Surprise!" Ben sang. "There's a lot you don't know, old man, but we'll get to that," he said as he looked around the room at all the Shumen.

"Hello, everyone," he said joyfully. "For those that don't know me, I'm Ben Harman." He waved a hand. "Hi!"

MendipT looked decidedly nervous, wondering if he also knew, as Alice did, that he was present at Lydia's death and did nothing to prevent it.

He didn't want to even risk the chance, so without a moment's hesitation, MendipT pointed his weapon at Ben and pulled the trigger.

Some of the other Shumen were stunned, but others just copied him in firing their weapons. Lines of green and blue streamed through the air, all in Ben's direction.

Time seemed to stand still, but instead of being imbued with panic, Ben's face was a picture of calm. It wasn't his time to die right then. He knew it.

Thrusting his arms to the ground, he pushed his chest forward, and the green and blue lasers simply dispersed as they hit him. Not only that, a strong wind seemed to discharge from him and he imagined what it was like for Moses as God parted the Red Sea.

The wind blew back toward the Shumen, throwing them up in the air, their bodies clattering against the wall. This included MendipT, who quickly pointed his weapon up and shouted,

"Fire!"

Those who'd previously just stood still, now fired their weapons at Ben, and just as before, they ended up clattering into the walls, clutching their relevant, hurting body parts. The streams just dissipating around Ben's body.

No one else tried firing after that. Not even MendipT, who was nursing more injuries than most, having felt the wrath of Esme earlier.

Ben stood tall, looking around, almost teasing anyone else to try it.

"As I was saying..." he continued, decidedly looking at Charles. "There's a lot, you don't know about me. I now see, so clearly. In fact, I've never been so clear. Old man...that is what your friend, Margaret called you, is it not?"

If he was waiting for a response, he didn't get one. However, he couldn't help but notice a subtle pang of guilt wash over the Guardian's face.

"You have opened my eyes to my many mistakes—to my many misbeliefs. And now is the time to right those wrongs, at least the ones I have control over," said Ben.

He glanced around again at the Shumen. All remained motionless, unwilling to take the risk of enduring further harm or even facing death at the mercy of this formidable and mysterious force.

"You need to be ashamed of your duplicitousness, especially with Margaret. Alice is my daughter," he exclaimed.

There was an audible gasp from most of the Shumen who had only just heard about Alice and that she was dangerous. They did not know what that meant about her father, having just experienced his wrath and not wanting to find out what else he could do.

"My daughter, given to me by God, is not your property to do with what you like. We are a family, and she is under my protection. Touch her at your peril."

He stopped and again looked around at everyone in the room, leaving no one who did not feel the strength of his resolve.

"Here's what's going to happen. I'm going to walk out of here and leave the Complex with my daughter. You are going to sort out your problems amongst yourselves and carry on living your lives, just as you agreed to when Sendo appointed you to your respective positions."

Ben looked across at Charles to see if he had anything to say. He did. He moved to a station—to lean on it more than anything.

"You don't know what you are doing. I know what you truly believe and this is not it. I know your grandpa holds more sway over you than—"

"Enough!" Ben said firmly but calmly. "You do not know my beliefs. I didn't have too much of an idea about them myself, to be honest. But I could not be more clear now. And that's why I have to do what I have to do."

He looked around the bridge, stepping closer to the door. It opened.

"Let's hope you all have the courage to do the right thing, too," he said as his departing words, as he walked out and thought he heard an enormous sigh of relief. He ran back towards Annex A, which he hoped would lead to his Trans-Portal to freedom.

Adrenaline still pumping inside him, Ben was panting by the time he reached the docking bay. He quickly entered the airlock, continuing to puff. Despite his growing abilities, he was still human.

Inside, as he spotted Esme's face through the porthole, a warm feeling radiated within him. This woman was most definitely growing on him, though right now, reuniting with Alice was foremost on his mind.

When the pressure was set, Esme opened the door and a desperate Ben rushed to his daughter, hugging her real—still sleeping body—for the first time in over six months.

"Monkey!" he called out as tears of joy streamed from his face.

"Not so hard, Dad. I hurt all over," she grimaced, her face slowly transitioning to a beaming smile, as Ben loosened his grip but still held on to his baby daughter. She would always be his baby, his little Monkey.

Esme locked in the coordinates for home and set the ship to depart, knowing she would soon need Ben or Alice to take over; only their power could trigger the ships' FTL drives.

Looking over her shoulder lovingly at the scene before her, so pleased to see two people she'd grown to love, be reunited, she felt blessed that God allowed her to play a role in their story. When she got a moment, she would need to patch in her mother. Margaret would dearly want to know the rescue was a success.

"Hey guys. Sorry to interrupt, but there's a ship in the docking bay. I'm not sure they're keen for us to leave. I know you don't have your strength, Alice, but we need to FTL somehow." Alice smiled as she glanced at Ben.

He planted a kiss on her forehead, then got up.

"Leave it to me, Monkey. You recoup your strength," he said smiling, as he moved over to the controls and the glowing begun.

"Er...that's new..." quizzed Esme.

"Yeah. There are a few new things around here," said Alice, smiling as she raised herself up, holding on to a bar attached to the wall.

"You don't need to..." said Esme, still very much concerned as Alice politely waved her away.

The ship moved to light speed as they all gazed out the window; the Complex vanished before them and tiny pinpricks of light became streams before resolving back into yellow balls of fire.

In that moment, Ben's mind was filled with a galaxy of thoughts, twinkling and whirling like stars in the night sky.

He glanced at his daughter, and Esme, and judging by their expressions, he guessed it was the same for them too. Translating thoughts into words was currently unnecessary. That could wait.

For now, he turned around to gaze out the window, letting himself bask in the never failing beauty of space, safe in the knowledge he finally had his daughter back.

# CHAPTER 59

## NEW DAWN

6 MONTHS LATER

Laying back, he breathed in the scent of freshly cut grass, his head resting on her lap. A delicate hand rested on his chest, whilst another stroked his head.

Through his closed eyes, Ben could see the sun beaming through an almost cloudless sky, the burnt orange ever so slowly fading in, charting the path from day to evening.

"It's time," Lydia said.

He felt her hands move to his temples, as the soporific sound of his deceased wife's voice travelled to his ears, whilst the scent of rosemary touched his nostrils.

He knew she was right. Sitting here with her, he'd had a sense that this would be the end. They'd chatted a lot about Alice, naturally, but his initial hesitation in discussing his feelings for Esme hadn't been warranted. Lydia responded with grace and alacrity that epitomised why he loved her so much, and why he found it so difficult to leave her—even virtually.

"I know," he responded, tipping his head to gaze at his feet through his squinting eyes. "Will I ever see you again?" he asked with a touch of hope.

She didn't respond immediately, giving him pause for thought.

"You won't need to," she said eventually. "You know you have my blessing. She's a keeper. Treat her as well as you treated me, and you'll be fine," Lydia encouraged. Then, as his eyes fully opened, he saw her staring back down at him, her finger pointing in mock consternation. "But...treat yourself well too by putting God first," she admonished.

"I'll try," Ben smiled, feeling more content than he'd felt before, especially knowing it might be the last time he would see his wife again. A sense of peace washed over him unexpectedly.

"Dad?" A young girl's voice came out of nowhere. Ben furrowed his brow, trying to ease his confusion.

He felt his wife's hands push his shoulders, beckoning him to get up.

"My love, it's time. She's calling you," Lydia whispered.

"Dad," the voice called out again.

Ben stood, bringing Lydia up with him as they faced each other. A tear descended his cheek as their lips met, arms entwined around each other in a tight embrace. Then he felt Lydia push back, her arms still holding his waist. His, caressing her shoulders.

"Goodbye, my love. It's been my pleasure," she said as her hand took his and, raising it to his head, she tapped it on his ear, triggering the NCep device. A low drone and flash of light brought Ben back to reality.

"Dad! Dinner's ready!" Alice shouted from another room.

"I'm coming, Monkey," he shouted back as he wiped his cheeks before pulling the NCep fully out, dropping it on the table. A little disorientated, he headed to the bathroom to clean up before dinner.

Margaret Flint's house always reminded Ben of his grandparents' place. It wasn't so much the size or layout. He described it as having a homely ambience of learning which he revelled in. There were many shelves containing books of all shapes, sizes, ages and genres, and quite a few in the legal category because of Margaret's work.

Since returning from the Complex, Ben had been more open about his LinerVerse obsession. In fact, Margaret, Esme, and Alice, knew he'd been in the study attempting to close out this part of his life. He'd told Alice about seeing her mother, which she'd found strange at first, but in time she understood.

But he was yet to broach the subject with Esme. He'd also given a rough synopsis to Margaret, but the burgeoning relationship that he felt was clearly developing with Esme, made it more difficult to open up to her.

It was the right thing to do. He knew that. If God wanted him to move on, Ben believed that this Godly woman was a clear sign. Esme's clear love for Alice only reinforced his belief. And, having been through, and survived the trial of the Complex, well...it was obvious, right?

He splashed water over his face then wiped it with a towel. Yes, it was obvious. He cared for her and he had to tell her the truth. Lydia's blessing was the final puzzle piece. Looking at himself in the mirror, he felt more assured now as he made his way down to the dining room, right into a buzz of activity.

An elegant dining table was laid out with an array of foods. Carrots, of which Ben could definitely smell, were honey roasted, parsnips, sweet peas, and corn and his favourite, Yorkshire Puddings. Sunday dinners at the Flints' were heaven for him.

"Hey, Dad," said Alice, putting down a bowl of potatoes to embrace her father, giving him a side hug before carrying on fixing the last items for the table. He saw Esme look up from pouring some liquid in the glasses around each place setting. She was beautiful.

"Hey. OK?" she said hesitantly.

"Yeah. Good, thanks," he said, smiling, hoping to mask the butterflies flitting about in his stomach. "Can I do anything?"

At that moment, Margaret glided in from the kitchen.

"Typical. Now you ask when we're all done!" She said with mock consternation.

"Oops. Sorry!" Ben replied as he rolled his eyes.

"Just sit tight and we'll get started. I hope you're hungry," she said as he sat next to Alice, opposite Esme.

"Famished, to be honest. I could eat a Cassowary," he joked.

"Dad!" Moaned Alice.

"What? What's wrong with Cassowary? I've heard it's a delicacy in some parts," he retorted.

"Well, we've got lamb, and you can serve up," Margaret replied as she handed Ben the knives and went to sit down opposite him.

After saying grace, Ben began carving up the lamb as the buzz of conversation resonated around him. Alice, Esme, and Margaret immediately started chatting away whilst serving each other, taking the lamb Ben was placing on the serving plate and adding to it the assortment of sumptuous food displayed on the table.

Ben was using the slicing of the lamb to work through how to bring up the subject of the virtual relationship with his ex-wife. Though despite being nearly a decade since her death, he still wasn't comfortable with the term, 'ex-wife.'

He thought whether to get Esme alone before he told her, but then, on the other hand, having the support of the others could really help. But then she might question why she was the last to know.

'Oh, I can't win either way,' he thought frustratedly as he placed the last slices of meat on the serving plate before transferring a few to his own plate.

He felt Esme's eyes on him. "You look deep in thought," she said. Margaret and Alice kept talking, something about the Shumen on the Complex he vaguely heard.

"Hmmm. Yes, I am. Listen Es. I have something to tell you," he started, ignoring the rumination's in his gut.

"Yeah?" she replied. "Is it about Lydia?"

He looked at her pointedly; his cheeks pursed. Her response gave him hope.

"In a way," he said. "I know we're not an item as such, but I've wanted to tell you since we got back that I have been seeing Lydia in LeV8. I know it's only virtual, but as you and I are getting closer, I felt it right that I should tell you. But what I was doing earlier...as in before dinner, was actually ending it, and I don't intend to see her again."

He paused, waiting for some kind of response, and noticed that Alice and Margaret were now silent, glancing casually his way. "What do you think?" He asked her.

Esme, swallowed. Smiling, she moved her hand over his. Ben watched her as she looked over at her mother first, then at Alice, almost as though asking permission before speaking. They both smiled at her.

"I know," she said.

"How long?" Ben asked, thinking he should be puzzled but actually feeling relief.

"Alice told me a few weeks back, and I'm sorry, but I didn't think it was my place to bring it up," she replied. Ben raised his eyebrows at his daughter, still admiring the supernatural wisdom in one so young.

"That's fine," he said before looking decidedly at Alice. "Good thinking, Monkey," he nodded. She smiled back.

"But thank you for telling me," Esme continued. "I know it can't have been easy, but I'm glad you did. It must have been tough to end it," she said as she removed her hand to continue eating.

"Yeah. You could say that. But with all that's happened this last several months, I'm learning to let go. I realised I was treating her as an idol, and I don't need anything coming between me and God. She's gone, and it's time to move on," he declared.

As he paused, he noticed Margaret looking in his direction like a proud parent.

"That sounds very wise, Ben," she said. "The Lord gives, and the Lord takes away. But blessed be His name."

"Amen!" Esme and Alice said together, smiling at each other.

"I do have one question though…" said Esme.

"What's that?" Ben replied as his eyebrows creased.

"Will you still use LeV8 again—even without her?" She asked.

Ben, thought for a while, looking down at his rapidly emptying plate. Normally, he'd have a burst of dopamine, even at the mention of LeV8. The anticipation of jacking in was so great. However, now, whether it was to do with his newly discovered powers, or whether his faith was growing in a way that he didn't rely on the LinerVerse for his fix, he wasn't sure. But either way, he was glad the last four months at least had proved his desire has been significantly sated. He finished the last of his meal, placing his cutlery neatly on the plate, feeling content.

"That's a good question, Es," he replied thoughtfully, staring at his plate. "I simply don't have the need at the moment. It was discontentment that drove me to it, but now I have my Monkey back…" he said looking at Alice, "I'm clear about Lydia, and I'm enjoying getting to know you more, I feel like I have peace again. That's not to say I won't use it again as I'm sure it will come in useful for work, but just not at the moment."

"Makes sense," said Esme.

"So, Dad," Alice chimed in excitedly. "Wanna show them what you can now do?"

Ben rolled his eyes at his daughter. Then he concentrated, staring at a spot on the far wall.

"Here," said Ben. Esme and Margaret looked at each other, then back to Ben. Both were confused.

"No. Here!" They both swung their heads round to the sofa at the far end of the room, the direction of the second voice, watching another Ben sitting back casually on the sofa, miming smoking a pipe.

"Wow! You can do that too? That's amazing and so difficult to tell it's not real," Margaret, said, switching her gaze between both Bens comparing them.

"How does it feel?" Esme quizzed.

"It kinda feels normal now, though I don't know how Ali keeps it up for so long," said the Ben on the sofa. "I feel drained just bilocating for a few minutes," Ben one finished.

"You'll get used to it as you learn to control it even more," comforted Alice.

Ben took a deep breath as his alternate version disappeared. He scratched his head, still trying to process his new capabilities, thankful to now be able to discuss things freely with Alice. They'd even helped each other to hone and control their abilities more, and certainly he was getting stronger all the time. But he was still very often baffled at the strength Alice seemed to command.

It made him continue to ponder Charles' fearful words. Words he would never forget, and if he was honest, sent a chill down his spine.

"Underestimate her power at your peril," he'd said.

But that would have to wait for another day. Right now Ben was content: overjoyed to have his daughter back, to have made peace with Lydia, and with his growing closeness to Esme, the chance at family again.

THE END

# COMING SOON

Thank you for taking the time to read my debut novel *Awaken*. It's been 14 years in the making! I hope you enjoyed journeying with Ben, Alice, Lydia, Esme, and the gang.

*Fall*, is the second book of the Aberration series. We go back in time as it focuses on Shemia Dryers—Alice's grandmother —who also has the aberration in her genes that enables super-natural abilities.

Make sure you're subscribed to my mailing list to keep up to date with *Fall* along with new short stories.

Subscribe at: https://richardmlalchan.com/

## ACKNOWLEDGEMENTS

A book is rarely produced in a vacuum, and as such, there are many people to whom I owe a great debt of gratitude.

First and foremost: God—without whom, none of this would have been possible.

> *"For in him we live, and move, and have our being."* Acts 17:28.

Thanks to every one of my Kickstarter crowdfunding backers, some listed on the website at richardmlalchan.com/backers. A special mention for M. Mootoo and Hugh O'Neil. Thank you all for taking a punt on my debut novel.

Huge thanks to all my family, but especially my sister Rache for constant encouragement and inspiration over the years, beta reading, and feedback—and along with Tom for letting me have my creative getaways in their place in Norfolk. Much needed!

Susannah Carras, the first person to ever look at the manuscript in its most early (and awful!) stage. My original Creatives Hub crew and my wonderful solopreneurs community, Conekto Pro, both of which provided accountability to complete various drafts.

Thanks to my dear friends, Aaron and Rosy Paul, for such

valuable feedback on the second draft and a constant source of encouragement from the beginning. Susan Perks for providing insightful feedback and encouragement. Everyone else on my mailing list, some who have been part of my journey for over ten years.

Thanks to Nick Russell-Pavier, my very first editor way back in 2014 (when the book was called GREEN.) His feedback was vital to take the manuscript to the next level. Amelia Winters, whose insight really helped to knock the final draft into shape, and Tiffiny Spire my proofreader for adding a much needed set of eyes over the final manuscript. I must thank Abbie Emmons, who I've never conversed with, but whose YouTube channel has significantly helped my writing.

Thanks to the insanely talented Marcus Silversides (@marcussilversides) cover designer—and so much more. Andy Scott (@andyphotohello) for producing the wonderful crowdfunding video.

I will no doubt have neglected to mention some people. But you know who you are. Thanks for your input.

And finally, with all the amazing support I received from various professionals, all errors and mistakes are solely my responsibility and do not reflect on anyone else.

# ABOUT THE AUTHOR

Richard Lalchan grew up watching Space 1999, Buck Rogers and Blake's 7, before progressing to reading Arthur C. Clarke and Philip K. Dick. It was too late after that. He was hooked on sci-fi.

However, feeling a void in science-fiction with a Christian worldview, he has made it his mission to fill that gap with his debut novel, Awaken, part of the Aberration series.

Outside of reading and writing, Richard keeps himself busy as part of a close-knit supportive, church family. He loves coaching solopreneurs (claritycoach.net,) and hosting networking events (bit.ly/StAlbansBuzz.) He lives in Watford, UK, and doesn't have any cats.

instagram.com/richardmlalchan

linkedin.com/in/rmlalchan

BV - #0072 - 190824 - C0 - 203/127/20 - PB - 9781738531608 - Matt Lamination